TOM CLANCY
TARGET ACQUIRED

TOM CLANCY
TARGET ACQUIRED

DON BENTLEY

THORNDIKE PRESS
A part of Gale, a Cengage Company

Thorndike Press, a part of Gale, a Cengage Company.

LIBRARY OF CONGRESS CIP DATA ON FILE.
CATALOGUING IN PUBLICATION FOR THIS BOOK
IS AVAILABLE FROM THE LIBRARY OF CONGRESS.

ISBN-13: 978-1-4328-8716-2 (hardcover alk. paper)

Published in 2021 by arrangement with G. P. Putnam's Sons, an imprint of Penguin Publishing Group, a division of Penguin Random House LLC.

Printed in Mexico
Print Number: 01   Print Year: 2021

PRINCIPAL CHARACTERS

United States Government
Jack Ryan: President of the United States
Mary Pat Foley: Director of national intelligence

The Campus
John Clark: Director of operations
Domingo "Ding" Chavez: Assistant director of operations
Gavin Biery: Director of information technology
Jack Ryan, Jr.: Operations officer / senior analyst
Lisanne Robertson: Former director of transportation

Operational Detachment Alpha (ODA) 555
Captain Alex Brown
Master Sergeant Cary Marks
Sergeant First Class Jad Mustafa
Doug "Crumdog" Crum: Medic

Sergeant First Class Brian Martin
Staff Sergeant Greg Glass
Staff Sergeant Jeff Mishler

<u>**Shin Bet Officers**</u>
Tal Levy
Dudu

<u>**Other Characters**</u>
Dr. Cathy Ryan: First Lady of the United States
General Farhad Ahmadi: Iranian Quds Force
Darien Moradi: Iranian Ministry of Intelligence and Security (MOIS)
Katerina Sidorova: Wagner Group
Peter Beltz: CIA case officer
Dr. Rebecka Schweigart: American scientist
Tommy Schweigart: Son of Dr. Schweigart
Captain Natalie "Daisy" Smith: Air Force F-35 pilot

PROLOGUE

Al Tanf Outpost
Syria

"Why are we here again?" Master Sergeant Cary Marks said, shifting his weight for what seemed like the hundredth time.

The two-man sniper hide site that Cary and his spotter were nestled beneath offered a number of advantages to its occupants, not the least of which being near invisibility in both the thermal and visual spectrums. It was the closest thing to a Harry Potter cloak he'd seen in his decade and a half of service with 5th Special Forces Group.

But for all the hide site's technical prowess, it didn't make the Syrian soil any more comfortable.

"Because we're Special Forces," Sergeant First Class Jad Mustafa said, tuning the focus on his M151 spotting scope. "That means we get to do special shit."

As always, Jad's gift of understatement

had reared its ugly head. *Special shit* didn't come anywhere close to capturing the pure and unadulterated joy that had been the last twelve hours. Per the techniques, tactics, and procedures Cary and his fellow long tabbers had perfected during their countless combat deployments in support of the never-ending war on terror, he and Jad had infiltrated about 0300 local time.

The hour had not been randomly chosen. BMNT, or Begin Morning Nautical Twilight, was at 0500. This was the time of day when the human eye could start to discern objects from shadows. Even after thousands of years of civilization, human beings were still attuned to the world around them. Though they might not recognize it as such, the average person's circadian rhythms programmed them to feel restless around dawn.

With that in mind, Cary and Jad had wormed their way into the shallow depression they now occupied while the rest of their world was fast asleep. And though the rocky soil and surrounding scrub brush had provided exactly the hide hole they'd been hoping for, the accommodations were not exactly five-star.

The two men had made camp on a sand flea nest.

A large one.

Green Berets might be renowned for their ability to destroy enemy forces much larger than their organic twelve-man A-teams, but this was a different kind of battle. Cary had been waging a bloody war of attrition against the little beasties for the last several hours, but the pecker fleas were winning.

"Goddamn it, Jad," Cary said, trying to ignore the burning sensation dangerously close to his right testicle. "Can't you just ask some of your cousins for help?"

"Hey, now," Jad said. "Just because a bunch of biters are munching their way up your leg doesn't mean you need to get all cranky. Besides, I'm Libyan, not Syrian, you uneducated hick."

The language exchanged between the two special operators was harsh, but the sentiment behind it was anything but. The two men couldn't have looked more different. Cary Marks was a blue-eyed, blond-haired farm boy from New England whose vowels gave away his Yankee roots under moments of duress. Jad Mustafa's dark complexion and SoCal surfer accent made him Cary's polar opposite. Jad was suave where Cary was simple, and Jad's teammates often kidded him about being a SEAL in disguise due to his affinity for hair gel and fashionable clothes.

But despite their differences, the men were opposite sides of the same coin. Physically, their years serving on an Operational Detachment Alpha, or ODA, team had given them bodies uniquely suited to their type of work. Both boasted wide shoulders, broad backs, and well-developed chests complemented by an endurance athlete's lung capacity.

Mentally, the pair were even more alike. Though each man's upbringing and cultural heritage was radically different, this wasn't important. As with most men and women who served in the armed forces, and certainly those within the Special Operations community, differences in skin color and nationality ceased to matter long ago. In the Army there was but a single skin color — green — and just one blood type — red.

After half a dozen shared combat deployments, Cary and Jad were brothers in a way that superseded such trivial matters as birth parents or family lineage. Theirs was a familial bond conceived in the most arduous training the military offered, birthed in the fires of combat, and nurtured into the bone-deep trust shared only by men who've guarded each other's backs as bullets whipped past their heads.

10

The two Green Berets might pick at each other, but woe to the uninformed observer who tried to come between them.

"That's funny," Cary said, panning his SIG Sauer TANGO6T riflescope across his sector, " 'cause when we were in Iraq, I'm pretty damn sure you said you were Lebanese."

"That's because you listen about as well as you shoot. Which we both know is for shit. Without me as your spotter, you'd — wait a minute now. Boss, I think I've got something."

The change in Jad's tone was unmistakable. Though Cary had whiled away countless uncomfortable hours shoulder to shoulder with his barrel-chested spotter in more combat theaters than he cared to count, the half-Lebanese, half-Syrian, and all-American Green Beret knew not to mix business with pleasure.

As soon as Jad called Cary *boss,* the time for joking was over.

"Whatcha got, brother?" Cary said.

"Convoy of three Land Cruisers headed toward the front gate. Shift three hundred meters west of point Alpha and you'll see 'em."

Cary swung his rifle to the prescribed azimuth and turned on the laser range finder mounted to his scope ring. In that instant, the stifling heat, glaring sun, tired muscles, and even the merciless pecker fleas gnawing their way up his inner thigh were forgotten. This was no longer a game of hide in the dirt and hope for the best. The convoy of factory-new vehicles with tinted windows, sparkling paint jobs, and shiny black tires didn't fit the surroundings.

They were an anomaly.

And anomalies were what Cary was paid to notice.

Though, to be fair, nothing about the fortress the men were surveilling approached normal. And in Syria, that was saying something. Rather than the traditional stucco walls that denoted a compound or the concrete-and-cinder-block houses that signified more modern accommodations, the structure one thousand meters distant was unique.

As in Cary hadn't seen anything like it anywhere.

Earthen berms that stretched fifteen feet tall and ten wide formed something more reminiscent of a medieval castle than a Middle Eastern homestead. The sand and dirt had been bulldozed into a natural barrier and flattened on top into a plateau wide enough to situate fighting positions equipped with crew-served weapons. Earlier that morning, Cary had watched stupefied as vehicles drove on top of the densely packed barriers, bringing to mind the stories of chariot races atop the walls of the biblical city of Jericho.

Cary hadn't seen any chariots yet, but after hours of logging the occupants' comings and goings, he wouldn't be surprised. Unlike the hodgepodge of vehicles common to Syria's many militias and self-proclaimed armies, the earthen fortress's occupants had a motor pool with a surprising amount of sophistication.

Cary had already noted half a dozen technical vehicles, but on closer inspection, the converted Hilux trucks didn't have the hodgepodge look he'd expected. Traditionally, militia groups paired their vehicles with outsized weapons like DShK antiaircraft machine guns or M40 recoilless rifles. Matches like this were just as likely to destroy the host vehicle as the target at which they were aimed.

No, what Cary had observed reflected a customized integration between vehicle and armament. The compound's weapons tech wasn't some fly-by-night machinist recruited into turning out weapons of war. The Hiluxes prowling the fortress's walls

13

resembled something that might have been produced in a 5th Special Forces Group motor pool back in Kentucky.

This was, to say the least, troubling.

And that was before he'd seen the Humvees.

About two hours into his watch, Cary had gotten the shock of his life when a pair of up-armored Hummers had taken a turn around the south side of the compound. The vehicles still had U.S. markings, leading him to believe he was seeing an American patrol. He'd been on the verge of calling in his discovery when the doors had opened and Syrians poured out. Promised mystery visitor aside, the presence of American Humvees was worth investigating by itself.

Unfortunately, he didn't get the chance.

Cary and Jad had planned their observation post after spending hours poring over satellite and drone imagery, searching for a spot that would offer both concealment and line of sight into the fortress.

They'd managed only one of the two goals.

Biting fleas aside, Cary was pretty happy with the seclusion offered by their vantage point. But visibility inside the compound was a big miss. He could see some of the buildings on the far side of the fortress, but the walls were just too steep to get eyes on much more. After disgorging their passengers and loading up the old guard shift, the Hummers drove back along the wall and then took a ramp to the fortress's interior, where they promptly disappeared from view.

Even so, Cary had elected to remain in position. Mystery Hummers aside, the sniper's nest offered a commanding view of the roads approaching the compound, and the Agency asset who'd been the genesis of this operation had been firm on this point. The important visitors the asset claimed were coming would be approaching from the west in tricked-out black SUVs.

And here they were.

"Who do you think these guys are?" Cary said.

"Fuck if I know, boss. The folks inside are a cult, right?"

"That's what the intel folks believe," Cary said, cheek still welded to his rifle's stock.

The CIA case officer had tried his best to explain, but Cary was still a bit iffy about what was going on behind the earthen walls. Something about an apocalyptic cult. If he remembered correctly, the head dude was convinced he was an ancient Shia imam reincarnated.

15

Or something like that.

Like most Green Berets, Cary was an expert on a good many things. That said, weighing in on whether the head crazy on the other side of the Jericho walls really was a holy man reborn was a bit outside his wheelhouse. Then again, as long as the cult members kept to themselves, Cary didn't really care whether the guy inside thought he was Muhammad, Jesus, or Elvis.

As was the case with most of the men and women who made a living going into harm's way, as long as the people in question weren't bothering anyone, Cary was a big fan of live and let live. There were already plenty of malcontents actively working to visit hellfire and brimstone on America's sons and daughters.

No sense creating any new ones.

But based on what Cary had observed, the folks inside the compound didn't much look like they intended to keep to themselves. People content to peacefully wait in seclusion for the end of times didn't usually arm themselves with crew-served weapons and American Humvees. And the thing most apocalyptic cults had in common was an unwillingness to sit passively by while their prophecy unfolded. In fact, many of them believed their leader had a role to play in bringing about the end of the world.

And that role usually involved the shedding of innocent blood.

In this case, the Agency spook asked the Green Berets to keep the compound under surveillance in an attempt to learn how the crazies intended to bring about the apocalypse. And, perhaps more important, whether they had help.

If Cary had to guess, the cult's plan for world destruction probably had something to do with murderous pecker fleas. But guessing wasn't the same thing as knowing. The asset said the people who were arming the cultists would arrive in a trio of black vehicles.

And here they were.

Hallelujah.

"Satellite uplink ready?" Cary said, holding his aim point on the center vehicle.

Cary didn't know who these guys were, but statistically, the middle vehicle in a convoy usually had the best chance of surviving an IED. If there was an Important Person in this motorcade, that's where he'd be.

"Negative on the uplink," Jad said. "We're getting interference from somewhere."

Given that the two snipers had just checked in with their team leader via satellite uplink less than thirty minutes ago, Cary didn't think the sudden loss of connection was a coincidence. In the two-plus decades since the war on terror had kicked off in earnest, tactical technology had progressed by leaps and bounds. While the United States had been behind many of the most exponential advances, America's adversaries had done a respectable job of trying to thwart the technology overmatch.

Case in point, terrorist organizations didn't have fifth-generation fighters equipped with smart bombs, but more and more were using equipment that jammed the GPS signal that guided smart bombs to their targets. By the same token, the bad guys in Cary's weapon's sight probably didn't have a constellation of geosynchronous cubesats to ensure uninterrupted communications.

But they just might possess the ability to jam the necessary wavelengths.

Either way, this wasn't Cary's concern. In the lexicon of Green Berets, he was an Eighteen Charlie — a Special Forces engineer specializing in demolition. Jad, on the other hand, was an Eighteen Echo — a communications expert capable of fashioning a radio from a coat hanger, car battery, and calculator.

Or at least it seemed that way to Cary. If there was a way to reestablish the satellite uplink, Jad would do it. Otherwise the sniper team would do things the old-fashioned way — take pictures and then wait until nightfall to exfil and carry the intelligence they'd gathered back to the COP, or combat outpost, they called home.

"Roger that," Cary said, maintaining his sight picture on the rear passenger's window. "Keep recording."

In addition to riding in the middle vehicle, Important People usually sat in the back, behind the front passenger's seat. This allowed the muscle on the passenger side of the vehicle to take care of business while the precious cargo hunkered down behind armored doors and Kevlar-reinforced seats.

While this little excursion had been briefed solely as a sneak-and-peek, Cary viewed every operation as one mistake away from going kinetic. That way, when the inevitable happened and steel started flying, he was prepared rather than surprised. Already the part of his mind occupied by the black magic practiced by every good sniper was considering *dope, terminal ballistics, Coriolis effect, hold, relative wind,* and a host of other arcane-sounding words.

In layman's terms, Cary's fire-control-computer of a brain was calculating all the environmental factors that might or might not affect a shot he might or might not ever have to take. As his instructor had told him during the first day of Special Operations Target Interdiction Course, pressing the trigger was the easiest part of the job.

It was everything that happened prior that separated a sniper from a shooter.

A slight breeze tickled Cary's cheek, probably no more than two or three miles per hour. Even so, it might be worth asking Jad for a formal wind check just in case things didn't go according to plan. That was the second-most-important lesson he'd learned at sniper school — nothing ever went according to plan.

This truism applied to both sides of the battlefield.

As if to drive this notion home, a blast of dirt and rubber erupted from beneath the SUV as the front tire exploded. A second later, the breeze carried the sharp *pop* to Cary's ears.

"Looks like someone forgot to pick up their tire spikes," Jad said. "Sucks for our guy."

"Yep," Cary said. "But great for us. Get ready for the money shot."

"Come on, darling," Jad whispered, "hike

up your skirt."

At first the SUV's driver seemed determined to roll through the checkpoint. Then physics stepped in. The front tire was done. Not only was the wheel deflated, but the rubber had disintegrated around the rim. The engine revved, and the wheel spun, churning away what was left in black spongy chunks, but the truck wasn't going anywhere.

"No run-flats," Jad said.

"Nope," Cary said. "Looks like he's going to try and ride in on the rim."

"Not going to work," Jad said. "Too sandy."

Once again, his spotter proved prescient. The now rubberless rim spun impotently, throwing up a fountain of stones and dirt as the vehicle settled into the soil. After several seconds spent trying to rock the truck free, the roaring engine idled.

"Protection detail fucked this one up," Cary said. "They should have evaced the principal by now. If this had been an ambush, the middle vehicle would already be toast."

"Hard to find good help," Jad said. "Okay, here we go."

The passenger-side doors of the lead and trail vehicles opened in unison, releasing a scrum of gun-toting occupants who swarmed over the middle vehicle. Only once the screen was fully in place did the rear passenger door open.

"All right, beautiful," Jad said, "let me see your face."

Cary increased the magnification on his optic, centering it on the opening door. A moment later a bearded face swam into view.

A familiar bearded face.

"Well, son of a bitch," Cary said. "Look who's slumming with the locals."

"You recognize him?" Jad said.

"Indeed I do. Contrary to popular belief, you Syrians do not all look alike."

"I'm not Syrian, you racist son of a bitch. I'm Libyan. Now, tell me who we're seeing before I whoop your farm-boy ass."

"That, my uneducated friend, is General Farhad Ahmadi."

"As in commander of the Iranian Quds Force?"

"One and the same."

"What's he doing with a cult hell-bent on bringing about the apocalypse?"

"Nothing good."

1

Shuk Hacarmel Open-Air Market
Tel Aviv, Israel

Jack Ryan, Jr., took another bite of falafel, hunching his broad shoulders to protect his prize against the press of hundreds of bodies. At six-foot-two and two hundred twenty pounds, Jack was a big man even by American standards. In Israel, he towered over most of the crowd. Even so, he still felt like a lion guarding its prey from a pack of circling wild dogs.

Jack smiled at the image, expertly using a thick forearm to guide a chattering trio of teenagers away from his dripping food. Wild dogs on the savannah would try to rob the lion of his food, despite their small size. But the crowd that ebbed and flowed up the narrow confines of HaCarmel Street was absent the malicious intent of an African predator, regardless of how small. Over the last decade or so, Jack had become adept at

23

reading crowds, and this one radiated benevolence.

The Mediterranean sun shone from a sky the kind of perfect blue usually seen only in Photoshopped travel brochures, bathing the crowd in soothing light. The air was warm without the stickiness of the hot season, while the faint smell of salt water blowing in from the ocean just blocks away mingled with spicy scents of food cooking in the countless booths lining the street. Jack caught bits and pieces of a handful of languages as vendors and potential buyers argued over prices and wares.

Jack was no stranger to foreign locales, but there was something inherently magical about Tel Aviv. The city felt electric, full of entrepreneurs whose agile minds and unbounded dreams rivaled those of Silicon Valley. Here, in the Middle East's only democracy, the weather was excellent, the women beautiful, the people friendly, and the food fantastic. In short, the perfect vacation city.

But Jack wasn't on vacation.

As if on cue, a man settled into a plastic seat adjacent to a table at the opposite side of the alley. He was late forties to early fifties, with a full head of blond hair that was just beginning to gray at the temples. The

24

man dusted off the table with the fastidious nature of someone unaccustomed to the grit and dirt common to open-air markets. Once he'd cleared the spot in front of him of all debris real and imaginary, he flagged down a waiter.

The proprietor came over with a smile and the man ordered a coffee in English before adding the obligatory *toda,* thank you. The waiter smiled again before leaving to fetch the man's order.

Just another foreigner in a diverse, multinational crowd.

But to Jack's practiced eye, the man still seemed out of place.

It wasn't so much his fair complexion in the sea of olive-toned skin or his attire. Though the majority of the shoppers were Israeli or Arab, plenty of Europeans mingled with the natives. And the man had done a fairly respectable job of incorporating local fashion. He wore a button-down shirt in the local style, open at the collar so that a tuft of chest hair poked through, and jeans and sensible shoes.

No, it wasn't the man's wardrobe or genetics. His actions were the problem. Rather than the laissez-faire attitude coupled with liberal shoving that pervaded the rest of the afternoon shoppers, the man was clearly on edge. His head moved with sharp, bird-like movements as he looked from one end of the alley to the other, scrutinizing each passerby like he was a man on a mission.

Which he was.

But he was supposed to be behaving as if he wasn't.

Popping the last bite of falafel into his mouth, Jack dusted off his hands and then slid his cell from his pocket. Opening the notes app, Jack began to annotate his initial impressions. Tel Aviv was already one of his favorite cities, and while he'd like to do nothing more than go for a run along the beach and admire the local talent, that wasn't why he was here.

Technically.

Espionage was a tricky business. Even with mind-numbing advances in technology, running an agent or asset was still a deeply personal endeavor. As such, much of it was based on impressions, or gut feelings, and right now the man who'd just ordered a coffee was acting like he'd consumed far too much caffeine already.

The man's drink came Mediterranean-style, pitch-black and piping-hot, in a small glass cup. The man acknowledged the waiter with a curt nod and a handful of shekels.

Then, with a start, he seemed to remember the leather satchel hanging across his chest. With quick, furtive movements the man yanked the bag over his head and placed it at his feet, glancing left and right as he did so, as if trying to determine if someone was paying attention.

Someone was.

Jack.

Jack thumbed a couple more notes into his cell before dropping the device back into his pocket. Had he really ever been that green? He answered his unspoken question with a chuckle.

Without a doubt.

Fortunately, Jack's teachers were some of the very best in the business. Warriors like John Clark and Domingo Chavez, plank holders in the storied Rainbow team, had been his tactics and firearms instructors. Master spy Mary Pat Foley, current director of national intelligence and onetime CIA case officer famous for running an agent nestled in the bowels of the Kremlin, had coached him through the finer points of clandestine tradecraft.

Though Jack had never attended the CIA's school for fledgling clandestine operatives known as The Farm, he'd been through a different school of hard knocks staffed by a cadre that was no less prestigious. But the apprentice asset slurping his coffee had none of this training. He wasn't an intelligence professional. He was simply someone with access to information the CIA deemed valuable. If this was a different vocation, Jack might be tempted to offer the newbie a bit of grace.

But it wasn't.

Those who played the game of espionage did so for keeps, and Jack had the scars to prove it. In the rough-and-tumble clandestine world, doing your job well meant that you lived, while the consolation prize for second place was often a body bag. This was why it was imperative to determine if the potential asset had the required operational chops *before* lives were truly on the line.

Jack glanced at his watch. According to the pre-mission briefing, the fun should commence in exactly five minutes. Since this was Jack's first joint operation with the Agency, he wasn't sure how closely Langley's boys and girls adhered to timelines. But if he had to guess, things would be wired down to the second. Peter Beltz, the case officer calling the shots, had served with Jack's mentor, Ding Chavez, back when both men were young soldiers in the

Ninjas, 3rd Battalion, 17th Infantry Regiment.

Military men loved their timelines.

Across the alley, the man with the satchel lifted his coffee to his lips, but then slammed the glass back on the table without drinking, craning his neck to focus on something to Jack's right. The scalding liquid cascaded over the cup's rim, leaving a brown puddle on the table's white plastic surface.

Jack winced.

The violent motion had undoubtedly upset the collection of grounds settled at the bottom of the cup, rendering it undrinkable. But the travesty that had just occurred went beyond the now ruined cup of coffee. The would-be asset's actions were attracting attention. The sharp sound of glass on plastic caused several people to turn toward the commotion's source. At the same time, the shop's owner left his perch behind the bar to see if his singular customer required a refill.

Even worse, the man seemed unaware of the notice he was attracting. When the waiter reached his table, responding to the disturbance by sopping up the rapidly growing spill with a checkered cloth, the man couldn't have cared less. Instead, his attention was focused over Jack's right shoulder.

Which was entirely the wrong direction.

Jack sighed as he mentally added additional comments to his running critique, now trying to find something positive to offset the growing negatives.

The asset's contact window didn't open for another five minutes, and this was important. Doctrinally, the time before the window opened was allocated to ensuring that the asset hadn't been followed and that the meeting site wasn't under surveillance. A good asset used this period to attempt to identify other intelligence professionals while remaining inconspicuous.

But instead of calmly drinking coffee while committing the faces of seemingly random passersby to memory, the man was almost vibrating with tension. A counter-intelligence FBI agent straight out of the Academy would have keyed off the asset's nerves from a dozen feet away. To Jack, the man might as well have been a strobe light.

And the real fun hadn't even begun.

2

"See the pretty colors?"

The question, posed by a female voice, cut through the marketplace's hustle and bustle. Or perhaps the American accent just made the words more noticeable. Jack shifted his attention toward the unexpected interruption. A woman and child were standing in front of a booth selling brightly colored fabrics to his left.

The woman was several years older than Jack, probably late thirties, with a runner's trim build. She was wearing shorts, a tank top, and athletic shoes, and her chestnut-colored hair was arranged in a messy bun.

The travel attire of moms the world over.

"Which is your favorite?" the woman said, running her fingers along a length of fabric dyed a brilliant green.

Her questions were directed toward a boy who looked to be about seven or eight. Like his mom, the boy was dressed for a day outside, in shorts, a Marvel T-shirt, and running shoes. A Cincinnati Reds baseball cap, worn at a jaunty angle to permit a mass of brown curls to escape the bill, completed his wardrobe.

But this is where the similarities ended.

Unlike his mom, who seemed to be genuinely taken by the sights and sounds of the bustling market, the boy wasn't focused on his surroundings. But not because he was heeding the siren song of a cell phone or some other form of hypnotizing electronics.

This was something different.

Though he held tightly to his mother's hand, the boy was concentrating on the ground. His gaze swept left and right, as if the trash and debris were interesting, but too slippery to capture his attention.

"Are you hungry?" the woman said, allowing the shimmering fabric to slip from her fingers, much to the vendor's dismay. "Want some ice cream?"

With this question, Jack fully expected the boy's blank expression to transform into a smile. While it had been a long time since he'd been that age, Jack could sympathize with the boy's plight. His parents had also recognized the value of exposing their four children to other cultures, and some of Jack's earliest memories involved trudging through English museums during his dad's rotation with the British Secret Intelligence Service.

Not any toddler's idea of fun.

Still, the magic words *ice cream* could usually transform even the most dreary day. But to judge from the boy's reaction, his mother might as well have been asking him if he'd like to spend the day browsing the Old Masters section in the Tel Aviv Museum of Art. He kept his head down, his face expressionless, while his gaze roved across the ground, settling on nothing.

Squatting so that she was eye level with the child, the woman tried again. "Ice cream, Tommy? Mommy needs to know."

Tommy's head suddenly stopped, his eyes fixated on something past his mom's right shoe. Reaching pudgy fingers into his back pocket, he produced a Captain America figure. Without breaking eye contact with whatever bit of grit had captured his attention, Tommy dipped the figure forward twice, approximating a nod.

"Okay," the woman said, cupping her son's face in both hands. "Ice cream it is."

The woman smiled brightly at Tommy for a beat before standing, tracing his chubby cheeks with her fingertips.

In that moment, Jack understood. Growing up, he'd had a boyhood friend on the autism spectrum. As mother and son faded into the crowd, the boy shoved Captain America into his rear pocket, but not quite deeply enough. A collision with a passerby dislodged the action figure, sending the toy tumbling to the dirty concrete.

Without thinking, Jack was out of his seat, slicing through the crowd toward the fallen figure.

Jack had met Aaron in kindergarten. He was high-functioning, enough so that casual acquaintances probably wouldn't have recognized the symptoms. But he did have a few unusual qualities that his no-nonsense mother had termed quirks. One of these was a corroded penny he carried everywhere. In the fourth grade, a schoolyard bully had stolen the penny in a misguided attempt to make Aaron cry. Misguided, because the bully had been the one in tears after Jack had fallen on his friend's oppressor like thunder.

Jack and the bully had both been sent to the principal's office, and in true Ryan fashion, Jack Senior had been the one to attend the mandatory parent-teacher conference. Jack never did learn what was said behind those closed doors, but he'd also never forgotten the conversation during the

34

car ride home.

"Son, you broke the school's no-fighting policy, so you're suspended. That's the way life works. But sometimes a good man has to be willing to pay a price for doing what's right."

As Jack scooped the action figure from the grimy concrete, it wasn't a seven-year-old boy with curly brown hair and a ballcap that he saw. It was Aaron. Aaron and his penny crusted with green corrosion.

"Ma'am," Jack said, touching the woman on the shoulder. "I think your son dropped this."

The woman turned, her eyes going from Jack to the Captain America figure in his outstretched hand.

"Oh, goodness, thank you," the woman said, taking the toy from Jack with the reverence it deserved. "Here you go, buddy," she said, offering the figure to Tommy with a smile. "It wouldn't have been good to lose this, would it?"

Tommy released his mother's hand in favor of taking Captain America in both of his. His fingers flew over the figure, performing a frantic triage as his gaze remained focused on his feet. Only once he was certain that no harm had come to his friend was the superhero returned to his back pocket.

Still looking down, Tommy murmured two words.

"Thank you."

The woman stifled a gasp as she looked from her son to Jack, her face now radiant. She began to speak, the words trickling out at first but quickly becoming a deluge. Jack felt the warmth of her happiness, but he wasn't paying attention to what she said because he was focused on something else.

A man bearing down on her from behind.

A man with a knife.

3

In skilled hands at close range, a knife was a much more fearsome weapon than a gun.

The man stalking Tommy's mom was less than three yards away.

If pressed, Jack couldn't have articulated exactly how he knew what the man intended to do with the six-inch folding blade. He just did. Perhaps in the same manner that a sheepdog instinctively recognized a threat to the sheep, whether that threat approached on two legs or four.

Jack understood what the man represented with the primal part of his being. The part honed by years of training alongside some of the world's deadliest men and women. In the span of a single heartbeat, Jack had identified the wolf. Now it was time to do what sheepdogs did.

Protect the sheep.

Lunging past the woman, Jack hip-checked her out of the way as he intercepted the blade inches from her kidney. Jack gripped the attacker's wrist with both hands while interposing his linebacker-sized frame between the mom and knifeman. Jack was aware of the mom tumbling to the ground as a line of fire opened across his forearm. But these neurological inputs were muted, as if shrouded by a foggy haze. Instead, the sum of his existence was laser-focused on just one thing — staying alive.

The flickering steel reversed course, hunting Jack's abdomen in a blur of silver as the knifeman shook off Jack's wrist lock. As he'd been taught, Jack sacrificed a second forearm, this time his left, to parry the knife away from his vulnerable abdomen.

Another line of fire, this time accompanied by the sticky sensation of blood curling down his arm.

Chasing the blade, Jack crashed the knifeman, attempting to immobilize the knife arm by pinning it against the attacker's torso. Now Jack was body-to-body with the attacker. He could smell the man's sour odor, hear his rasping breath, and feel his muscles harden.

This was the intimate, visceral nature of hand-to-hand combat that movies omitted.

Jack compressed the knifeman's arm against the man's rock-hard torso, coming nose-to-nose with the attacker's Asian features and cold, dark eyes. Jack was tempted to go for the wrist again, but didn't. Instead, he kept the knife immobilized while launching a knee at the man's leg, aiming for the sciatic nerve.

In the half a dozen seconds they'd been grappling, Jack had been subconsciously assessing his opponent. The man was good, maybe better than Jack. A wrist lock alone wouldn't be effective unless the knifeman had something else to think about.

Like pain radiating down his leg.

Jack hammered the man's leg with two rapid strikes, picturing his patella snapping the offender's tibia in two. But instead of turning away to take the blows on his meaty hamstring, the knifeman rotated toward Jack. This meant that Jack's knee bludgeoned the man's quadriceps, but the attacker bore the attack with nothing more than a hiss of displeasure.

Then Jack understood why.

While Jack had been doing his best to shatter the assassin's leg, the Asian had switched the knife from his pinned left hand to his free right. Now that hand was a blur of motion headed for Jack's rib cage.

Leaping back, Jack planted his feet, and locked both hands on the knifeman's left arm. Snapping his heavy shoulders in an ever-tightening arc, Jack ripped the attacker's arm across his own body and shot his rear leg across the circle of violence he'd perpetrated.

While unorthodox, the maneuver was an effective substitute for a shoulder throw. Between the amount of energy Jack harnessed by torquing his shoulders and waist through a vicious arc and the attacker's own forward momentum, the throw should have generated enough force to dislocate the knifeman's shoulder while snapping his wrist in the process.

The operative words were *should have.*

Once again, the attacker seemed to defy physics. Nimbly leaping over Jack's blocking leg, the knifeman somehow slipped his hips around Jack's. Then, rather than fight the power generated by the corded muscles in Jack's back and shoulders, the attacker went with the throw, catapulting himself headlong into the crowd and ripping his arm from Jack's grasp.

In the time it took Jack to process what had just happened, the man was back on his feet, no worse for the wear, minus the knife Jack had stripped from him. And then he reached into his pocket and extracted a second blade.

His backup knife.

Of course.

Spying the original blade where it had fallen to the cobblestone street, Jack scooped up the weapon. As his fingers touched the hardened plastic handle, Jack dropped into a knife fighter's crouch, expecting the Asian to be on top of him. But the assassin was nowhere to be seen. Jack scanned the crowd for the attacker, trying to understand why the assassin had ceded the advantage.

Then a pistol pressed into the small of his back, and Jack wondered no longer.

4

"Who are you?"

"Already told you," Jack said, shifting his weight in an attempt to get more comfortable. This was a losing battle for two reasons. One, Israelis didn't design their chairs with meaty Americans in mind. Two, interrogation rooms weren't known for their comfortable furniture.

"Tell us one more time."

This time the request was softer, more like casual conversation between friends, and Jack felt inclined to answer. He'd already spent more than an hour going over his story and wanted to bring this part of his Israeli adventure to a close. But more important, the second questioner didn't seem to believe that Jack was responsible for the attempted knifing.

It also didn't hurt that she was pretty easy on the eyes. Who needed the good cop/bad cop routine when one of the interrogators could give Gal Gadot a run for her money?

"My name is John Patrick Ryan, Jr.," Jack said, directing both his gaze and his answer solely toward the female interrogator seated across the metal table. This was partly to encourage the woman into thinking that her efforts to establish a bond were succeeding and partly to annoy the shit out of her male partner. Besides, her olive skin, dark eyes, and sun-streaked brown hair were far more interesting than the interrogation room's off-white cinder-block walls and scuffed linoleum floor.

Her partner more mirrored the room's uninspiring decor. He had a squat, stocky build and his hair was cropped to brown stubble on his shiny skull. His lips were set in a permanent scowl, and he was constantly clenching and unclenching his fists as if he was searching for a neck to throttle.

Like Jack's, for instance.

The woman's disarming appearance aside, the man stalking back and forth across the narrow room behind her more resembled a caricature of the organization that held Jack in custody. The organization's official name was long and not easily understood by non–Hebrew speakers, but its abbreviation was known well enough. *Shin Bet* — Israel's internal security service.

"Why are you in Israel, Jack?"

The question again came from the woman. She smiled as she spoke, as if she and Jack were friends knowingly exchanging falsehoods to avoid an embarrassing topic.

How's your mom doing?

Great — never better.

"Sightseeing," Jack said, shifting in the chair for the hundredth time. "We've been over this already." The chair's steel frame seemed determined to put his ass cheeks to sleep.

"Bear with me, Jack," the woman said. "We're almost done."

Her smile widened as she spoke, revealing twin dimples. Jack didn't smile back, but it wasn't easy. He wondered just how many hardened terrorists she'd cracked with her bright eyes, sunny personality, and heart-stopping smile.

The Shin Bet officer was pretty without being intimidatingly beautiful. The kind of woman a man wanted to talk with, just to feel the warmth of her undivided attention. Her brooding, muscle-bound partner aside, Jack's intuition said that she was the more dangerous of the pair.

"I'm done talking," Jack said, leaning forward, his posture challenging. "Someone

44

tried to kill an American woman, and I stopped him. A simple thank-you would have been enough. Instead, your jackass of a partner shoved a pistol into my back, and the bad guy got away. We've been over this three times. I'm not doing it a fourth. Either release me or let me speak to my embassy."

"You think you're a tough guy because you're American?" the woman's partner said, looming over her shoulder.

"Nope," Jack said, his Irish temper rising. "I'm a tough guy because I'm a tough guy. Want to see?"

The man lunged across the table, grabbing Jack's shirt collar.

"You're in my country now, Jack Ryan," the man said, rolling his knuckles into a cross-collar choke. "Your constitution doesn't protect you here."

"Shit or get off the pot," Jack said, locking eyes with the man. "Your choice."

The man's face darkened, and for a moment, Jack thought the Shin Bet agent would take him up on his offer. Then a female voice cut through the testosterone with a string of Hebrew. The man barked a reply, but the tension on Jack's collar didn't get any tighter.

"Listen to Mom," Jack said. "She's trying to keep you from getting hurt."

45

The man's face mottled red. He slammed Jack back into the chair, but instead of applying the choke his fingers so obviously craved, he released Jack's shirt and stepped backward.

"You Americans," the man said, dusting off his hands, "such arrogant pricks."

"Maybe," Jack said. "But that woman's alive because of me. More than I can say for you."

The Shin Bet officer took a stutter step forward, but once again the woman intervened. What she said was incomprehensible, but Jack understood the gist all the same. The man rolled his shoulders and turned his head from side to side, cracking his neck.

Then he made for the exit.

"Good talk," Jack said, as the man opened the door.

He looked over his shoulder, dark eyes finding Jack's.

"Go to the airport and get on the first plane heading somewhere else," the man said. "Anywhere else."

"Thanks for the advice, Sparky," Jack said. "Now let me offer some in return — fuck off."

The man glared at Jack before storming through the door and banging it closed behind him.

46

"You and Dudu certainly seemed to hit it off," the woman said, another smile brightening her face.

"Don't take this the wrong way," Jack said, "but your partner is an asshat."

The woman tilted back her head and laughed, the bubbly sound bringing a smile to Jack's face in return.

"Asshat," she said, wiping tears from her eyes, "I must remember that."

"Glad I could help with your English," Jack said. "Now, as much fun as this has been, I'd really like to get back to sightseeing."

"Yes, yes," the woman said, waving away Jack's concern. "My country has many amazing sights. Can I point you toward anything in particular?"

"I have a degree in history," Jack said, "so there's not much in Israel that doesn't interest me."

"Well, then," the woman said, getting to her feet, "perhaps you'd like a local to show you around?"

She smiled again as she asked the question, but this time there was something more behind her eyes. Something . . . interesting.

"Do you make that offer to everyone you interrogate?" Jack said.

"Oh, Jack. This was just a friendly conversation. If you were being interrogated, you'd know."

The woman's lips might still have been smiling, but her eyes weren't.

"Okay," Jack said, pushing himself out of the chair. "As much as I'd like to take you up on that, I'm going to pass. I've had about all the excitement I can stomach. Besides, I need to see to these."

Jack lifted his arms, showing the twin bandages on his forearms. The knife cuts had been fairly shallow, but Jack knew from experience that assassin's blades were seldom clean. The Shin Bet medics had done a respectable job of patching him up, but Jack wanted to stop by a pharmacy on the way back to his Airbnb and take a look for himself.

"Too bad," she said, opening the interrogation room door. "If you change your mind, give me a ring."

The woman passed a card to Jack. The name *Tal Levy* was printed in dark ink with a 972 telephone number written beneath.

Nothing else.

"Thanks, Tal," Jack said. "I'll keep your offer in mind."

"Do more than that," Tal said. "My partner might have let his emotions get the better of him, but he wasn't wrong. Our nations are friendly, but it's still bad form to operate on allied soil without coordination. I'd strongly suggest calling the number on that card if you intend to leave your residence at Shefer Street for anywhere other than the airport. I'd hate for any more misadventures to mar your stay."

A final smile accompanied her words, but Tal's flirty attitude was gone, replaced by something else.

Steel.

5

Jack pondered Tal's parting words as he waited for his server. Like intelligence offices the world over, the Shin Bet station to which Jack had been taken didn't exactly advertise its presence. Located on a leafy, tree-lined boulevard close to the ocean, the nondescript building competed with trendy clothing stores on one side of the street and cafés with tables arranged for outdoor seating on the other.

People strolled along the pedestrian area as the sun's light softened, casting writhing shadows through the eucalyptus branches. Bikes competed with motor scooters as Israelis wrapped up work and headed for their flats, never suspecting that they were passing by one of the outstations belonging to their nation's feared intelligence apparatus.

But Jack knew. And if Tal's inference was to be believed, the Shin Bet now knew about him. Like it or not, that changed things.

Jack considered the cardboard box sitting on the table in front of him as he thought about his next move. As per protocol, the Shin Bet agents had confiscated his personal items after taking him into custody. A dour-faced security guard had returned them in an unassuming box as Jack had left the building. He'd kept the box unopened while putting some physical distance between himself and the Shin Bet station.

Now it was time to decide what to do next.

The waiter wandered over, and Jack ordered a cappuccino. The server frowned and asked Jack to repeat his order, as if unsure of his English. Jack reiterated that he had indeed said *cappuccino*. In Italy the blasphemy of ordering that particular coffee this late in the day would not have been tolerated, but the Israeli waiter was much too polite to comment on the American's obvious lack of sophistication.

Jack had traveled extensively enough to know that anywhere other than America, espresso was the only acceptable form of caffeine after eleven a.m. Even so, the jet lag and stress of an operation gone sideways were starting to catch up with him and he craved the frothy drink. Besides, what was the point of being American if you didn't use the stereotype to your advantage?

Jack waited for the man to leave before sliding his thumbnail into the tape binding the box and then shaking the contents onto the table. His phone fell out first. Jack eyed the electronic device before placing it back in the container. He'd spent about an hour separated from the device while in Shin Bet custody. That was probably fifty-nine minutes too long. The cell was undoubtedly compromised, and this, combined with Tal's less-than-subtle implication, made his next moves somewhat more difficult.

The irony was that while Jack often worked as a clandestine operative for The Campus, the organization was a private entity and technically outside the umbrella of the American intelligence community. Jack was not a CIA officer, or member of any sanctioned intelligence agency, for that matter. He did not draw a government paycheck and therefore was not bound by the unwritten rule that required that he declare himself when working on allied soil.

Usually.

But this trip was different. It was actually supposed to be Ding Chavez, not Jack, observing the CIA asset-validation exercise. The man in charge of the exercise, Peter

52

Beltz, had asked Ding to serve as an outside observer. While Peter didn't know that Ding, like Jack, was a Campus operative, he figured that when his friend had vanished from the Army's ranks without a trace, he'd been "sheep-dipped" to one intelligence organization or another.

When Campus OPTEMPO necessitated a last-minute change in plans, Ding had asked Jack to pinch-hit. Jack had been only too happy to oblige for a number of reasons. For one, Jack respected Ding immensely. The significance of the Rainbow Six legend vouching for Jack's competency to a former comrade-in-arms wasn't trivial. Jack had sought the respect of the senior members of The Campus, and this gesture by Ding meant he was well on his way.

Second, the personal sacrifices Jack was making for his dual life were substantial. His father had already met and married his mother and welcomed Sally to the family by the time he was Jack's age. While Jack certainly didn't feel like he was having a midlife crisis, he was keenly aware that forty loomed much closer than twenty. As his mother, Cathy Ryan, reminded him at every opportunity, not only was Jack still single, but he didn't even have any real prospects.

Or at least not any serious ones. Before

leaving for Tel Aviv, Jack had delighted his mother and father by bringing a friend home for dinner. A female friend. Lisanne Robertson had her Lebanese mother's olive skin and dark curly hair, and her American father's sense of humor. Like Jack, she'd also worked for The Campus, but her operational career had recently been cut short by a bullet that had almost ended her life. Now that they were no longer coworkers, Jack thought there might just be something more to their relationship, but it was still much too early to tell.

Even so, Jack's parents' marriage had always been a source of inspiration. He'd taken for granted that he'd marry and have a brood of his own once he'd met the right woman. But more and more, Jack realized that the career he'd spent his twenties trying to attain was now the very thing holding him back from the family he so desired. It was hard to find and maintain a relationship with a normal girl when his definition of work-life balance meant dividing time between his "white" job as a financial analyst with Hendley Associates and his off-the-books work as a Campus operative.

Not exactly a fertile hunting ground for the future Mrs. Ryan.

So when Ding offered an all-expense-paid

trip to Israel in exchange for observing an asset-validation exercise, Jack had jumped at the chance. His work for Peter was scheduled to last an afternoon at best, and he'd intended to divide the remainder of his weeklong visit between playing tourist to the Holy Land's historical sites and surfing. There was something about being on a surfboard that brought the world into focus.

Jack had succeeded in his goal of moving from a desk at The Campus to becoming a full-fledged operative because he'd focused the analytical skills he'd inherited from his overachieving parents on the problem at hand. He'd developed a plan, put in the hard work, and now, almost ten years later, he'd achieved what he'd sought.

He'd intended to spend some secluded time in Israel examining his personal life with the same intensity he'd applied to his professional, but without the distractions offered by The Campus, his parents, or even Lisanne.

Unfortunately, the Asian knifeman had thrown a wrench into that plan.

The asset-validation exercise was undoubtedly over, but Jack had no intention of reaching out to Peter. The Shin Bet might have already made Peter and his team, but if not, Jack wasn't going to give them any help. With his operational reasons for remaining in Israel gone, Jack was left with the option of playing tourist.

But here, too, Tal's warning resounded like a ringing bell.

I'd hate for any more misadventures to mar your stay.

Though Jack wasn't sure what she was hinting at, her warning wasn't exactly subtle. If he intended to remain in Israel, he needed to retain the Shin Bet officer as a tour guide. And while traipsing through Israel in Tal's company wasn't the worst thing he could imagine, Jack also knew he wouldn't be the first man to allow a beautiful woman's smile to circumvent his common sense.

Tal was an intelligence officer for one of the world's most aggressive services. Yes, Israel was an ally of the United States, but honor among spies, even those of friendly nations, was more romantic notion than reality.

Besides, it would be better for Jack's cover if Tal continued to believe he was an undeclared intelligence officer rather than an operative for a private entity. Even spies from adversarial nations were offered some professional courtesy. But if the Shin Bet officer discovered that Jack worked for The

Campus, anything could happen.

Viewed from this vantage point, the most conservative course of action would be for Jack to bring his Israeli vacation to a close. There was no operational reason to stay, and the risk of giving away Peter's team, or even information about The Campus, wasn't worth nosing around Tel Aviv. Soul-searching via surfing would have to wait.

Jack was headed home.

Or at least that's what he thought.

Picking up his passport from the pile of pocket litter and other debris that had fallen from the box, Jack found something underneath. The Captain America action hero. The toy must have tumbled from Tommy's pocket during the confrontation with the Asian assassin.

Jack spun the character through his fingers, examining the toy from all angles.

Other than a couple of nicks in the plastic and a wobbly back leg, old Cap wasn't any worse for wear. Even more important, there was nothing remarkable about the figure. No colorful additions to Cap's costume rendered in marker, no initials melted into the back with a soldering iron. It could have been one of the millions of action figures on the market — as easy to replace as a quick trip to Walmart.

Except Jack knew that it wasn't.

Not really.

In an instant, he was back to Aaron and his green-crusted penny. His friend had memorized every crevice and cranny on the corroded piece of copper. Aaron knew his talisman by touch. He had an almost telepathic link to the one-cent piece, and Tommy undoubtedly felt the same way about the lost action figure. Where most people would see just another battered superhero, Tommy would be able to read the dings and nicks the way a forensic examiner read fingerprints.

Cap couldn't be replaced, because he was irreplaceable.

Jack placed the action figure next to his passport and examined them both. One represented the rational course of action, while the other a flight of fantasy. Jack was a covert operative. A ghost. Someone who made his living by flying under the radar, and as Tal had made clear in no uncertain terms, there was nothing under-the-radar about his current heat status.

He was burned, no two ways about it. The smart play, the only play, was to catch an Uber to the airport and jump on a flight home. He'd fulfilled his end of the bargain both to Ding and Peter.

58

Sometimes discretion really was the better part of valor.

Except that when Jack looked at the object perched on the table next to his passport, he no longer saw a cheap plastic toy. He saw a curly-haired boy with tears streaming down his face, trying to pry his penny free from the schoolyard bully's dirty fist.

Sometimes a good man has to be willing to pay a price for doing what's right.

Jack smiled as he threw a handful of shekels onto the table before grabbing both the passport and the action figure. The next direct flight to the States didn't leave for another four hours. Plenty of time to run an errand on his way to the airport. And if the detour meant pissing off Tal and her partner, that was too damned bad. Worst-case scenario, Jack would get a second chance to talk to a beautiful woman.

What could go wrong with that?

6

Al Tanf Outpost
Syria

"Say that one more time?"

Cary gave a long sigh, looking from the man asking the question to his commander, seated directly behind and to the left of the questioner. Cary raised his eyebrows, giving Captain Alex Brown his best *Do I really have to deal with this shit?* look.

As team leaders went, Captain Brown was pretty switched on. Unlike some of the officers Cary had served with, Alex saw his role as an A-team leader as the pinnacle of his career rather than just a stepping-stone to bigger and better things. In a break with tradition, Alex had been an Apache helicopter pilot prior to attending the grueling selection process required of all those who had aspirations of someday wearing the Army's coveted green beret.

This unorthodox career path opened Alex

up to untold amounts of ribbing from his contemporaries, but also a degree of begrudging respect from his men. After all, as anyone who'd served in the infantry for longer than a day could attest, aviators had things pretty damned cushy, all things considered. Someone who traded the hot meals, eight hours of crew rest, and not-insubstantial flight pay that accompanied the Army's silver aviator wings for a hundred-pound rucksack and endless nights sleeping in the mud was not on a mission to make general officer.

No, men like Alex Brown were exactly the type of leaders Cary had hoped to find when he'd joined the ranks of the Green Berets. This was why, when Captain Brown met Cary's look of exasperation with an understanding nod but a gesture with his hand to continue, Cary exhaled his breath in a noisy rush and began his story again.

For the third time.

"Like I said before," Cary said, keeping his tone civil while making no attempt to hide his grimace of frustration, "Sergeant Mustafa and I saw General Ahmadi enter the compound at 1300 local time. When we broke station three hours ago, he was still inside."

"And you're sure it was him?" the CIA

61

case officer said.

Cary stared at the man standing in front of him before answering. In the way of soldiers everywhere, he compared the man to his own commanding officer and found the intelligence operative wanting.

While Alex looked like the Special Operations officer he was, the Agency man had a spare build, which he compensated for with his oversized condescending attitude. The intelligence officer's narrow features seemed to be set in a perpetual sneer, and his diction was distinctly professorial, as if he were teaching a graduate-level course in international relations rather than tracking down his nation's enemies. Everything from the man's stance to his manner of asking questions was patronizing.

Simply put, Cary didn't like him, and he figured the feeling was probably mutual.

"What's your name again?" Cary said, no longer attempting a civil tone.

"Bill. Bill Jones."

"Of course it is," Cary said. "I guess all the John Does were taken. Here's the thing, *Bill.* I'm a Special Operations–trained sniper. Most people think that means I'm a good shot, and that's true. But it's also a bit like saying that a NASCAR driver is really good at parallel parking. Shooting is part of my job, but not the main part. A sniper's primary function is observation. Seeing and remembering things. Things that may not seem to be important at the time, but could be critical when a pair of MH-60s loaded with assaulters is thirty seconds out from a target. I'm not trying to be a jackass, Bill, but if I tell you that General Farhad Ahmadi walked through the compound gates, he fucking did. Got it?"

Cary felt the flush that came when he was truly angry building at the base of his neck at about the same time Jad, who was seated next to him, kicked him in the shin.

Okay, so maybe that last sentence was a bit too much, but damned if this CIA or OGA, or whatever the hell secret squirrel acronym they were now using, wasn't getting under his skin. In Cary's experience, CIA case officers came in two variants: field spooks and desk drivers. If this debriefing session was any indication, the man currently known as Bill Jones definitely fell into the latter category.

"I think what Sergeant Marks is trying to say is that he and Sergeant Mustafa both had ample time to observe the target and independently confirmed his identity. Is that about right, boys?"

The interruption came from Captain

Brown, who was doing exactly what good officers were supposed to do — stepping into the breach on behalf of his men. The former aviator's stock took another jump in Cary's eyes. Turning back to the Agency operative, Cary opened his mouth to follow his commander's salvo, but Jad beat him to the punch.

"Exactly right, sir," Jad said, folding his arms across his massive chest. "And our satellite link and recording equipment both taking a shit right exactly when Ahmadi's convoy arrived only adds credence."

"What do you mean?" Bill said, his pinched features narrowing.

"I see it like this," Jad said, his surfer's drawl somehow at odds with the serious-ness of the situation. "You Agency boys have been using drones of one kind or another to remotely smoke targets of opportunity with absolute impunity for the last two decades. We both know the dumb jihadis died a long time ago. The ones that are left are smart, and I think they may have figured out how to rebalance what has been up until now a pretty lopsided battlefield. I recalibrated both our radio and the digital recorder as soon as we returned to base. They're both fine. But both pieces of equipment failed at the exact moment a high-value target rolled into our sightline. It doesn't take a genius to guess why."

"Enlighten me," Bill said.

"You sent us in instead of using an Agency drone for a reason," Jad said. "I'm assuming that reason has something to do with the drone's performance. Either the video stream crapped out as the bird arrived on station over the compound or the drone lost its satellite navigational fix and had to return to base. How am I doing so far?"

Bill didn't say anything. He didn't have to. His expression spoke volumes.

"Now," Jad said, taking the case officer's silence as affirmation, "I'm shit for flying drones, but I do know a thing or two about the RF spectrum. I think someone has developed the ability to burn out the military frequency bands using a high-energy pulse rather than persistent jamming, otherwise we would have picked up the interference on our own SIGINT devices. That would account for our loss of comms, and if the jammer was putting out enough juice, it could scramble our video equipment as well. The video recorders we use are top-of-the-line, which means they're commercial off the shelf. They perform a hell of a lot better than the shit the government buys, but because they weren't built with this mission in mind, their circuitry isn't hardened to mil standards. The amount of juice the bad guys must be throwing into the atmosphere in that micro-pulse could easily bleed from the sat radio into the attached peripherals."

"So the general's vehicle is equipped with some kind of customized jammer," Cary said.

In addition to being hands down the best spotter he'd ever worked with, Jad was also a gifted Echo. Unfortunately, when he talked radios, Jad sometimes forgot that not everyone had the equivalent of a degree in RF engineering from MIT.

"Isn't that what I just said?" Jad said, a look of genuine confusion on his face.

"Focus, gents," Alex said. "Jad, do you mean that our local David Koresh has access to this pulse jammer, too?"

"Not necessarily," Jad said, smiling as the conversation came back to one of his two favorite topics. "Just stating the facts, sir. I leave the wild-ass guesses to people like Bill."

This time it was Cary who kicked his teammate in the shin, though his heart really wasn't in it. Despite his impressive size and formidable appearance, Jad was as easygoing as they came. If the Agency pencil pusher had managed to piss off the nicest man in all of 5th Special Forces Group, there really was no hope for him.

Even so, Cary was a master sergeant. He'd already been boarded for sergeant major twice without success. In its bureaucratic way, the Army had let him know that he had climbed as high on the career ladder as he was liable to go. That knowledge came with both pluses and minuses.

On the minus side, he wouldn't be bringing home an E-9's retirement pay when he finally decided to stop kicking in doors in favor of heading back to the family maple syrup business in New Hampshire. On the plus side, his days of worrying about a politically incorrect attitude affecting his chances of promotion were a thing of the past.

Not so with his spotter. Jad was still a sergeant first class, or E-7 in military parlance. He needed to be promoted once more before retiring, and bullshit spats with government partners had a way of making it into a soldier's promotion files. Cary opened his mouth, preparing to take the heat off his spotter with another smartass comment, but again his team leader rode to the rescue.

"Mr. Jones," Alex said, interposing himself

between his men and the Agency officer. "Is there anything else? If not, let's wrap this up. My guys have had a long day and will undoubtedly have another long one tomorrow."

Damn, but Captain Brown was on it. As much as Cary hated to admit it, the young officer's directness was refreshing. Perhaps Special Operations should be recruiting more Apache aviators to fill their ranks.

Bill looked from Alex to the two knuckle draggers and seemed to remember where he was for the first time. Because of the sensitivity and urgency surrounding their report, Bill had come over to the 5th Group compound rather than making the snipers troop across the road to the CIA's collection of buildings.

As such, this debriefing was taking place in the team room, one of the more sacrosanct spaces in an ODA's environment. This is where team members serviced and stored their gear, conducted pre-mission briefings and post-operations debriefings, and generally gathered to shoot the shit and keep one another company.

In other words, the ramshackle collection of battered tables, broken chairs, and chain-link-enclosed gear lockers, and the pictures of former team members killed in action hanging over the obligatory miniature bar in the room's back corner, were hallowed ground. An outsider did not come into the holy of holies and question the integrity or professional competence of team members.

Not without consequences, anyway.

Bill cleared his throat before speaking. This time his words came without condescension dripping from each syllable. Not an apology exactly, but maybe a start.

"My asset's reporting is . . . at odds with what your men saw," Bill said.

It didn't pass unnoticed to Cary that the Agency man had said *saw* without a couple of adjacent words that might have substantially watered down the verb. Again, not an apology per se, but things did seem to be moving in the right direction.

"Interesting," Alex said. "What did your asset report?"

Now it was the Agency man who sighed before replying. "He said that the visitor was one of the local Syrian militia leaders coming to pay his respects. Because of the influence the cult's leader exerts on the local community, quite a few of the tribal chieftains have been trying to make inroads with him."

"How reliable is your asset?" Alex said.

Bill shot the former aviator a distasteful

look before replying. The new spirit of détente notwithstanding, Alex had just done the equivalent of challenging the case officer to a dick-measuring contest.

A spy's worth was directly tied to the accuracy and value of the reporting he or she obtained from their assets. An asset who reported false information was of zero value, a sentiment that applied doubly to their handler, who hadn't been able to determine the veracity of the so-called intelligence before passing it on.

And that was only the tip of the iceberg. An asset discovered to be lying had a cascading effect in that every bit of reporting the man or woman had ever provided now had to be called into question and either independently verified or, as was more often the case, discarded. This was not how junior CIA case officers successfully advanced through the ranks to the rarefied air of Langley's Seventh Floor.

Bill's defeated expression seemed to indicate that there was quite a bit of previous reporting on the line.

"His other reporting has been validated to an extent," Bill said, clearly hedging, "but this discrepancy isn't one we can ignore. Setting that aside, if Ahmadi did stop by, it wasn't for a social visit. We need to know what he's doing there and why. We need eyes inside that compound."

"Maybe we can kill two birds with one stone," Jad said.

Cary looked at his spotter, trying to understand what the man was suggesting.

Then he knew.

"No fucking way," Cary said, shaking his head. "Not going to happen."

"Come on, boss," Jad said, "you said it yourself. Maybe my cousins know a thing or two."

"I also said you should make Jocelyne an honest woman, but you don't listen for shit about that. Why start now?"

"Hey, guys," Alex said, "what if for a minute we pretended like I was your team leader. What gives?"

"My spotter was out in the sun too long today, sir," Cary said. "He must have suffered heat stroke, because the words coming out of his big mouth make zero sense."

"Please excuse my friend, sir," Jad said, talking over Cary. "He sometimes forgets he's my team sergeant and not my mother. I happen to be a native Arabic speaker who spent my first twelve years in the local neighborhood. Bill here wants to know whether or not his asset is legit, and we all want to know why the Quds Force commander has suddenly taken an interest in an apocalyptic cult. I'm simply suggesting that I put my good looks and linguistic badassery to use by taking a look around inside."

"I like it," Bill said.

"Absolutely fucking not," Cary countered.

"Again," Alex said, holding up his hand, "I think I read somewhere that I'm actually in charge. Bill, Bob, John, or whatever the fuck your name is — Jad is my responsibility. Mine. I don't put the lives of my men in jeopardy on a whim. Don't get me wrong, we do some pretty hinky shit around here — there's a reason why we're called Special Forces. But we don't do half-assed. Not now. Not ever. So, if you want to use one of mine on an operation, I'm all ears. But the op gets planned and controlled from here. Otherwise, we are done talking. Capeesh?"

Bill grimaced like he'd bitten into a rotten peach, but he nodded all the same.

"And you," Alex said, turning to Cary. "Enough with the Mother Goose shit. Give me just a little bit of credit. If we do this, it will be done right. And before you ask, yes, you will be the one providing overwatch for Jad. Tracking?"

Cary paused for a moment and then slowly nodded. "Yes, sir. I get it."

"Good," Alex said, turning back to Bill. "Now, assuming Sergeant Mustafa was cleared to participate in this operation. How would it go down?"

"According to my asset," Bill said, "the VIP will be back tomorrow. It would be great if Sergeant Mustafa could tell us why."

Which was exactly what Cary was afraid he would say. Sometimes he absolutely hated being right.

7

Tel Aviv, Israel

The man known as Jonathan Mills kept a warm smile plastered on his friendly face as his stomach churned. This was the moment of truth. The instant in time in which all the work from the previous six months either bore fruit or exploded in his face. In the lexicon of businessmen everywhere, this was *the close.* The final interaction determining whether the person he'd been working agreed to the terms of the deal.

Or not.

If Jonathan was a corporate salesman, this would be where he met or missed his yearly quota. But he was not a businessman. He was a spy. In his line of work, a missed pitch didn't equate to an anemic bonus or a poor performance review. It meant death. The potential asset's death for sure, and potentially Jonathan's as well, depending on how badly he'd misjudged the situation.

While the profession of espionage has always been a bit more rough-and-tumble than selling stocks, in the more civilized rules that guided the interactions of the world's superpowers, an unsuccessful pitch rarely resulted in anyone's death. But the country Jonathan was operating against had never been known for its genteel civility, especially with regard to adversarial intelligence services.

"I'm very grateful for your help," Jonathan said, smiling so broadly his teeth hurt. "It's people like you and I who are able to help our countries move past the petty squabbles of today in favor of the lasting relationships of tomorrow. We are patriots."

Except that the bespectacled, middle-aged man sitting across the table from Jonathan was not anyone's idea of a patriot. He was a mid-level manager with three unremarkable children and a plain-looking wife. If that had been all, the man's tragic but all-too-common existence would have probably never come to Jonathan's attention.

But that wasn't all.

Not by a long shot.

In addition to his pedantic family life and dead-end career, the dark-haired man had another aspect to his existence. One that Jonathan had found infinitely more interesting. The ordinary-looking man had rather extraordinary taste in women. Specifically, younger women with a yearning for the finer things in life. The kind of things a manager who'd been passed over for a lucrative promotion in his booming technology start-up in favor of a wunderkind half his age could not afford.

At least not without a little help.

Like all good case officers, Jonathan understood that the bespectacled man's motivation went beyond just providing his newest arm candy with an IWC Portofino watch. He was angry. *Pissed off* might be a better description. At almost fifty years old, Jonathan's quarry had finally come to the realization that all men eventually reach — his professional life had peaked and was now on the decline.

It wasn't just that the plush assignments were no longer offered to him. No, the latest promotion he'd pursued had gone to a man-child barely out of university. The kind of spoiled creature who expected a six-figure salary just for showing up to work each day and then bitterly complained when he didn't get one. Except this time the spoiled creature had scored big, leaving the bespectacled man to digitally shout the situation's injustice to his social media followers.

If he'd had any.

And while this phenomenon was not uncommon in Tel Aviv, also known as the Silicon Valley of the Middle East, it still didn't rise to the level of Jonathan's attention. After all, in a city in which new start-up dreams were conceived each and every day, it was inevitable that a few ended in nightmares. Even overleveraged and angry, there was nothing particularly interesting about Jonathan's mild-mannered companion.

Not without his second job, anyway.

The bespectacled man's additional job was just that — a distraction that took him away from his hot start-up one day a week. But what a distraction it was. Like many in Israel's professional workforce, the man was an IDF reservist. A citizen soldier, as it were. Except that this man did not report to an Army base and draw a Tavor rifle while pretending to be a warrior.

No, his reserve duty was much more interesting.

The bespectacled man, Yossi Cohen, took a sip of coffee as his pale eyes studied his tablemate. Jonathan knew what the other man saw — the epitome of a serious, yet harmless, American. Jonathan had blue eyes, a shock of blond hair that he wore long, spilling over his forehead in curly waves, and chubby cheeks that framed an ever-present smile. Though he was in his late thirties, Jonathan projected an earnestness more in line with the naïveté often ascribed to youth.

Or Americans.

Jonathan knew that it was this naïveté, this childish innocence, that put Yossi at ease, allowing him to believe that he, not Jonathan, was the one who was dictating the terms of their relationship. And this was completely fine with the man known as Jonathan who was not in the least bit naïve.

Not that Yossi needed to know this troublesome detail.

"Tell me again what you will do with the information," Yossi said.

His expression was deadpan, completely devoid of emotion. They might as well have been discussing the beautiful Israeli weather, to judge from the bored look on his face. Except the long, elegant fingers of his right hand were in constant motion, first spinning his coffee cup on its saucer, then tapping out a quiet staccato on the table's edge.

The fingers said there was more at stake here than just idle gossip.

"Sure," Jonathan said with another radiant smile. "Our two countries are at an impasse because of politics. You and I are going to shortcut the bureaucratic bullshit. You give me the software hooks, and I'll network your system into our current architecture. Then I'll set up an off-the-books demonstration for my friend at the PEO weapons office. He's promised me that if he can verify the system's capabilities, he'll push the necessary customs paperwork through. In a month, two months tops, the U.S. Army will finish the procurement they started. We'll sell more systems, Israel will have an overseas customer, and American servicemembers will have the protection they need. Everyone wins."

Yossi stared back without speaking. As if he were weighing Jonathan's words. As if he wasn't already doing the conversion from dollars to shekels in his head. As if he hadn't already visited a designer boutique on Rothschild Boulevard last night to shop for his blond girlfriend with the big tits who lived in Florentin. Not to be confused with the brunette with the shapely ass who preferred the Neve Tzedek section of Tel Aviv.

For a man with as many women as Yossi, it wouldn't do to confuse one mistress's taste for another's.

That kind of thing could land a man in trouble.

"I'm not entirely comfortable with this," Yossi said, "but I also am not the sort to let bureaucracy stand in the way of keeping our American allies safe."

"A man after my own heart," Jonathan said. "And believe me, the last thing I want to do is make you uneasy. So how about this — why don't we make our arrangement official? I'll hire you as a consultant. My company already has a Technology Assistance Agreement in place with the Maf'at. We can add you to the paperwork tonight. Of course we'd need to pay you a reasonable salary just to keep this all on the up-and-up. How about ten thousand a week? You've been helping me for the last couple months, so let's do a lump sum of one hundred thousand dollars to get caught up. Will that work?"

For once there was a crack in the man with the face of stone. One hundred thousand dollars was double what they'd flirted with in the dance of betrayal up until now. But the man known as Jonathan was supposedly an American businessman, and Americans were nothing if not generous.

"Yes," Yossi said, gulping to hide his surprise. "I would feel much better if this was documented."

"Of course, of course," Jonathan said, waving away Yossi's concerns. "I'll send an e-mail back to the office as soon as I get to the airport and have my assistant send over one of our boilerplate agreements to get things kicked off. That said, I don't want to wait on paperwork. Why don't we get the payment out of the way now, and the contract can catch up later this afternoon? What account would you like the money wired into?"

Yossi rattled off a string of numbers and Jonathan dutifully entered them into his phone. A moment later Jonathan hit the send button and Yossi's phone chimed in return.

"Well, I guess that's that," Jonathan said. "So how about those hooks?"

Without so much as a twitch, Yossi reached into his pocket, removed a thumb drive, and slid it across the table.

"Excellent," Jonathan said, collecting the memory stick. "Thank you again for your help. You have my gratitude as well as that of the American people. You've just made both our nations safer."

In truth, Yossi had done nothing of the sort. But that didn't bother Jonathan in the least. Mainly because the man known as

Jonathan was not a businessman.
And he certainly wasn't American.

82

8

The man formerly known as Jonathan Mills edged into the shadows offered by the narrow alleyway, making his way deeper into the predominantly Arab village of Ajami located in the southern portion of Tel Aviv. Men who looked like Jonathan weren't typically seen among the brown faces who inhabited the multitude of dwellings stacked on top of one another in haphazard fashion like the perennial Leaning Tower of Pisa.

Then again, few men were like Jonathan.

For starters, the man formerly known as Jonathan Mills wasn't American, or Canadian, or even European, for that matter. At least not in any sense of the word that mattered. Though he spoke English with a midwestern accent, Jonathan had never set foot on American soil. He did have his mother's looks and language, but beneath the curly blond hair and fair skin, he was his father's child through and through. And his father hated Americans with a passion unmatched by any other country save one.

Israel.

So it was with no small amount of satisfaction that Jonathan selected a door at the end of the alley, gave two quick knocks followed by two longer raps, and then stole inside. The pair of men waiting in the dimly lit room beyond held pistols.

Both were pointed at Jonathan.

He understood.

Jonathan had been mistaken for someone else his entire life. On the first day of school he'd realized that he looked completely different from his classmates. In the days that followed, he'd been subject to taunts and torments from the other children. But this had also been part of his father's plan. A career employee of the Iranian Ministry of Intelligence and Security, or MOIS, Jonathan's father had seen in his progeny a once-in-a-lifetime opportunity. Now, almost thirty years later, that opportunity was on the cusp of being realized.

But only if the two imbeciles with guns didn't shoot him first.

"*As-salamu alaikum,* brothers," Jonathan said, his hands raised chest level, palms facing the gunmen. "I believe you have something for me."

84

"Who are you?" the nearest man said, his eyes squinting in the darkness.

The man's face was pinched and drawn, bringing to mind a rat. Jonathan instinctively didn't like him. He looked like he should be nosing around on the floor for a scrap of cheese, and his finger foolishly rested on the pistol's trigger. Jonathan decided then and there that regardless of what happened in the next several seconds, the man's time on earth was rapidly drawing to a close.

"I was told to knock four times on the front door before entering," Jonathan said, keeping his smile in place. "I hope there weren't too many other men given the same instructions."

Though Jonathan's Arabic was flawless, Ratface scrunched up his nose as if he didn't understand. Which might just be true. Hamas foot soldiers weren't known for their intelligence.

"You look American," Ratface said, edging a step closer.

"That's the point, you idiot," Jonathan said, allowing his smile to fray.

"What did you call me?" Ratface said, now standing close enough to punctuate each word by jabbing the pistol's barrel into Jonathan's chest.

Though metal stabbing into his breast-bone was hardly a charming feeling, Jonathan endured the unpleasantness exactly twice. On the third time, Jonathan slapped his hands together, sandwiching the pistol's muzzle between them, while jerking up and to the left.

Ratface's wrist snapped and the pistol discharged.

Though Ratface's companion didn't know it, Jonathan had actually done the man a favor. Since Jonathan was right-handed, he typically performed this particular disarming technique to his dominant side, which meant the new bullet hole in the plaster wall would have resided in the man's head instead.

But Jonathan was not a barbarian. Besides, as much as he detested hired help, he needed at least one of these goons for what came next.

Ratface, on the other hand, was completely expendable.

Between the muzzle blast from the unexpected pistol discharge and the equally unexpected lightning bolt of pain from his snapped wrist, Ratface was looking a bit dazed and confused. He'd reacted to the *pop* of his radius snapping like a turkey's wishbone by cradling the wounded wrist against his chest with his good hand, leaving his lower body unprotected.

Jonathan capitalized on this oversight by punting Ratface squarely between his spindly legs.

The would-be tough guy reacted predictably, crumpling into the fetal position. From there, it was a simple matter for Jonathan to step forward, place the pistol against the groaning man's head, and pull the trigger. Or at least that's what he'd intended to do. But just as his finger began to take the slack from the trigger, a voice interrupted him.

"Wait!"

Though screamed, the exclamation was more plea than command, and this saved Ratface's life. If the *wait* had been an order, Jonathan would have squeezed the trigger in the smooth, even motion for which he'd been trained and then probably done the same to Ratface's compatriot, help be damned.

But something about the other man's plaintive tone gave Jonathan pause.

Jonathan lived by wits, and right now, his intuition told him to delay the fool's execution.

At least for the moment, anyway.

"Why?" Jonathan said. His pistol was still squarely affixed to Ratface's head, and his index finger still held tension right at the trigger's breaking point. Less than a millimeter of additional pressure and Ratface's brains would be decorating the floor.

"Because he's my brother," the second man said. "The man who briefed us didn't say you'd look like an American. My brother was just being cautious. Don't kill him. Please."

Jonathan weighed the man's words, testing their veracity, while pressing the pistol harder into Ratface's forehead, dimpling the skin.

The brother's explanation was plausible — probably true, even. Jonathan's appearance was his greatest asset, allowing him to move unmolested through target countries in a manner in which his father's people never could. These Arabs were low-level operatives. Operational security certainly dictated that they know as little about Jonathan as possible, including his appearance. As Jonathan knew from personal experience, the Israeli intelligence apparatus was a fearsome adversary.

Even so, Jonathan's instinct said that Ratface was a liability, and in Jonathan's line of work, liabilities were handled in just one way.

"Please," the second man said again, as if

hearing Jonathan's thoughts.

Shifting his attention from Ratface, Jonathan looked at the brother. Slim, perhaps five years younger than his sibling, with dark hair and an honest face. His hands were lifted above his head, his pistol angled up and away from Jonathan. Unlike Ratface, there was no cruelty in his expression. This was the thinker. The intellectual who had probably bailed his older, headstrong brother out of too many problems to count. An older brother he was risking his life to save.

Jonathan would have given much to have had such a brother.

With a sigh, Jonathan lowered his pistol and took a step away from a still-kneeling Ratface.

"Get me the device," Jonathan said. "Now."

The younger brother bobbed his head and practically ran for the back room. A moment later, he reappeared holding an innocuous-looking box. Reaching into his pocket, Jonathan took out the thumb drive Yossi had given him and tossed it to the brother.

"Put that in the slot," Jonathan said, "and push the button."

The young man did as instructed. For a

moment, nothing happened. Then a single LED on the side of the box glowed green. A second later the acrid smell of an electrical short filled the apartment as a thin column of gray smoke drifted up from the device.

"I'm sorry, I'm sorry," the brother said, holding the still-smoldering box up as if it were a burnt offering. "I did what you said."

"And because of that, your brother lives," Jonathan said, backing slowly from the apartment, his pistol swinging from one man to the other. "For now. But if you want him to stay that way, you need to do one more thing."

"What?"

"Forget you ever saw me."

And with that, Jonathan slipped from the apartment as silently as the wisps of smoke escaped from the box.

9

The man who'd called himself Jonathan was not a Jonathan at all. His name was Darien Moradi, and while his accent and features came from his mother, Persian blood coursed through his veins. At this moment, this ancient blood was warning him that he needed to get a grip on his emotions before he made a mistake that was less survivable than the two Palestinian morons he'd left in the apartment.

Even at its most tame, the game of espionage was not hospitable to second chances.

And nothing about an Iranian intelligence officer operating in Israel was tame.

Slipping into the alleyway in front of the apartment, Darien realized that he still had the Arab's pistol stuffed into his waistband. Swallowing a curse, he stared at the garbage littering both sides of the moldy cinderblock walls, looking for a way to remedy his oversight.

Though it was surrounded on all sides by enemies, Israel had a positively byzantine approach to personal weapons. The general populace was not permitted to own one. Period. Anyone found carrying an unauthorized weapon would be a prime target for a Shin Bet interrogation cell, regardless of how wide his smile.

Darien needed to ditch the pistol.

Fast.

Striding across the fetid water puddling in the street, Darien made for a promising pile of garbage. As per the less-than-pleasant smells emanating from the stacks of plastic bags, this particular heap hadn't been disturbed for quite some time.

Perfect.

After a final check to ensure he was alone, Darien removed the pistol from his pants, ejected the magazine, and racked the slide, catching the shiny bullet as it tumbled through the air.

Though children probably frequented the alley, he hadn't rendered the weapon safe because of humanitarian concerns. They might share a common enemy in Israel, but Arabs and Persians were hardly friends. In fact, Darien had a feeling that, were it not for the Jews, Hezbollah and Hamas would be at each other's throats.

No, Darien had a much more practical reason for ensuring the weapon wasn't accidentally discharged. Gunshot wounds drew police, and the last thing Darien wanted was one of the many pairs of unseen eyes peeking through the curtained windows overlooking the alley to report a blond-haired, blue-eyed American to the Israel Police. This was why he'd spared Ratface's life back in the apartment, instead of putting the creature out of his misery as he'd so clearly deserved.

At least that's what Darien told himself.

Sticking the bullet into his pocket, he poked through the trash heap until he found an unclosed bag. He then disassembled the pistol, wiped it clean, and shoved the components into the mass of squishy, half-decomposed rubbish. Once the gun's pieces were completely hidden from view, Darien sanitized the remaining round and dropped it into the bag.

Then he dusted off his hands, trying not to think about what he'd been rummaging through. Breathing with his mouth, he tied the ends of the bag together and started toward the pool of light shining from the mouth of the alley.

Now that he'd put the encounter in the apartment behind him, it was time to get his head back in the game. By now, the data on the thumb drive had been decrypted and was in his countrymen's hands. Phase two of his operation was about to begin, and Darien had somewhere to be. Fortunately, what came next should be a walk in the park compared to the last several hours. For the first time since setting foot on Israeli soil, Darien finally felt like he could breathe.

Until an Israeli police car pulled past the alley.

10

Unlike police the world over, law enforcement officers in Israel do not turn on their lights just when they anticipate pulling someone over. Instead, cruisers constantly have their light bar activated as they go about their business. Darien's handlers had warned him about this unique cultural phenomenon before he'd infiltrated the Zionist state, so at first he wasn't overly alarmed when red and blue strobing lights cast writhing shadows across the alley.

At first.

But worry reasserted itself when the police sedan stopped at the mouth of the alleyway, reversed direction, and then headed straight for Darien.

Darien hated the Jews with the best of his countrymen, but that didn't mean he couldn't admire their culture. Right now, a particularly apt Yiddish proverb sprang to mind — *men plan and God laughs.*

Though if there were any laughing from Darien, it would be the sort that precedes hysteria. First, he'd had to deal with the Arab brothers who between them had the equivalent of half a brain. Now he had the great fortune to make the acquaintance of the Israel Police.

Wonderful.

The car eased to a stop about two meters away as the driver flicked on the headlights, spotlighting Darien against the dank concrete. Suppressing a sigh, Darien smiled his best clueless American grin and gave a little wave. He could have tried to run, but there was no point. The alley was probably a dead end, and no one outruns radio waves.

His best defense was to play to the Israelis' assumptions. He was an American tourist who'd lost his way. He was delighted to see the police.

At least that's how Darien hoped the encounter would go.

The police cruiser's doors swung open, and two patrol officers exited — a man and a woman. The woman was about five-foot-two and slightly built. The man was bigger, but still no match for Darien's American-sized frame.

Though he'd never met his mother's family, Darien would someday like to, if for

96

nothing more than to thank them for their genes. The Great Satan they might be, but when it came to going toe to toe with Israelis, American size and strength was greatly appreciated.

"Howdy," Darien said, as the two officers approached. "Sure glad to see you."

He was smiling so wide his lips hurt, but as it had many times before, the ruse seemed to work. Israelis were a suspicious people by nature, and the ones who staffed the law enforcement and intelligence communities doubly so and with good reason. Still, it was hard to see an American tourist as danger-ous in this context.

Much like a puppy who's found its way into a neighbor's home, the best thing to do is gently put the well-meaning animal back outside while making a few chastening noises. Why waste your time disciplining the dog when it didn't have the capacity to understand what it had done wrong in the first place?

"Are you lost?" the man said.

His English, while good, was accented, and Darien felt an immediate sense of relief. Israel enjoyed one of the greatest propa-ganda programs ever conceived under the guise of something known as Taglit-Birthright Israel, or the birthright trip, as it

97

was more commonly called. Originally founded in December of 1999, the program financed trips to Israel for Jewish American teenagers paid for by wealthy Jewish businessmen and other donors.

The program's benefits were twofold: First, most anyone who participated left Israel with an overwhelming positive impression of the Jewish homeland. Second, a good number of Americans decided to return to Israel after graduating from high school to join the IDF and earn their Israeli citizenship. Running into one of these Americans who had made *aliyah* was Darien's biggest fear.

For non-Americans, he could play the American stereotype to a tee. But if he encountered someone born and raised in the United States, Darien knew his legend had limitations. Fortunately, the Israeli's thick accent reassured Darien that he had nothing to worry about.

Until the woman began to speak.

"You're American?" she said. "Me too. Where you from?"

And that was the million-dollar question.

Even people who'd never traveled to America could usually name three states — New York, California, and Texas. To the uninitiated, everyone from New York was sophisticated and probably a snob, while Californians were laid back and smooth. Texans, on the other hand, were unfailingly polite patriots and generally harmless.

Accordingly, Darien had cultivated a Texas persona.

"Texas," Darien said. "Fort Worth."

"No kidding," the woman said. "I'm from Arlington. Where'd you go to high school?"

Darien had never set foot in America, much less Fort Worth, Texas. Even so, he was an excellent case officer, and excellent case officers always backstopped their stories.

"James Martin," Darien said. "Graduated fifteen years ago. You?"

"Arlington High," the woman answered, taking a step closer. "I graduated about the same time. I think our football teams played each other at state that year. Remember?"

"Sorry," Darien said. "Believe it or not, I'm not much of a football fan. I know that's sacrilegious, but there it is."

The woman smiled, but Darien was not assuaged. As they'd been talking, her male partner had taken up a position off Darien's right shoulder while the woman remained at a forty-five-degree angle to his left. In short, the two of them formed the base of a triangle with Darien at its point. This setup was advantageous to the two police officers for a number of reasons, the least of which being that their vantage points now offered them intersecting fields of fire.

"What are you doing in this alley?" the woman said.

She was small in stature, had a slim build, and was quite pretty. But she was also a Jew, which meant her nimble mind was already working on ways to catch Darien in a lie. Time to go on the offensive.

"Got turned around somehow," Darien said. "Is the park back that way?"

He gestured over the male officer's shoulder and the man instinctively looked where Darien was pointing.

Which was a mistake.

A mistake the policeman realized he was making as he turned his head. To his credit, his sixth sense seemed to tell him something was amiss while his head was still in motion. Unfortunately for him, by then Darien's elbow had already connected with his temple.

While Darien was not an expert on Texas high schools, his MOIS cadre had ensured that he was adept at a much more useful discipline — unarmed combat. Darien snapped his hip into the strike, picturing his elbow entering the man's skull and exiting through his mouth in a spray of blood and gore. And while he hadn't put enough force behind the blow to accomplish that, the strike was more than adequate enough to bounce the policeman's brain around his cranium.

As the policeman crumpled, Darien caught his falling body and stepped behind him, using the concussed cop's unresponsive form to shield himself from his partner. While the Jewess drew her firearm and racked the slide to chamber a round with admirable speed, she hesitated when confronted with her partner's limp form.

Contrary to the movies, shooting in a hostage scenario was a daunting task. One misplaced motion and the nine-millimeter round intended for Darien would wind up in her partner instead.

But Darien was under no such constraint.

Stripping the policeman's pistol from his holster one-handed, Darien racked the slide on the officer's web belt and fired a single round. At this distance, he really couldn't miss. The slug took the former American squarely in the chest.

She collapsed.

Releasing his hold on her partner, Darien allowed the man to slump forward, putting a single round in the back of his head as he fell. The pistol's report was deafening in the alley's narrow confines, but that couldn't be helped.

In any case, Darien had one more loose end to tie off.

Edging around the bloody mess that had been, until moments before, a breathing human being, Darien towered over the female officer. As he'd suspected, she'd been wearing a vest, and it appeared to have done its job. While she was gasping for breath, in considerable pain, she was still alive.

Which was unfortunate.

"Please," the woman said, holding her hand out, palm up. "I —"

Darien fired the gun twice, and the encounter was over.

Darien might someday second-guess his decision to spare the Palestinian brothers, but he did know one thing for sure. The world was a better place with two less Jews inhabiting it.

Taking out his cell, Darien dialed the brothers. He hoped the smarter of the two would answer. The phone rang once, twice, three times. On the fourth, someone picked up.

"Yes?"

"There's a mess outside," Darien said as he strode into the shadows. "Clean it up."

Darien ended the call without waiting for a reply, but he felt confident the men would heed his instructions. They knew what he was capable of and the two murdered Israeli police officers would only reinforce their thinking. After all, cleaning up dead bodies was preferable to becoming one.

11

"Hey good-lookin' — whatcha got cookin'?"

Jack smiled in spite of himself. This was partially because, while he considered his life a bit more interesting than the average American's, he'd never heard Johnny Cash sung with a Hebrew accent. But that only accounted for part of his smile. The majority of it had something to do with the ray of sunshine with twin dimples smiling at him from the driver's seat of a Toyota Corolla.

"Use that line often?" Jack said, crossing from the street corner on which he'd been standing.

"First time," Tal said with another grin. "It would be wasted on an Israeli boy. I had to wait for the right American to come along."

Jack leaned against the door frame. He could smell an intoxicating blend of coconut and vanilla. He wasn't sure if the scent was body lotion, shampoo, or something else.

He didn't care. All he knew was that the inside of the car smelled like heaven.

"Are you getting in, or do I need to find another American?" Tal said.

"Getting in," Jack said. "Definitely getting in."

Tal replied with another dazzling smile. Jack pondered the very real possibility that he was losing his mind, but found himself scrambling toward the passenger door anyway. A throaty growl snapped him out of his revelry as Tal redlined the engine just as he was rounding the hood. Jack jumped, and he could hear a peal of feminine laughter over the engine noise.

Definitely losing his mind.

Upon deciding that he was going to try to find the woman and Tommy before leaving Israel, Jack had bitten the bullet and called Tal. After all, he was probably already under both passive and active Shin Bet surveillance. Israel was surrounded by Islamic militants willing to trade their own lives for Jewish corpses. By this metric, Israel's domestic intelligence service was constantly on war footing. As such, Jack had no illusions about his ability to elude the organization's watchful stare. Instead, he decided to subscribe to the maxim *If you can't beat 'em, might as well join 'em.*

Besides, finding the two Americans would be much easier with the Shin Bet's considerable resources.

And then there was the other reason.

Intelligence operative or not, Tal was a pleasant diversion from what until now had been a fairly disastrous trip. That said, only a fool let a pretty smile distract him from what was undoubtedly a capable intelligence officer. Unfortunately, as the KGB's infamous success with honey traps had proven, the world was full of fools.

And most of them possessed both X and Y chromosomes.

"Oooh, this one's my favorite," Tal said, cranking up the radio's volume as Jack belted himself into the passenger seat. A familiar, haunting baritone filled the car, waxing poetically about a ring of fire.

"You really like Johnny Cash?" Jack said.

"Love him," Tal said, sliding the car into drive and accelerating into traffic with the casual lack of self-preservation common to all Israeli motorists. "But I only bring out this playlist for special occasions. I'm more of a red dirt country fan. Are you from Texas?"

"Baltimore," Jack said with a smile. "Sorry."

"Ah," Tal said, shaking her head in mock

disappointment. "My first American, and he's not even a cowboy. Such a shame."

"Does that mean dinner's off?" Jack said.

Tal turned from the maze of vehicles to give him an appraising glance, and Jack felt his pulse quicken. This was partially because a car slid in front of them with a complete disregard of traffic norms more akin to a Daytona racetrack than a busy city thoroughfare. But only partially. The real reason he was having trouble forming coherent thoughts had more to do with the intensity of the brown eyes evaluating him like he was a slab of meat.

He should have felt offended.

He didn't.

"No," Tal said, shifting her attention back to the road just in time to switch lanes to a chorus of several pissed-off horns. "I think you'll do. What made you call? I didn't expect to hear from you so soon."

Implied but left unsaid by the Shin Bet officer was that Jack would have called her eventually. She was probably right.

"Here's the deal," Jack said, digging Captain America from his pocket. "I need to find the woman from the market."

"Why?" Tal said, threading her way through the stop-and-go traffic like she had feet instead of inches to spare between her car and her fellow commuters.

"Her son dropped this," Jack said, setting Captain America on the dashboard. "He'll want it back."

Tal glanced at the action figure before giving Jack another look, this one also appraising, but for perhaps a different reason.

"I thought you didn't know her," Tal said.

"I don't. But her son reminded me of a childhood friend. I think the action figure is important to her son. Important in a way that a replacement toy won't be. I'd like to return it, but I don't know where they're staying or the mother's name. But I *do* know someone in the Shin Bet."

"Are you sure you're not a cowboy, Jack Ryan?" Tal said.

"The older I get, the less sure I am about anything. But I'm about as city as they come."

"I guess you're right," Tal said with a mock sigh. "A cowboy would have made a pass at me by now."

"Don't take this the wrong way," Jack said with a laugh, "but what would you know about cowboys?"

"Much," Tal said, brown eyes warming to the topic. "My father taught at an American university in Montana while I was a child. He fell in love with country music and cowboy movies. It's how I learned English."

"Who's your favorite cowboy?" Jack said.

"Real cowboy? Probably George Strait. Movie cowboy? That's easy — John Wayne. *A man's got to do what a man's got to do.*"

Tal pitched her voice low as she spoke, doing a fair mimic of the Duke's distinctive drawl, and Jack found himself laughing again.

"That's pretty good," Jack said. "Are all Shin Bet officers this talented?"

"Jack Ryan, I am unlike anyone you will ever meet," Tal said, suddenly serious. "Is returning a lost toy the only reason you called me?"

"Nope," Jack said. "I was hoping you might know a good place to eat."

"Ah, you are wise, Jack Ryan. If there's one thing I love more than cowboys, it's food. First, I will make a call about the woman. Then we will have a dinner you will never forget."

"Great," Jack said. "But just so you know, cowboys don't eat hummus."

"Then it's a good thing you are not a cowboy."

12

Thirty minutes and a series of hair-raising lane changes later, they were seated at a quiet table overlooking the Mediterranean. A warm ocean breeze was rolling off the water, bringing with it the smells of salt water and grilling meat. The air tugged at Tal's blond-streaked hair with invisible fingers, tousling her thick curls.

Jack expected her to pull her hair back with one of the endless rubber bands or hair clips women always seemed to carry, but the Shin Bet officer surprised him once again. Turning her face into the breeze, Tal closed her eyes and breathed deeply.

"I love the ocean," she said.

"I thought you loved cowboys," Jack said.

"I love a great many things, Jack Ryan. Ah — food."

The waiter had appeared as they'd sat down, but Tal had sent him scurrying away with a long burst of Hebrew before he'd even had a chance to speak. Jack had tried to add in a request or two of his own, but the Shin Bet officer overruled him. She'd stated in unequivocal terms that since Jack was a guest in her country, he would eat and drink what she ordered.

Jack had protested, but more because he thought Tal expected it than because of any real sense of disappointment. In truth, he enjoyed just about everything. Besides, he liked tweaking the Israeli spitfire.

The waiter deposited the first course on the table with a flourish that would have won awards at a five-star restaurant. Six bowls of hummus, each garnished with fresh olives, along with a basket of warm pita bread. Next came glasses of wine as well as bottles of beer and sparkling water.

Not a bad start to the evening.

Jack wanted to pretend that the hummus starter annoyed him, but the bread smelled too good. Ripping a slice in two, he dunked the warm pita in the first available bowl and took a heaping mouthful.

Heaven.

"You like it?" Tal said, eyes sparkling.

"Love it," Jack said, going back for a second helping. "As long as we both understand that hummus alone is not a proper meal."

111

Tal opened her mouth to reply when the shrill ring of her phone interrupted. Fishing into her purse, she retrieved the handset.

"Ha-lo," Tal said, holding the phone to her ear.

Jack could hear a male voice on the other end, but the Hebrew words were indecipherable. Tal nodded twice, asked a single question, and then ended the call after receiving the answer.

"That was the office," Tal said, dropping the handset back into her purse. "We have an address for your friend."

"That was fast," Jack said, tearing off another chunk of pita.

"We are the Shin Bet. Fast is what we do."

Jack started to speak, but forgot what he was going to say. A white contrail streaked into the blue Mediterranean sky just behind Tal's right shoulder.

"Rocket," Jack said, rising to his feet.

Tal spun in her chair, saw the smoke trail, and cursed. "It's coming from Gaza."

"What now?" Jack said.

"Now you get a firsthand demonstration of Israeli technology."

"The Iron Dome?" Jack said.

Tal nodded. "Although the system does have limitations — namely, cost. Each interceptor has a price tag of more than forty thousand dollars, so unless the rocket's trajectory shows that it's going to hit a populated area, the computer controlling the interceptors will not trigger a launch."

An air-raid siren underscored Tal's words. The warbling sound made Jack feel as if he were on set in a World War II movie rather than in present-day Tel Aviv. But his fellow diners didn't seem overly concerned by the warning.

"Don't take this the wrong way," Jack said as the contrail continued to climb, "but shouldn't we be heading to a bunker or something?"

"What, and miss the show?" Tal said.

Her smile was just as bright but, to Jack's eye, seemed a bit fixed.

"Five years ago, maybe even two, everyone would be running for shelter. But I'm afraid the Iron Dome has made us complacent. The interceptors' effectiveness means that rocket attacks are down. When the jihadis do launch, they send the projectiles up in waves in the hopes of overwhelming the system. A single rocket is nothing to worry about."

"It will be if it hits near us," Jack said.

"Watch and learn, Jack Ryan."

The contrail reached its zenith and then started arcing back toward earth. A rocket

113

scientist Jack was not, but it didn't take a physicist to see that the white finger was pointing right at them.

"It must be an optical illusion," Tal said, echoing his thoughts. "If we were in danger, an interceptor would have launched by now."

Jack was about to make the case about discretion being the better part of valor when a streak of fire rose from the skyline behind them.

"Better late than never," Jack said, watching as the Tamir interceptor surged skyward at better than Mach 2.5.

"Relax," Tal said, the first bit of worry coloring her voice. "You're about to see something amazing."

She was right, but probably not in the way that she meant. The incoming rocket's contrail did do something both amazing and awful.

It changed course.

"That thing's guided," Jack said, reaching across the table to grab Tal's hand. "We need to seek cover. Now."

"There's no need," Tal said, shaking her head. "I told you."

Jack was done arguing. While Tal looked heavenward, Jack grabbed her by the waist and lifted her from her chair.

114

"Hey," Tal said, squirming away. "I said —"

But whatever it was she intended to say, Jack didn't hear it. Probably because he'd slung the Shin Bet officer over his shoulder in a modified fireman's carry. But that was only part of the reason. Even if Tal had been able to talk with one of Jack's broad shoulders digging into her diaphragm, he probably wouldn't have heard her over a peculiar buzzing that sounded equally like ripping paper and hissing cat.

In other words, the acoustic signature of a missile on terminal approach.

Jack risked a glance skyward as he made for the relative shelter of a parked car. What he saw wasn't good. The white smoke trail was now angled straight toward them. The Iron Dome interceptor, on the other hand, seemed to be on a one-way trip to the moon. As the buzzing became a full-fledged roar, Jack dumped Tal against the vehicle and covered the slight woman's body with his own.

A second later, the missile impacted.

13

One moment Jack's face was inches from Tal's flashing brown eyes. The next, he and the Israel intelligence officer were a jumble of intertwined limbs. Jack had a split second to think about how nice her muscular body felt against his chest. Then she jabbed him in the solar plexus and expertly slid from beneath him as he tried to catch his breath.

Jack knew his spunky mother had made his father work for her hand, but even the indomitable Cathy Ryan hadn't spear-handed her future husband. Maybe he ought to listen to his mom and settle down with a nice Catholic girl after all.

Assuming, of course, he made it out of Israel alive.

"You're welcome," Jack said, rolling to his knees.

Tal was already on her feet, surveying the scene over the hood of the car.

"We should be dead," Tal said.

"Like I said," Jack said, getting to his feet. "You're welcome."

"Yes, yes," Tal said, waving away his words with slender fingers. "You were right about the rocket. But the blast radius was much too small. To reach Tel Aviv from Gaza, the terrorists would have used a locally made M-75 rocket or perhaps an Iranian Fajr. These munitions have ten-kilogram high-explosive warheads. We should have felt the shock wave from here."

Jack stood, turned to survey the devastation, and realized Tal had a point. The rocket had impacted next to a kiosk selling newspapers and tourist knickknacks about twenty meters away. While the air was filled with a blizzard of torn newspaper and the kiosk's metal frame leaned at an oblique angle, the structure was still largely intact.

Even more surprising, the two cars parked on the street catty-corner to the newspaper stand were both untouched.

As Jack watched, an Arab man stumbled out of the kiosk and immediately sank to his knees. Tal ran toward him and Jack followed, but their help wasn't needed. The man was shaken, and perhaps even concussed, but he wasn't even bloody. A moment later Jack realized that the man was on his knees because he was praying, not due to injuries.

All things considered, Jack thought the shopkeeper might be onto something.

"Do you see the rocket?" Jack asked. "Maybe it didn't detonate."

Tal shook her head as she slowly walked around the kiosk.

"Wait," Tal said, stopping on the far side of the structure. "I see it. The fin's sticking up from the roof. Get everyone back."

The Shin Bet officer pulled out her phone as she spoke and punched in a number. Jack jerked the Arab man to his feet and then shouted at the crowd of onlookers to move back. To his surprise, they listened. Though a handful of people wanted to congregate near the kiosk, the majority of the crowd was clumping together across the street, a safe distance away.

At least Jack assumed the hundred or so feet constituted a safe distance. Rocket warheads weren't exactly his specialty. Fortunately, two police cars rolled up, and the uniformed men set up an honest perimeter.

Relieved that his brief career in crowd control was over, Jack turned back toward the kiosk, searching for Tal. A moment later he saw the diminutive brunette on the far side of the street, speaking with yet another

118

police officer. Edging around the Israelis in front of him, Jack eased out of the crowd toward Tal.

One of the policemen intercepted him. Though Jack had about six inches and probably close to one hundred pounds on the officer, the Israeli showed no intention of backing down. Bowing up to Jack, the officer planted a hand on his chest and pushed him back, all the while yammering at him in Hebrew. With a potentially live rocket still sprouting from the kiosk, Jack figured that this wasn't the time to argue.

"Tal," Jack shouted, ignoring the fireball in front of him. "Tal."

The second time she heard her name, the Shin Bet officer turned. Seeing Jack, she ended her conversation and started toward him.

She made it two steps before the rocket detonated.

14

Once again, Jack found himself in a tangle of limbs with an Israeli. This time, the Hebrew speaker was decidedly male and smelled of stale coffee and cigarettes.

In other words, the sensation wasn't nearly as pleasant.

Jack slid from beneath the police officer and struggled to his feet. And that was when he realized that things had gone from bad to worse in a blink of an eye. As familiar as he now was with the average Israeli's lively personality, Jack should have been on the receiving end of a torrent of Hebrew, or, more likely, a less endearing form of Tal's spear hand to his solar plexus.

Instead, the policeman was positively compliant.

Because he was dead.

A six-inch chunk of steel protruded from the center of the man's back.

At first Jack went into triage mode, assessing the policeman's airway and breathing on his way to feeling for a pulse. But he was operating on autopilot. One look at the man's sightless eyes, and Jack knew his efforts were in vain. Like a marksman's crossbow bolt, the chunk of steel had entered the Israeli's body almost directly between the shoulder blades, snapping the spine in two before plunging through the chest cavity. No amount of battlefield trauma medicine could save a casualty who no longer had functioning lungs.

Jack turned to survey the blast radius and swore. He'd certainly seen his fair share of death, but this was different. The pavement was slick with blood and strewn with body parts, while the kiosk was a smoldering pile of rubble.

In that moment, Jack realized that the jihadis who'd launched the instrument of death had just sunk their equivalent of a hole in one. Short of detonating in a crowded movie theater, Jack couldn't think of a more lucrative target. The aluminum from which the flimsy structure had been constructed had sheared into millions of razor-sharp lightweight projectiles scattered in all directions by the shock wave like paper borne on a tornado.

Jack's eyes raced from crumpled form to

crumpled form until he saw a mop of sun-streaked brown hair puddled on the concrete. Sprinting across the street, he dropped to his knees next to the facedown Shin Bet operative and cursed again. Her blood-darkened hair suggested that Tal had also been caught in the explosion's kill zone.

Steeling himself, Jack eased Tal onto her back.

The unseen hands that had guided the killing steel into the policeman's chest cavity had seemingly pushed the same instruments of death away from Tal. Though her face was smeared with blood, most of it didn't seem to belong to her. Jack's probing fingers found a couple of superficial cuts, probably from flying glass and other debris, but nothing serious.

"Tal, can you hear me?" Jack said.

The Shin Bet officer's eyelids fluttered, and she let out a low moan followed by a barely audible stream of Hebrew.

"Tal," Jack said, stroking her cheek.

Her eyes fluttered open, and then she convulsed. This time Jack was ready. He batted the spear hand away before Tal's hardened fingers found something soft.

The woman must be hell to wake up next to.

"Tal," Jack said, cupping her chin, "it's

me. Jack."

Tal's liquid eyes swam into his, and Jack found himself reassessing his earlier conclusion. Maybe this wouldn't be such a bad way to start the morning after all.

"Jaaaack," Tal said, dragging out his name.

She wasn't exactly slurring her words, but the blast wave had clearly rung her bell. Explosively generated shock waves were tricky things. The concussive force they generated increased exponentially the closer one stood to their epicenter. Oftentimes, the damage blast waves inflicted on the soft tissue of a person's internal organs was difficult to diagnose without an MRI.

"I'm here," Jack said, shifting Tal so that he could cradle her head in his lap. "Can you hear me?"

"Everything hurts," Tal said, her eyes sliding closed.

"Uh-uh," Jack said, lightly slapping her cheek. "You've got to stay awake. I think you've got a concussion."

Sirens screamed from every direction as emergency vehicles arrived, first responders leaping from the trucks before they'd fully stopped moving. In its short history, the nation of Israel had become adept at a good many things. Some of those things, like the innovation that powered Tel Aviv, were sources of national pride. Others sprang from national necessity.

Responding to mass casualty events fell into the latter category.

But in this case, the plethora of white-clad men and women absolved Jack of some of the guilt he felt for attending to the slumped Shin Bet officer while potentially more seriously injured casualties lay within reach. The feeling of the Israeli lying in his arms and the smell of her coconut-scented brown skin aside, the danger of Tal slipping into a coma was a real concern. Jack needed to keep the Shin Bet officer talking until she was triaged by a medical professional.

"Jack," Tal said again.

"Right here," Jack said.

Her pronunciation sounded better, but he shaded her eyes to check dilation just in case. Her pupils dutifully expanded and contracted.

So far so good.

"Don't take this the wrong way," Tal said. "But you're a lousy dinner date."

15

Darien surveyed the explosion's aftermath from his vantage point across the street. There was some irony to the fact that he'd been close enough to the explosion to be cut by flying glass, but it couldn't be helped. He'd mitigated the situation as best he could, choosing a restaurant with table-high concrete barriers and an overhead cover of thick Jerusalem limestone.

But concrete and barriers hadn't shielded him from the Arab rocket's poorly designed guidance system. No matter. The operational margins were razor-thin — the tightest timelines Darien had ever tried to maintain in his not-insignificant career. Before Darien's superiors authorized the second phase, they wanted to be damned sure the reward was going to be worth the inevitable price. Someone needed to verify that the software functioned correctly.

That someone was Darien.

Even so, his vantage point had been a little closer to the action than even he'd anticipated. As par for the course, the rocket had strayed from its intended trajectory.

Significantly.

The eggheads back in Tehran had assured Darien that the computed point of impact would bring the projectile no closer than two hundred fifty meters from his chosen vantage point. Which was interesting, since the rocket had crashed into a kiosk scarcely twenty-five meters away.

Fortunately, while he'd acquiesced to General Ahmadi's demand that he document the Iron Dome interceptor's flight path from directly beneath what should have been the intercept point, Darien had held firm to his stipulation of a delayed-action fuse. This precaution had provided Darien with the time necessary to duck behind a brick wall before the warhead detonated.

Not so for the Jews who'd tried to help the stunned Arab to safety.

But the destruction caused by the rocket was an afterthought. The important thing, the reason why Darien had put himself in harm's way to begin with, was the four seconds of video he'd shot with his cell phone's camera.

Selecting the correct file, Darien posted it

to YouTube, where it joined a dozen others. But the YouTube channel Darien had selected featured one important subscriber the rest of the videos making their way to the Internet did not.

Standing, Darien joined the throng of patrons moving away from the gore-filled streets and cries of the wounded. As Darien fell in with the crowd, his phone vibrated. Consulting the device, he activated the modified Telegram app and keyed in his encryption.

A single word awaited.

Approved.

With a smile, Darien pocketed the phone. The real fun was about to begin.

16

"Surfer, this is Reaper Seven," Cary said. "If you can hear me, scratch your ear."

Cary watched through his optic as Jad brought a hand up to his right ear and gave it a scratch. Then, with his fingers safely hidden behind his mound of curly black hair, he turned the scratch into a one-fingered salute.

"I think he hears us."

The comment came from Doug Crum, and the sound of the team medic's voice made Cary uneasy. Not because of anything old Crumdog had said. The fast-talking Ohio boy had been on the team for almost ten years, and as far as Cary was concerned, there was no finer medic the world over.

No, what made Cary uneasy was that it should have been Jad's voice, not Doug's, that he heard just inches from his left elbow.

128

But Jad was one thousand meters away, entering a compound full of people who wanted to bring about the end of the world in the company of a CIA asset who might or might not be completely full of shit.

Other than that, Cary had nothing to worry about.

"He's gonna be fine. You'll see."

Cary grunted but didn't speak.

The fact that Doug was trying to reassure him instead of busting his balls about Ohio State football was telling enough. If the indomitable Crumdog was worried, this whole operation was a bad fucking idea. Unfortunately, the time for second-guessing had long since come and gone.

For better or worse, Jad was in the mix.

"All elements, this is Reaper Seven," Cary said. "Surfer is Cruise, I say again, Cruise."

Radio transmissions during operations were always tricky. Listening for, and responding to, long, detailed instructions took the operators' minds off what they were really supposed to be concentrating on — the battlefield.

To that end, simple status updates were usually done via brevity codes — one-word call signs designed to let everyone on the radio net know exactly what was happening with as little chatter as possible. In an operation in which multiple brevity words would be transmitted over a period of time, they often had a theme. In this case, that theme was Cary's favorite actors. *Cruise* meant that Jad had successfully entered the compound. *Reeves* was the next brevity code the team was listening for, indicating that Jad was through security.

By the same token, *Kidman* was the one word everyone had memorized and no one wanted to hear. If that one came across the radio, the mission had gone to shit.

"Reaper Six confirms Cruise."

The sound of Captain Alex Brown's voice echoing the brevity code did much to untangle the knots in Cary's stomach. Doctrinally, the team leader should be in Cary's position — on a hilltop with eyes on Jad as he rode shotgun in a Toyota truck.

But once again Alex had proved why he was uniquely suited to be a Special Forces A-team leader.

Alex knew that what Jad was doing, while necessary, also upset the interpersonal dynamics that were so crucial to the team of twelve men whose lives depended on one another. Accordingly, he'd asked his team sergeant how he could best help rather than dictating his role in the operation.

After a moment of thought, Cary had

answered truthfully that the rear security position would be the best place. From there, Alex could concentrate on coordinating with the team's external assets and running interference between the men on the ground and their supervisors sitting in an air-conditioned TOC thirty miles away from the action.

Alex had readily agreed. Now the sound of his team leader's voice reminded Cary that Jad wasn't alone. Less than a kilometer away, Alex was watching out for the entire team with all the force multipliers unique to a Special Operations element. As al-Qaeda and the Taliban had learned the hard way in the months following 9/11, an A-team brought a considerable arsenal to the fight.

"Reaper Seven, Reaper Fourteen, Surfer's truck is pulling over."

"Fourteen, this is Seven. Roger that. We knew this was going to happen. Stay frosty."

As expected of an Operational Detachment Alpha team sergeant, Cary relayed his instructions in the calm, no-nonsense radio voice he'd spent his entire career cultivating. Soldiers keyed off the emotions of their leaders, and there was nothing that sent a tactical unit into a high hover like a leader losing his shit over the radio.

But inside, Cary felt anything but calm.

Bill, the numbnuts CIA case officer who'd foisted this mission on Cary's team, had assured Alex that Jad would have no problems with the compound's security. According to his asset, the cultists had a big construction project in the works on the southeast side of the facility. To keep the work going, the crazies had been paying locals to truck in raw materials, like sacks of quick-drying concrete, cinder blocks, lumber, and other odds and ends.

The asset had been bringing in supplies once a day for the last week, always with a different laborer. Jad would fill in as his hired hand and use the opportunity to clandestinely take pictures as well as eyeball whatever the cultists were doing. Hopefully, General Ahmadi would make another appearance. But even if the Quds Force commander didn't show, Jad should be able to sniff out what the crazies had up their sleeves.

Simple.

Or at least it had seemed that way in the team room eight hours prior. Now, as two men armed with AK-47s motioned for Jad to get out of the car, nothing about this operation seemed simple.

"Reaper Seven, Fourteen, Surfer is out of

the car. The two military-aged males are both keyed on him."

"Reaper Seven copies all," Cary said. "I designate the MAM with the blue shirt as target Sierra One. His partner is Sierra Two. Confirm, over."

"Reaper Fourteen has Sierra One."

"Reaper Eleven has Sierra Two."

"Reaper Seven, roger. Surfer's duress signal is hands interlaced on top of his head. You see that, drop your target. Otherwise, I clear all fires. Surfer's a smooth operator. He's got this."

Cary's radio transmission was answered by multiple *Roger*s. Cool and calm. That was the name of the game, even though his own fingers itched to be holding the stock of his Barrett Advanced Sniper Rifle. It's not that he doubted the abilities of the team's other two snipers, far from it. But Jad was his spotter and it felt wrong that Cary wasn't the one holding a bead on the head of one of the two men threatening his friend.

But this is what it meant to be the team sergeant instead of just another shooter.

"Everything's gonna be fine, everything's gonna be fine," Doug said, whispering the mantra over and over like he was praying the Rosary.

"For Christ's sake, Crumdog," Cary said, adjusting the focus on his variable power scope. "You're putting knots in my stomach. Knock that shit off."

"Sorry, boss," Doug said. "It's Jad down there. It's fucking Jad."

Cary opened his mouth, but the snappy comeback he had planned turned to dust on his tongue. Cary watched through the precision offered by his Horus reticle as Sierra 1 grabbed Jad by the shirt, chattering at him in Arabic. At the same time, Sierra 2 pointed his AK-47 at the asset and motioned him out of the truck.

Like all Green Berets, Cary had spent twenty-six weeks at the conclusion of the Special Forces Qualification Course learning a language that would be beneficial to his new life. Since he was being assigned to 5th Special Forces Group, Cary had been taught Arabic. While he was by no means fluent, he was picking up enough of the conversation through Jad's mic to understand that the guards were not happy about something.

And that was a problem.

An even bigger problem was the fact that Sierra 1's fingers were inches away from the listening device concealed in Jad's shirt.

"Surfer's hands are still free," Cary said,

"and he has not given the duress signal. I say again, he has not given the duress signal. Shooters are weapons hold. Acknowledge."

"Reaper Fourteen, roger."

"Reaper Eleven, roger."

The snipers' rapid acknowledgment was a good sign, but Cary wasn't fooled. The psychological profile used to screen potential Green Berets was heavy on independent thought and action, as fitting for operatives who lived and worked far from the flagpole. But this independence came at a price. Cary didn't doubt for a moment that if one of the shooters thought the situation was getting out of hand, he would fire.

Cary would do the same thing in their shoes.

"Reaper Seven, this is Reaper Six, over."

"Go for Seven," Cary said.

"Roger Seven, our TERP is providing a real-time translation. Those two knuckleheads are pissed about the quality of wood the asset trucked in yesterday. A bunch of the boards were warped. The TERP thinks this is just a negotiating technique, over."

"Roger that, Six," Cary said. "It'd better be. If the asset fucks this up because he's trying to skim some off the top by selling the crazies shitty wood, I will hold Bill, Bob, or whatever the fuck his name is personally

135

responsible."

"Understood, Seven," Alex said, "and since Bill is standing right next to me, I think he's tracking, too."

His team leader's words brought a smile to Cary's face, and he felt some of the tension leave his body. On the screen, the harsh body language and angry tones had de-escalated into something that more resembled everyday bargaining at the bazaar than an encounter that would lead to death. After a final tongue-lashing, both Jad and the asset were allowed back in the truck and waved toward the construction site.

Cary released the breath he hadn't realized he'd been holding in a noisy rush of air. Beside him, Doug's whispers faded to silence. The radio was still active as the eight other members of the team monitored Jad's progress across the compound from their respective observation posts.

While Cary had chosen the rock outcropping where he and Doug were hidden for the view it offered of the compound's interior, it still didn't provide a completely unobstructed sight line. At several points, obstacles obscured the truck and Cary had to chart Jad's position via brevity words called out by his fellow Green Berets. Then came the one he'd been waiting for.

"Surfer is Garner. I say again, Jennifer Garner."

Cary acknowledged the radio call with two clicks of his transmit button while fiddling with the display, dividing it in half as he selected a second video source. This imagery came courtesy of a tiny wireless button camera on Jad's shirt.

Two days ago, the cult members had erected a set of tents covering the construction site, and Bill the CIA officer didn't think it was to shade the workers. For once, Cary agreed. The cultists might be crazy, but that didn't mean they were dumb. Chances were those tarps were protecting something important from prying eyes in the form of orbiting satellites or loitering drones.

Jad was about to put this theory to the test.

Cary waited as the staticky video resolved into recognizable images as the digital amplifier situated with Reaper 11 decoded the video stream and boosted the signal. All at once, a series of symmetrical indentations roughed into the soil and framed by lengths of wood swam into view.

The shaky video showed plots laid out in a grid that spanned a hundred-meter footprint, with each indentation equidistant from its neighbor. The depressions were too small to serve as building foundations, but Cary had done enough construction work on the family farm to recognize a rough-in for concrete when he saw one.

"What the hell are those?" Doug said, pointing at the screen.

"Don't know," Cary said, "but I have a feeling we're going to find out."

17

Tel Aviv, Israel

Darien studied himself in the mirror, checking the results of his transformation. While his jovial face remained, little else of Jonathan Mills was present. The unruly blond curls were absent and so were the blue eyes and about two inches of height.

Jonathan had gone the way of a multitude of other aliases Darien had employed in his long and storied career. The wig and contact lenses were in a trash bag at his feet, along with the specially designed platform shoes. But most important, the carefree bohemian personality that accompanied them was also banished to the dustbin of Darien's operational mind.

In their place was the man currently staring back at him from the mirror.

While Jonathan's carefree locks had grabbed and held the eye, the muddy brown hair parted to the left side of his head with a surgeon's precision didn't attract attention. Or at least not the same kind Jonathan would have relished. No, the no-nonsense haircut paired with dark eyes and conservative yet expensive linen slacks and a button-down shirt worn open at the neck spoke of something else. Precision matched with maturity. A professional's wardrobe.

But not just any professional.

A venture capitalist.

Darien studied his appearance, looking at the apparition not as an extension of himself, but as a projection of who he wanted the world to see. The handsome, accomplished man staring back at him looked the part. Almost. Something was missing. Something hard to articulate, but necessary all the same.

Gravitas.

A VC manager successful enough to fly halfway around the world in search of new ideas to invest in needed to look the part. Eyeing the open box resting on the counter to his left, Darien selected a bottle, opened it, and dabbed the contents on a fine-bristled brush. Next, he stroked the liquid through his sideburns and temples with an artist's precision. After five or six strokes, he again consulted his reflection.

This time he nodded.

The patches of gray conveyed exactly the right message. The man standing before him was still in his prime, but had earned his exalted reputation by burning the midnight oil. As the salt-and-pepper hair attested, his professional success, while merited, had not come easy. This was a man who had endured the jealousy of his contemporaries, while succeeding where they had not.

In short, a man uncannily like the woman he was scheduled to meet.

Darien clenched and unclenched his fists, trying to burn off the adrenaline still coursing through him.

Contrary to spy novels, the vast majority of an espionage practitioner's life was spent in boredom. Crash meetings with excitable assets were part of the game, but these instances were the exception rather than the rule. Wet work was even rarer. A good spy swam through the sea of humanity without notice, just another unremarkable fish among an ocean of many.

Dead bodies, on the other hand, had the opposite effect. Darien had certainly been involved in his share of assassinations, but these operations were meticulously planned and executed only when there truly were no other options. And once the deed was done, the operations team was spirited out of country before their victim's body had begun to cool.

Usually.

But this operation was different, and in Darien's experience, different was not good. He'd once heard it said that there were bold pilots, and old pilots, but no old bold pilots. This was doubly true for those who practiced the art of espionage. And yet here he was, preparing for another high-risk operation in the same country where he'd broken an asset's wrist, killed two Israeli police officers, and watched a missile impact just twenty-five meters away.

Each of these heat-state-increasing actions had been conducted in Israel, the most dangerous adversary his country had ever known. A nation that had crafted a national strategy around the notion of striking first and asking questions later. Was the risk posed by the final phase of this operation truly worth the reward?

Darien took a deep breath, let it out, and gazed at his reflection, knowing the answer. This was the operational opportunity of a lifetime. Even if what happened next burned him so badly that he would never be able to leave Iran again, it would be worth it. In one fell swoop, Darien would bring Israel to its knees while stripping America of the technological invincibility it had enjoyed for far too long. This was the reason why he'd joined the Ministry of Intelligence to begin with. When this operation was successful, Darien would return home a hero.

If he was willing to do what was necessary.

And that was the question. Was he willing to risk everything?

As Darien's father had told him since he was old enough to understand, this was the purpose for which he'd been created. The reason why he'd been granted his mother's American face and tongue and his father's Persian soul and courage. This unique combination was a gift that would someday allow him to operate where his fellow countrymen feared to tread.

Israel.

And not only that, Darien possessed the means to finally accomplish what the politicians and mullahs had been promising since the Islamic Republic of Iran's founding more than four decades ago. Until this moment, their promises to push Israel into the sea had been nothing but empty words.

Not anymore.

Darien had the chance to make good on the threats uttered by untold lips. Where Arab and Persian alike had failed, where

the Nazis had stumbled, Darien could right
the historical wrong forced upon the Middle
East at the conclusion of World War II. If he
were successful, the Quds Day holiday
would finally be a day of joy in truth instead
of just the pretend world his countrymen
inhabited. Darien would be the one to
transform a nation's tears into laughter
while ushering in a new alliance that would
permanently check the influence of the
United States and her lapdogs.

The day of reckoning was finally here.

Nodding at his reflection, Darien snapped
the makeup bag closed.

He was ready.

18

Jack stepped into the lobby of the Hilton Tel Aviv and paused, impressed with the view in spite of himself. With more hours on international flights than most commuters had miles, Jack had seen his fair share of foreign locales and luxury hotels. Accordingly, he'd learned long ago to avoid tourist destinations in favor of living like the locals. He rarely stayed in hotels, and when he did, he purposefully chose ones that didn't cater to Westerners.

The Hilton was the opposite of this philosophy. First opened for business in 1965, the establishment was constructed primarily with foreign tourists in mind. With easy access to the Hilton Beach, shuttles running to and from Ben Gurion Airport, staff who spoke impeccable English, daily tours of Israel's stunning list of attractions, and restaurants that served both Western and Mediterranean cuisine, the hotel had a reputation as a one-stop shop for travelers who appreciated a little handholding.

In other words, the perfect spot for an American mother and her special-needs child.

In spite of the hotel's sterling reputation and its commanding view of the Mediterranean from a prime stretch of real estate on Hilton Beach, Jack had come to Tel Aviv with about as much intention of visiting the hotel as he had of frequenting the McDonald's located two kilometers south. This wasn't to say that Jack was some sort of foodie snob. But he did believe that when in Rome, do as the Romans. With this in mind, he was certain he'd dislike the hotel the moment he strode into the lobby.

He was wrong.

The lobby was breathtaking. The entire space was designed to showcase the view through the floor-to-ceiling windows making up the far wall. The blue Mediterranean sparkled invitingly through the glass, and once again Jack felt a yearning for the feeling of a surfboard between his legs as he sat bobbing in the warm water.

The customary check-in desks loomed to his left, with a concierge's stand to his right. But rather than the ritzy, out-of-place feeling most high-end hotels generated, the

Hilton's lobby did nothing to try to detract from the beckoning ocean. Jack wasn't a student of architecture, but even he could see that this space was something magical. As if the hotel's builders had been trying to communicate that the real jewel of Tel Aviv was just outside the hotel's steel doors. Therefore, any time spent inside the hotel should be both pleasant and brief.

Jack could sympathize.

Snapping out of his reverie, Jack looked at the check-in clerks and concierge desk, weighing his options. After attempting to follow Tal to the hospital, her partner had let Jack know in no uncertain terms that his presence wasn't wanted. Rather than go head-to-head with the Shin Bet goon, Jack had decided to search for Tommy and his mother on his own.

He'd come to the hotel on a hunch. Getting into their quarry's head was a skill set honed by all good intelligence officers. Jack didn't know where Tommy and his mother were staying, and normally that wouldn't be a problem. A single call to Gavin Biery, The Campus's hacker extraordinaire, and Jack would know everything about the mystery woman in minutes. From there, it would be child's play to determine where she and her son were staying.

But Jack was hesitant to make use of The Campus's resources normally at his disposal. Tal had been unflinching in her assessment of Jack and the attention his presence on Israeli soil was drawing. His phone was compromised, and though he hadn't spotted a tail, Jack had to believe he was a target of surveillance, electronic or otherwise.

Unlike the softer, gentler Western services, Israel's two premier intelligence organizations, Shin Bet and Mossad, thwarted attacks intent on maiming or killing Israeli citizens daily. As Israeli politicians patiently explained to the rest of the world time and time again, Israel was a nation surrounded by enemies. In the world's only Jewish state, threats weren't abstract or launched from a nation thousands of miles away.

No, in Israel terrorist cells formed, planned, and tried to execute bombings from enclaves in the West Bank or the Gaza Strip, literally a stone's throw from their Jewish targets. With this in mind, the intelligence services charged with protecting the nation of Israel and her people didn't bother with the niceties common to their Western counterparts. The Mossad and Shin Bet played for keeps.

As such, Jack was operating under the assumption that he was completely burned, which in turn meant that every and all communication between himself and the outside world was being monitored. He had no intention of further confirming or denying Tal's suspicions by letting the Shin Bet listen in on his call to Gavin.

For the remainder of Jack's time on Israeli soil, The Campus didn't exist. But by no means was Jack helpless. He'd been trained by the best in the business and served alongside legends.

It was time to put that training and experience to work.

After a moment more of thought, Jack headed for the concierge's desk. The man behind the desk was tall and thin, with the build of a marathoner. Even so, in yet another mark of a great hotel, his suit fit his frame perfectly. He smiled as Jack approached, asking, "Can I help you?" in flawless English.

"I hope so," Jack said, reaching into his pocket. "By the way, your English is excellent. Were you raised in America?"

"No, sir," the concierge said with another smile. "My mother was an English teacher. She practiced her lessons at home, and my sister and I were her willing, and sometimes unwilling, pupils."

"I feel your pain," Jack said with a laugh. "My father was a history professor. While most families talked sports around the dinner table, we discussed Alexander the Great. Anyway, I could use your help."

Jack withdrew the Captain America figure from his pocket and set it atop the concierge's desk. "I met a mother and her child briefly in the marketplace a couple hours ago. She's American with brown hair. About five-foot-five with a trim build. Probably in her thirties. I'd guess her son is about seven or eight. He was wearing a baseball cap and shorts, and he dropped this. I was hoping to return it."

As Jack spoke, the man's smile slowly vanished, his lips compressing into a hard line.

"I'm sorry, sir," the concierge said, "but for security reasons, we can't discuss our guests. I hope you understand."

"I understand completely," Jack said, "and I apologize for not being clear. The child is special-needs. Probably autistic. Growing up, I had a friend with the same condition. This toy looks cheap, but based on my experience, I think the boy considers it irreplaceable. I'm not asking for personal information. In fact, I'm not asking for anything at all. I just want you to return the figure to the mother if she's staying here. I'd be happy to compensate you for your trouble."

Jack withdrew a twenty-dollar bill from his pocket and set it next to the action figure.

The man stared at the action figure and then Jack for a long moment before coming to a decision.

"As I said before," the man said, clasping his hands behind his back as he took a step away from both the figurine and Jack's money. "We can't discuss our guests. But I can tell you that a woman and child just headed out to the beach. If you hurry, you can probably catch them."

"Toda," Jack said, grabbing both the bill and the action figure. "I appreciate it."

"There's nothing to appreciate, sir."

Jack nodded his thanks and headed for the doors on the far side of the lobby. Once again, Ding was right. A little human-to-human interaction trumped technology every time.

19

Jack stepped from the lobby onto the beach and once again regretted his decision to adhere to Tal's ultimatum. A warm breeze smelling of salt, grilling meat, and faintly of fish slapped Jack in the face while surf lapped against the white sand less than one hundred yards away. Jack crossed over a two-lane biking and running trail, dodging a pair of joggers traveling in one direction and a brunette wearing roller skates and little else heading in the other.

Rather than give in to the seductive embrace of jetlag-induced sleep, Jack had found this same jogging path on his first morning in Israel. He'd followed it along the ocean from Jaffa all the way north to the Tel Aviv marina. The trail really was a feat of engineering, plodding past stretches of open beach interspersed with nightclubs, restaurants, volleyball courts, cafés, and high-end boutique shops. Every couple of kilometers, permanent exercise equipment sprouted from the sand, fashioned out of steel and coated thick with paint to resist the corrosive salt water.

But this time it wasn't beauties sunbathing, pedestrians ambling along the path, or even the ocean's whispering that caught Jack's attention. It was the sight of a mother and child standing in the ankle-deep surf to his right.

He'd found them.

Jack thought of calling out but didn't. Between the dozens of conversations in half as many languages and the gusting wind, the chances of his words reaching their target were slim. Besides, even if she heard him, Jack didn't know how the woman would react.

Last time she'd seen him, Jack had been in the fight of his life with an Asian assassin. Even though he'd been protecting her at the time, he couldn't help but think his presence now might be a wee bit of a shock. No, Jack would approach, surrender the toy, and bid her farewell.

Then it was back to Ben Gurion Airport and a flight to somewhere else.

Jack let his mind drift for the moment as he considered where that flight to somewhere else might take him. God knew that

153

he had more than his share of vacation time coming after the nonstop OPTEMPO of the last few years, and the idea of spending some time on a surfboard had really taken hold. What if instead of flying west, he headed south or southeast? He was already halfway around the world; maybe it was time to finally take that trip to South Africa, or Australia, or New Zealand.

Jack paused, turning his face to the sun as he closed his eyes, breathing in the salty air. Though his father now spent his time surrounded by armed men and women while working out of the world's most exclusive office, there was a time when Jack Ryan, Sr., could walk the streets unrecognized. When the work he did as a CIA analyst was known to but a select few, long before he'd entered the high-profile world of national politics. In those days, Junior remembered hiking a length of the Appalachian Trail with his father.

The section they'd chosen wound through the mountains of Dahlonega, Georgia, not far from where the Army's legendary Ranger School taught its pupils the finer points of mountaineering. On day three of their hike, father and son came to a break in the canopy permitting an unobstructed view into the valley below.

Jack was about fifteen at the time and was walking point. He'd come across the gap in the trees first, indicating the breathtaking vista to his father before continuing up the steep incline. The straps of his pack bit into his still-widening shoulders, and he'd hunched forward into the load, not realizing that his father wasn't with him until he'd hiked another fifty meters. Backtracking, Jack had found Senior standing motionless, still contemplating the view. Sensing that something magical was happening, Jack had silently joined his father.

After a moment, Senior had draped a rugged arm across Junior.

"I appreciate the majesty of God's creation more the older I get," Senior said, still captivated by the view. "Don't get me wrong, I've always enjoyed being outside. But there's something about places like this that resonate with a man's soul. We were created to experience wonder, Jack. But to find it, you have to be willing to look."

At fifteen, Jack had little reference for what his father had been trying to communicate. But by thirty, he'd begun to understand. Whether it was a wife and a family, or a day spent bobbing in the ocean's embrace, there had to be more to life than kicking down doors and chasing bad guys.

As his dad had been trying to tell him on the side of a mountain long ago, every job, no matter how noble, was still just a means to an end.

Jack was beginning to think that he'd spent far too long focusing on the means, to the detriment of the end.

That needed to change.

Opening his eyes, Jack greeted the world with a smile. A smile that lasted for just a fraction of a second. He might have taken the first step toward reconciling his professional life with his personal, but the scale was far from balanced. Fifty meters away, a mother and child splashed in the surf. But unlike the pastoral scene Jack had just relived, the little boy was going to have a completely different memory. Angling toward the pair like a wolf culling its prey from the herd was the Asian man.

And this time he had a gun.

20

Spotting a concealed pistol, much like carrying one, was an art form. To most people frequenting the Tel Aviv beach, the Asian man's intent wasn't quite as easy to deduce. But Jack was not most people. Sure, the assassin was bearing down on a woman and child without the easy smile worn by most of the sunbathers, but frowning certainly wasn't a crime.

Then there was his dress. While the majority of the beachgoers were in either swimwear or athletic clothing, the man's attire was decidedly less festive. His short-sleeved button-down shirt, cargo pants, and hiking boots definitely looked like they belonged on the boardwalk rather than the beach.

But again, this was not necessarily a red flag. The breeze blowing off the ocean fractured into countless swirling eddies gusting past the rows of lifeguard stands, shops, and shelters lining the sand. Boardwalk strollers frequently darted across the no-man's-land between sand and concrete, chasing errant papers or napkins, torn from their grasp by the teasing wind.

But there was another, more serious tell that set the Asian apart from everyone else. The way he walked. Or, more specifically, the way he walked carrying a rolled-up windbreaker in his left hand. Rather than allowing the garment to pendulum back and forth with his natural stride, the jacket, and the hand holding it, hovered in place along the length of his left thigh.

Because the jacket concealed a gun.

For the second time in less than eight hours, Jack's fingers longed for the comforting grip of the Glock 43 he usually carried. He'd entered Israel clean since this was a non-Campus-sanctioned operation. Strangely enough, the Asian man didn't seem to care about Israel's restrictive gun-control laws.

Imagine that.

Even as Jack vowed to never leave home without his pistol again, he was already spinning through scenarios. A hit in a public place was more the operandi of a suicide bomber than a skillful assassin. Only someone incredibly foolish or exceedingly desperate would attempt to murder another

158

human being in front of fifty eyewitnesses.

While Jack couldn't speak to the Asian man's mind-set, he did know from their previous tangle that the assassin was not a threat to be taken lightly. Though Jack had kept the knifeman from the woman, the fight had been far from even. That he had sustained only superficial wounds could be attributed more to the assassin's surprise than to Jack's skill. The longer the altercation had continued, the more lopsided it had become. If the Shin Bet officers hadn't intervened when they did, Jack's wounds would have been much more extensive.

Perhaps even fatal.

The assassin was not a simple thug and wouldn't employ his pistol with a "spray and pray" mentality. He was surgical. Precise. And since he'd melted back into the crowd of bystanders after the appearance of the Shin Bet officers, he was probably also without a suicide bomber's desire to accompany his victim into the afterlife.

This meant that if the man planned on dispatching the mother in broad daylight, his method of killing her would be no less exacting. His pistol would be compact, perhaps even disguised to look like something else, and definitely suppressed. This necessitated small-caliber bullets and subsonic loads.

But this stealth came with a price — the pistol's range. The gunman would have to close to almost contact-shot distance to ensure a mortal wound. Since a good thirty meters still separated the assassin and his target, Jack had time.

But not much.

While he was all in favor of grounding the man with a flying tackle and then duking it out, this time Jack decided to use the part of his anatomy that separated him from his cave-dwelling ancestors. His cerebral cortex. The Asian assassin had already proven to be a skilled combatant. The last thing Jack wanted to do was confront the man bare-handed.

This was a time to be smart rather than tough.

But a crowded Israeli beach didn't offer much in the way of weapons. At the thought of his location, Jack turned, scanning the crowd. Terrorism was a way of life here. Sometimes even a daily occurrence. With that in mind, it would serve to reason that the assassin wasn't the only armed person on the beach. Maybe Jack could recruit a good guy or two.

But a quick sweep of the boardwalk put that notion to rest. No overt security presence at all. This didn't mean that a plain-clothes security official wasn't concealed-carrying, but hidden weapons did Jack no good. By the time he figured out who was armed, Tommy would be motherless. No, stopping the slaughter remained Jack's responsibility.

But how?

Jack was running out of time. The Asian man was now less than twenty meters away. Jack needed to act. Conducting a final sweep of the beach, he found salvation.

It felt like karma.

To his right, a collection of brightly colored surfboards was clustered next to a wooden shack like psychedelic lawn ornaments. While even the short boards were much too long for what Jack had in mind, a dark-toned skimboard poked from the bottom of the pile. Grabbing the length of laminated wood, Jack sprinted toward the Asian man.

A shout let Jack know that his act of larceny hadn't gone unnoticed, but he figured he could deal with the upset proprietor later.

Assuming there was a later.

Jack was now to the left and slightly behind the Asian man, who was continuing his stalk toward the hapless pair. Jack

161

pumped his knees, leaning into the sprint, flashing back to his days as a high school linebacker. He pictured the assassin as an unwitting wide receiver he was about to level.

And then he was face-first in the sand.

Untangling himself from the pair of muscular arms that had brought him down, Jack found himself face-to-face with his bare-chested assaulter. Apparently, the surfboard rental shop's proprietor believed in actively deterring theft. The kid looked about twenty, with bronze skin and a shock of brown hair that fell across his eyes.

And he was angry.

Very angry.

While Jack could sympathize, he didn't have time to explain.

Slipping under a wild cross, Jack struck the kid in the throat, using the webbing between his thumb and index finger to soften the blow. Jack didn't put much behind the strike, aiming for shock and awe rather than injury. If the kid's startled expression was any indication, Jack seemed to have achieved his goal.

The torrent of angry Hebrew ceased as the kid grabbed his throat, coughing.

"Sorry," Jack said, rolling to his feet, "but I need this. I'll be back."

162

Jack picked up the sandy skimboard and turned back toward his target. His stomach clenched. The Asian man was now less than ten feet from the woman. An easy shot. The man's presence seemed to have pinged something on Tommy's radar. The boy turned from where he'd been watching the surf swirl around his feet to the looming assassin, his eyes going wide at the man's appearance.

For his part, the killer ignored the child completely, extending his left arm toward the kneeling mother's head.

It was going down, right here, right now.

And Jack was too far away to stop it.

Putting the fingers of one hand to his lips, Jack gave a piercing horse whistle shrill enough to raise the dead. And then, just to make sure the Asian man got the message, Jack screamed "Hey!" at the top of his lungs.

Ding was famous for saying that he'd rather be lucky than good, and while the sentiment had never really made sense to Jack before, it did now. Along with just about everyone else on the beach, the Asian man turned his head reflexively toward Jack. Which meant that he caught the skimboard Jack hurled like a javelin right between his eyes.

Part of Jack actually wanted to pause to

marvel at the sheer perfection of the throw. He could have tossed the board a thousand times and probably never achieved the same result. The length of wood had flown in a perfectly arcing trajectory, just like Nolan Ryan's famous fastball. Even from twenty feet away, Jack heard the assassin's nose shatter with a satisfying *crunch.*

If there was ever a time to appreciate a perfect trick shot, it was now.

Unfortunately, Jack couldn't afford to rest on his laurels. Instead, he was doing his best to follow the board's flight path. His six-foot-two-inch frame barreled into the dazed assassin like a runaway freight train. Jack had a split second to ponder another bit of wisdom, this time from his dad rather than Ding — *If you're going to be stupid, you'd better be tough* — before he slammed into the assassin, leading with his elbows.

Jack felt the jarring shock all the way down the length of his forearms as his stitches tore loose. Even his fingers tingled. A physics major Jack was not, but the amount of force generated by the bone-on-bone impact should have put the Asian man down for keeps.

But it didn't.

Even with blood streaming down his face and blinded by his own tears, the man had somehow still sensed Jack's devastating attack. At the last second, he'd bladed his body, turning the impact into a glancing blow. Instead of splitting the man's sternum, Jack had sent the assassin spinning toward the surf. Recovering his balance, Jack pivoted toward his opponent, intending to stomp the man's solar plexus into mush.

The assassin had other ideas.

A hand cleared the water.

A hand holding a gun.

Jack threw himself right as the pistol spit, the round snapping by his face. He landed next to the skimboard, and Jack grabbed the length of wood, jabbing it at the assassin's ruined nose. The man batted the thrust away, and his pistol coughed again. A bullet tore through the board, peppering Jack's cheek with splinters. Jack needed to take the pistol out of play.

Now.

Flopping down on top of the lacquered wood, Jack sandwiched the Asian man between the skimboard and the snarling surf. As bullets erupted in showers of wood chips, Jack spun atop the board's slick surface, turning his body perpendicular to the assassin's. He hammered a knee into the man's side while gripping the wrist holding the gun with both hands, slamming it against the sand. The assassin squirmed beneath him, but Jack's weight prevented him from bringing his non-firing arm to bear.

For the first time, Jack was getting the better of the assassin. While the soft sand kept Jack from bashing the man's wrist hard enough to free the pistol, the ocean was working in Jack's favor. The rolling breakers frothed over Jack's torso, spraying his eyes with stinging salt, but the foaming surf did far worse to the assassin. Each time a roller crashed ashore, the water completely submerged the Asian man's face.

It was hard to concentrate on fighting when you couldn't breathe.

Shifting his weight again, Jack worked the assassin's forearm into a figure-four arm bar. Once the pistol was immobilized, Jack wrenched his shoulders upward while pinning the assassin to the sand with a modified side control grappling position. Not exactly the type of form that would impress judges at a jiujitsu competition, but Jack was still alive and controlling the fight.

That would have to do.

But the gunman knew a thing or two about grappling. Twice he bridged his hips, trying to sweep Jack out of position while he curled his arm toward his own chest, negating the arm bar's leverage. Though he was at least twenty pounds lighter than Jack, the Asian man had a gymnast's core. He bucked like a bronco, and if they were on mats or even hard ground, his escape might have worked.

But not today.

The wet sand absorbed the energy the assassin was trying to generate, and Jack doubled down, slamming his chest against the slick skimboard. Finally, Jack's greater bulk and strength were starting to pay dividends. The skimboard distributed Jack's weight across the man's entire torso, flattening the assassin's shoulders to the ground as the board's edge knifed into the man's sternum.

The pistol fired again, the muted muzzle blast close enough to set Jack's ears ringing. But even the cocktail of hot gases scorching his face didn't distract Jack. Like a pit bull, he kept worrying the gunman's arm, tightening his hold, and locking down the man's elbow and forearm.

The Asian man was incredibly strong, and Jack grunted with the effort of peeling the assassin's arm away from his chest. Shifting position on the skimboard, Jack rocketed a knee toward the gunman's head. The assassin got his non-shooting arm in the way, deflecting some of the blow, but Jack's thick kneecap still connected with the gunman's temple, rocking his head.

For a split second, the tension in the gunman's arm slackened.

Jack pounced.

Twisting his shoulders, Jack engaged his traps, lats, and core as he wrenched the gunman's arm skyward, grunting with the effort. Then there was a *pop* that he felt as much as heard as the assassin's wrist gave way.

"You're mine now, motherfucker," Jack said as the pistol plopped into the surf beside him.

And that would have been true, if not for the chainsaw-like sound coming from behind him. Turning his head, Jack froze, trying to make sense of what he was seeing. At first, he saw only black.

Then Jack realized that the blackness was actually a boat.

The correct term was *rigid inflatable boat,* also known by its more common nomenclature of Zodiac. But Jack didn't have time to ponder the nuance of the watercraft's naming convention, because it was skipping across the waves straight at him.

Then the Zodiac's hard rubber hull crashed into his chest.

Sky chased sea as Jack cartwheeled through the air before landing heavily on his back. Coughing, Jack rolled over onto shaky knees, just in time to be hit full in the face with a second deluge of salt water to the high-pitched scream of a revving motor. Wiping the burning liquid from his eyes, Jack watched as the Zodiac tore back out to sea, bouncing from swell to swell.

He had no idea what had just happened, but the stretch of water where the assassin had been lying seconds before was now empty. On the plus side, for the moment, no one was trying to kill him.

It wasn't much of a win, but Jack would take it.

"Who are you?"

Jack turned toward the speaker to see Tommy's mom standing behind him, her arms wrapped around the little boy.

"I was just about to ask you the same question," Jack said.

21

Darien had never been more thankful to feel the pulsing of his cell phone.

"So sorry," Darien said with an apologetic smile. "Got to take this."

"Oui, oui," his companion said, waving Darien away. "Perhaps we can talk again later?"

"Looking forward to it," Darien said as he fished the phone from his pocket. "Ciao."

The detestable Frenchman had cornered Darien as he'd waited in line for a cocktail, attaching himself like a leech for the next thirty minutes. In his cover as a venture capitalist, Darien was used to listening to the prattle of self-important scientists convinced that they'd made the next life-altering discovery.

In fact, Darien welcomed a little arrogance. After all, he was a spy, and spies made their livelihood exploiting the bravado of others. Even so, the French researcher was in a class all his own. After being lectured for the third time about how disappointed his investors would be if Darien allowed another fund to beat him to the Frenchman's door, Darien was ready to snap the man's neck, consequences be damned.

Fortunately, his phone provided a much-needed interruption.

"Hello," Darien said, smiling as he worked his way from the ballroom in search of a quieter space to talk. Though Tel Aviv was quite a haul for the American scientists in attendance, the Israeli organizers had spared no expense to make their trip worthwhile. The Hilton Tel Aviv certainly knew how to throw a good party.

"We have a problem."

The words sent a shiver down Darien's spine for more reasons than one. The sound of the speaker's voice conjured up images of the weekend they'd spent in Vienna. A weekend in which they'd seen very little besides the confines of their hotel room and each other. But this delightful feeling was competing with the meaning behind the voice's words.

"Explain," Darien said.

Though the caller, like Darien, was fluent in a number of languages, the conversation

171

was conducted in English. This was not done for convenience's sake. The eyes of the army of signal-intercept officers laboring in the IDF's infamous Unit 8200 were ever watchful. Akin to the U.S. National Security Agency, Unit 8200 specialized in vacuuming up SIGINT, or signals intelligence.

And though the organization's capabilities were formidable, the men and women working were only human. This meant that they were cursed with a human's finite ability to process the plethora of information prioritized for their consumption by the horde of adaptive algorithms at work on their behalf. With this in mind, capturing English communications was a lower priority than electronic tidbits featuring conversations in threat languages.

Darien knew he couldn't completely hide from the Israelis' omnipotent-seeming collection capabilities. But perhaps he could seek shelter in a pile of secondary data while the analysts pursued other leads that seemed more promising. Much like a chameleon, Darien didn't aspire to invisibility. He just wanted to look less enticing than other potential prey.

"We are not the only interested party."

Darien processed the speaker's words as

another false smile slid onto his face. The pair of scientists from India were trying to catch his eye, and while the two women didn't have the pugnaciousness of the Frenchman, they were no less determined.

Pointing to his phone, Darien turned away from the researchers.

"Another recruitment?" Darien said, finally finding a quiet corner between the bathrooms and the foyer leading to the lobby. This had been his biggest fear. Though he'd successfully wooed his target to Israel, he knew that a fish this big would certainly tempt other fishermen.

"No. The new party seems intent on taking our player out of the game altogether."

Darien swallowed to cover the sudden dryness in his mouth. This was unexpected. As much as he would have preferred that the academic conference take place in Vienna or one of the other European Union countries whose lax border control was much more hospitable to spies, working in Israel had its benefits. Chief of those being that you had to be absolutely mad to try something kinetic on Israeli soil.

Or the kind of angry that came only from being double-crossed.

"Our friend survived the encounter?"

"Yes, but she's no longer coming to the party."

Darien considered the caller's words, thinking about their ramifications. Like a good case officer, he had prepared for contingencies. Even so, there was a difference between preparing and executing. As he thought, his gaze traveled across the hotel, settling on the Frenchman, who was even now corralling another VC representative into a one-way conversation.

That the scientist was a pompous ass who undoubtedly was overhyping his breakthrough was a given. But even so, Darien thought that the man would leave the conference with at least two new sources of funding for his fledgling laboratory. As Darien had learned time and time again, success didn't come to the bright or polite. It was bestowed on the ruthless few willing to do what others weren't.

Like Darien.

"Provide our guest with a personal invitation," Darien said, watching as the Frenchman secured a coveted business card from the surrendering investor. "Her attendance is mandatory."

22

"How's that ice cream, buddy?"

As before, the little boy didn't respond to Jack's question verbally. But he gave a pudgy thumbs-up with his left hand while pushing the melting clump of chocolate gelato around the plastic bowl with his right.

"You're pretty good with him."

Jack shrugged as he shifted his attention from boy to mother.

"I had a friend like him growing up."

"Like him how," the woman said, her tone taking a frostier turn.

"Hey, I didn't mean anything," Jack said, holding up his hands in surrender. "I just noticed how attached he was to old Cap there, and it reminded me of a kid I went to school with. Except for him, it was a penny. I could never see anything special about it, but to him —"

"— it was everything," the woman said, her voice warmer. "I'm sorry. It's been a

175

crazy day."

"No need to apologize. I'm just glad I could get Captain America back to you safe and sound."

At the mention of the superhero, the boy curled his fingers around the toy, as if to reassure himself that the figure really was back safe and sound. Currently, Cap was guarding the boy's ice-cream bowl. Tommy hadn't let the toy out of arm's reach since Jack had reunited the pair.

"Who are you," the woman said, unscrewing the cap on her water bottle.

Normalcy had returned to the beach almost before the Zodiac bearing the assassin had disappeared from view. Though several of the beachgoers had seen the scuffle, no one had been close enough to hear the suppressed pistol.

The boat's appearance had certainly caused a stir, but no bombs had exploded, and no armed terrorists had sprayed machine-gun fire into the crowd. By Israeli standards, the whole incident wasn't worth getting excited about. Someone had made noise about calling the police, but the woman had turned away all offers for help.

Except Jack's.

He'd asked if she and her son would join him at one of the many outdoor cafés that

176

bordered the beach, and she'd agreed. Jack had a feeling this was partly because of his American accent, and partly because when the man who's saved your life twice in the same day asks you to ice cream, you don't say no.

Now they were sitting at a covered table watching the surf wash over the same patch of sand that thirty minutes ago had been the site of a life-and-death struggle. The sun was setting, transforming the Mediterranean Sea into an ocean of burnished copper as the cafés, restaurants, and bars lining the beach glowed with soft light.

Surreal didn't even begin to cover how Jack was feeling.

"My name is Jack. Jack Ryan."

"That sounds like a superhero's name," the woman said.

Jack smiled. "I've got Irish blood, so it's basically the same thing."

The woman smiled in return, and once again Jack was struck by how much the simple gesture transformed her face. When they were fixed on you, her green eyes were captivating, but the rest of her features, while pleasant, were nothing memorable.

Until she smiled.

"I'm Becka Schweigart and this is my son, Tommy. Say hi to Jack, Tommy."

Once again, the boy gave no indication that he'd heard, but Captain America dipped his head in Tommy's chubby fingers.

"Great to meet you, Tommy," Jack said with a smile. Then he turned back to Becka, a more serious expression on his face. "You're a pretty popular girl. Any idea why someone might try to kill you twice in one day?"

Becka's smile became a frown.

"Why do you care?"

"I don't believe in just watching things happen," Jack said, holding up his bandaged forearms. "Look, you don't owe me anything. Say the word and I'll leave. But it seems to me that the men who are after you are both determined and well financed. That's not a good combination."

"Are you FBI?" Becka said.

"Nope," Jack said. "Just a Good Samaritan. But I have some friends who might be able to help. Why don't you tell me who you are, and why you're here. Then we'll figure the rest out together."

Becka looked at Jack in silence for a moment, her green eyes boring into his. Then she slowly nodded.

"I don't know why, but I feel like I can trust you," Becka said, settling back in her chair. "The truth is I have no idea why

178

someone is trying to kill me. I really don't."

"But you've talked with the FBI?" Jack said, pulling on the earlier thread.

"Yes, I —"

"Look, it's my favorite American cowboy." Jack turned to see Tal, Dudu, and a collection of rough-looking men.

They didn't look happy.

23

Ocean air spilled into the car, blanketing Jack in the scent of salt water. Relaxing in his seat, Jack closed his eyes and breathed deeply, trying to understand how things had gone so off track.

He'd been genuinely happy to see Tal up and about, but something between them had clearly changed. Though she'd led with her trademark flirty banter, it didn't last long.

Or, more specifically, Tal as the speaker didn't last long.

Before Jack could respond, Dudu had inserted himself between the two. In no uncertain terms he'd told Jack that his time in Israel was at a close. He was going to the airport, willingly or with help. One look at Dudu's henchmen had convinced Jack the Shin Bet officer wasn't bluffing.

The men were built like fire hydrants.

Jack hadn't had the pleasure of operating

with anyone from Israel before, but if he had to guess, the newcomers were on loan from Israel's fabled Sayeret Matkal, an elite commando unit only slightly less prestigious than the U.S. Army's Delta Force. Though the men weren't visibly carrying weapons, Jack knew scrappers when he saw them.

Besides, the men wore untucked shirts, which meant that Jericho pistols were within easy reach.

Becka didn't have Jack's tactical experience, but she seemed to recognize predators when she saw them. Turning from the Israeli paramilitary team to Jack, she'd asked just one question.

"What happens now?"

"Whatever they say," Jack had replied.

And what they'd said was to stand up slowly and head for the two cars parked on HaYarkon Street. Jack had tried to grab a word with Tal, but Dudu wasn't about to let that happen. He'd separated Jack from Becka and Tommy. Tal walked with the mother and son while the remainder of the team herded Jack in the same direction.

When they got to the street, Tal and two of the commandos bundled Becka into the lead vehicle while Jack, Dudu, and the remaining commandos piled into the second. Tal paused for a moment as she was getting in, catching Jack's eye over the car's roof. But she gave him nothing more than a sad smile before ducking inside.

That had been five minutes ago, and until now, the ride had passed in silence.

Perhaps it was time for that to change.

"Why are you doing this?" Jack said.

"You have only yourself to blame," Dudu said. "We offered you the chance to do the right thing. You refused."

"Your idea of the right thing is curious," Jack said, leaning forward. "I saved the American's life. Twice. Which was more than I can say for the vaunted Shin Bet or Sayeret."

The driver partially turned in his seat before Dudu arrested his motion with a burst of Hebrew. The man seemed on the verge of arguing, but didn't. Even so, the look he'd given Jack spoke volumes.

Jack had hit a nerve.

"All right," Dudu said, "you want to speak plainly. Let's. You are a CIA operative who is working in my country undeclared. Yes, you've saved that woman's life. But I hardly think it's a coincidence that you just happened to be nearby each time a killer targeted her. Either you and your team are using her as bait or you're simply incompetent. Both options are appalling."

182

Jack didn't bother to reply. Dudu was convinced he was a CIA officer, and while that wasn't true, it was close enough. In fact, the best thing Jack could do for both The Campus and the real CIA team he was augmenting was to allow Dudu to continue with his mistaken assumption.

The asset-validation exercise was long over. Hopefully by now the CIA operatives were in the wind. As much as he hated to admit it, Dudu and his team were infinitely better equipped to protect Becka and Tommy than Jack was. Not only was this their backyard, but they dealt with terrorist attacks every day. No, the best thing Jack could do was keep his mouth shut and get on an airplane heading west.

And yet . . .

"Do you at least know why she's being targeted?" Jack said.

"That's none of your concern," Dudu said, turning so that he was eye to eye with Jack. "Someone has tried to kill this woman twice on my watch, in my country. It is now a matter for Blue and White. You know what this means?"

"I do," Jack said as the car convoy turned left, trading the ocean for views of apartment buildings and restaurants. "Though from where I'm sitting, it's been a matter

183

for Blue and White this entire time. So far, you guys have come up with jack shit."

The lead car's brake lights glowed through the windshield as both vehicles slowed. Israel's traffic density was among the highest of any country's, and driving in Tel Aviv was a special kind of nightmare all its own. Still, commuters continued to flow past in the lanes heading the opposite direction, so maybe this would be a short delay.

"You Americans," Dudu said, shaking his head. "Forever convinced that —"

Jack tuned the Shin Bet officer out, his words relegated to the buzzing of an unpleasant insect. This wasn't because Jack didn't want to hear what Dudu had to say. Jack would be the first to admit that Americans tended to approach world problems with a healthy dose of optimism that often looked a lot like arrogance. But a more in-depth self-analysis would have to wait until later. The traffic on the opposite side of the boulevard had also stopped.

And that didn't feel right.

No sooner had the thought entered Jack's mind than squealing brakes and crunching steel gave him something else to ponder. The collision threw Jack against the seatback in front of him, torquing his neck and back. While fender benders in Israel were almost a daily occurrence given the country's congested roadways, this felt a tad more aggressive. Turning to look behind him, Jack saw three men exiting a van.

Men with masks and guns.

"Contact rear," Jack shouted, as the men flowed apart, taking up shooting positions at a forty-five-degree angle to the car's occupants — two on Jack's side and one opposite the driver.

While one part of Jack's mind tried to figure a way out of what was rapidly becoming a no-win situation, the other marveled at the tactical fluidity on display. The men's overwatch positions were perfectly chosen to provide maximum coverage of the car while at the same time deconflicting fires.

Whoever these guys were, they'd done this a time or two.

Dudu said something in Hebrew that Jack was pretty sure was inappropriate for mixed company, but in the time it took the Shin Bet officer to reach for the gun holstered at his waist, two of the shooters had pulled even with the front half of the car. Once again Jack found himself staring down a gun barrel.

"Hands on the dashboard," the shooter nearest Dudu shouted. "Now."

The command was given in accented English, but at the moment, Jack couldn't focus on the speaker's nationality. He was too busy watching to see if either Israeli went for their sidearm. For the moment, prudence seemed to win. Both men stretched out their arms, splaying their fingers across the car's dashboard. The shooter covering Jack gestured upward with his rifle's muzzle, and Jack obliged, placing his palms flat against the car's roof.

This was interesting. The ambushers had them dead to rights. In fact, the entire scenario would have been over by now if the shooters had come out of the van firing. But they hadn't. They wanted someone alive.

Jack had a feeling he knew who.

A flurry of motion at the lead car confirmed Jack's suspicions. A pair of shooters flanked the driver and passenger, rifles oriented forward so that stray bullets wouldn't accidentally catch the shooters guarding Jack's car.

But this is where the similarities ended. The facemask-clad gunman oriented on the lead car numbered four. Now Jack understood why. A gunman standing by the rear passenger side door wrenched it open, reached inside, and pulled Becka out by her hair.

His partner grabbed Tommy.

"Son of a bitch," Jack said, pounding his fist against the roof.

The facemasked gunmen were kidnapping the two, and all Jack could do was watch.

"Fuck," Jack said, punching the roof again.

The action caught the attention of the gunman opposite Jack's window. The man glided closer on silent feet, halving the distance between them as an audible metallic *click* announced that he'd moved his weapon's selector switch from *safe* to *fire.*

"Fuck, fuck, fuck," Jack screamed, punctuating each word with a strike to the roof.

The gunman moved even closer, poking his weapon's barrel through the open window until the muzzle was just inches from Jack's temple.

A human brain is not nearly as evolved as people think. Logically, the gunman knew that Jack was well within the effective range of his rifle even when he'd still been ten feet farther away. But instinct told the shooter to dominate the situation. To nip Jack's untoward behavior in the bud by reminding his hostage who was in control.

So he'd moved closer.

Time slowed as Jack weighed the opportunity he'd been given, weighing the risk versus reward. If a fellow Campus operative had been in the front seat, it would have been a no-brainer. But this time he wasn't betting his life on an unknown.

Jack turned his head a fraction of an inch, making eye contact with Dudu.

The Shin Bet officer stared back at him, his features relaxed, his expression blank.

And then he winked.

Slapping the shooter's rifle up and away, Jack pinned the barrel against the roof.

The weapon discharged, the three-round burst splintering the metal roof. The muzzle blast was deafening in the car's close confines, and the shock wave pummeled Jack's face and neck. Ignoring the gonging in his ears, Jack wrapped both hands around the barrel's plastic grip and jerked across his body, trying to tear the weapon from the gunman's grasp.

In a perfect world, this would have been enough to dislodge the weapon.

Jack did not live in a perfect world.

Instead, the rifle discharged again, and this time the burst shattered the windshield, inches from the back of the driver's head. This was still not progressing how Jack had intended. Additional gunshots echoed from the car. Dudu was no longer in the passenger seat beside him. Instead, he was firing his pistol over the crouched driver's shoulder, presumably at the second gunman.

Jack didn't know if the Shin Bet officer's rounds were hitting their mark or not. He was still in a fight for his life, and anything beyond the black rifle barrel squirming against the roof was pure distraction.

Jack shifted his grip on the rifle, trying to gain leverage, but it wasn't working. The element of surprise was gone, and the attacker had physics on his side. He was standing, while Jack was seated. This meant that he could put his full body weight behind his attempt to wrench the rifle free while Jack could not.

Time to change strategies.

Bunching his shoulders, Jack yanked the rifle to his left while torquing the weapon, hoping to twist the gun from his assailant's fingers. The gunman responded by rocking back on his heels, dragging the weapon down and away. Jack felt the gritty plastic sliding through his fingers and knew that this time, he couldn't maintain his hold.

So he didn't try.

Instead, he put his shoulder into the door

and slammed it open, driving with his legs. The steel battering ram smashed into the crouching gunman's face and knees, knocking him off balance and taking the rifle out of play.

Leaping from the car, Jack crashed into the reeling shooter, pinning the rifle lengthwise between their bodies. As the gunman struggled to free the weapon, Jack smashed him twice in the nose, rotating his shoulders into the punches. The first blow glanced off the gunman's chin, and Jack felt his hand go numb as the jarring bone-on-bone contact ran the length of his arm. But his follow-up cross landed right on the bridge of the shooter's nose. The familiar feeling of cartilage breaking beneath his knuckles was followed by a deluge of red as blood soaked through the gunman's facemask.

Bingo.

Jack made a grab for the rifle, but the shooter's sling hampered his efforts. Switching tactics, Jack stripped the dazed man's pistol from his drop holster, pressed the muzzle against the gunman's chest, and squeezed the trigger three times.

The shooter crumpled to the pavement.

One threat down.

Three to go.

Except that as Jack came to his feet with

the pistol at the high ready position, he saw that the Shin Bet officer and his commando driver hadn't exactly been idle. The shooter on Dudu's side of the window was down, but the gunman that had been covering the Sayeret Matkal commando was bleeding from a shoulder wound and still on his feet. The shooter was staggering toward the second van at the opposite side of the street as two of his comrades were providing covering fire.

Jack took shelter behind the car's rear wheel well as a fusillade of bullets smashed into the vehicle. To his right, Jack heard answering *pop*s as the Shin Bet officer and commando responded with their pistols. The Israelis' return fire was slower and much more disciplined. Traffic was still bumper to bumper on the other side of the street, and the risk of collateral damage was enormous.

Not to mention that an automatic assault rifle beats a semiautomatic pistol any day. Especially at these distances. To their credit, the Israelis weren't hunkered down riding out the storm, but neither were they racing into the street that separated their car from the getaway van. Jack didn't blame them. Leaving cover now would be suicide. But doing nothing meant that the bad guys

192

would vanish with Becka.

Unacceptable.

Leaning past the rear bumper, Jack ignored the buzzing sound of high-velocity rounds snapping by his head as he braced his right shoulder and arm against the vehicle's frame, steadying his aim. Jack had perfected his pistol skills with Chris Albanese, a former Secret Service marksmanship instructor.

Now it was time to put those lessons to work.

Finding his front sight post, Jack bladed the stubby notch on the gunman's legs. Hitting someone on the run took some doing. Hitting someone on the run at forty meters was a bitch. Hitting someone on the run at forty meters in the legs was damn near impossible.

But Jack had to try.

He brought his rear sights into alignment with the front sight post, then began his trigger press. He ignored the fact that this was a crazy shot, ignored the rifle rounds slamming into the car, and even ignored the ricochets pinging off the pavement. Jack's entire world narrowed to just two things: his sights and the slow, steady pressure he was applying to the trigger. He resisted the urge to look at his target after the shot broke, heeding Chris's tutelage by concentrating solely on his sights.

Only after the second shot did Jack check his work.

The gunman was sprawled on the concrete twenty meters from the getaway car, but it might as well have been two thousand. No way was he going to be able to cover the distance.

Jack had a prisoner.

The two gunmen providing covering fire seemed to reach the same conclusion. As one, they swiveled toward their wounded comrade and fired into his prone form. The wounded man jerked under the vicious onslaught and then lay still. Without so much as a second glance, the remaining gunmen piled into their van and peeled away.

Jack was back where he started — with nothing.

25

"Good shooting."

Dudu spoke reluctantly, as if the words had been dragged from his lips, but he still said them. Which was an improvement. Unfortunately, the Shin Bet officer's praise did little to salve Jack's toxic mood.

"Maybe," Jack said from where he was crouched over the gunman, "but he's still just as dead."

Jack had pulled off the gunman's mask, but other than a Caucasian face, the man's features hadn't told him anything. Probably to be expected, but frustrating all the same.

"We're alive," Dudu said. "That's something."

Jack nodded. "Yep. But Becka and Tommy are in trouble."

"Israel is a small country," Dudu said, squeezing Jack's shoulder, "and there's a reason why terrorists fear the Shin Bet. The kidnappers won't get far."

"Don't take this the wrong way," Jack said, "but from what I've seen so far, this crew is running roughshod over you and your Shin Bet."

Dudu's face clouded at Jack's remark, but a frantic shout in Hebrew brought the Shin Bet officer up short. Turning from the dead assassin to the lead car, Dudu barked a question. The Sayeret Matkal commando standing next to the car answered in another indecipherable stream of Hebrew. For once, Jack didn't need a translator.

The look on Dudu's face was translation enough.

Jack followed behind the Shin Bet officer's sprinting form, knowing what they'd find. Dudu stopped at the car, shouldering the commando out of the way. Crouching eye level with the driver's-side window, he peered into the interior. Then he stood and pounded his fist against the car's roof, denting the metal.

Jack slid past Dudu, steeled himself, and looked inside.

He wished he hadn't.

The driver was dead, and while this was shocking, if that had been the totality of the carnage Jack could have borne it. But it wasn't. Tal was sprawled across the front seat, half of her face missing. Only hours ago Jack had looked into those laughing brown eyes and wondered about what might have been if they'd met at a coffee shop instead of an interrogation room.

Now he'd never know.

Her Jericho pistol lay on the seat next to her, just beyond her grasping fingers. Opening the car door, Jack stretched past the driver and grabbed her gun. Then he reverently pressed the polymer grip into Tal's hand.

"What are you doing?" Dudu said.

"I have Irish blood," Jack said, turning to face the Israeli. "Irish warriors die with their weapon in their hands. She deserves the same."

Dudu looked back at Jack, his eyes blazing. For a moment Jack thought the Shin Bet officer might deck him. Instead, the man slowly nodded. "And what do the Irish do to their enemies?"

"Hunt them down."

"Irish and Israelis have much in common," Dudu said. He stared at Jack in silence until the shrieking of approaching sirens prodded him to action. "Go," Dudu said, "quickly. Otherwise, you'll be detained and questioned."

"Where?" Jack said.

Dudu shrugged his massive shoulders.

197

"That is up to you. If you head to the airport, I'll make sure you board unmolested. But if you have something else in mind, take this."

Dudu fished a phone from his pocket and offered it to Jack.

"The first stored number is mine," Dudu said. "Stay off the grid, but when I call, be ready to hunt."

Jack stared at the phone, considering his options. The smart play, the only play, was to head to the airport. This was not a Campus-sanctioned operation, and Jack was certainly way past his original charter of running an asset-validation exercise.

Did he want to help Becka and Tommy? Of course. But he had no idea who Becka was, let alone why she was in trouble. Not to mention that even though he'd saved her life twice, Becka was clearly still in danger. Anyone could see that his choice was clear — go to the airport and call it a day.

Except in his mind's eye, Jack kept returning to two things: Tal's lifeless eyes and the terrified look on Becka's face.

Sometimes a good man has to be willing to pay a price for doing what's right.

With a sigh, Jack took the phone.

"There's a coffee shop two blocks away," Dudu said as the first ambulance careened around the corner. "I'll pick you up when I'm ready."

"Better call instead," Jack said, dropping the phone in his pocket. "I won't be there."

"Where are you going, Jack Ryan?" Dudu said as Jack walked away.

"To get answers."

26

Jack worked through an abbreviated surveillance-detection route, or SDR, trying to temper his impatience with the need to stay operationally sound. It certainly wasn't lost on him that since the cell phone riding in his right pocket had been provided by an officer of Israel's internal security service, he might as well be wearing a strobing beacon strapped to his head. There was not an SDR in existence that could shake Israeli surveillance as long as he was in possession of Dudu's phone.

But it wasn't the Israelis Jack was worried about.

Walking down a side street protected by leafy sycamore figs and populated by chic stores and even trendier coffee shops, Jack looked for evidence of surveillance in the glass storefronts. Since this morning, Jack had survived three different encounters with men who harbored murder in their hearts.

That was a record, even for him. In the ensuing hours Jack had been reacting, moving from one potentially deadly situation to another. As such, he'd yet to take the time to engage his most deadly weapon.

His brain.

Stopping at a *sabich* shop, Jack ducked inside and read the menu. The woman behind the counter said something to him in Hebrew, to which Jack shook his head with a smile. Then he walked outside, doubled back on the direction he'd been traveling while crossing the street to a gelato shop.

Entering, he settled on a scoop of green ice cream that he hoped was a close cousin to pistachio before crossing the pedestrian causeway in favor of a narrow alley cutting between the streets. Emerging into yet another pedestrian area, Jack ducked into a small drugstore lined with patrons. Shuffling to the end of the line, he browsed the soap section, which, conveniently, offered him a view of the street outside.

Pedestrian traffic seemed normal. A father pushing a pair of twins in a stroller made way for a mother cycling past with her toddler strapped to a specially designed child's seat behind her. Across the avenue, a man and a woman got up from a table and

201

strolled over to where a scooter was parked. The man stepped onto the small, rectangular platform and the woman climbed aboard behind him, wrapping her arms around his waist. A moment later, he keyed the gas and they motored away.

Jack saw no familiar faces, or, perhaps more important, familiar shoes. As he'd learned from Mary Pat's tutelage, hair could be concealed with a hat, facial features could be broken up with glasses, and shirts could be covered with jackets. But shoes were a different matter. No one, spies included, wanted to walk around all day carrying a second pair of shoes, which by and large meant that surveillance teams tended to neglect that item in their wardrobes.

Accordingly, Jack had become somewhat of an expert at memorizing shoes. He shifted his attention lower, mentally cataloging the feet he saw walking to and fro on the cobblestone streets.

Nothing.

This didn't necessarily mean that Jack was clean, but he was fairly certain that assassins weren't lying in wait. Now it was time to make a decision.

Shuffling to his left to make way for another customer, Jack gave up on the soap in favor of the small rack of hardback books

202

as he turned the problem over in his head. Nothing made sense. Jack wasn't psychic, but like most espionage professionals, he was pretty good at reading people. If he'd had time to question her, Jack was certain that he could have sussed out why Becka was being targeted. But with nothing more than her name to go on, Jack was no closer to understanding what was at play.

Still, he did know one thing for sure — Becka wasn't an international woman of mystery. She might have come up on the wrong person's radar, but she was not an espionage professional. Tommy's presence alone was proof of that.

So why had the same Asian man tried to assassinate her twice? And why had her pursuers now changed tack from murder to kidnapping?

Jack picked up a book at random and leafed through the pages. An entry from Brad Taylor's Pike Logan series. Israelis had good literary taste. Espionage fiction aside, something about the change in the assassin's tactics bothered Jack. He couldn't pin it down at first, and then realization came like a lightning bolt from a clear sky.

"Holy shit," Jack said, slamming the book closed with a resounding *crack*. Ignoring the startled looks from his fellow patrons,

Jack placed the book back on the shelf next to the newest Mark Greaney Gray Man novel and hustled out the door.

The Asian assassin had targeted Becka twice. Each time, were it not for Jack's intervention, she would have been killed. But during the kidnapping, they'd gone to great pains to take Becka alive.

Why?

Because Becka's kidnappers were not the same people who'd been trying to kill her.

Jack thought this over as he cut through another series of alleys, heading west toward the beach, where he knew taxis would be much more plentiful. He tried to work through why two groups of armed men might be seeking Becka, but quickly gave up. Without understanding who Becka really was and what she represented, it was pointless to guess at her attackers' motives. He needed more information.

Time to up the stakes.

Emerging onto the boulevard, Jack merged with the flow of foot traffic, meandering parallel to the beach. For once, his attention wasn't captured by the breaking swells or girls sunning themselves in barely-there swimsuits. Instead, Jack's attention was occupied by something considerably more mundane — taxis.

Tel Aviv's reputation as a mini–Silicon Valley was aptly deserved. While a trendsetting company named Uber was making its American debut, an enterprising Israeli start-up was unleashing an app called Gett. Essentially Uber for taxis, it revolutionized Israel's transportation system, providing easy access for natives and tourists alike.

But now this technical innovation made it incredibly difficult for Jack to find a cab without using his phone. The first two taxis he approached drove off without a second glance. By the third, Jack had an epiphany. What better way to get the notice of people driven by innovative capitalism than by displaying a little innovation of his own? Reaching into his pocket, Jack withdrew a wad of American dollars.

As the next cab accelerated away from the curb, Jack took his life into his hands by stepping into the vehicle's path. The driver brought the car to a screeching halt, but before he could say something that would irrevocably damage relations between two allied nations, Jack shoved a stack of twenties at him.

"One hundred dollars to give me a ride," Jack said, playing up the loud-and-dumb American stereotype for all it was worth.

"Use the app," the driver responded in

flawless English.

"Lost my phone at the beach," Jack said, gesturing behind him. "I need to get back to my apartment. One hundred and fifty dollars. Please."

"What's the address?" the driver said.

Jack relayed the street number he'd memorized before boarding the long flight from Dulles.

"One hundred's fine," the driver said. "Get in."

"Thank you," Jack said, sliding into the backseat. He'd no sooner closed the door than the driver accelerated away from the curb, merging with the traffic with the fearlessness of a kamikaze pilot.

Which was an interesting comparison, because if Jack was wrong about where he was headed, death and destruction were certain to ensue.

27

"This is it," the driver said, easing over to the curb. "One hundred dollars."

"Keep the change," Jack said, passing the man one hundred fifty instead.

The number-one rule of working clandestinely was to be unremarkable and therefore unremembered. Unfortunately, in his need to find an anonymous taxi, Jack had already become memorable. There was nothing he could do about that.

But he could influence the way he was remembered. After all, a happy taxi driver with a fat tip in his pocket was a whole lot less inclined to talk with his coworkers about the jackass of an American who'd practically commandeered his car. Besides, it was the CIA's money, not his. And from what he knew about the world's premier intelligence agency, dollars were not something the Central Intelligence Agency had in short supply.

Climbing out of the cab, Jack crossed the street and began walking south, until the taxi pulled from the curb and turned and drove away. Once the vehicle was out of sight, Jack doubled back, this time crossing to the opposite side of the street. His eyes swept the landscape as he walked, for once not looking for surveillance.

Jack wasn't sure what he was searching for, but he was convinced he'd know it when he saw it. He was about to commit a major operational faux pas, and minimizing the ensuing damage was the least he could do.

After almost reaching the end of the street, Jack began to worry that what he was searching for couldn't be found. Then he discovered them. A cluster of bushes growing about thigh-high from a concrete-ringed planter. The branches sported bunches of bright pink flowers, and the plants brought some much-needed greenery to the otherwise bleak concrete-and-blacktop cityscape.

But Jack didn't key off the bushes because of their aesthetic appeal. He peered into the cluster of green, parting the plant's thick leaves to verify that the innermost roots were obscured from view. Once he confirmed his suspicion, Jack looked up and down the sidewalk. The street was still mostly deserted, with the exception of two men seated and engaged in a heated conversation in a coffee shop across the way.

Jack pulled the phone Dudu had given him from his pocket.

After a final, much more covert, look at his surroundings courtesy of the coffee shop's floor-to-ceiling bay window, Jack dropped to one knee and began tying his shoe. Except that in between fiddling with his already fastened laces, Jack slid the phone deep into the bush's sappy embrace.

Then he stood, brushed off his hands, and crossed the street a final time.

Walking past an empty café with the chairs stacked on top of the outdoor tables, Jack followed a cobblestone footpath that rambled by several trees sprouting from bricked-in enclaves. The path wound alongside the café and then meandered into a cul-de-sac of sorts, on which sat a small grocery store, a falafel stand with its metal grating already drawn down for the day, and a door leading to an adjacent apartment building.

Like most Tel Aviv residential areas, an obligatory bike stand sat in front of the building, half-full of bikes of varying shapes and sizes. The bikes looked inexpensive and were chained to the stand. In Jack's experience, these were the two qualities necessary for longevity on a Tel Aviv street. Owners of high-end bikes either stored them in their flats or had them stolen, no matter how ingenious the locking mechanism.

There was no middle ground.

Stooping next to a rusted hunk that looked like it had last carried a passenger when the most famous of Jews had been carrying his cross to Golgotha, Jack felt beneath its worn seat until his probing fingers encountered something metal.

A key.

Jack tore the key away from where it was taped to the torn fabric with a satisfying *rip* and headed toward the communal door. In the years he'd been living a double life as a financial analyst and covert operative, Jack had learned one infallible truth — no operation ever went as planned. Often this meant that the most important part of the operational brief was the portion the team hoped never to use — the contingency plan.

Though the asset-validation exercise wasn't an operation in the truest sense of the term, Peter had still briefed a contingency plan. In this case, it was fairly simple, but it existed all the same. If shit went sideways, rendezvous at the safe house. And if you lost your key in the rough and tumble that sometimes accompanied even the most benign of operations, get the spare from beneath the bicycle seat.

Once again Jack was grateful that Peter and Ding had both earned their spurs in the same organization.

Reaching the door, Jack pressed the key into the requisite slot, turned it, and felt the most wonderful of sensations — a lock disengaging. He leaned against the door, and it swung open on well-oiled hinges. Catching the metal handle, Jack eased it closed and then ignored the elevator in favor of a winding staircase. The safe house was a couple floors up, but Jack didn't mind the exercise. Besides, once you'd been trapped in an elevator with someone who wanted to kill you, stairs weren't so inconvenient.

Three flights of stairs later, Jack stood at the landing, peering down the hall.

Unlike a stereotypical safe house, the apartment complex wasn't decrepit, nor was the air filled with stale cigarette smoke. The hallway's tile was clean and uncracked, and the overhead lighting was uninterrupted and bright. No long shadows hid men in trench coats and fedoras waiting to complete a brush pass. The safe house sat above the now closed coffee shop, and the narrow hallway contained just two doors — one to

211

Jack's immediate left that led to a storage room and one at the far end of the hallway.

While the atmosphere wasn't exactly cheery, neither did it have the foreboding, murky feel of the safe houses Ding favored. And yet there was something that made Jack hesitate before strolling down the narrow hallway. An operational team was gathered behind the unassuming door twenty meters distant. And though this wasn't a slum in Beirut or a *banlieue* of Paris, Jack couldn't help feeling like he was entering the den of a wild animal.

A cornered wild animal.

Jack considered giving Peter a heads-up that he was coming, but didn't. This was a crash meeting in every sense of the word. Somewhere, a team of killers had Becka and Tommy, and at any moment, the phone Jack had hidden in the bushes could ring.

The clock was ticking.

Entering the hall, Jack walked to the far door and knocked twice. He heard a rustling, and then the door swung open revealing two things — Peter and the business end of a Glock 19.

212

28

"Jack," Peter said, surprise coloring his voice. "Come in."

Peter holstered the pistol in the back of his pants and shuffled right to make room for Jack, favoring his left leg as he did so.

Though he had to be at least twenty years older than Jack, the CIA operative was still built like the door kicker he'd once been. Muscular shoulders topped a broad chest and thick arms. Peter's receding hair was cropped close to the skull on top, but he still sported longish sideburns that were anathema to a classic military haircut. His eyes were a deep, startling blue seemingly at odds with his brown, weathered face.

If not for the awkward shuffle induced by his left leg, Peter would still look at home in a pair of MultiCams and a Crye Precision plate carrier. But as Ding had explained, a Taliban sniper had put Peter's operational days firmly behind him.

"Why are you here?" Peter said, shutting and locking the door behind them.

"Sorry," Jack said. "I know this is against protocol, but I need help."

"Sure," Peter said, waving Jack forward. "Come in, come in."

The entranceway passed through a tiny kitchen before emptying into a common area with a table to the right and a pair of couches and a chair framing a sliding glass door directly ahead. A narrow hallway trailed off to the left toward what Jack assumed were bedrooms and a bathroom.

The space had the cramped, lived-in feel of safe houses the world over. Paper plates and containers of takeout food were stacked on the table, and several bags lined the far wall, packed and ready for an emergency bugout should the occasion arise. The air smelled musky, with a trace of cigarette smoke, but as far as Jack could see, Peter was alone.

This was probably better, all things considered. Jack didn't know the former paramilitary officer well, which was to say that he didn't know him at all. Even so, it didn't take a shrink to deduce that the CIA operative was going to be less than happy with the turd Jack was about to drop in his operational punch bowl.

"Have a seat," Peter said, gesturing to the chair flanking the sliding glass door. "Want a beer?"

"No, thanks," Jack said, trying to keep the regret out of his voice.

The truth was he would love a beer, but he didn't mix alcohol and work. Especially when that work potentially involved putting steel on target. Dudu's parting words hadn't been the least bit ambiguous. When the cell phone rang, Jack intended to be ready.

Thinking of the cell phone nestled in the bushes reminded Jack that this meeting had a sense of urgency for more reasons than one. All of this would be for naught if Dudu called while Jack was up here jaw-jacking with Peter. Best to keep things moving. So rather than take the offered seat, Jack remained standing.

"Look, I'm sorry for coming here unannounced. But things are a bit crazy."

"No shit," Peter said. "One moment I'm running another uneventful asset-validation exercise, the next you're going hand to hand with Jet Li. What the hell happened?"

Jack shook his head. "I don't honestly know. I was watching the meet go down when a child the next stall over dropped something. An action figure. I went to hand it back to his mom and this Asian dude

215

came from nowhere with a knife."

"I saw," Peter said, crossing his arms across his massive chest. "You did all right, by the way. Looks like he nicked you once or twice, but that's still good, considering. I'll take a gunfight over a tussle with a good knifeman any day. You're damn lucky you didn't eat that blade."

Jack shrugged. "Sometimes it's better to be lucky than good. Anyway, if that was the end of the story, I'd either be surfing Maravi Beach or sitting in a plane somewhere over the Atlantic by now. But it's not."

"What do you mean?" Peter said.

"The Shin Bet rolled me up. They let me go pretty quickly once the woman, Becka, told them what had happened, but not before one of the agents read me the riot act about operating as an undeclared intelligence officer on Israeli soil."

"Holy shit," Peter said. "How'd that go?"

"About as well as you'd expect. We danced around for a bit before they told me it would be best if my Israeli vacation came to an end."

"Guess you didn't take their advice," Peter said.

Jack nodded. "You could say that. Believe it or not, I had every intention of unassing this place. The last thing I wanted to do was to compromise you or your team."

"But," Peter said.

"But I didn't see the harm in returning the kid's action figure on the way to the airport."

"Famous last words."

Jack nodded again. "I guess. I found the kid and his mom. But I also found Jet Li."

"Goddamn," Peter said, shaking his head. "Another go with the knife?"

"Gun this time. I stopped him from killing the mom. But before I could get my hands on him, a Zodiac extracted him."

"What did you stumble into?"

"That's the question," Jack said. "And one I still can't answer. The mom and kid were kidnapped on the way to the airport. Two Israelis were killed in the fray."

"You've had a rough go of it, kid," Peter said, scratching his bristly hair with a ham-sized hand. "But why are you here?"

"Not sure," Jack said. "Frankly, I wasn't expecting you to still be in town. The asset-validation exercise ended hours ago. That's plenty of time for you and your team to exfil. But here you are . . ."

Jack let the end of the sentence trail off as he watched the CIA operative.

Waiting.

His answer to Peter had been truthful.

217

Jack didn't know exactly why he was here. He'd tried to explain it away as a chance liaison with a U.S. operational team, or perhaps a mechanism for engaging the intelligence agency's considerable analytical capabilities. But neither of these explanations rang true. Jack was at the safe house because his gut told him this was the next rock he needed to turn over.

Jack's instincts had become more refined over the years. At first he'd resisted the idea of operating by his gut, but Ding had weighed in with the opposite perspective. Much like hours putting lead downrange and long sessions in the combatives annex perfected an operative's ability to fight and shoot, running surveillance-detection routes, recruiting assets, and coordinating complex operations trained the mind.

And not just the conscious portion.

Like it or not, Jack's subconscious was along for the ride. This link to a more primeval period of human history, when daily survival depended on a hunter-gatherer's ability to make split-second decisions, still lurked in the human brain. The primitive, evolutionary relic might be of little use to the modern cubicle dweller, but Jack didn't work in an office.

As Ding had made clear, every good

operator developed some sort of sixth sense, and Jack's had pointed him toward the CIA safe house. Now the body language emanating from the mountain of a man who was one of his mentor's oldest friends indicated that Jack's intuition had proven correct. Something else was going on here.

29

Peter unwound his arms and steepled his fingers, chest level. This was known as the interview stance. It was commonly used by law enforcement personnel to keep their hands ready even though their stance appeared to be nonconfrontational.

The key word was *appeared.*

Jack resisted the urge to arrange his hands in a similar pose, but he did widen his stance and transfer his weight to the balls of his feet. He didn't know what was happening, but the building tension suggested it wasn't good. Yet again he'd brought just his hands to a knife fight. Or potentially a gunfight. He'd already survived both today.

But even cats ran out of lives eventually.

"Okay," Peter said, radiating nervous energy, "let me lay this on you. We aren't just here for an asset-validation exercise."

"You don't say," Jack said. He forced a smile while looking at the stocky operator, developing his own contingency plan.

If Peter went for a gun, Jack was done. But if, like many operators, Peter's default close-in weapon was something sharp, Jack had a sliver of a chance. To employ a knife, Peter would have to close ground, potentially exposing his gimp leg.

Jack pictured how this would go, imagining himself devastating Peter's wounded leg with a Muay Thai kick. It wasn't the best plan, but it would have to do. In no scenario did Jack intend to get into a grappling match with an armed man who outweighed him by at least twenty pounds.

"Sorry for the runaround," Peter said. "The validation exercise was for real, but it was also part of a deception plan. Something to divert the Mossad or Shin Bet while the other part of my team got after our real purpose."

"Which was?" Jack said.

Jack edged to his right as he spoke, trying to move out of the corner into which Peter had herded him. Peter hadn't attempted to close the gap between them, but the paramilitary officer was still sparking like a live wire. Besides, in this case, distance was Jack's friend. Given Peter's size, there was a better-than-even chance the commando would absorb the kick and keep on coming.

Taking out his leg wouldn't help if Peter got his meat hooks into Jack and dragged him to the floor.

"Did you get a good look at the knife-man?" Peter said.

"I was close enough to smell what he had for lunch."

"Then you saw his nationality?"

Jack shrugged. "We didn't exactly exchange hellos, but I'd guess he was Asian."

"Chinese. The MSS."

"The Ministry of State Security?" Jack said. "You serious?"

"As a heart attack."

Jack frowned. He hadn't seen that one coming. "Why would Chinese intelligence be interested in a woman and her son?"

"Not the son. The woman. How much do you know about her?"

Jack shook his head. "Not much more than her name — Becka Schweigart."

Peter seemed to relax at Jack's answer, hands drifting toward his waist. The CIA officer still felt twitchy, but Jack was no longer getting the vibe that he wanted to grab Jack's throat and start squeezing.

Progress.

"She was being modest," Peter said. "Her name is *Doctor* Rebecka Schweigart."

"A doctor?" Jack said, trying to reconcile

the nervous wreck of a woman he'd led off the beach with his analytical, no-nonsense mother. Granted, not everyone was an accomplished surgeon like Cathy Ryan, but Jack still would have expected more from a doctor.

"Not a medical doctor," Peter said, seeing Jack's confusion. "Becka's a scientist. Her doctorate is in applied physics."

"Why is that important?" Jack said.

"Because she's the reason we're here. What do you know about Chinese industrial capabilities?"

"Enough to understand they're not our friends. The U.S. lobbied for the Chinese to be granted membership in the World Trade Organization back in the nineties. It was supposed to lead them down the path to capitalism. Instead, China's been buying, copying, bullying, or outright stealing intellectual property from other nations ever since. Far from normalizing the Chinese Communists, the free-trade nations have created an eight-hundred-pound gorilla with the buying power of one-point-four billion people. China's a disaster."

Peter's posture edged down another notch as he nodded along with Jack. "That's right. The Chinese Communist Party has been siphoning off trade secrets for the last thirty years. Take their J-20 stealth fighter. They don't have the expertise required to manufacture a true fifth-generation fighter, but agency analysts believe that bird is a solid four-point-five. So tell me — how does a country make the exponential leap from a third-generation rattletrap to a fighter that flies circles around what most of our NATO allies can field?"

"Espionage," Jack said.

"That's half the answer," Peter said. "The other half is scientists like your Dr. Schweigart. China has been flooding Western schools with graduate students who bring home U.S. technology by the bucketload. And what the Chinese students can't steal, the Chinese Communist Party acquires through grants to top universities and scientists. Hell, a recent FBI investigation found that dozens of hard-science laboratories at the University of Texas were funded by Chinese dollars in the guise of talent-recruitment plans. And that doesn't count the scientists who willingly work for the Chinese."

Jack felt his stomach sink. "Does Becka?"

"We don't know," Peter said, cracking his giant knuckles. "That's part of what we were trying to find out. Here's what we do know: Like many hotshot university professors,

224

Becka founded a private laboratory affiliated with her university."

"I thought professors were supposed to teach," Jack said.

"Maybe if your specialty is English. But researchers in the hard sciences like Becka want a way to monetize their research. It's really a win-win for everyone. Professors get access to the university's talent pool and facilities while reaping the financial rewards of their research. Schools benefit from the buzz surrounding the innovative technology generated under their banner. A good laboratory is a huge recruiting tool for the university, and Becka's lab isn't just good. It's fantastic. The work she's doing out of a little school in Kansas has the boys and girls at MIT and Stanford all playing catch-up."

"What work?" Jack said.

Peter shook his head. "My last science class was sophomore year of high school. Here's what I do know: Professor Schweigart's expertise lies in material science — specifically, coatings capable of bonding to any material. Coatings that can be tuned to either scatter or transmit RF energy."

"I studied history and economics," Jack said. "Can you dumb that down for the liberal arts major?"

"Stealth in a bottle," Peter said. "If our

225

analysts are right, Becka's figured out a way to manufacture a spray-on coating that provides radar-defeating properties."

"Holy shit," Jack said, as the gravity of Becka's discovery finally became clear. "And she's selling this capability to the Chinese?"

"Not sure," Peter said. "Sometimes scientists are willing participants and sometimes they're duped. Becka's been under surveillance since she arrived in-country. The Chinese aren't stupid. We've been cracking down on their Confucius Institutes, so they know the American people are waking up to their blatant espionage. With this in mind, we've seen a shift in the way their case officers operate. Meetings between handler and asset are now held in countries not quite as concerned with countering the Chinese threat."

"Like Israel," Jack said.

Peter shrugged. "I've got nothing against the Israelis, but they aren't going to wade into a great power struggle between the U.S. and China. I'm not saying our Jewish friends are complicit, but I also don't think they give two shits if an MSS case officer meets with their American asset in Tel Aviv."

Jack thought about what Peter was implying. It made sense. Like all nations, Israel was primarily concerned with its own survival. And though the United States and the Middle East's only democracy saw eye to eye on a wide range of issues, there had been some rough points in their relationship. The United States had even imposed sanctions for a period of time after Israel had sold armed drones to China.

Still, much about what the CIA officer was suggesting didn't feel right. Take Becka herself. She had exhibited none of the self-awareness or street smarts of a trained asset. Instead, she'd behaved like a mom with her special-needs son on a much-needed vacation.

Then there was Tommy.

While legendary operative Mary Pat Foley was famous for running joint intelligence operations with her husband while living behind the Iron Curtain, they were both Farm-trained CIA case officers. And even then, Jack couldn't imagine Mary Pat endangering one of her children by using them as a prop. Becka was a scientist, not an intelligence officer. She had none of Mary Pat's skills and all of her maternal instinct. Becka wouldn't knowingly put Tommy's life at risk.

But that wasn't all that was bothering Jack.

"I hear you," Jack said, eyeing Peter. "But if Becka is working for the Chinese, why did they try to kill her?"

Jack had been careful to ask the question in as off-the-cuff a manner as possible. Even so, his words changed the room's dynamics. Once again Jack could feel tension radiating from the operator like heat from a potbellied stove. Something was still simmering below the surface, and the pot was about to boil over.

"Here's the thing," Peter said. "We're in trouble."

"We?"

"My team."

"Where is your team, Peter?" Jack said.

Peter stared at Jack for a long moment. Jack kept his face carefully blank, but his heart was racing. Two teams hunting Becka. One who wanted her dead, one who wanted her alive. While it was true that the man who Jack had tangled with twice was Asian, Jack had no idea if he was really Chinese.

What was also true was that Jack hadn't seen the faces of any of the other men. The Zodiac team had come and gone too fast for Jack to get a look, and the shooters who'd kidnapped Becka and Tommy had all been wearing masks. But the one Jack had unmasked hadn't been Asian.

He'd been Caucasian.

Just like Peter.

228

"How well do you know Ding?" Peter said, breaking into Jack's thoughts.

"Pretty well," Jack said.

"How well is 'pretty well'?"

Jack paused, considering how to answer. The question about Ding threw him off track. Peter was clearly nervous about something, and his behavior, combined with Jack's evolving hypothesis about Becka, didn't mix well. But if Peter and his team were the killers Jack was afraid they might be, why ask about Ding?

Jack replayed the quick conversation he'd had with Ding prior to his departure for Israel. He couldn't remember the exact words his friend has used to describe his relationship with Peter, but he did recall one phrase verbatim.

I vouch for Peter.

In the clandestine community, the sentiment behind this sentence meant more than the words implied. Vouching for someone was the equivalent of saying that you could trust them with your life. That your honor was an extension of theirs, much like the mafiosi of old. Essentially, it meant that Jack should see Peter as Ding. What would Jack do if it were Ding asking him the question?

Tell him the truth.

Taking a breath, Jack put aside his suspicions and trusted Ding.

"Domingo Chavez is my mentor," Jack said. "We work in the same organization, and I owe him everything. When he asked me to take this assignment, he vouched for you. As far as I'm concerned, you are Ding."

Peter blew out a long breath, and the tension leaked from his body like air from a balloon.

"Okay, kid," Peter said, "I'm a little over my skis on this one. I don't think Dr. Schweigart is a Chinese asset. At least not anymore."

"Anymore?" Jack said.

Peter nodded. "When she first came to Israel, we weren't sure. The FBI had been keeping an eye on her stateside for some time. They knew the Chinese were nosing around, but couldn't figure out if the MSS was gearing up for an initial approach or was already running her. Then she booked a trip to Israel."

"Which put her out of the Bureau's reach," Jack said.

Peter nodded again. "Yep. So the FBI passed the intelligence to the CIA."

"And who says fibbies and spooks don't get along?"

Peter smiled. "You might want to reserve judgment until you hear the rest of the story. Anyway, the Agency wasn't big on running an active surveillance mission in Israel because . . ."

"It's Israel," Jack said.

"That's right. When it comes to counterespionage, the Israelis are ruthless. We knew they'd key in on a foreign team running an operation in their backyard."

"So you gave them the asset-validation exercise to focus on," Jack said. "I get it. But why not try and run a joint operation with the Shin Bet?"

"Good question, kid. This is where things get sticky." Peter took out his cell, swiped a couple times, and then held up the handset for Jack to see.

"Know this guy?"

Jack looked at the screen and then slowly shook his head. The picture was of an unremarkable middle-aged man with muddy brown hair and dark eyes. "Never seen him before in my life."

"That's because he doesn't exist," Peter said.

"Come again?" Jack said.

"Dr. Schweigart isn't here on vacation. At least not completely. Tel Aviv University is holding an academic conference in her area of specialization. Giant brains are flying in from all over the globe to attend. This guy's on the confirmed list, too. He runs a VC that invests in laboratories like the one Dr. Schweigart is forming."

"She's looking for investors?" Jack said.

"Without a doubt. But I think her interest might be beyond just the professional. The hotel has in-room childcare, and she reserved a sitter for the night. She and this dashing captain of industry have plans to meet after the conference social."

Peter made the statement in a matter-of-fact manner, but Jack still felt defensive on Becka's behalf.

"She's a grown woman," Jack said. "Her business is her business."

"Couldn't agree more," Peter said. "There's just one problem — this guy isn't who he says he is."

"What's that mean?" Jack said. "He doesn't actually run a VC?"

"The technology fund he reps exists. In fact, it's made several investments in the work of scientists just like Dr. Schweigart. He's the shady part of the equation."

"In what way?" Jack said.

"He's backstopped pretty well, but one of our desk jockeys graduated from the same MBA program this guy lists on his résumé. The alumni network is pretty tight, so our guy put out some feelers. Nobody in Casanova's graduating class remembers him."

Jack thought through the implications. "He's an intelligence officer running a honey trap?"

"That's my guess," Peter said. "He's definitely not Asian, and he speaks English with an American accent."

Jack studied the picture, considering. The man could pass for a number of different nationalities.

Including Israeli.

"You think he's Mossad?" Jack said.

Peter shrugged. "Like I said, the Israelis are ruthless. But if the recruitment was happening on Israeli soil, it would probably be Shin Bet rather than the Mossad that made the approach. Regardless, if our mystery man is Israeli, there's no reason for him to impersonate an American. Plenty of VC funds in Tel Aviv looking to plow money into American start-ups. No, if I had to guess, this guy's another team's star player. We knew that the Chinese were interested in the good doctor. Word is they're working on their own version of the technology. I think the FBI was wrong, and Becka got pitched by the MSS back in the States. She either didn't know it or didn't report it. Either way, she must have turned them down. Now the Chinese want to take her off the table."

"And you used her as a dangle?" Jack said, his blood pressure rising. "To draw out the Chinese or anyone else interested in her? Brilliant. Right up until you sons of bitches lost her."

"Easy now, kid," Peter said. "Was it a bad decision? Absolutely, and I take full responsibility for it. But we haven't lost her. At least not completely."

"What do you mean?" Jack said.

"We beaconed her. The device has extended-life batteries and only transmits when it's interrogated. It's very hard to detect."

"How do you know she still has it?" Jack said. "If her captors are from an intelligence service, they'll search for the beacon. Even if they don't find it, they won't let her keep anything of her own. Not even her underwear."

"This isn't our first rodeo, kid," Peter said. "Dr. Schweigart isn't the one carrying the beacon."

Jack stared at Peter. "The Captain America figure. You put your beacon in her autistic son's toy?"

"Don't be getting all high and mighty," Peter said. "A beacon isn't much good if the bad guys find it, now, is it? We had to use something that she'd take everywhere."

"Then what are we waiting for?" Jack said. "Interrogate the beacon."

"Love to. The rest of my team's crawling all over Tel Aviv as we speak, but they haven't had any luck. Our best guess is that the beacon is out of range of our transmitters."

"Then she's gone," Jack said.

"Maybe not," Peter said. "If we had some friends with a stronger transmitter . . ."

"Oh, for fuck's sake," Jack said. "You ran this operation without telling the Israelis, and now you want me to go to them for help?"

"Like I said, kid. We're in trouble."

Jack looked at Peter, thinking. The Israelis were going to be radioactive when they found out their suspicions about Jack were correct, even if he hadn't been in the know. Friendly nations ran undeclared intelligence operations on each other's soil all the time. The key was to give your allies plausible deniability by not fucking things up in the process. This little adventure was turning out to be a cluster of epic proportions.

That aside, Becka and Tommy's lives were on the line. If Jack needed to go to the Israelis with his hat in his hand, so be it.

"Okay," Jack said, "here's how it's going

235

to work. Give me everything you've got on this mystery man who might just be a spy, as well as the beacon's info. I'll pay a visit to my Israeli friends. But this happened because of your team's fuckup. You need to make things right."

"Ding vouched for me for a reason, kid," Peter said. "I don't need a reminder of what I owe to who. Find the girl and her son. If the Israelis get squeamish and you need some hitters, give me a ring. My boys and I will be ready."

Jack was still pissed, but he nodded all the same. What's done was done. Scores could be settled later. Now he needed to focus on getting to the people who'd kidnapped Becka and Tommy before they slipped away. That was still a tall order, but at least now he had somewhere to start.

And a phone call to make.

30

"Hello?"

The voice on the other end of the cell phone radiated equal parts fatigue and anger. Jack understood. Though he'd known the smiling Shin Bet agent for only a matter of hours, Tal had wormed her way into his heart. He couldn't imagine how her friends and comrades must feel knowing that one-of-a-kind smile would never again warm up the room.

"It's Jack," Jack said, holding the phone to his ear as he surveyed the road in front of him.

"Jack," Dudu said, the word sounding like gravel in his mouth. "I told you I would call you."

"And I told you I was going to find answers. I did."

"What?"

"In person," Jack said. "Pick me up. Corner of —"

"I gave you that phone," Dudu said, the gruffness returning to his voice. "I know where you are. Walk west two blocks, then look for a silver taxi. Show them the address I'm texting. They will bring you to me."

It turned out *bring you to me* was an invitation to a place a bit more prestigious than the nondescript building where Jack had initially made his acquaintance with Tal and her beefier partner. The taxi deposited Jack in front of a building that virtually screamed *Government* with a capital *G*. Cyclone fence topped with triple-strand barbed wire, roving guards, and cameras everywhere.

If the previous site had been the Shin Bet's idea of flying under the radar, this building's purpose was to shout to the world that serious matters were decided inside its multistory façade. To Jack's practiced eye, the structure in front of him looked like Israel's answer to the Hoover Building.

Bad guys beware.

As he was trying to decide if he should make his way over to talk to the less-than-friendly-looking guard behind the bulletproof glass or just give Dudu another ring, the blast-proof metal door swung open and Dudu strode out.

238

"What do you have?" the Shin Bet man asked.

Once again Jack felt that he was playing the role of troublesome asset more than operational partner. Which was fine. He'd hardly given the Israeli much to go on, and the professional feeling of distrust between them was mutual. Still, Jack was smart enough to know that this was no longer his party. If he wanted to go to the dance, he needed to prove he was a worthwhile date.

"I can find her," Jack said.

"How?" Dudu said.

"She has a beacon," Jack said.

"Why?"

The moment of truth. Jack had been walking a tightrope since his first interaction with Tal and Dudu. From the beginning, the Shin Bet officers had seemed to know that he was more than just an American tourist. During their talk following Tal's death, Dudu had intimated as much again. Jack hadn't discouraged the Shin Bet agents' conclusions, but he hadn't confirmed them, either.

And there was a reason why.

Jack worked for an intelligence organization not even officially acknowledged by his own government. He certainly couldn't come out to a foreign intelligence officer.

And then there was Peter's team to consider. Sure, the Shin Bet seemed to have Peter's men in its collective crosshairs, but thinking someone was a spy wasn't the same as knowing.

That said, Jack wasn't a novice in the world of case officers and agents, either. As the old field hands liked to say, you had to pay to play. Wanting to help find the people who'd killed Tal and kidnapped Becka and Tommy wouldn't be enough to gain entrance to the intimidating building.

You had to pay to play.

"Becka's a person of interest to the U.S. government," Jack said, beginning the age-old dance practiced by espionage professionals since the dawn of time. Flirt enough to keep your suitor interested, but don't give away everything on the first date.

"Yes, yes," Dudu said, waving his hand for Jack to speak faster. "We know she's a scientist, and that she was here to attend the academic conference. This is not news."

"Not just any scientist," Jack said. "She's developed something novel in the material-science realm. I've got a liberal arts degree, so I can't give you specifics, but my people are calling it stealth in a bottle."

Jack was willing to bet that Dudu was an exceptional poker player. His face never changed expression and neither did his eyes widen. The perfect blank stare.

Almost.

The fingers of Dudu's right hand, which until now had been urging Jack's story forward, froze. Jack had the Israeli's attention.

"Does she know about the beacon?" Dudu said.

Jack shook his head. "No. She's unwitting."

"Why do this to her?"

Here again, Jack had to tread lightly. As much as people liked to romanticize otherwise, there were no true alliances between nations. Only shared interests. Jack believed that he and Dudu both shared an interest in seeing Becka rescued and Tal's killers brought to justice. But if Becka's discovery really was that disruptive to current stealth technology, the interests of the United States and the sovereign nation of Israel might quickly diverge.

Jack needed to ensure that didn't happen.

"We thought that she was being targeted by a foreign intelligence service, but we weren't sure. The FBI had been keeping tabs on her and her work. When she made plans to travel to Israel, responsibility for her passed to my organization. We beaconed her rather than running physical surveillance so as not to run the risk of alerting a countersurveillance team."

"You wanted to use her to identify the service targeting her?" Dudu said.

"That was the intent," Jack said. "It didn't work out that way."

"If you'd just come to us," Dudu said, shaking his head.

"Maybe we should have," Jack said. "But what's done is done. Here's what I know — our scientist is gone, and Tal is dead. The question is, what are you and I going to do about it?"

"Now you're ready for a joint operation?" Dudu said, a flush creeping up his bull neck. "After everything has gone to shit?"

"I'm not talking about my government. I'm talking about me. I want to help."

"How?"

"I'll give you the beacon. But I get to be part of the rescue operation."

"Why?" Dudu said. "The woman was captured on Israeli soil, and Israelis died protecting her. This is a problem for Blue and White. Not some American cowboy."

At the word *cowboy*, Jack saw a smiling brunette with twin dimples. A smiling brunette now missing half of her face. With this image firmly in mind, Jack didn't have

242

to work to bring the required hardness to his voice for what he said next.

"This is personal for me, too, Dudu. I want to get Becka and her son back. But I also want to be there when the son of a bitch who killed Tal takes a round between the eyes."

Dudu stared at Jack for a long moment, his face as expressionless as a slab of granite. Then he spoke.

"I think you may be part Israeli, Jack Ryan. Follow me, and for God's sake, touch nothing."

31

Jack had assumed the *touch nothing* instruction had been for dramatic effect. It wasn't. Dudu had been literally cautioning him to touch nothing inside the looming building, and it didn't take Jack long to discover why. From the time he'd entered the vestibule entranceway complete with a magnetometer, full-body scanner, and a couple other devices whose function Jack couldn't begin to fathom, he'd been approached no less than three times by employees attempting to gain a sample of his DNA.

The first attempt had been pretty straightforward — a security person who'd buttonholed Jack with an outstretched swab and a smile on her face. Dudu had shut this down with a spat of Hebrew that, while incomprehensible, was unmistakable in its tone. The woman acquiesced with a frown, but the cunning look in her brown eyes said that this game was far from over. Next was an outstretched badge that Jack moved to take without thinking. Once again Dudu intervened on his behalf, intercepting the plastic and clipping the badge to Jack's shirt himself.

After that, Jack got the message. The folks here did not take kindly to visitors. And the visitors that did make an appearance probably gave false names. With that in mind, the Israelis were doing their damnedest to lock down the biometrics of their American guest, and Dudu was doing his level best to thwart their plan.

Once again Jack found himself revising his estimation of the Shin Bet agent. His initial assessment of Dudu as a knuckle-dragging pain in the ass still seemed to be correct, but Jack was now in the circle of trust. This meant that the former commando's belligerence was directed elsewhere.

Jack remained silent throughout the initial encounters, content to let Dudu pull his weight. But once they crossed the marble foyer to a pair of elevators and the doors slid shut, Jack decided to break his silence.

"What the hell?" Jack said, eyeing the Shin Bet officer.

Dudu shrugged his massive shoulders. "We're Israeli — espionage is in our blood. Touch nothing and your cover should remain intact."

" 'Should'?" Jack said.

Another shrug. "Like I said, we're Israeli."

Dudu's silence after the last statement seemed to indicate that as far as he was concerned, the issue was closed. But from Jack's perspective, the topic was a long way from being tabled. Jack had never been to Langley before, but he'd heard Ding talk about visiting Mary Pat at Langley when she'd still been an Agency employee. While CIA security was robust, they drew the line at clandestine attempts to obtain a saliva sample.

Jack didn't know how Dudu had explained his presence to the security personnel, but it certainly wasn't the standard liaison-officer drill Jack would have used if their roles had been reversed. He was about to press the issue further when the elevator doors whisked open, revealing their destination.

In spite of himself, Jack was impressed. When your father was the President of the United States, life did come with a few perks. One of those was seeing firsthand the famous government buildings that most people experienced only through books and movies. While Jack had found the Executive Residence to be a bit small for his taste, the five-thousand-square-foot John F. Kennedy Conference Room, otherwise known as the Situation Room, more than lived up to the hype.

In the decades after the September 11 attacks, the space had been completely retrofitted. Unlike the often-stuffy air that accompanied the unglamorous workspaces in the West Wing, the Situation Room really did look like the command center for the most powerful man or woman on earth.

From the plush upholstered leather chairs that ringed the glossy brown table, the President and his staff could view live ISR footage from any sensor on the planet, watch in real time as Delta Force assaulters snatched a high-value target, and peer through an Apache helicopter's thermal sensor. From that basement bunker, admirals and generals could command and control the nation's fighting men and women almost down to the individual-soldier level. It really was the equivalent of the bridge on the starship *Enterprise.*

But the Situation Room didn't hold a candle to where Jack now found himself.

He was standing on a balcony overlooking a bullpen. Rows upon rows of desks were occupied by men and women wearing headsets and typing on computers. Additional people flitted from workstation to workstation like bees buzzing among flowers. Murmurs from dozens of muted conversations filled the air, but as impressive as the bullpen on the ground floor seemed, it was the front of the room that captured Jack's attention.

Three massive flat screens took up the entire wall, stretching from floor to ceiling.

Hebrew characters adorned the top of each screen, which appeared to be displaying live feeds from orbiting aircraft or drones. Except the giant displays showed more than just Predator porn. Like a wide-screen TV's picture-in-picture, the UAV feed occupied only a small portion of the mammoth displays. The rest consisted of topical maps overlaid with operational graphics, link diagrams, and pop-up windows containing all manner of information.

Jack didn't fully grasp what was being presented, but like a caveman stumbling across a spacecraft, he could tell that it was infinitely complex.

"Welcome," Dudu said, clearly enjoying Jack's reaction.

"What is this?" Jack said.

"Israel's nerve center. We based it on your own National Counterterrorism Center. Contrary to what the rest of the world believes, the decisions that govern the security of our nation aren't made in the prime minister's office or Mossad headquarters. They happen here."

Jack watched as windows on the gigantic screens opened and closed, cycling from topic to topic as the work product of countless analysts was displayed in real time.

"Who controls this?" Jack said.

"They do," Dudu said, gesturing over his shoulder.

Turning, Jack saw yet another level to the amphitheater. But unlike the bullpen, this tier was occupied by men and women in dresses and suits.

The people in charge.

"What now?" Jack said.

"We talk to her," Dudu said, indicating a petite blonde with her hair pulled back in a bun, sitting at the edge of the platform. "If she agrees with your proposal, we get to work."

"And if she doesn't?" Jack said.

Another massive shrug.

"Don't touch anything on the way out."

32

Jack followed Dudu up the winding open staircase leading to the amphitheater's second floor, trying to figure out how he was going to explain this to Ding at the inevitable post-mission debriefing. It wasn't so much that Jack was up to his eyeballs in trouble — that actually was par for the course. No, it was more of *where* Jack's adventures had landed him.

So then my new Shin Bet friend took me into Israel's version of the NCTC.

Yep, that story was definitely going to need a little finessing. Fortunately, Jack was saved from that painful line of thought as he mounted the final step and came face-to-face with the diminutive blonde. Up close, Jack could see the woman was older than he'd first thought. Fine wrinkles webbed from her startlingly blue eyes and streaks of gray accented her hair. Her mouth was ringed with laugh lines, which was a bit ironic, because nothing about her demeanor suggested that she was in a humorous mood.

"Who are you?" the woman said.

Her Slavic accent suggested that Israel was her adopted rather than birth home. This in itself was not unusual in a country in which fully a third of the population were once immigrants. Still, the way the woman was peering at Jack over the rim of her frameless glasses while perched on the edge of a backless stool suggested that she'd acclimated to her adopted country quite well. Jack felt like he was standing in front of a bird of prey sizing up its next meal. Dudu began to speak in Hebrew, no doubt attempting to answer her question, but the woman stopped him midsentence with a single upraised finger.

"I wasn't asking you," the woman said, never taking her eyes off Jack, "though we will have words later. I was asking *him.*"

The emphasis she put on the word *him* put Jack in mind of a particularly repugnant insect.

"My name is Jack," Jack said. "I'm here to help you find the kidnapped American." Though he towered over the woman, he still had to fight the urge to fidget. In an instant, he understood why. He was facing off with the Israeli version of his mother.

"Of course you're here to help," the woman said. "Americans always want to help. Tell me, Jack the American, why do I need your help?"

"Ma'am," Jack said, putting a bit of steel into his voice, "your setup here is very impressive. Probably the best I've ever seen, and believe me, that counts for something. But a friend of mine once said that the best technology in the world is worthless without HUMINT. From where I'm standing, you've got a lot of pretty lights, but jack shit when it comes to actionable intelligence."

Dudu stiffened, but Jack ignored the Shin Bet agent. Diplomacy might have a time and place, but this wasn't it. A woman who knew the secret to stealth in a bottle and her little boy were in the hands of killers. Making nice with the Israelis would have to wait for later.

"This friend," the woman said, speaking each word with a surgeon's precision. "What is his name?"

"*Her* name is Mary Pat Foley," Jack said. "Ring a bell?"

"Perhaps," the woman said. She still watched Jack with an expressionless mask, but her gaze now seemed to hold more curiosity than annoyance. "But even if I know that name, I don't know yours. Who are you?"

"The man with the frequency that will activate the missing woman's beacon. Would you like it?"

Dudu muttered under his breath, but once again Jack ignored his friend. In for a penny, in for a pound.

"Give it to me," the woman said.

"Gladly," Jack said, "as soon as you give me your word I can accompany the team you send to extract her."

Now the woman's thin lips did curve into a smile. But not the one Jack had been picturing.

"Why would I agree to this nonsense?"

"Because that's my price," Jack said, "and you're going to pay it."

The woman's porcelain features flushed, her blue eyes glittering. She started to reply, but Jack interrupted her.

"I don't mean to be disrespectful," Jack said, "but I'm not a diplomat and time is short, so let's speak plainly. By my count, you have at least two different paramilitary teams operating on your soil. That means your domestic security service has a problem. That problem could be incompetence, a mole, or something else entirely. I've never operated with the Shin Bet before, but their reputation is not one of incompetence.

253

Which means something else is at play here. I don't know what that something is, and I'm willing to bet you don't know, either. But I suspect debriefing the captured American would help point you in the right direction."

"Give me the beacon's information," the woman said. "We're perfectly capable of rescuing the professor without your help."

"I go with the assault team or you get nothing," Jack said. "She may have been kidnapped on Israeli soil, but Becka has knowledge deemed critical by my government. I'm willing to bet that one of our special-mission units is already heading this way, bringing the full weight and power of the United States with them. As soon as the wheels of their jet touch Ben Gurion's runway, your role in this affair will be an afterthought. We can do this together right now, or you can watch as this becomes an American operation. Your choice."

For a long moment, the woman said nothing. Even so, Jack had to force himself not to take a step backward under the weight of her fury. Courage was the only recourse when facing a lioness unarmed. A single hesitation, a single show of weakness, and all would be lost. The silence stretched as the woman tapped a slender finger against her thin lips.

Then she spoke.

"A man with no last name and important friends walks into my house and demands my help," she said. "Even Americans aren't usually this impudent."

The woman's eyes widened.

"You look familiar, Jack with no last name," she said. "But this is Israel, not America."

"I understand," Jack said.

The woman nodded. "Then who is this kidnapped American to you?"

"Before this morning?" Jack said. "No one."

"Then why do this for someone you scarcely know?"

This time it was Jack's turn to pause as he considered his answer. As the words formed in his mind, his thoughts weren't of a professor who'd discovered something that might upset the world's balance of power. Instead, Jack was picturing chubby fingers wrapped around a battered action figure.

"Because it's the right thing to do," Jack said, locking eyes with the seated lioness.

"You Americans," the woman said, shaking her head. "Boy Scouts to the end. All right, Jack with no last name. You may accompany the rescue operation. Satisfied? Or

255

would you like my answer written on official letterhead?"

"That won't be necessary, ma'am," Jack said, ignoring the woman's sarcasm. "Your word is assurance enough."

The woman waved a hand at one of the hovering technicians, and Jack provided him with the information needed to interrogate the beacon. The man verified Jack's instructions and then passed them to a bullpen worker. For several long seconds the group waited in silence. Dudu nervously shifted from one foot to the other while Jack corralled his heaving stomach, trying to maintain his best poker face.

Then the tech spoke.

"We have the beacon."

"Show me," the woman said.

The image in the centermost screen blurred as the scale changed, zooming out and then centering on new coordinates. A moment later the pixels steadied and the beacon's location appeared as a single pinpoint of cobalt, pulsing like an accusing finger.

The woman laughed, while Jack swallowed a curse. Contrary to what he'd assumed, the beacon wasn't in Tel Aviv.

It wasn't even in Israel.

"Well, Jack the American," the woman

said, "you're going on a trip. I'm sure you won't mind. No visit to the Middle East is complete without a stop in Lebanon."

33

"What now?" Jack said once the echoes of the woman's laughter had faded.

"Now?" the woman said, her lips still stretched into a smile. "Now your American special-mission unit can try its hand at what passes for diplomacy in this part of the world. As far as the nation of Israel is concerned, this affair is now America's problem."

Jack swallowed, considering. On the map in the center of the room, the blue dot continued to flash, mocking him. Or maybe it was an indigo-hued lighthouse trying to warn him against dashing himself on dangerous rocks. In any case, it was clear from the woman's willingness to cede control of the entire fiasco that she had no desire to send forces into Beirut.

Jack understood. In the annals of Israeli history, there were few cities as polarizing as Beirut. In the 7.6-square-mile city of 2.2

million rested some of the Jewish state's most audacious successes side by side with its most humiliating defeats. Beirut was where an Israeli commando team led by a future prime minister came ashore dressed as women and singlehandedly brought justice. Justice in the form of a bullets to the skulls of the terrorists responsible for the murder of defenseless Israeli athletes during the 1972 Olympics.

In the same vein, Beirut was also the city that Israel had laid siege to and occupied at different times during the turbulent years since the Jewish state's modern founding. In the disastrous Second Lebanon War, which took place in 2006, Israel attacked Beirut's Rafic Hariri International Airport to support an invasion of southern Lebanon designed to uproot Hezbollah once and for all. Though perhaps a tactical success, the Israeli effort failed its strategic goal of ending Hezbollah's presence in Lebanon.

At the war's conclusion, Hezbollah lived to fight another day, while several Israeli military and civilian leaders were fired or forced to resign. Lebanon's capital was just 147 miles from Jerusalem. A mere fifteen-minute flight by airplane. But to the Israeli people, Beirut might as well have existed in another universe.

Still, Jack knew that he couldn't wait for SEAL Team 6 or the Army's Delta Force to show up and save the day. Time was of the essence, and every minute that Becka remained in the hands of her captors was an opportunity for her captors to discover the beacon or, even worse, move her beyond America's operational reach. Conducting a hostage rescue in Iraq or Syria was one thing. But going to war with Iran or China was something else entirely. Jack needed this woman to act now, while a rescue was still within the realm of the possible.

Which meant he had to try a different approach.

"The kidnappers who have Becka murdered a Shin Bet officer," Jack said. "Will her death go unanswered?"

"You misunderstand me," the woman said, her smile now gone. "Those who have harmed us will pay for what they did. But it will be at a time and place of our choosing. We are not the United States of America, Jack. We cannot afford to stumble into wars halfheartedly. Like your country, we were once proud. And like you, we were humbled. Our national humiliation took place during the Second Lebanon War. I will not authorize a mission just to sate our need for vengeance. We must be smarter than that."

"Not even if the men holding Dr. Schweigart represent a clear and present danger to the nation of Israel?" Jack said.

The woman frowned, her eyebrows narrowing. Once again Jack found himself confronting a bird of prey.

"Jack the American," the woman said, "what are you not telling me?"

"Much," Jack said. "Just as I'm sure there's much you're not sharing with me. But there is one additional detail about Becka's kidnapping you might find interesting."

Jack took a breath before continuing, as if to draw out the moment. He needed the woman's attention solely focused on what he was about to say. But that wasn't why Jack paused. Instead, he was summoning the required courage for what was to come.

You have to pay to play.

"I have a picture of the intelligence officer who we believe targeted Dr. Schweigart," Jack said, pulling out his phone and scrolling to the picture Peter had provided. "He was scheduled to meet her in Israel, right under the Shin Bet's nose."

"Pictures of spies are nice," the woman said, "and I would love to have this one. My internal security service is fearsome, but also fallible. If you're right, and a spy was

261

operating undetected in our midst, I find that concerning. But a single spy unaccounted for is a far cry from a clear and present danger to my nation."

"This man speaks English with an American accent," Jack said. "He looks like a farm boy from Idaho. These traits are valuable for a cover operative. In your country, I'd say they're priceless."

"What's your point?" the woman said, her eyes narrowing.

"My point is that you don't risk an operative with these unique qualities on a single operation," Jack said. "My guess is that he's probably been to Israel before. Run this picture through your security databases. If there are no other hits, you have nothing to worry about. But if I'm right, then he's probably running other assets in Israel. Highly placed assets with information sensitive enough to justify an intelligence service sending their most valuable intelligence officer to debrief them. Tell me, ma'am, what Israeli national secrets do you think this farm boy from Idaho came to collect?"

This time the silence in the auditorium was absolute. The woman stared at Jack, her face blank. After a long moment, she nodded.

"Give me the picture," the woman said,

"and we will run it. If it is as you say, I'll phone the prime minister and recommend the course of action you suggest. But if my analysts come back with nothing, you leave here empty-handed. Agreed?"

"Agreed," Jack said.

Again the woman waved her hand, and a technician materialized by Jack's side. Jack wiped off his phone before handing it over, and the technician bore it away with a reverence normally reserved for holy relics. The next several moments passed with excruciating slowness as Jack tried to maintain a self-assured expression while his racing heart and churning stomach suggested otherwise.

Then the technician returned.

Heading directly for the seated woman, the man bent and whispered into her ear. The woman stared into the bullpen as she listened, her expression blank. After the man finished speaking, she offered a single nod before returning her attention to Jack.

"Looks like you'll be getting a tour of Beirut after all, Jack the American. I hope you won't regret it."

Jack answered with the confident smile for which Ryans were known. And this was just as well, because words probably would have failed him. There were many places he

hoped to someday see.
Beirut wasn't on the list.

34

The rush of wind through the Black Hawk's open doors should have felt refreshing. It didn't. Instead, the heavy, salt-tinged night air felt oppressive, like a wet blanket. For the past several days, the ocean had been taunting Jack, its green foamy water beckoning. But now he would have been just fine standing on the beach and staring at the water from afar.

Perhaps that was because the sea was less than ten feet below the Black Hawk's tires.

Jack had always considered flying nap of the earth in a helicopter something to check off his bucket list, but right about now he was rapidly coming around to his father's view of aircraft. Namely, that they were best enjoyed from the ground.

As if able to hear Jack's disparaging thoughts, the helicopter banked hard to the right. Jack found himself staring at nothing but frothing ocean as the blur of the rotor blades dipped to what seemed like just inches above churning swells. A particularly troublesome wave crested over the landing gear, drenching Jack in spray.

Then they were straight and level again, though Jack's stomach begged to differ.

"How are you?" Dudu said, screaming his words over the roaring wind and twin turbine engines providing the 2,000-shaft horsepower needed to keep the aircraft aloft.

"Swell," Jack screamed back. "Just swell."

For once he was glad that he wasn't on a headset sharing the same channel as the aircraft's crew and the ten heavily armed commandos strapped into the jump seats next to him. Even to Jack, his voice sounded a bit off. Tossing his cookies was one thing, but sounding shaken to a squad of unknown men you were about to follow into combat was unthinkable. Better to just unfasten his restraint harness and drop into the roiling ocean.

"Five minutes," Dudu said, squeezing Jack's biceps as he shouted. "Five minutes to target."

Jack nodded. This time he wasn't worried as much about his voice giving him away. Instead, he was terrified that if he quit gritting his teeth and clenching his stomach, the quick meal he'd wolfed down before boarding the helicopter would end up all over Dudu's shirt. What in the hell did it say about modern combat that Jack would rather be in a firefight with Hezbollah than sitting in this chopper?

Or maybe that was part of the plan. If the ingress was rough enough, the assaulters would hit the ground looking for someone to throat-punch. Based on the threat assessment Jack had received during the lightning-fast mission rehearsal, there would be no shortage of throats to punch. Assuming, of course, the rapidly maneuvering Black Hawk managed to get feet dry without plowing into a rogue wave.

Then again, the alternative was even more stark.

Since the disastrous Second Lebanon War, Beirut's Hezbollah occupiers had become a de facto nation-state of their own. Gone was the rudimentary militia armed with little more than AK-47s, RPGs, and a fierce devotion to Allah. Now the Shia terrorists employed the best technology their Iranian benefactors could provide. Russian next-generation thermal sights, antitank missiles, sniper rifles, and even shoulder-launched surface-to-air missiles were all common-place in Lebanon.

And those were just the armaments that

Mossad had confirmed. More troubling were the rumors of Russian-made integrated air defense systems popping up across the city.

Jack and his new friends weren't conducting a limited operation against a technologically overmatched foe. They were doing the equivalent of invading a nation-state. One potentially able to detect their approach and respond with aircraft-killing munitions long before the pair of helicopters streaking over the water ever got close enough to discharge their cargo of killers.

Hence the Israeli pilots' attempt to turn their Black Hawks into speedboats.

But the operation's success didn't depend solely on stealth. The Israelis firmly believed that the best defense was a good offense. Jack and the team of Sayeret Matkal commandos were not the only IDF assets sweeping in from the Mediterranean Sea.

"Look," Dudu said, pointing toward the tablet strapped to his leg. "The diversionary force is inbound."

Jack hunched over the Shin Bet officer's shoulder, watching as blue icons edged ever closer to the area bounded by operational graphics denoting their objective. Like much of Israel's defense tech, the handheld tablet was an improvement on an existing

U.S. product. It showed a common operating picture that was a compilation of UAV footage and graphical overlays along with the real-time positions of friendly aircraft and vehicles. In short, it allowed the user to watch an operation unfold, which, to be fair, was a good summation of Jack's role in this entire endeavor — observer.

"Are they F-35s?" Jack said, the blue icons captivating him despite his stomach's queasiness.

"Lo," Dudu said, shaking his head. "F-15s. We want to get their attention, remember?"

Jack remembered. Though he had no role in planning the operation, he'd been allowed to stand in the back as the leader of each task-organized element briefed their portion of the mission. Dudu had been kind enough to translate, and Jack had to admit that, for a plan thrown together in less than two hours' time, the operation was impressive.

Then again, Israel was a country surrounded by enemies intent on her destruction. The many elements of the IDF were used to integrating seamlessly on little notice. Israel's numerous foes necessitated constant vigilance and an uncanny ability to adapt to changing circumstances.

This mission was no exception.

"One minute," Dudu said.

Jack nodded, appreciating the update but not needing it. The helicopter's cabin was abuzz with action as men chambered rounds, conducted comms checks, situated gear, and prepared to go into battle. It was a scene Jack had witnessed many times before, but for once he was not a part of the tight-knit brotherhood of warriors about to go into harm's way.

Though she had acquiesced to his request to accompany the commandos charged with Becka's rescue, the formidable defense minister did not surrender unconditionally. Much to Jack's chagrin, she'd held firm to a few conditions of her own. The most tiresome one, in Jack's opinion, was her insistence that he proceed with the team unarmed.

In hindsight, she'd probably been trying to call Jack's bluff. Disprove his promise that he would accept any restrictions as long as he was allowed to insert with the commandos. But in a surprise to them both, Jack had instantly agreed to her terms. He'd already gotten what he wanted, and the clock was ticking. Negotiating with an Israeli was a fool's errand.

Except that hitting a hot landing zone unarmed was starting to look less smart with every second his helicopter grew closer to Beirut. It wasn't that Jack didn't trust his new comrades-in-arms — Sayeret Matkal had one of the best operational records of any team of commandos in the world. No, as Sean Connery had so aptly put it, there was just something fundamentally wrong with bringing a knife to a gunfight.

"Here, my friend," Dudu said. "I thought you might want this."

Jack looked up from the tablet to see Dudu offering him a pistol, butt-first. Though a Jericho pistol wasn't his firearm of choice, beggars couldn't be choosers. Besides, the weapon was reliable and chambered in a man-stopping .45-caliber round. If he was going to have to use an unfamiliar firearm, Jack at least wanted one designed to punch big holes in his intended target.

"Thank you," Jack said, accepting the Jericho and press-checking the weapon to ensure that it was loaded. "I appreciate it."

Dudu gave another one of his famous shrugs. "Think nothing of it. Politicians have their rules, but in the end, the warriors going into battle should decide what is best. True?"

Jack nodded. Most definitely true. He thought about how his dad would react to Dudu's statement and decided the old man would agree.

Unlike most American politicians, Jack Ryan, Sr., had been a Marine long before he'd given up his career at the CIA for presidential politics. His father believed in providing strategic direction while delegating the tactical decisions to the war fighters on the ground. For a moment, Jack's mind wandered as he considered what his dad would think if he knew that at this moment his eldest son was sitting shoulder to shoulder with a team of Israeli commandos heading into Lebanon.

Then the helicopter flared and the time for thinking was over.

35

The Black Hawk piled into the earth with the grace of a hippopotamus belly-flopping from a high dive. Then again, Jack couldn't exactly fault the pilots' eagerness to get their bird on the ground and their cargo discharged.

Though the twin GE turboshaft engines were still howling just feet above his head, Jack could hear explosions rumbling through the air. The Israeli misdirection effort was in full force, and while the chopper had landed without incident, the Black Hawk pilots still had a harrowing flight through Lebanese airspace before they were feet-wet and home-free. While skimming wave tops hadn't been a ton of fun, Jack almost preferred another helicopter ride to what he and the team of assaulters had in store for them next.

Almost.

Jack reflexively ducked beneath the Black

Hawk's blades as he exited the cabin. He thought about turning to give the pilots a thumbs-up once he was clear, but the sudden change in engine noise indicated that it wasn't needed. A gust of downwash blasted him with grit and dirt, turning his pants and shirt into makeshift sails. Then both the primary and alternate helicopters thundered overhead, clawing for altitude like homesick angels. A moment later, they vanished from sight, leaving Jack and ten Israeli commandos alone.

In a stadium.

In his tenure with The Campus, Jack had been on some unique operations. Hell, any op with Ding at the helm was bound to be unique in some form or fashion. But this boondoggle might just take the cake. Jack was standing in the middle of a soccer field, surrounded on all sides by the more than forty-seven thousand empty seats of Camille Chamoun Stadium.

At least Jack hoped the seats were empty.

Turning a stadium into a clandestine landing zone really was a stroke of operational genius, just as long as the stadium wasn't occupied. Otherwise, he and his Israeli counterparts stood a good chance of giving new meaning to the term *shooting fish in a barrel.*

"Come, Jack," Dudu said, gripping Jack's shoulder. "We must go."

On this, Jack agreed wholeheartedly. In addition to conducting the insertion in Black Hawks that looked suspiciously like the stealth helicopters SEAL Team 6 had used on the bin Laden raid, the defense minister had come up with a couple of other interesting ideas to keep the Lebanese and their Hezbollah parasites off balance during the insertion phase of the operation. Namely a pair of Hermes 900 UAVs that were emptying their stock of precision-guided munitions into a known Hezbollah surface-to-surface missile cache.

As the defense minister had told Jack in no uncertain terms, the nation of Israel was not about to provoke a third Lebanon War just to rescue a single American woman and apprehend a spy. With that in mind, there were limits to what she, as the minister of defense, was willing to authorize. For example, F-15s flying provocative sorties just outside Lebanese airspace were acceptable. So were drone attacks against known Hezbollah strong points. But penetrating Lebanon with the sizable force needed to escort and provide combat search and rescue, or CSAR, for a conventional infiltration was something else.

A pair of stealth Black Hawks landing in an unoccupied stadium was a good compromise.

But what came with that compromise was the knowledge that Jack and his Sayeret Matkal team were utterly and completely on their own. If shit went sideways, the cavalry wasn't coming. This in turn meant that the team wanted to transition through the high-risk areas of the operation as rapidly as possible.

Areas like a stadium, for instance.

"Coming," Jack said, trotting after the disappearing commandos.

While the Sayeret Matkal was undoubtedly one of the finest close-quarters battle elements ever to hold a weapon, the unit wasn't originally conceived for direct-action missions like the American Delta Force was. In fact, *sayeret* translates to "reconnaissance" in English, and the organization's founders staffed the team accordingly.

Originally envisioned as an element capable of operating deep inside enemy territory, the men who formed the unit's first incarnation were chosen for reasons beyond just intestinal fortitude or martial skills. Specifically, the founders were looking for Israelis who could pass as Arabs. Shooters who spoke the language like natives and wouldn't look out of place in a *souk* or mosque.

Now, sixty-some years later, the unit's charter had changed drastically, but there still existed a detachment whose mission was different from her sister elements. A unit staffed with men who swore in Arabic when punched and prayed the *salah* like devout Muslims.

In short, the kind of men comfortable in the villages and homes of their enemies. It was in the company of these warriors that Jack now found himself. Which was a good thing, since the stadium in which they'd landed was barely a fifteen-minute drive from Hezbollah's operational headquarters.

Jack caught up with Dudu as the commandos reached the stadium's interior, trading the soccer pitch's openness for the close confines and narrow hallways designed to funnel thousands of people to and from their seats. For some perverse reason, the pitted concrete walls felt comforting. Though engaging in a gunfight within the stadium's constricting corridors would be disastrous, Jack drew reassurance from the fact that he was no longer standing exposed on a wide-open field.

A murmur in Arabic followed by an upraised, clenched fist brought the group to a halt. Though still at the rear of the group, Jack could see a kind of gray, dirty light filtering from the gated entrance ahead.

"What are we waiting for?" Jack whispered.

A moment ago, Jack had been grateful for the warren of twisting tunnels. Now all he could think about was how one well-placed grenade would shatter the entire team.

Amazing how fast perspectives changed.

"Our contact," Dudu whispered back. "He's a Mossad asset."

As had happened since he'd first listened to the Sayeret team leader flesh out the extraction plan, Jack's mind flashed back to another time when elements of this same organization had clandestinely infiltrated Beirut with death on their minds. Back then, Mossad case officers had been waiting with stolen vehicles to pick up the commandos and ferry them to their targets.

This time it wasn't an Israeli waiting on the other side of the fence.

"There's no one from Mossad to meet us?" Jack said, voicing his thoughts.

"No Mossad officers in-country," Dudu said. "This operation was a bit last-minute."

Touché.

Not for the first time, Jack found himself wishing he was carrying something a bit more robust than a .45-caliber pistol. Then again, the commandos weren't armed all that more heavily. The operating environment in Lebanon prohibited the assaulters' preferred modus operandi, which would have entailed fast-roping from the Black Hawk onto target, clearing the structure in a blur of flash-bangs and suppressed rifles, and then winging away, hostages in hand, while F-35 sorties provided top cover.

Instead, the men would have to rely on subterfuge and stealth. This meant that the ten assaulters were wearing normal clothes and carrying easily hidden weapons. In this case, IWI-manufactured Uzis chambered in nine-millimeter. While the submachine gun was more than adequate for close fights, it was not a rifle, and therefore lacked a rifle's punch or ability to reach out and touch someone at two or three hundred meters.

Normally, this wouldn't be a concern, as an operation of this magnitude would have two, potentially three, sniper teams in overwatch. However, as Jack was quickly learning, nothing about this mission was normal.

"Street is clear," Dudu said. "We're moving."

Jack nodded, trying to keep his breathing slow and steady, as his thoughts raced. Though he'd been in some hairy ops with his Campus compatriots, Jack had never felt so out of sorts. Thanks to Dudu, Jack had a pistol, but he was still little more than a glorified observer.

All small-unit tactics had elements in common, but the way they were executed varied widely from element to element. Case in point, the TTPs, or tactics, techniques, and procedures, that SEAL Team 6 employed while clearing a structure were similar, but by no means identical, to those used by their Army brethren, Operational Detachment Delta, or Delta Force. And those two Tier One organizations were part of the same military and shared the same language.

Jack had almost zero commonality with the Sayeret Matkal commandos. Their movement techniques, weapons employment tactics, and hand and arm signals were a mystery. For the first time in his life, Jack felt completely and utterly disconnected. And the shooting hadn't even started.

Yet.

"Stay close," Dudu said.

Jack squeezed the Shin Bet officer's shoulder twice in response, defaulting to his own CQB training. Though the team wasn't stacked outside a door about to breach, Jack couldn't shake the feeling that they were just as exposed. Perhaps it was the view he'd glimpsed as they'd rounded the corner.

Israelis in general tended to be slighter in stature than their American counterparts, and Jack was taller than most of his countrymen. As such, even from his position as tail-end Charlie, Jack had no problems seeing over the commandos' heads and shoulders. What he saw made his stomach clench. The lead commando was working the lock on the accordion-style gate barring the stadium's entrance while numbers two and three in the stack provided security with their Uzis.

On the other side of the gate, Beirut loomed.

According to the pre-mission brief, the team was exiting on the eastern side of the stadium. The facility was bounded by a north–south-running highway to the west and wide, unobstructed pedestrian areas to the north and south. To the east, a narrow road snaked around the stadium's periphery, branching into multiple secondary roads providing both access to Highway 51 to the west and several entry points to Hezbollah-controlled territory to the south and east.

But this access did not come without a price.

To the east, overlooking the stadium, stood row upon row of apartment complexes. A busy mosque was nestled among the side streets on the other side of the apartments, while a Palestinian refugee camp was barely a ten-minute walk to the southeast. Though Israeli cyberwarriors had done their job and the entire city of Beirut was temporarily without power, the darkness was not comforting. The team of ten marginally armed commandos was incredibly exposed.

As Jack watched, an ambulance pulled to a stop next to the curb.

"Shit," Jack said, flattening himself against the concrete wall.

"Lo, lo, lo," Dudu said, shaking his head. "That's our contact."

As if on cue, the ambulance's headlights doused. A moment later, the driver exited the ambulance, popped the vehicle's hood, and ducked beneath it. After several long seconds, he emerged, edging around the bumper until he was standing on the sidewalk next to the passenger door. Taking his phone from his pocket, the driver appeared to make a call. Though he was too far away to hear the man's words, his voice's cadence and his expressive hand gestures suggested the conversation wasn't a pleasant one.

With a disgusted shake of his head, the man stuffed the phone back into his pocket. Then Jack saw a tiny flame flare to life as he lit a cigarette. After taking a long pull, the man squatted on the sidewalk, even with the front tire.

"All clear," Dudu said. "Let's go."

Number one eased the door open to an impossibly loud screech of metal. In moments like this, adrenaline-heightened senses magnified everything, but Jack still cringed. Secondary explosions thundered to the southeast, lighting up the horizon and directing attention away from the stadium and its Israeli visitors. Even so, Jack felt antsy. The sooner he and his new friends were across the linear danger area posed by the pedestrian mall outside the stadium and inside the back of the ambulance, the better.

The Israelis covered the open ground at a fast walk in a loose, staggered formation, trying to ride the line between moving expeditiously and running, which would certainly draw attention. Numbers one and two in the formation crossed the halfway point between the stadium and the waiting ambulance, and Jack breathed a sigh of relief.

Then the night erupted in gunfire.

36

Jack instinctively dropped to the ground, trying to ignore the familiar buzzing sound of inbound rounds in favor of locating the shooters. The concrete jungle formed by the stadium played hell with the rifles' acoustics, and the retorts echoed from seemingly everywhere. Even on flat, unobstructed terrain a sniper was hard to locate by sound alone. Then Jack saw flashes to his left, solving the mystery of where the attackers were hiding.

That was the good news.

The bad news was that the shooters had picked a perfect place to trigger an ambush — a parking lot about one hundred meters northeast of the stadium's entrance. Jack recalled eyeing the spot during the rushed pre-mission briefing. Satellite imagery showed a series of knee-high concrete barriers to funnel traffic. Now Jack had a feeling those same structures were being put to good use by his unseen attackers.

A series of groans to his left demanded Jack's attention, announcing the rest of the bad news. At least three members of the team were on the ground, unmoving. Dudu and the surviving commandos were returning fire with their Uzis in short, controlled bursts, but Jack knew they were effectively spitting into the wind.

An Uzi fired a nine-millimeter pistol round — deadly for up-close work, but just short of useless for any engagement beyond about fifty yards. Not to mention that since the shooters had initiated in darkness, their rifles must be equipped with thermal or low-light sights. Not only were Jack and his teams sitting ducks, but they were out-manned, outgunned, and blind to boot. If something didn't shift the engagement in their favor, this was going to be the most one-sided battle since Custer's.

Another commando spun and fell to the ground, his Uzi slipping from his fingers.

Vaulting to his feet, Jack scooped up the wounded man's Uzi and fired a burst toward the snipers while sprinting toward the still-waiting ambulance. Like everyone else near the kill zone, the ambulance's driver was doing his best to become one with the dirty concrete. But unlike the commandos, the Mossad asset wasn't directly in the line of fire, thanks to the hulking ambulance.

And that gave Jack an idea.

The Uzi's magazine ran dry just as Jack reached the ambulance, and he dropped the machine pistol. He'd been under no illusions about his ability to place accurate fire on his attackers, but that hadn't been his goal.

The snipers probably thought that a lone gunman firing his Uzi while running was no danger to them, but thinking wasn't the same as knowing. Especially when the three-inch tongue of fire blossoming from the Uzi's barrel was getting ever closer. In a gunfight, sometimes violence of action really did trump superior firepower.

And sometimes, you just got lucky.

Right about now, Jack wasn't real choosy about which was which. He was just happy to have reached the ambulance alive. A sentiment the Mossad asset didn't seem to share.

"Get in," Jack screamed, pointing at the ambulance.

If he spoke English, the prostrate man wasn't acting like it. Instead, he waved his arm in Jack's direction as if shooing him away, while keeping his face pressed against the concrete. Jack considered using his .45

to motivate the man, but didn't. The snipers were still firing into the kill zone, which meant Israelis were still dying.

Time to go to work.

Yanking open the passenger door, Jack hopped into the ambulance and crawled across to the driver's seat. Settling behind the steering wheel, he reached for the starter, only to find that the keys weren't in the ignition.

Well, shit.

"Keys," Jack said, turning to the asset still prostrate on the ground.

The man looked up and shook his head as though Jack were speaking Swahili. Fair enough. Discerning the subtleties of an unfamiliar language was always difficult, and, like most tasks, difficult edged toward impossible when bullets started flying.

"Clés de voiture," Jack said, trading English for French as he made a turning motion with his fingers. Many Lebanese spoke a unique language called Levantine Arabic which was heavily influenced by French. While Jack's Arabic was passable, he felt much more comfortable with French.

Apparently, so did the asset.

"Pare-soleil," the man said.

Now Jack was the one devoting precious brain cells to translating as opposed to stay-

287

ing alive. The window to his left ruptured in a spray of glass. What had begun as a good display of initiative was rapidly stalling as the unseen snipers peppered the ambulance, forcing Jack to duck beneath the dashboard.

This wasn't going as planned.

"Pare-soleil," the man said again, pointing upward.

Jack got it. Smacking the visor above his head, he was rewarded with the tingle of metal on metal as a set of keys fell into his hand. Shoving the correct one into the ignition, Jack turned the motor over and smiled as the engine coughed.

Slamming the gearshift into reverse, Jack stomped on the gas.

Tires squealed as the ambulance roared backward as another volley of fire ripped through the cabin. Crouching lower in the seat, Jack peered in the side-view mirror, attempting to navigate. A moment later, a stray round fractured the glass into a million pieces.

Abandoning any pretense of precision driving, Jack wrenched the wheel to the right, sending the back wheels onto the curb. Then he slammed the gearshift into park, crawled to the passenger side of the ambulance, and tumbled to the ground. As he'd hoped, the ambulance was now positioned between the commandos and the snipers. The vehicle was still drawing bullets like flies to horse manure, but the Sayeret Matkal operatives now had a brief window of calm.

A window Jack intended to exploit.

Reaching over, Jack grabbed the Mossad asset by the scruff of the neck and hauled him to his feet. "Help me," Jack said, pointing toward the wounded commandos splayed across the concrete, "now."

The spindly-looking man seemed on the verge of arguing when a round ricocheted off the pavement, drilling him in the posterior. While the impact didn't draw blood, it did provide the Lebanese with a much-needed boost of motivation. Unbidden, one of Ding's sayings came to mind: When all else fails, kick 'em in the ass.

Of the original ten-man team, four were laid out on the concrete, unmoving. Two more were hit, but seemed ambulatory. The final four were miraculously untouched.

Thankfully, one of these men was Dudu.

"Dudu," Jack said, shouting to his friend. "Help me get them in the vehicle."

"No," Dudu said between bursts from his Uzi. "Get them to the stadium."

In a heartbeat, Jack understood. Out in the open with half of their members incapacitated or wounded, the Israelis were sitting ducks. But falling back to the stadium's narrow confines would at least negate the advantage offered by the snipers' long guns. Not to mention that the Black Hawks were probably inbound for a hot exfil. Or at least Jack hoped they were. Last stands tended to play well in the movies, but they weren't too keen in real life.

Just ask Davy Crockett.

Pointing the asset toward a prone Israeli, Jack ran to another commando and hoisted him into a fireman's carry. Then he turned toward the stadium, legs pumping as bullets zipped past his head. Crashing through the accordion gate, Jack placed the Israeli on the ground only to find himself alone. Cursing, Jack headed back into the firefight to see the asset struggling to drag a commando to safety while Dudu and the remaining Israelis traded fire with the snipers.

This wasn't working.

Ignoring the wounded, Jack sprinted for the ambulance. "Come on," Jack said, tapping Dudu on the shoulder as he ran past. To his surprise, the Israeli listened. Diving into the still-open passenger door, Jack crawled into the driver's seat. Crouching below the dashboard, Jack oriented the steering wheel toward the snipers, shifted into drive, and floored the gas pedal.

"Dudu," Jack said as the ambulance picked up speed, "you any good with that Uzi?"

"Better than you are with that pistol," Dudu said, swapping his partially spent magazine for a fresh one.

"Little bit far for a pistol engagement," Jack said, ducking as the windshield spider-webbed under a barrage of incoming rounds. "So let's get closer."

Dudu mumbled a response that Jack couldn't hear over the *ping, ping, ping* of rifle rounds aerating the cabin. The ambulance's headlights were still off, so Jack had no problem picking out the cluster of muzzle flashes coming from his eleven o'clock.

Spinning the wheel to the left, Jack centered the hood on the snipers and willed the ambulance to go faster even though the tactical part of his brain screamed that he'd never close the distance in time. As if to give voice to his thoughts, Dudu grunted and his Uzi clattered to the floor.

Not good.

"Can you still shoot?" Jack said.

"For now," Dudu said, gritting his teeth as he scooped the machine pistol from the floor one-handed. "But whatever you're going to do," Dudu said, "do it quickly."

Jack didn't bother to answer. Instead, he turned on the headlights and triggered the high beams. Only one lamp responded, but it was enough. Twenty thousand candlepower split the darkness, catching the men crouching behind rifles full in the face.

As Jack had suspected, the shooters had night-vision devices mounted to their rifles, and their earlier technological overmatch suddenly became a liability. Those using light-intensifying optics rolled away from their long guns, hands pressed against their eyes. Even the one or two equipped with thermals or serving as spotters were unprepared for the sudden transition from darkness to light. For one glorious second, six enemy combatants were completely and utterly vulnerable.

A second was long enough.

The Shin Bet officer and former Sayeret commando emptied the submachine gun in one long trigger pull, causing the shooters to jerk and spasm as nine-millimeter rounds tore through their unprotected bodies. Jack felt the ambulance's front wheels crest the curb, and then he was in their midst, plowing through gunmen like bowling pins.

Steeling himself against the sickening *thump*s as the van's tires exacted revenge for the dead or wounded Israelis, Jack slammed on the brakes just before his bumper smashed into the far concrete wall. Hopping out of the vehicle, Jericho pistol in hand, Jack went to work until Dudu grabbed his shoulder.

"Come," Dudu said. "The birds are inbound. We're going home."

Home.

The word rolled around in Jack's mind as he watched Dudu climb into the ambulance, favoring his wounded shoulder. Home for Jack was six thousand miles away, sitting around the White House family residence while eating Mom's apple pie. Home was the place you went after your work was done.

But Jack's work wasn't done. Not by a long shot. Becka and her son were still somewhere in this city, in the hands of hard men. Maybe Peter was right and Becka was reaping what she'd sown. Jack wasn't God. He didn't know the hearts of men — or women, for that matter. But Jack didn't have to be omniscient to understand that a seven-year-old autistic boy didn't deserve to be in the company of killers, regardless of who his mother was or what she'd done.

Home was still somewhere Jack intended to go, but not just yet.

"I'm not coming," Jack said, waving Dudu off.

"What do you mean?" Dudu said. "You can't do this alone."

"I know," Jack said. "But I can't leave. Not yet."

The big Shin Bet officer paused half in and half out of the ambulance, caught between his desire to see what remained of his team back to Israel and his responsibility to his strange American friend. Then the sound of distant police sirens solidified his indecision.

"*Behatzlacha,* my friend," Dudu said, "and take this. You're going to need it more than me."

Jack caught the thrown bag instinctively. But before he could say anything else, Dudu slammed the driver's door shut and threw the ambulance into gear. Then the engine revved and the battered vehicle reversed over the curb and headed across the street, leaving Jack standing amid a pile of torn bodies.

For a moment, the starkness of the situation crashed down on his shoulders, and Jack wanted to chase the ambulance's disappearing taillights. But he didn't. Instead, he reloaded his pistol, thumbed on the safety, and tucked the weapon into his pants.

After a final look at the carnage, Jack ran across the street and pulled the unharmed Mossad asset to his feet. Then he turned his back on the Israelis and Hezbollah assassins alike. The infil might not have gone according to plan, but Jack was in Beirut just like he'd asked.

It was time to get down to business.

37

Jack ghosted through the darkness, following the Mossad asset. He angled away from the chorus of sirens hurtling toward the ambush site, while distractedly listening for the deep *whump* of the Black Hawk's rotors. But he didn't devote much mental energy to the task.

This wasn't because Jack didn't care about Dudu and the rest of the stricken team. He'd actually grown to like the burly commando despite their rough start, and he genuinely hoped they made it back to Israel alive. No, the reason why Jack wasn't fervently scanning the night skies for the helicopter's shadowy black shape was much more practical — his attention was now singularly focused on his own survival.

Passing a couple walking along the street, Jack instinctively looked down and to the right, shielding his face as his mind raced. The assault team had obviously been betrayed. The ambushers had been lying in wait, perfectly positioned. This was no chance engagement with a random Hezbollah patrol. Jack and the Israeli commandos had been set up.

But who were their attackers?

If the gunmen had been Lebanese military, Jack's goose was good and cooked. While not on the same level as near peer nations like the Russians, when it came to catching a spy within the confines of their country, the Lebanese still represented a nation-state and the resources that came along with it. If this were the case, Jack was operating in hostile territory without an operational safety net. He might be clean now, but he wouldn't last long.

And then there was the other option.

Hezbollah.

This contingency, while not good, wasn't quite as stark as the first. Hezbollah did control large swaths of Beirut and acted as a de facto national government in some of the areas it occupied. In the fifteen years since the last Israeli-Hezbollah war on Lebanese soil, the Shia militia had built upon its paramilitary capabilities to become the most powerful non-nation-state in the world. In addition to a standing army of more than 25,000 soldiers, the terror group possessed an estimated 150,000 rockets and missiles poised to rain down death and destruction on Jewish soil.

But they didn't control all of Beirut. For now, anyway, the would-be jihadis lived under an uneasy truce with their Lebanese hosts. If the snipers had been Hezbollah, Jack was probably still a hunted man, but he was not wanted by every member of Lebanon's Internal Security Forces Directorate, which included the national police and other paramilitary units.

But that was a big *if.*

Jack had effectively burned the ships when he'd left Dudu and the stricken commandos to forge ahead. In fact, operating untethered to the Israelis might just be a blessing in disguise. Someone on the Israeli side of the house was compromised, of that Jack was certain. And while it was impossible to be completely sure of anyone, Jack assumed that everyone who'd been on the receiving end of the ambush was clean.

This included the Mossad asset, Gebran. The slightly built man didn't look like much, but he'd kept his head during a firefight. That was endorsement enough for Jack. After leaving Dudu behind, Jack had offered Gebran sanctuary in the United States for him and his family in exchange

298

for his help. The ambulance driver had been only too happy to oblige.

Jack wanted to believe that Gebran's rapid change of allegiances was a credit to his smooth pitch, but he had a feeling that the former Mossad asset was just focused on survival. That was fine. Survival tended to be a wonderful motivator.

"What now," Gebran said, pausing as Jack caught up.

Jack's first priority had been to put distance between himself and the scene of the ambush as quickly as possible. An encounter with a local who would later tie Jack to the Israeli incursion would be just as dangerous as a run-in with Hezbollah or the national police. With this in mind, he'd asked Gebran to lead them to a place where they could lie low, and the former asset had quickly obliged.

After paralleling Highway 51 north for several blocks, the men had followed an underpass heading west beneath the busy road. From there, it was a simple matter to duck into one of the many patches of trees lining the vacant lots. Gebran had found a cluster of cedars that offered a large enough space between their intertwining trunks for the men to squat unseen at their base.

For the first time since the ambush, Jack

stopped to catch his breath. He needed to start thinking instead of just reacting. While he still believed his decision to remain in Beirut was correct, he had to start dealing with the repercussions. Ever since things had first gone wrong in HaCarmel Market what seemed like an eternity ago, Jack had bent over backward not to involve The Campus. Partly due to operational security, or OPSEC, considerations, but Jack had to admit that there was also another motivating factor at work. One that was a bit more insidious.

Pride.

Ding had offered this operation to Jack instead of to one of the more senior Campus operatives, and Jack took this as both a vote of trust and an opportunity to prove himself. A chance to show that he was capable of working without training wheels or oversight. That he truly could function alone and unafraid.

Well, alone, anyway.

But rescuing Becka and her superhero-loving son would take more than just a single Campus operative equipped with a pure heart and a Jericho pistol. Time to see what exactly Dudu had left him. Opening the Israeli's messenger bag, Jack peered inside. He wasn't sure what he'd been hoping for, but a second magazine for the Jericho and a cell phone seemed a bit underwhelming.

Then again, beggars couldn't be choosers. Withdrawing the magazine, Jack conducted a combat reload and then placed the half-spent one in his back pocket. The phone was an even bigger letdown. While he'd figured that the Israeli version of the NSA Suite B–encrypted EMI-hardened BlackBerry his father carried was probably out of the question, Jack had hoped for more than just a Samsung knockoff.

Powering on the device, Jack saw a normal home screen with recognizable icons in English. If there was something special about this phone, it wasn't readily apparent. Jack swiped from one screen to another, looking for a hint to the phone's purpose. Nothing. If the phone's covert aspects were camouflaged in germane apps, they would stay that way. Jack had neither the time nor the inclination to discover them.

As espionage tools went, the phone was a bust.

And then, as if the device could read Jack's mind, it vibrated. Swiping back to the home screen, Jack saw that the messaging app now registered an unread text. Thumbing the appropriate icon, Jack was

301

rewarded with a hyperlink. He paused, his thumb poised over the gibberish string of text and numbers, wary of what often befell the naïve who clicked on unknown links.

Then his lips twisted into a smile. He was hunkered down in a stand of trees, hiding from Hezbollah, the national police, and everyone in between, with only a Lebanese ambulance driver for company. Somewhere out there, a kidnapped American scientist with the power to upset the world's balance of power was being held by unknown gunmen. From this perspective, clicking on an unverified link was a pretty manageable risk.

Jack stabbed the link with his index finger. A moment later, the phone's display transformed into a familiar picture — an overhead shot of Beirut with a pulsing blue icon denoting the beacon.

He didn't know what kind of beer Dudu drank, but Jack would be delivering a case of it once he got out of this mess. Thanks to the Shin Bet officer, stumbling block number one had just been overcome. Jack now had a real-time fix on Becka.

Time to plow through stumbling block two.

Clicking back to the phone app, Jack dialed a number from memory and listened to it ring while doing the time conversion in his head. Beirut was seven hours ahead of Eastern Time. No reason why a normal person wouldn't be available right now. Unfortunately, the person he was calling wasn't exactly normal.

The phone rang five more times and Jack was on the verge of thumbing the disconnect button, when a distracted voice answered.

"Hello?"

And just like that, Jack was back in the game.

38

"Hey, Gavin," Jack said, holding the phone against his ear as he peered past the trees. "It's Jack."

"Jack! How are you, buddy? How's Tel Aviv?"

The sound of Gavin Biery's high-pitched voice brought a smile to Jack's face despite his surroundings. Though his official title was IT director of Hendley Associates, Gavin also doubled as The Campus's hacker. The plump, perpetually single keyboard ninja didn't have a tactical bone in his body, but Jack already felt the odds shifting in his favor. Gavin's coding skills were terrifying.

"That's the thing," Jack said, eyeing a scrawny cat nosing around the outside of the glen, "I'm not in Tel Aviv anymore. I'm in Beirut."

"Come on, man!" Gavin said, his exclamation loud enough to make Jack pull the handset away from his ear. "That's camping, plain and simple. The noobs are making this board unbearable."

"Gavin," Jack said. "Did you hear what I said?"

"What? Oh, sorry, Jack. My crew and I are getting in some final reps. The Call of Duty tournament's in five days, so we're pretty much in pregame isolation. You're lucky I even answered. How's Tel Aviv?"

"Gavin," Jack said, adding a bit of steel to his voice. "Put the video game controller down. Now. I'm in Beirut. As in Lebanon. I need your help."

"Lebanon? Holy crap, Jack. Why didn't you say so?"

Jack felt his temper rachet up a notch, but he pushed the anger away. Gavin was exactly what he appeared to be — a once-in-a-generation cyberwarrior with the absent-minded professor's social skills. As Jack had learned early in his Campus career, getting frustrated with Gavin wasn't worth the oxygen. Although Gavin had done fieldwork a handful of times, he wasn't truly an operator. As such, he'd never understand what it was like to be huddled in a stand of trees with a Mossad asset for company and a dead man's blood on your shoes.

But that was okay. At this moment, Jack

305

didn't need another shooter. He needed an electronic wizard capable of bringing ones and zeroes to heel from more than six thousand miles away. He needed Gavin.

And Gavin was exactly what he got.

"Beirut, got it, Jack. Is this phone clean?"

"No," Jack said.

"Okay, no worries. Let me patch you through something I've been tinkering with. It's an algorithm that will both mask your cell's Mobile Identification Number and give us end-to-end encryption. Basically, my answer to ad-hoc COV COMS. I mean, it's not NSA Suite B–encrypted, but if someone's trying to localize your signal or listen to our conversation, their job is going to get a heck of a lot harder."

Though he had only the slightest idea what Gavin was talking about, Jack made appreciative noises all the same. He needn't have bothered. Gavin was muttering, which meant he was already in the zone. Nothing Jack could say would penetrate the hacker's ironclad concentration until he'd finished whatever the hell he was doing. At this point, Jack was just along for the ride.

An electronic tone chimed in Jack's ear, followed by a high-pitched squeal. Then the distortion that had been plaguing the call suddenly vanished.

306

"That's better," Gavin said, his voice sounding like he was standing next to Jack instead of an ocean away. "Now that I cleaned up that mess, we can talk freely."

"Mess?" Jack said.

"Yep. Some Hezbollah jackwagons were trying to eavesdrop. They were pretty close to geolocating the phone, but I just sent them on a wild-goose chase. With any luck, they'll spend the next couple days chasing their tail in Baghdad. And don't get me started on the embedded Israeli firmware. Luckily, I was able to sandbox the operating system and wall off the malware. So, what can I do for you?"

Jack paused, considering the information that Gavin had just offhandedly relayed. Hezbollah had been moments away from compromising an Israeli-issued operational phone. Jack knew that the Iranian-supported proxy's technological prowess had grown by leaps and bounds since the Second Lebanon War, but the Israelis had some of the best SIGINT and cyber-capabilities in the world. Not to mention that Jack had activated the phone only two minutes prior. There was only one way an adversary could compromise a hardened device that quickly: betrayal.

"Jack? You still there?"

"Sorry, buddy," Jack said. "Zoned out for a minute. I'm in the shit up to my neck."

"Just another day in the office, huh?"

Gavin meant the line as a joke, but the words fell flat. This was *not* just another day at the office. Not even close.

"Here's the thing, buddy," Jack said, shifting positions so that he had a better view of the narrow street on the other side of the trees. "The Campus doesn't know about this operation. At least not yet."

"Oh," Gavin said, taking a moment to digest the new information. "So you're working for another agency?"

Jack considered giving his friend the answer he wanted, but didn't. Jack knew he had a history of going off the reservation, but this was a cluster even by his standards. Gavin needed to understand exactly what he was getting into.

"Nope," Jack said. "Right now, I'm operating solo. That means any help you give me will be off the books as well. Understand?"

"I understand that my friend is asking for help. That's all I need. Stop talking in circles and lay it on me. There'll be hell to pay if I don't rejoin practice soon. This tournament's for money, Jack."

Jack laughed. Operator or not, he'd take the potato-shaped keyboard warrior any day of the week. Coworkers were great, but Gavin was so much more than that. The hacker was willing to climb into the mud, no questions asked. He was a friend.

"All right," Jack said, savoring what was coming next. "Here's what I need. One: I'm gonna make some calls from this phone. I'll need them to be both secure and untraceable. Got it?"

"Come on, Jack. I already told you — the handset now has end-to-end encryption. Give me something hard."

"Okay," Jack said with a smile. "I'm logged in to some sort of GPS app. I need you to access it as well, in case I lose this phone and you have to resend me the link."

"Done and done. I cloned your phone the moment you said you were in trouble. That means I'm watching the same GPS feed you're seeing."

"Excellent," Jack said. "This last one's a bit of a doozy."

"For Pete's sake, Jack, just spit it out. My teammates are already talking about replacing me with the alternate. Trust me, if that doofus John Dixon takes my place, they won't make it out of the first bracket."

"All right, all right," Jack said. "Here's what I need."

Jack explained what he wanted to do in

the most technical terms he was able. Which was to say he mostly referenced things he'd read in Vince Flynn novels. Even so, Gavin quickly understood what Jack needed, and perhaps more important, he never questioned the request's sanity.

Jack found his friend's support equal parts comforting and terrifying. Comforting because Jack now had someone besides the onetime Mossad asset in his corner. Terrifying because this was normally the time when Ding would have injected a bit of operational sanity.

Then again, maybe a little crazy was just what the doctor ordered right about now.

"Got it, Jack," Gavin said. "I think I'm tracking. I've actually been fiddling around with something that might be able to accomplish exactly what you need. I call it the Eye of Sauron."

"The what?" Jack said.

"You know, from *Lord of the Rings?*"

"No," Jack said, "I don't."

"Seriously? They made the books into movies, for crying out loud."

"Focus, Gavin."

"Okay, okay. Give me an hour and I'll get the Eye up and running on your phone. I can probably do it in thirty minutes, but

310

you always tell me to be conservative. How's that?"

"Perfect," Jack said. "Just perfect."

"Great. Oh, and Jack, one more thing — YOU SHALL NOT PASS."

"What?"

"Aw, come on, Jack. Seriously?"

"Gavin!"

"Okay, okay. Thirty minutes. Bye."

The line went dead.

39

"Hello?"

Jack paused before answering. Though he'd rehearsed what he was going to say several times, he'd felt more at ease pulling Israeli commandos from the ambush's kill zone than he did right now. That was the effect John Terrence Clark had on people.

"Hey, Mr. C. It's me, Jack."

"Jack? Where the hell you calling from? I don't recognize the number."

"Beirut, sir."

In other circumstances, Jack might have been able to attribute the long silence on the other end of the line to a bad connection. But that wasn't the case. True to form, Gavin's new piece of digital wizardry was delivering crystal-clear communication all the way back to Alexandria, Virginia. No, the unnerving silence had a much more ominous cause.

John Clark was pissed.

"Did you say Beirut?" Clark asked.

"Yes, sir," Jack said, his heart rate accelerating.

Calling John T. Clark a legend was a bit like saying that Superman was strong. Words alone did not do the man justice. While Clark's current Campus title was the innocuous-sounding director of operations, his résumé was full of names that weren't so hard to decipher. Inaugural commander of Rainbow Six, CIA paramilitary officer, Vietnam-era Navy SEAL, SOG veteran, and personal friend to the President of the United States, who also happened to be Jack's father.

And then there was the title that prompted this call: Jack's boss.

"Is the line secure?" Clark said.

"As secure as Gavin could make it. He loaded my phone with a new encryption system. Your phone was pulled into the ad hoc network the moment you answered."

"Swell," Clark said, not bothering to disguise the irritation in his voice. "Then I may as well bite the bullet. What the hell are you doing in Beirut, Junior?"

"It's a bit of a long story, sir," Jack said, eyeing the flashing blue icon. It was still stationary. For now. "I was pinch-hitting for Ding on an asset-validation exercise —"

"That part I remember," Clark said. "But as I recall, the exercise was slated to run in Tel Aviv. Last time I checked, that city is in an entirely different country."

"True enough, Mr. C. Like I said, long story. The CliffsNotes version is that an American citizen and her son were kidnapped, and I'm trying to get them back."

"Kidnapped? By who? Hezbollah?"

"This is where it gets sticky, sir. I don't know who has them. The CIA team leader thought multiple intelligence services were targeting her. The Chinese tried to kill her twice, so I'm pretty sure it's not them. But it could be just about anyone else."

"Holy hell, Junior. Who is this woman?"

Even though he'd turned down the speaker's volume in anticipation of his boss's reaction, Clark's voice still carried farther than Jack would have liked. Fortunately, he'd had the presence of mind to post Gebran across the street as a lookout. This was partly for security's sake and partly to keep the former Mossad asset from overhearing the phone call. Nothing about the conversation thus far would have inspired confidence in the shaken ambulance driver.

"Her name is Dr. Becka Schweigart, Mr. C. She's a physicist who may have discovered stealth in a bottle. Like I said, sir, it's complicated."

"I feel like I'm shoveling shit in a manure pile. The deeper I go, the worse it smells. Can you at least tell me why you're trying to chase this woman down instead of the Israelis?"

"The Israelis are involved. Or at least they were. The Sayeret Matkal team I inserted with exfilled after we were ambushed on the LZ. I stayed behind."

"Goddamn, Jack. Are you telling me you're hunting a snatch team solo in Hezbollah-controlled territory?"

"Not exactly solo, sir. I've got a Mossad asset helping me. Though I guess he's my asset now. Anyway, the scientist is beaconed, so finding her isn't the problem. It's the whole kicking-down-the-door-and-shooting-her-captors-in-the-face part I could use help with."

"Is that all you need? Well, why didn't you say so? I'm sure I can have some Campus folks in position in about SIXTEEN FUCKING HOURS!"

"Actually, sir, I think there's already a special-mission unit wheels up. But they're still twelve hours out, best case. But the Agency team who was running the asset-validation exercise are all former hitters. Special Operations guys sheep-dipped to

315

the CIA. I talked with the team leader, and his men are ready to go. They just need transportation from the Israelis. I was hoping that maybe you could run this by Mary Pat and ask her to lean on them for me? I've already met their defense minister, so I'm sure she'll remember me."

The silence stretched again, but Jack no longer felt the apprehension he'd wrestled with earlier. In fact, he was strangely at peace. Was he out over his skis? Maybe a little. Okay, a lot. But as he replayed the events thus far, everything he'd done was operationally sound. Clark was fond of saying that what separated the U.S. military from its counterparts was a bias toward action. In other words, pick a compass azimuth and move out.

If nothing else, Jack had seized the shit out of the initiative.

"Well, hell," Clark said, "I do believe my junior-most operator is either all grown up or lost his ever-loving mind. For both of our sakes, I'm hoping it's the former. I'll get on the horn with Mary Pat, but you are authorized to continue with surveillance only. That's it. No kicking-down-doors shit. Agreed?"

"Absolutely, Mr. C.," Jack said.

"All right, then," Clark said. "Keep your

powder dry and your head down. I'll be back in touch directly. Out here."

Clark ended the connection.

One of the many things Jack had learned from his mentors was how to hear what you wanted to hear in a set of orders. For example, Clark had made it abundantly clear that he didn't want Jack breaching a safe house without his consent.

But he hadn't said anything about what to do if the door just happened to open on its own.

40

Jack stared at the pulsing blue icon. The rhythmic flashes seemed to be mocking him, daring Jack to investigate their source, which is exactly what he wanted to do. His penchant toward action was one of the things that drove him toward the operational side of The Campus in the first place. Analyzing numbers was all fine and good, but columns of digits alone couldn't sate his appetite. He needed something he could sink his teeth into.

Like the beckoning icon.

Jack stifled a yawn and took another swallow of strong coffee.

Passing the darkness in a copse of cedars wasn't exactly conducive to a good night's sleep, but Jack hadn't had much of a choice. Though he'd wanted nothing more than to see where the flashing beacon led, he'd decided to wait until the sun rose and the streets filled with pedestrians. By his way of thinking, the anonymity offered by the early-morning work crowd was better suited to his purposes.

Once people had begun to appear on the sidewalks and shops, Jack had left the safety of the trees, making his way to his current location — a café across the street from the multistory building where the beacon resided. He really wanted to pull open the building's grimy doors and take a look inside, but he didn't. Maybe this was what being all grown up felt like.

If so, he wasn't impressed.

But as much as the icon's siren song called to him, Jack stayed put. His adversaries had been one step ahead of him the entire operation. He'd sent Dudu home with instructions to radio that Jack was on the Black Hawk with the returning commandos, hoping to buy himself time if the leak really was within the Shin Bet. But if the operation was compromised somewhere else, Jack was in a world of trouble.

To be fair, Jack wasn't exactly playing things safe, mole or no mole. In keeping with the spirit of what he'd promised Mr. C., Jack did not intend to try a one-man rescue. However, if the beacon started to move, he'd have to reassess. He was not foolish enough to believe that the transmitting device's battery would last forever. By his count, Israeli drones had been continuously interrogating the beacon for several hours. At some point, he'd have to risk going to less frequent transmissions in exchange for prolonging the beacon's life.

And then there was the second, more serious contingency. What if the people holding Becka and Tommy decided to move them? Jack was not in any sense of the word equipped to conduct active surveillance, even if he had access to a vehicle. Besides, there was no guarantee that kidnappers wouldn't move Becka somewhere beyond Jack's operational reach. No, if the beacon either stopped flashing or started to move, Jack would have to make some hard decisions.

This was why, counter to what he'd said to Clark, Jack was not going to just wait for the cavalry. Every plan needed a contingency, and to develop one, Jack needed information. Who was holding Becka and Tommy, how many kidnappers were there, where exactly in the building were they being held, and what was the building's layout?

All of these questions would have to be answered before a team of shooters could attempt a rescue, whether that team consisted of Peter and his men or the special-mission unit already en route from the States. The operators needed actionable intelligence and Jack intended to get it.

"More coffee, sir?"

"Non," Jack said with a smile.

The pretty waitress had posed the question in French, so Jack had answered in kind. With his blue eyes, Jack wasn't going to pass for a local, so he'd used Beirut's second, unofficial language. There were still degrees to being a foreigner, and in a city once known as the Paris of the Middle East, there were worse things to be taken for than French.

Like American.

"What about your friend?" the waitress said, gesturing over Jack's shoulder.

Jack turned to see Gebran crossing the street toward them. One look at the former Mossad asset's face told Jack all that he needed to know.

"Merci beaucoup," Jack said with a smile.

The waitress nodded with a smile of her own and then headed inside just as Gebran settled into the opposite chair.

"How'd it go?" Jack said as the man fumbled in his shirt pocket for cigarettes and lighter.

While the asset had outwardly recovered from the ambush's trauma, Jack knew that action of that magnitude still left scars, visible or not. With this in mind, Jack bore the cloud of rapidly expanding smoke without complaint, even though Jack's Turkish coffee now tasted a good deal less appealing. Besides, to Jack's way of thinking, the man's nervous habit vouched for his veracity. Anyone not shaken by the grisly scene back at the stadium would merit a second look, and right now, Jack had more than enough suspects to go around.

"Fine," the man said between puffs. "It went fine."

Jack let the comment lie for a beat before pressing into the silence. "You know I'm not Israeli, right?"

The man gazed at Jack for a moment before shrugging his narrow shoulders. "So?"

"So I'm not as direct as our Jewish friends, but even I am going to need a bit more information. I know this operation hasn't gone as planned, but I meant what I said earlier. If you help me, you'll find that my nation makes a much better friend than enemy. Okay?"

Gebran's fingers shook as he took another long drag, but he nodded all the same. Not the most wholehearted acknowledgment Jack had ever received from a would-be asset, but it would have to do.

"Good," Jack said. "What did you find?"

The pretty waitress chose that moment to reappear, setting a cup of coffee in front of Gebran. Though Jack wasn't her intended target, he still felt the warmth of her smile. The effect on Gebran was instantaneous. The asset stopped trembling, and his lips found an answering grin. Strong coffee and promised riches were all well and good, but at the end of the day, nothing warmed a man's soul like the smile of a beautiful woman.

The waitress spoke a sentence or two of Arabic to Gebran, which he answered in kind. With a final appraising look, the woman sauntered back inside, and Gebran tracked her movement over Jack's shoulder with hungry eyes. Forget ambulance drivers. The Mossad's money would be much better spent on pretty baristas.

Jack took a swallow of coffee, waiting for the woman's spell to fade before again prompting his asset.

"Gebran, what did you find?" Jack said.

The man looked at Jack with a startled expression, as if surprised to see the American sitting across from him. But then his brain seemed to come back online as the waitress's exotic perfume faded.

"The building isn't controlled by Hezbollah," Gebran said, his answer delivered in a clinical, no-nonsense manner. "Or at least it doesn't appear to be. I talked to the building manager about renting an apartment, and he gave me a tour of the vacant space and wanted me to sign a lease on the spot. Hezbollah-controlled properties tend to be a bit choosier about their tenants. The organization usually leases out the entire building. In the rare cases when they do have vacancies, there's a strict vetting process for potential occupants."

"So Becka's kidnappers aren't Hezbollah?"

Gebran shrugged. "I didn't say that. All I'm saying is that if they had your victims, why wouldn't they stash them in a building they controlled?"

Jack leaned back in his chair as he considered Gebran's statement. *Why, indeed?* Two answers came readily enough, even though Jack didn't particularly like them. Either someone other than Hezbollah had pulled off the kidnapping or the flashing beacon was a trap.

Or both.

Occam's razor was referenced by military strategists the world over for a reason. Most of the time the simplest explanation really was the correct one. But thinking so wasn't the same as knowing so. Still, the pulsing icon was the only tie Jack had to Becka and Tommy. He couldn't afford to ignore it, trap or no. But that didn't mean he had to waltz into a spiderweb unaware, either. For better or worse, the next link in this chain lay within the building across the street.

Which meant that Jack needed a way inside.

Not for the first time, Jack wondered why Becka's kidnappers had moved her to Beirut. If her captors were Chinese MSS officers, relocating her to Lebanon made zero sense. If they were Hezbollah, why not relocate to the heart of their territory three miles to the south? The simplest explanation was that someone else, someone Jack had yet to identify, had kidnapped the scientist.

But who?

And why?

An independent player? Someone who wanted to auction the physicist off to the highest bidder?

This new line of possibility seemed much more plausible. If Becka really had discovered stealth in a bottle, a number of bad actors would be willing to pay for her expertise. But who would have the operational

325

resources and savvy to carry out a snatch mission in Israel?

And then there was the question Jack really didn't want to ask: Was Becka complicit in any of this? Jack didn't for a moment believe she'd staged her own kidnapping, but maybe the scientist wasn't quite as naïve to the ways of espionage as she'd let on. Peter had characterized Becka as an opportunist. A mercenary who wielded a computer instead of a rifle.

Perhaps, but Jack didn't think so. He'd seen the confusion and fear in her eyes when the Asian assassin had tried to kill her. Jack would stake his life on the notion that Becka had no idea what was waiting for her in Tel Aviv. She loved her little boy, and Jack couldn't imagine her willingly putting Tommy's life in danger.

Regardless, according to the beacon, Becka was across the street. But even if this was true, she wouldn't be there long. Thanks to years spent stalking high-value targets in Iraq, the United States had developed manhunting technologies and tactics that often seemed more science fiction than fact. Even ensconced in Beirut, just minutes from a Hezbollah-controlled suburb, Becka was well within America's operational umbrella.

Which meant that her captors would have

to move her.

Soon.

As if summoned by Jack's thoughts, an SUV with dark tinted windows pulled up across the street. The luxury vehicle's doors eased open on well-oiled hinges and four men exited.

Men with guns.

41

Contrary to what Mr. C. might think, Jack didn't always believe he was right. In fact, there were times when he was quite happy to be proven wrong. When bad guys went down easier than planned, for instance. Or even when the new recipe his mom seemed to be burning in the White House's family residence actually turned out to be quite tasty. Sometimes Jack was positively delighted to be proven wrong.

This would have been one of those times.

The three men took up positions around the car, AK-47s secured in tactical slings as their hard eyes scrutinized everything. Jack was closest to the man guarding the driver's side of the car, and he felt the shooter's gaze sweep over him, lingering for a moment before moving to his fellow diners.

Gebran was shrouded in a halo of smoke, and as much as the clinging, acrid cloud irritated Jack's sinuses, he was temporarily grateful for the ambulance driver's vice. Smoke attracted attention, something an assassin would be doing everything in his power to avoid. Accordingly, bodyguard number one noted Jack's presence, but dismissed him and his smokestack of a companion in favor of less obvious threats.

Jack felt simultaneously relieved and apprehensive. Relieved that he had managed to slide under the gunman's radar, but apprehensive that the bodyguard was well enough trained to note, and then summarily dismiss, Jack. These men were not random jihadis who'd taken a one-day course in principal protection. They were professionals, meaning one of two things: Either the men were from the Radwan Unit, the Special Operations wing of Hezbollah, or they were something else.

Something more dangerous.

"Can I have one?" Jack said, gesturing toward Gebran's cigarettes.

The asset nodded, and Jack snatched the pack, shook out a cigarette, and lit it with Gebran's lighter. The smoke burned a trail of fire from his mouth to his nasal passages, and Jack did his best not to gag while focusing his attention on the vehicle's rear door. As he puffed on his cigarette, Jack picked up his phone, turning the device so that the camera had an unobstructed view of the SUV.

Then he activated the Eye of Sauron.

Knowing who the men were trying to protect might go a long way toward helping Jack understand who held Becka and Tommy. Even if it was a crew of unknowns offering the scientist to the highest bidder, identifying the sharks circling the bait was important. If Jack could snap a clandestine picture or two, Gavin could use The Campus's impressive database to do a little facial-recognition magic.

And then there was the little goody the Campus hacker had magically placed on Jack's phone. There'd been no way to perform a dry run on the quickly conjured program, so Jack activated the app and hoped for the best. Not for the first time, Jack considered the parallel between what Gavin did and witchcraft. Except with magic, at least there was some pageantry to go along with the spell.

When he used Gavin's magic, Jack just pushed a button and hoped for the best.

The rear passenger exited, and Jack swore instead of snapping a picture. He didn't need a Campus analyst to identify the man. The person was none other than General Farhad Ahmadi — commander of the Quds

Force expeditionary unit and fomenter of terrorist violence worldwide.

Prior to September 11, Iran, through its Quds Force operatives and Hezbollah proxies, had been responsible for more American deaths than any Sunni-based terrorist organization. After the tragic events in New York, that balance shifted firmly to the Sunni column. But from the invasion of Iraq onward, Ahmadi had been working overtime to run up the score for his team. The devastatingly effective EFPs, or explosively formed penetrators, that had maimed or killed scores of Americans was a wholly Iranian invention. And if that had been Ahmadi's sole contribution to the Shia insurgencies, the bombs would have been evil enough.

But they weren't. Not by a long shot.

Iranian Quds Force operatives had implemented a series of ratlines used to funnel thousands of foreign fighters into Iraq from all over the globe. On more than one occasion, American and Iranian operatives had actually traded fire. In fact, one of the worst massacres of U.S. soldiers happened in 2007 at the hands of Iranian Quds Force operatives posing as American security forces. The Iranian influence in Iraq was so detrimental and pervasive that none other than General David Petraeus once remarked that the United States had gone to war with the wrong Middle East nation.

And Ahmadi hadn't been satisfied with just killing Americans in Iraq. No, under the general's able leadership, Iran had expanded its targeted killings across the globe, spanning countries from the Middle East to South America. In a particularly brazen, and fortunately unsuccessful, operation, Iranian operatives even tried to assassinate the Saudi ambassador on U.S. soil. In short, the man exiting the Range Rover was the Iranian version of Osama bin Laden, except that he operated with the implicit backing of a nation-state.

And Jack was seated less than fifty feet away.

Clark's thoughts on his proclivity for impulsive decisions aside, Jack remembered another infamous story from the never-ending war on terror. During a CIA operation in Sudan back in the nineties, Osama bin Laden had been centered in a Ground Branch sniper's crosshairs while the operator had waited for authorization to shoot.

It never came.

Would the world have turned out differently if the shooter had squeezed the trigger? There was no way of knowing. Even so,

Jack had a hard time imagining a future more terrible than four planes destroyed, almost three thousand Americans dead, and an economy devastated.

Not to mention the disastrous Iraq War that had followed.

This was a once-in-a-lifetime opportunity, and there was no way Jack was going to allow it to pass him by. The question was how to leverage Ahmadi's presence. As loath as he was to go directly to his father, perhaps this was a time to involve the President of the United States. Deniability and separation between Jack Senior and the undeclared, semi-legal intelligence apparatus known as The Campus was all well and good, but Jack knew his dad.

John Patrick Ryan, Sr., was the epitome of Cincinnatus, the Roman soldier citizen who'd led his nation in a time of emergency before returning to life as a farmer. Senior might be President, but he didn't have a political bone in his body. Jack's father would never allow potential political fallout to prevent him from doing the right thing. In this case, the right thing was to end Ahmadi's reign of terror by ending his life.

The question was how.

Here again the Israeli phone with Gavin's new COV COMS program saved the day.

Like all of Senior's children, Jack knew the number to his father's direct line, but this wasn't an option. Not while sitting in Beirut, anyway. Between Hezbollah's ever-improving SIGINT capabilities and the pooled resources of Israel, Lebanon, Iran, and a host of other nations actively targeting the city's airwaves, Jack wasn't going to call his father on an open line. But thanks to Gavin's new algorithms, he didn't have to worry about eavesdroppers.

When this was over, Jack was going to take the chubby keyboard warrior out for a night on the town. Though knowing Gavin's culinary palate, that was more likely to be burgers at McDonald's than porterhouses at Ruth's Chris Steak House. Gavin could sling bytes with the best of them, but the guy subsisted on Cheetos and Mountain Dew.

Jack snapped a couple pictures as Ahmadi paused to button up his sport coat before allowing his bodyguards to escort him into the apartment building. Either the general really was as cool as a cucumber as everyone suggested, or the Iranian felt remarkably safe in Lebanon.

Even so, Jack now had the irrefutable proof of the man's presence.

Acting decisively regardless of the political

ramifications was one thing, but liquidating a human being solely on someone's say-so was something else, even if that someone happened to be your son. Jack ensured that the Sauron app was still active, and then activated the phone's digital dialing pad.

With his thumbs poised over the numbers, Jack was about to begin dialing when he noticed that his phone had lost all service. While not entirely surprising, this new development was concerning. Like most countries that boasted less-than-stable infrastructures, loss of cell or Internet service wasn't exactly unexpected.

But this wasn't that.

Rather than a gradual diminishment of the all-important cell signal bars or the fluctuating Wi-Fi symbol that announced a less-than-steady connection, Jack's loss of service had been much more abrupt. One moment both cell and Wi-Fi were alive and well, the next the words *no service* were stamped across the top of the screen. It was as if someone had just turned off the switch to the national grid, except that Jack was reasonably sure that Lebanon's grid didn't have this level of sophistication.

Which left a much less palatable option. Someone had just compromised his ability to connect to the outside world.

Not good.

Jack looked from his phone to Gebran, intending to tell his asset it was time to move. The man's expression stopped him cold. While the ambulance driver might not be Special Operations material, he'd kept his head during a bloody ambush. But that was then. Now the asset's features were contorted into a mask of terror. His cigarette trembled, scattering ash across the table as he struggled to swallow.

Dropping the phone to the table, Jack went for his pistol.

He was fast, Ding had seen to that.

But not fast enough.

As Jack's fingers found the Jericho's grip, a ring of cold steel pressed into the back of his head.

"I wouldn't," came the waitress's familiar voice, this time in perfect English. "You have such a pretty face. I'd hate to splatter it all over your friend's chest."

So much for the smile of a beautiful woman.

42

"I think there's been a mistake," Jack said, vying for time while considering his options.

None of them were good.

The waitress laughed, a musical sound that Jack would have found enchanting if not for the gun barrel resting inches from his brainpan.

"I don't doubt it," the waitress said. "A situation like this is usually the result of countless mistakes. But if you mean that I'm holding a gun to the head of the wrong man, don't waste your breath. I've been serving tables for the last two hours, waiting for you to show. I *hate* serving tables."

The inflection the waitress gave to the word *hate* gave Jack a half-second warning, but it wasn't enough. No sooner had his brain processed her tone than the back of his head was burning where she'd clubbed him with the pistol. Jack had been manhandled a time or two, but a good pistol-whipping wasn't really something for which you could prepare yourself. The pain flared in white-lightning bolts from the base of his skull, and Jack put both hands on the table to keep from face-planting into his coffee.

He was in no condition to stop the waitress from retrieving his Jericho.

"Sorry," the waitress said, her voice now coming from Jack's right, "but I needed to nip whatever you were thinking in the bud. If you'll just sit tight, my friends will be along any minute."

"Who are your friends?" Jack said, attempting to keep the woman talking as he squinted against the pain.

But the next voice Jack heard didn't belong to the waitress. The timbre was decidedly male, and the tone was unfamiliar.

Unfortunately, the words were easily understood.

"It's a pleasure to make your acquaintance, my American comrade."

Jack opened his eyes and sighed. The voice might be unfamiliar, but the man it belonged to wasn't.

General Ahmadi was standing across from him.

And he was smiling.

43

"Forgive the accommodations," General Ahmadi said, gesturing at the apartment, "but I haven't entertained many American intelligence operatives. In fact, I believe you are the very first."

"I don't know what you're talking about," Jack said, his response automatic as his brain struggled to make sense of what was happening.

He was handcuffed to a chair in the common area of a sparsely furnished apartment on the building's fourth floor. Gebran sat, similarly secured, beside him. The cool breeze tickled his neck, trickling past the flimsy curtains leading to a balcony behind him. To his left was a small kitchen. To his right, a narrow hallway disappeared from view.

The room felt cramped, and not just because of the apartment's meager square footage. Every spare inch seemed to be occupied by bodies. In addition to the general and his bodyguards, the waitress smiled at him from across the room, a hulking Caucasian man at her side. Two more men of similar girth lurked out of sight between Jack and the beckoning balcony.

He'd been trying to place the waitress's accent since she'd first spoken to him in English, and now he had it. Upon entering the apartment, she'd snapped off a quick command to the trio of steroid users, and unless Jack missed his guess, she'd spoken Russian. This little tidbit dovetailed nicely with the identity of the Slavic-featured shooter Jack had unmasked at the ambush site.

While he might have just ascertained the nationality of Becka and Tommy's kidnappers, Jack still didn't know why they were in Beirut. The Russian SVR was a ruthless and capable intelligence service, but it wasn't known for lending its operational prowess to anyone, especially the Iranians. To Jack's way of thinking, the relationship here was strangely inverted.

And then there was the guest of honor. Standing on the other side of the waitress with his arms nonchalantly crossed over his chest was none other than the man of the hour — the fake venture capitalist who

Becka had traveled to Israel to meet.

But the story of what was happening here was captured as much by who wasn't present as by who was. Nowhere among the shabby furniture and dismal furnishings did Jack see Becka or Tommy. If he dedicated enough brainpower to the task, Jack was certain he could reason out what was going on by reading the room's attendees like so many tea leaves.

Unfortunately, something else demanded his attention.

"Tell me your name," General Ahmadi said.

From the moment he'd joined The Campus as an operational asset, this scenario had been Jack's worst nightmare. While his athleticism and impressive intellect would have made Jack a natural recruit for any of the three-letter agencies dedicated to the clandestine world, The Campus was something unique. Existing outside the lines of authority that governed even the blackest of government entities, The Campus was a place for seasoned professionals recruited away from positions within the Special Operations and intelligence communities.

And then there was Jack.

Jack knew he'd been admitted to The Campus's ranks for just one reason — his father was Jack Patrick Ryan, Sr. And while Junior would have never been allowed to work in the field if Clark hadn't signed off on his progress, it was Jack's genealogy that had opened the door to this shadowy life.

But his legacy was still a double-edged sword. His father sat behind the Resolute Desk and had at his fingertips the power to turn the world to ash. Without children of his own, Jack could only tangentially understand the love a parent felt for their child. Even so, he'd long ago made the decision that if ever faced with a choice between death or handing his father's enemies a club with which they could beat the nation he loved into submission, Jack would choose the former.

Now it looked like his resolve would be put to the test.

"Come, now," Ahmadi said, pulling up a chair across from Jack. "Denying the obvious won't help."

"What do you mean?" Jack said.

He asked the question, not because he expected an answer, but because he needed time. Time to assess the situation. Time to understand what had gone so horribly wrong. And, most important, time to once more go on the offensive.

But time wasn't his to control.

"I mean that denying that you are an American intelligence officer does neither of us any good. I know many things about you already. I know that you came here with the Israelis, but were too brave or too stupid to flee with them. I know that you are seeking the American scientist. I even know that your first name is Jack. What I don't know is your last name. Tell me. Now."

"Why?" Jack said.

"So that I can have your nation's undivided attention."

44

"I don't understand," Jack said.

"And I don't care," Ahmadi said. "Tell me your last name."

"No."

"I was hoping we could act like reasonable men," Ahmadi said, shaking his head in disappointment. "I was wrong."

Turning over his shoulder, the Iranian delivered a harsh-sounding stream of Russian. A male voice answered in the same language. Then a door opened and Jack heard feet coming down the narrow hallway to his right. Multiple pairs of feet. A moment later, a hulking Slavic thug shepherded two more guests into the common area.

Becka and Tommy.

The sight of the scientist with her arms wrapped protectively around her son's shoulders broke something within Jack. This wasn't the first century. The sins of the mother, whether real or imagined, no longer fell upon the head of her autistic son.

But Tommy was here in a room full of killers all the same.

The boy's vacant stare panned across the apartment, but his eyes brightened when they found Jack.

"Hey, buddy," Jack said, forcing a smile. "How's it going?"

"Want to go home," Tommy said, locking gazes with Jack as if they were the only people in the room. "Now."

"You will," Jack said. "Real soon."

Becka stirred, but as she opened her mouth to speak, the guard backhanded her. The *smack* of his knuckles hitting her face echoed across the small room. To her credit, Becka didn't cry out, but the red splotches across her cheeks indicated that this wasn't the first time she'd been hit. Tommy observed the incident in silence, but when his eyes next found Jack's, they were filled with tears.

"Stop," Jack said, shifting his attention from Tommy to Ahmadi. "Now."

"How very American of you," General Ahmadi said, "but you are in no position to make demands. Your last name, please."

Jack stared back at the Iranian in silence.

"Very well," Ahmadi said.

A second stream of Russian, this time

directed at the waitress. Without replying, she raised her pistol and fired twice in a blur of motion. Jack lurched as blood sprayed across his face, convinced for an instant he'd been the target. Then he realized the gurgling sound was coming from the chair next to him. Turning, Jack watched as the life drained from Gebran's eyes.

"Son of a bitch," Jack said, struggling against his bonds.

One of the guards standing behind him fired a quick jab into Jack's temple, causing him to see stars. When his vision cleared, he ceased struggling. The barista was again brandishing her pistol.

This time the barrel was pointed at Tommy.

"As you've probably guessed," Ahmadi said, "I need what Dr. Schweigart has inside her head. But her son's brains are completely expendable. I know the good professor would rather keep them intact, but whether or not that happens is completely up to you. Your last name. I won't ask again."

Jack breathed in.

Breathed out.

Looked at Becka.

Smiled at Tommy.

In a situation like this, Jack would normally give his assumed name without a second thought. But there was nothing normal about this operation. Like it or not, the cocky Iranian general had been one step ahead of him the entire time. Jack had no doubt that the entire endeavor had been compromised from start to finish. But how far had the mole penetrated? Far enough to be able to distinguish Jack's true name from his legend? Jack had just one chance, and if he chose incorrectly, Tommy would pay the price.

Viewed from that perspective, it wasn't much of a choice at all.

Jack cleared his throat and looked into the Iranian's laughing eyes.

"It's Ryan. Jack Ryan."

second thought. But there was nothing
normal about this operation. Take it or not,
the cocky Iranian general had been one step
ahead of him the entire time. Jack had no
doubt that the entire endeavor had been
compromised from start to finish. But how
far had the mole penetrated? Far enough to

45

Over the course of his campus career, Jack
had been in a tight spot or two. Truth be
told, he'd probably experienced more close
calls in his decade or so of service than most
clandestine operatives encountered in their
entire career. This was partly due to the
nature of The Campus's work.

Former Senator Gerry Hendley had
brought the organization to life in order to
provide the President with an operational
capability beyond what currently existed.
With minimal government oversight, an
almost unlimited budget, and a reporting
structure completely outside the federal
government, Campus operatives went where
others wouldn't and did what they could
not.

But with this tremendous freedom came
tremendous risk.

Unlike a traditional espionage or covert
paramilitary mission, a Campus operation

was executed with minimal planning and sometimes zero notice. Whereas their counterparts in the CIA's storied Ground Branch had the luxury of building a replica of a targeted compound in its entirety before executing a direct-action mission, Campus operatives worked on much tighter timelines.

In short, this was far from Jack's first rodeo.

Even so, he couldn't think of a time when the stakes had been higher. While Jack certainly didn't seek out danger, risks to his own safety were something he'd come to accept. Indeed, operational risk had cut a little too close to home during his last assignment, as Lisanne could attest. Only in the movies did warriors who ran toward the sound of gunfire always return safe.

But this was still something different. It wasn't just his safety or that of Becka and Tommy that was at stake. The wily Iranian had wanted Jack's name for a reason, and it wasn't because he was updating his Christmas card list. No, if Jack had to guess, the Quds Force general wanted to use a captured intelligence officer to maximum effect by including his name with his picture when the inevitable ransom demands arrived at the U.S. embassy in Baghdad.

Except that Jack wasn't just any intelligence officer, as much as he tried to pretend otherwise. So far, Ahmadi didn't seem to know what he had in Jack. But when the diplomatic cables reached the DNI's attention, Mary Pat sure as shit would. So while General Ahmadi had probably intended to use Jack's capture to force Americans operating in Iraq or Syria to take their collective eye off the ball, he stood to do far more than that. If Jack's father learned that his eldest son was in the hands of terrorists, the repercussions could be world-changing.

No matter how this played out, something was coming. Something that Ahmadi intended to accomplish while U.S. decision-makers were preoccupied with recovering a captured intelligence operative. And this diversion would now be exponentially more effective, since the captured operative also happened to be the President's son.

But that was only half of the problem.

The other half was that Jack had seen his captors' faces. No matter how things shaped up between the President of the United States and the terrorists holding his son, Jack wasn't leaving the apartment alive. He needed to flip the script.

But he wasn't sure how.

After giving up his name, Jack had watched what unfolded next with the professional interest of a man who'd had a hand in more than one black-bag operation. General Ahmadi had smiled the grin of the victorious and then vacated the apartment with Becka, Tommy, the waitress, and the phony VC in tow. But not before plucking the Captain America toy from Tommy's fingers and tossing it at Jack's feet.

So much for the beacon.

Then it was just Jack and his two new friends — the Russian 'roid boys.

Next came the obligatory roughing up, consisting of a couple jabs to Jack's face delivered by the larger Russian thug. Though the blows hurt, the giant administered the strikes with the cold precision of a man trying to make a statement rather than a zealot's wild rage.

Jack's suspicions were confirmed when the thug paused to inspect his handiwork after a particularly solid shot to Jack's eye. Grabbing Jack by the hair, the Russian had jerked Jack's head left and right before grunting with what seemed like approval. Then he'd pulled his pistol and placed it against Jack's temple while his partner played the role of photographer.

Satisfied, the photographer nodded and

thumbed the phone. Then the men turned toward Jack. Jack understood what was going to happen, and the realization brought with it a certain amount of clarity. His earlier escape plans had been burdened by contingencies beyond his control. Did the men intend to move him? If so, how? Should he wait to act or take his chances?

Now those questions were meaningless.

He wasn't leaving the apartment alive.

Groaning, Jack hunched as far forward as his bonds would allow. "Something's not right."

The guard closest to Jack laughed before saying something to his partner. Both men chuckled. Not the reaction Jack had tried to provoke.

"Hey," Jack said, putting a bit more strain into his voice. "I need to go to the bathroom. Now."

More smirks.

"Your choice," Jack said, "but this room's about to get unpleasant. Understand?"

It was clear that they didn't. As escape plans went, this wasn't one for the books.

"Come on," Jack said, "surely you two dumb shits understand what I'm saying. WC, *baño, Toiletten, toilettes.*"

A linguist Jack was not, but short of the impressive number of languages in which he could inquire about the availability of beer, asking for the bathroom was his second-greatest foreign-language attribute. In his experience, if you added those two necessities to *please, thank you,* and *Your eyes look pretty in that dress,* you had a country licked. Unfortunately, his Russian vocabulary wasn't quite up to par.

"How about *hamam*?" Jack said. "Does that ring a bell? I've got half a dozen other languages to try, but we don't have time."

Still no reaction.

Time to sell the performance.

Bearing down on his already sore abdominals, Jack produced indisputable, audible proof of his distress. This got the guards' attention. Leaving a man to marinate in his own blood and piss was one thing, but even Russian thugs had limits. They set upon Jack as a pair. The larger one fired a warm-up right cross into Jack's jaw, while his comrade went to work on the handcuffs.

Jack had seen the blow coming, and managed to turn with the punch, but it still rang his bell. Then he heard the metallic *click* as the handcuffs released. A moment later, he was on his feet as the men herded him toward the bathroom. One thug shoved a pistol into Jack's back, while the second grabbed a handful of Jack's thick hair and jerked him forward.

Not ideal, but it beat dying handcuffed to a chair.

He hoped.

Contrary to popular belief, hair wasn't an effective restraint mechanism. The body had plenty of other natural handholds in which force applied in the right direction and magnitude could exert an inordinate amount of control. A person's hair wasn't on this list for one simple reason — the hold relied on pain, not physics, to ensure compliance. Presented with an equal and opposing force, the hair follicles would separate from the scalp, eliminating the control mechanism.

It just hurt like a son of a bitch.

Then again, so did dying.

46

Jack had learned hand-to-hand combat from the best. Fighters for whom surviving by their fists wasn't just an abstract concept debated after a few too many brews. As one such instructor had told Jack after nearly cracking his ribs with an elbow strike, The Campus's school of hard knocks wouldn't equip you for a career as a Golden Gloves boxer. But it might just keep you alive in an elevator full of people who wanted to kill you.

Or a cramped apartment.

Unlike the hand-to-hand combat regimes taught at other government paramilitary organizations, Campus instructors were not devotees of a particular martial art. Jack had certainly learned how to pass guard and absorb punishing thigh kicks, but his time in the fight house yielded no colored belts. He wasn't learning a martial art, how to defend himself, or even how to fight, per se.

Instead, he'd been taught how to kill or incapacitate his opponent as quickly and violently as possible.

Jack was ready for what was about to happen.

He was hoping his guards were not.

The key to fighting more than one attacker at the same time was simple — don't. Two trained fighters almost always successfully overwhelmed a single man. If the way that thug one had distracted Jack with the blow to the jaw while thug two worked his handcuffs were any indication, the pair had done this before.

Which made them confident.

Which Jack intended to exploit.

But first he had to even the odds.

Groaning, Jack wrapped his hands around his stomach and stumbled. Or at least appeared to stumble. His center of gravity settled, leaving the thug holding Jack's hair with a choice. He could arrest Jack's fall by yanking on the hair, or allow Jack to continue falling and risk losing his hold. The Russian chose option one, threading his stubby fingers into Jack's hair and jerking.

Which hurt.

A lot.

But not as much as it could have. Jack exploded upward from coiled legs, tucking his chin as he erupted. He speared the crown of his head into where he pictured the guard's chin.

Flesh met flesh with devastating results.

The *crunch* of cartilage reverberated across Jack's scalp as he shattered his captor's nose instead. The tension on his hair lessened, but what followed next would be a bitch all the same. Jack spun toward his captor, gritting his teeth as hair follicles parted company with his head. He used the pain as motivation, again slamming his forehead into the Russian's damaged nose.

A fountain of blood cascaded from the guard's shattered nose and mouth.

Grabbing two fistfuls of the semiconscious Russian's shirt, Jack slammed the flaccid man into his partner. The second man fired his pistol. Though Jack had tucked his head into his victim's chest, the pistol's discharge was still a doozy. The muzzle blast hit Jack with an invisible haymaker, buckling his knees.

Fighting the nausea, Jack snatched the wrist holding the pistol and wrenched downward, using the first man's shoulder as the fulcrum for an ad hoc arm bar. For an instant, the gunman kept Jack suspended in midair. Then gravity won. The man's wrist broke with a wet-sounding *crack* and the pistol clattered to the floor.

Abandoning both Russians, Jack grabbed the pistol and fired from position two, the pistol tucked close to his side. He walked rounds into both men's chest cavities, angling the muzzle up as he fired. Then the fight was over.

Jack was covered in blood, but alive.

By Campus standards, this constituted success.

Struggling to his feet, Jack wanted to search the bodies, but didn't. The fight had been as loud as it had been visceral. Beirut wasn't the most pedestrian of cities, but this much noise would still be noticed. The neighbors were probably already on the phone with representatives from Hezbollah or the local police.

Either option would put a damper on Jack's escape.

Stepping over the bodies, Jack paused at the gunman's corpse. The man's jacket had fallen open, revealing a magazine holder with two refills nestled in the plastic pockets. Jack grabbed them both and combat-reloaded the pistol on the way to the door before stuffing the two remaining magazines into his front pocket. Robby Jackson, a former F-14 driver and one of his dad's closest friends, liked to say that a good fighter pilot never turned down gas or bullets.

Jack figured that advice also applied to gunfighters.

Reaching the apartment door, Jack peered through the peephole. Haste was all well and good, but everything would be for naught if more bad guys were waiting. Fortunately, Jack's quick peek showed nothing but an empty, dimly lit hallway.

But it wouldn't stay empty for long.

Pulling open the door, Jack led with the pistol in his off hand. The hallway to the left and stairwell were clear.

The right not so much.

Unfortunately, a stabbing sensation in his right thigh was his first indication that all was not well. Looking down, Jack saw a large syringe held in place by slender, feminine fingers.

"The thing about tall men," came a Russian-accented voice, "is that they don't usually look down. I think that's because they don't believe anything smaller than them is a threat. Am I right?"

Jack tried to bring his weapon to bear, but his muscles weren't cooperating. Helpless to stop his pistol from sliding out of his rubbery fingers, Jack pushed past the waitress. Or tried to. But his leg muscles had plans of their own. His hamstrings and quads turned to jelly, and he followed his pistol to the floor.

Lying on his back, Jack stared into the waitress's sparkling eyes.

"You killed my men," she said, staring at Jack like he was a bug she was about to crush. "That was a mistake."

Jack tried to respond, but his lips and tongue decided to join the mutiny.

Then darkness claimed him.

47

Al Tanf Outpost
Syria

"Listen up, boys," Master Sergeant Cary Marks said, eyeing the men in front of him, " 'cause this one's gonna be a doozy."

As befitting an operations order briefing, the gathering was being held in the team room. Accordingly, the battered folding tables that made up the men's workspace were covered in spit cups, coffee mugs, weapon parts, batteries, pieces of kit in various states of disassembly, gun oil, and the ever-present green leader books filled with blank paper and bound with the snot-green-colored covers that gave them their name.

Along the wall, safely outside the danger zone posed by spilling coffee or dip spit, sat several laptops onto which were loaded maps of the team's AO, or area of operation. The front of the room sported an enormous TV, which was primarily used to watch ESPN or play first-person shooter games. Today, the screen was actually accomplishing its government-sanctioned job by displaying operational graphics overlaid upon terrain maps projected from one of the laptops.

The twelve men who made up ODA 555, otherwise known as Triple Nickel, were scattered across the room in various states of dress. As Cary surveyed the group, he saw everything from Crumdog's shorts, flip-flops, and Ohio State T-shirt to Brandon Durrant's cowboy boots, Wrangler jeans, and pearly-snap shirt.

The sight of his men gathered together warmed Cary's heart. But the levity and trash talk that normally accompanied such a gathering was conspicuously absent. The intel update CIA Bill had provided moments ago would have sobered a drunk.

Cary's earlier assessment had been right in one regard — the preformed plots the cultists had excavated were meant for concrete. What he'd gotten wrong was their purpose. According to Bill, the newly cured slabs were indeed meant to act as a foundation. A foundation for a convoy of trucks bearing Iranian-manufactured cruise missiles. As Bill had so aptly stated at the conclusion of his briefing, no one knew what the Hoveyzeh cruise missiles were carrying for warheads.

But they probably weren't Christmas presents.

With a range in excess of 1,300 kilometers and a configurable payload capable of handling high explosives, cluster munitions, or even biological or chemical agents, the weapons were dangerous in Iranian hands. In the inventory of a cult predicated upon bringing about the apocalypse, the Hoveyzehs were the equivalent of a tank of gasoline just waiting for a match. The National Command Authority had decreed that the weapons needed to go, and Triple Nickel got the job.

Ordinarily, this would have been a fairly simple operation. The truck-mounted MLRS, or multiple launch rocket systems, housing the missiles were certainly vulnerable to air attack, but here the cultists made things tricky. While the several hundred military-aged males making up the bulk of the cult leader's followers were certainly legitimate targets, the same could not be said of their wives and children who lived in the compound alongside them.

This was why Cary and his men were once again serving as their nation's eyes and ears.

"Let me get this straight," Crumdog said.

"Because the bad guys decided to use women and children as human shields, we're going to risk our lives so none of them get hurt. Do I have that right?"

Alex prepared to respond, but Cary held up a hand indicating that he'd field this one.

His team leader wisely deferred.

"Check it out, stud," Cary said, letting his irritation seep through. "That long tab on your shoulder says *Special Forces* for a reason. If this mission was easy, the SEALs would have it. But it's not, so headquarters called the adults. Just so we're clear, the people in this room always come first in my battlefield calculus. But our job is unconventional warfare. That means winning the trust of the local population, and that's damn hard when the Air Force accidentally massacres a bunch of women and children. So we're going to put eyes on those missiles, and we will clear the drop. Tracking?"

"Like a bloodhound," Crum said. "But what if potential collateral damage keeps us from clearing the drop?"

"I'll take that one," Alex said, walking to the front of the room. "First off, the Air Force will be using a new toy on this op. A sortie of F-15s will be dropping GBU-53/B mini glide bombs. These suckers weigh in at just two hundred pounds, so their warhead effects are much smaller than a standard two-thousand-pound JDAM. Also, GBUs can track to a laser spot, which gives them even greater accuracy."

"And I assume we'll be the ones lasing the target?" Crum said.

"And who said Ohio boys were dumb?" Alex said with a smile. "That's correct. The team will be arrayed in positions Alpha One through Alpha Five."

Alex pointed to the TV screen as he talked, indicating the terrain features with the sight lines into the compound's interior.

"Alpha One through Three will be fire support positions augmented with our two ground mobility vehicles, and one MRZR all-terrain vehicle. Crew-served weapons will be mounted on each mobility platform. Alpha Four will be the alternate lase. Alpha Five will have primary responsibility for guiding the missiles onto target. I'll be a terrain feature back at Bravo One with our Quick Reactionary Force and indirect fire assets. Questions?"

The QRF that Alex referred to was comprised of an assortment of Kurdish fighters with some Free Syrian Army folks thrown in for good measure. Cary was not always impressed with the quality of the indigenous forces he and his teammates were tasked to train, but the Kurds were hell on wheels. Having them at his back made Cary feel better already.

"Just one," Jad said, leaning forward in his chair. "Alpha Five is pretty close to the compound. Who's taking that sucker?"

"You and me, brother," Cary said.

"My man," Jad said with a smile. "I wouldn't have it any other way."

As usual, Jad's infectious enthusiasm prompted laughter from the rest of the team, and Cary felt himself smiling as well. Though the operation was risky, the people who gravitated toward careers in Special Operations weren't risk-averse. Selection standards were incredibly high, precisely because the job was so dangerous.

Even so, something his spotter had said resonated with Cary. Alpha Five was extremely close to the compound, but it couldn't be helped. The plateau offered the best view of the missiles and the greatest situational awareness of the dormitories where the women and children lived. If the cultists really did have the ability to disrupt electronic transmissions, Cary wanted to be close enough to see what the cultists were doing with his own two eyes.

He just hoped that sentiment didn't go both ways.

48

Beirut, Lebanon

Darien watched Beirut's modernity give way to peasant hovels as he followed Highway 30 southeast. In many ways, the experience was like traveling back in time as the industrial age gave way to an agrarian society little changed since the Bedouin nomads first inhabited the land.

The metamorphosis was not a pleasant one.

Because of where his Western looks allowed him to operate, Darien had grown accustomed to a certain level of modernity. He didn't need a Starbucks on every corner, but water that came out of the tap drinkable and in both hot and cold varieties was but one of the many conveniences he'd begun to take for granted. As he journeyed farther into the countryside, passing villages consisting of mud-brick homes constructed around a single common well, he couldn't help but think that he wasn't so much traveling back in time as viewing the future should General Ahmadi's plan succeed.

Darien was a spy. A field man to the bone. He'd learned long ago to leave the machinations and scheming that grew out of the tactical recruitments to those who viewed the world from the safety of their ivory towers. Though he detested having his decisions second-guessed by headquarters as much as the next field operative, this had happened less and less as his career had progressed. Darien went where his fellow countrymen feared to tread. The assets he produced and intelligence he garnered were untouchable. By extension, so was he.

Until now.

"Why so quiet?"

The question was benign, but the feminine voice asking it still sent shivers down Darien's spine. As a person who compromised human beings for a living, Darien was all too aware of the role sex played in motivating potential assets.

Especially men.

"Just daydreaming," Darien said, evading the question.

But Katerina Sidorova was not one to be put off by an evasive answer. A trait shared by most former SVR operatives.

"Then I hope your daydreams are good," Katerina said, stretching in the seat beside him. "I thought perhaps you might be contemplating your next role."

"And what would that be?" Darien said.

"Dead man."

Darien snapped from the road to his companion, taking her measure.

As always, the sight of Katerina made his heart stutter. With a pale complexion and dirty-blond hair, she wasn't the stuff of magazine covers. Even so, there was something about the intensity of her presence that a camera could never capture. A magnetism that drew the observer to her captivating eyes.

He'd first spotted those pale blue eyes examining him from across a Viennese café nine months ago. Then Katerina had looked more like a mousy librarian than an operative of Russia's feared foreign intelligence service. But even though she'd hidden her figure behind baggy clothes and her luxurious curly hair beneath a bland wig, she hadn't been able to disguise her eyes.

At least not from him.

But now those eyes exuded none of the sexual intensity Darien usually saw lurking within their depths. Instead, Katerina was looking at him in an almost clinical manner. As if she were a scientist and he an insect pinned to a tray for study.

"What do you mean?" Darien said, turning back to the road. As much as he enjoyed the sight of Katerina, focusing on her tended to decrease his capacity for reasoned thought.

Drastically.

"It's pretty simple," Katerina said, threading her fingers through Darien's hair. "I suspected his intent from the beginning, but I wasn't sure. Now that he ordered you to do this, I am."

She punctuated *this* with a hand wave encompassing the car, Darien, and the asphalt that stretched out before them like an endless black ribbon. Darien knew to whom she was referring. Truth be told, he'd harbored some of the same misgivings. Even so, he wanted to hear her reasoning without clouding her opinion with his own.

"Who?" Darien said, eyes on the road. "Who wants to kill me?"

"General Ahmadi, of course."

General Farhad Ahmadi — the Quds Force expeditionary commander and favorite of the grand ayatollah. The general had a deserved reputation for tactical brilliance. He'd single-handedly masterminded the Shia uprisings in Iraq that had thrown the country into chaos while simultaneously funneling foreign fighters and the armored vehicle–killing IEDs into Iraq by the bushel. Were it not for the unpopular American surge, Iraq would already be an extension of Iran.

What he hadn't been able to accomplish with brute force Ahmadi was now gaining through bribery, political machinations, and targeted assassinations. Already the Iraqi prime minister had invited Iranian peace-keepers into his country under the pretext of assisting the beleaguered Iraqi national police with uprisings spawned by various Sunni militias. The crafty old fox had achieved what his predecessors had not despite fighting a fruitless eight-year war against Iraq in the 1980s.

Iranian soldiers were operating openly on Iraqi soil.

But that didn't mean the general was without blind spots. In Darien's opinion, one of them was Ahmadi's manic obsession with wiping Israel from the face of the earth. To Darien's way of thinking, his homeland was on the brink of culminating the long journey that had begun when student revolutionaries had toppled the corrupt shah during a 1979 uprising.

With a bit more of the general's finesse

and a few more staged Sunni uprisings, the Iranian presence in Iraq would shift from temporary troops in an advisory role to a permanent garrison housing an occupying force. When that happened, the Islamic Republic of Iran would finally realize its goal of establishing a land bridge across the Middle East, starting in Tehran and crossing Iraq, Syria, and Lebanon, to end at the Mediterranean's warm waters.

And Ahmadi was jeopardizing all of this with a harebrained scheme to destroy the Jewish state.

At least Darien thought the plan harebrained. The Ayatollah, of course, loved it. But that was neither here nor there. With the cleric's backing, the Quds Force commander had trumped Darien's MOIS supervisors. Ahmadi had demanded their best spy for an operation planned for Israeli soil, and the cowards had handed Darien over like a lamb to be slaughtered. The insanity of the operation aside, one did not buck the supreme leader of Iran and expect to live a long and fruitful life.

Even so, Darien had taken the audacious goal that the Quds Force commander had given him and executed it flawlessly. Dr. Rebecka Schweigart, and the invaluable knowledge she was carrying inside her brain, had been taken off the board and no one had any reason to suspect the Iranians.

Darien had executed a near-perfect operation.

But perhaps not near perfect enough for Ahmadi.

"Why do you think he wants to kill me?" Darien said.

"My sweet, innocent boy," Katerina said, purring the words as she sidled up against Darien. "You think in terms of tactical success or failure, but your General Ahmadi plays the long game. Yes, we successfully snatched the scientist, but her disappearance will not go unnoticed. Someone must take the blame for her, for Jack Ryan's death, and for what is to come. My darling, that someone is you."

Darien shifted his hips to the left, pressing against the door. The movement wasn't much, but it created space enough to insulate himself from Katerina's touch. In a way that only a spy could, Darien understood that he now stood at the edge of a precipice, and it would take the totality of his mental facilities to see himself across the looming abyss. Now more than ever, he needed clarity of thought without the Russian's influence.

Attribution had been Darien's driving

consideration during the planning phase of the operation. It was why Katerina was seated next to him in the passenger seat instead of one of Ahmadi's Quds Force thugs and why the masked shooters who'd so ably snatched the scientist from the Israelis' clutches spoke Russian instead of Arabic or Farsi.

Several months ago, Katerina had left the SVR for a position in the Wagner Group — the Russian equivalent of the American mercenary company formerly known as Blackwater. Except instead of just the usual collection of former Spetsnaz Special Operations shooters, Wagner had recently opened its ranks to former intelligence operatives like Katerina.

For Darien, the organization's unique charter offered an unmatched competency — the ability to conduct kinetic operations with the precision expected of Special Operations veterans backed by actionable intelligence collected by Moscow-trained intelligence officers. For a spy charged with the seemingly impossible task of clandestinely kidnapping a high-value target from beneath Shin Bet's nose, hiring Katerina, and by extension the Wagner Group, had been a no-brainer.

But if he were honest, Darien would have

374

to admit that the operation had not gone flawlessly. He was not the only one who'd seen the academic conference as an opportunity to access the scientist and her game-changing ideas. The Chinese had been determined to neutralize Schweigart, and the Americans had obviously had her under surveillance as well. Darien was willing to wager that either the Mossad or Shin Bet, or both, had also been considering an approach.

Instead of the simple disappearance from her hotel that Darien had envisioned, Becka had been kidnapped in broad daylight. Even worse, Israelis had been killed in the process, and for that there would be retribution.

And then there was the ill-thought-out kidnapping of the American intelligence officer Jack Ryan, again ordered by Ahmadi. At first the old fox had wanted to give Ryan to Hezbollah as a way to distract the Americans. To tie up critical resources in what undoubtedly would become a massive push by the U.S. intelligence apparatus to locate and rescue their kidnapped operative.

But then the general had changed his mind.

After leaving the apartment and securing the scientist and her son with his Quds

Force entourage, Ahmadi had ordered Darien to undertake this current course of madness. In retrospect, it was a good thing he had, since the American had proven more resourceful than anyone would have expected. Were it not for Katerina's skill, Ryan might well have escaped the Wagner Group's safe house, and the repercussions for what Darien had done on Ahmadi's behalf would have been felt that much sooner.

But what had started as a clean, nonattributional mission had now morphed into the kind of high-profile debacle normally associated with overseas Quds Force activity. Except that when other intelligence services began the task of sifting through what had happened for the inevitable blame game foisted upon them by their political masters, the forensic evidence would point to just one man.

Darien.

Put in that perspective, Darien had no doubt that crafty General Ahmadi was setting up the spy he'd never liked as the fall guy for the coming blowback. And when it came to patsies, history had proven that most straw men were unable to refute the blame laid at their feet.

Mostly because they were already dead.

"Let's assume you're right," Darien said, choosing his words carefully. "What would you do in my shoes?"

"When your current friends betray you, you must find new ones."

"Like you?" Darien said, playing along.

Though he'd had a variation of this same conversation hundreds of times with potential assets, it felt completely different to sit on the other side of the negotiating table. And that's exactly what this was, a negotiation for Darien's most valuable asset — his life.

"You've already got me, darling," Katerina said, her tone now deadly serious. "I know that you still don't believe it, but it's true. I love you. But my love alone is not enough to save you. To protect yourself against a nation-state, you need a nation-state. I realize your General Ahmadi is a ruthless man who fears few who walk the earth, but I guarantee you that there is one world leader he will not cross."

"And why would this world leader protect me?" Darien said.

"Let's just say that he has a soft spot for former intelligence officers, because he is one."

"I thought there was no such thing as former KGB."

"Semantics," Katerina said with a smile. "The important thing is that once you are in his employ, you will enjoy the mantle of his protection. The United States is a powerful nation, truthfully, more capable than mine. But American Presidents come and go — that is their weakness. In my country, the tsar is forever. And he never forgets."

"That is a very generous offer," Darien said, feeling his way through the conversation like a blind man navigating a minefield. "But I didn't know that the tsar of Russia had use for an Iranian spy."

"He doesn't. Not directly. But the Wagner Group has a great need for talent such as yours. I'm sure you'll find the salary quite satisfactory. It's triple what you're currently paid. And that's just the tip of the iceberg. There are many more . . . *intangible* benefits."

Katerina pressed against him again, and this time Darien didn't move away. He was a spy. He lied for a living. And men who lied for a living quickly became adept at spotting untruth in others. As he'd listened to Katerina, he'd heard the veracity of her words. Ahmadi was setting Darien up to take the fall. Even if Darien managed to see his way through the coming storm, he would still have a target on his back. And Ahmadi had the ear of the Ayatollah himself.

Sooner or later Darien would get his due.

"So this job offer you referenced," Darien said, sliding his hand along Katerina's thigh. "Is there an interview process?"

"Yes," Katerina said, wiggling closer, "but you've already passed it with flying colors. Your future employer requires just one thing. Call it a show of your commitment."

"What would that be?" Darien said, already knowing the answer.

"The scientist," Katerina said. "Where is she?"

And there it was. The proverbial hook. Though he didn't like it, Darien knew that this was part of the deal. A high-level recruitment was risky, even for the Russian tsar. To bear the risk, the Russians needed to know that their newest employee had burned the proverbial ships. And nothing said "burn the ships" like giving up the location of his country's most prized acquisition.

For a long moment, Darien considered. Everything. Growing up as the only child of an American mother and Persian father. The poverty of his upbringing and the ridicule he'd endured as a child for his American looks and Western blood. His recruitment by the Iranian Ministry of Intelligence and Security followed by the risks he'd taken, the men he'd killed, and the women he'd seduced, all at his country's behest. And for what? So that the collection of turban-wearing bearded men who ruled his nation with an iron fist could now cast him away like a dog?

No.

"She's still in Beirut," Darien said, providing the safe house's address. "Quds Force operatives are guarding her. An Iranian cargo ship will be docking tomorrow. She'll be put on board and smuggled back to Iran by sea. A much longer process than simply flying her to Tehran, but —"

"There will be no incriminating flights between Beirut and Iran when the inevitable hunt to find her begins," Katerina said with a smile. "You really have thought of everything, my love. Fortunately, there just so happen to be some Wagner Group employees still in Beirut. Make a call to your Quds Force friends. Tell them you're assigning my mercenaries to augment their security. My comrades will take care of the rest. This time tomorrow, the good scientist will still be on a freighter, but it will be bound for Russia."

"Sounds like I wasn't the only one who thought of everything," Darien said with a smile. "We'll make a great team."

"Yes, we will," Katerina said, sliding onto his lap. "Now, why don't you pull off the road for a bit? It's time to consummate this new arrangement."

Darien did exactly as he was told.

49

Several delightful hours later, Darien slowed the car as they crested a hill.

"Our friends are already here," Darien said.

Katerina's metamorphosis was instantaneous. A moment before, she'd been a carefree girl on a scenic drive through the countryside. Now she was a trained operative. Even Katerina's posture changed. Her soft edges somehow seemed to harden as her bearing became more erect.

Darien felt himself undergo a similar change. Now that he was out from beneath the Jews' watchful eyes, he'd returned to carrying his two weapons of choice — a small blade sheathed beneath his left shirtsleeve and a Glock secured in an inside-the-waistband holster.

He touched both as the car coasted down the hill.

"Early is not good, my love," Katerina

said, checking the two-shot Derringer-type pistol she carried at the base of her spine. "Be ready."

Katerina didn't say what to be ready for. She didn't have to. Though Darien enjoyed her flirty persona, this was the woman he'd fallen for. The case officer with a lethal mind that matched her magnetic personality. A fellow professional who was his equal in both intellect and operational prowess. Like all spies, Darien had been trained to operate alone and had come to crave the solitary nature of his work.

No longer.

With Katerina at his side, he felt both fulfilled and invincible. Now it was time to put those feelings to the test.

"What does it mean?" Darien said.

"Don't know," Katerina said. "Not an outright ambush. Otherwise they would have already initiated. They might still want us dead, but they want to talk first."

"Or maybe they just want to make sure our passenger isn't hurt in the crossfire," Darien said, braking as he nosed the car up against the two trucks.

The hill's incline was quite steep, almost a forty percent grade. Darien would have to put on the parking brake to ensure the car didn't roll. Strange place for a meet. Unless . . .

"See if you can spot another shooter," Darien said as he set the parking brake with a squeal of metal on metal. "Look below the military crest of the hill."

Katerina was too well trained to turn in her seat. Instead, she angled the passenger-side mirror.

"Got him," Katerina said. "My side. In a hide site just beneath the lip of the hill. Great spot. He's got line of sight on the entire road as well as —"

"Us," Darien said, finishing her thought. "If this is an ambush, it will happen after they confirm we have Ryan. Stay in the car and keep an eye on the sniper. If you see him shift his focus from the road to me, beep the horn. I'll take care of the rest."

"You are very brave, my darling," Katerina said, unhooking her seatbelt, "but also very foolish. Your concern for my safety is touching, but misplaced. I am a veteran of the Sluzhba Vneshney Razvedki. I'm quite competent at my job. Besides, we all know how these *mudak* view women."

Darien reached across the car to grab Katerina's hand, but found himself grasping air instead. In one fluid motion Katerina popped open the door and slid from the car.

With a curse, Darien released his own seat-belt and followed, still trying to come to terms with the muddle the Russian made of his thoughts.

For the first time in his life, he wasn't the one with the golden tongue. The person who charmed others into betraying their country. As he caught Katerina's eye, the half-formed thoughts he'd tried to put into words solidified. His reticence to allow her to leave the relative safety offered by the car wasn't because he doubted her abilities. Far from it. It was because he wasn't at all certain that he could imagine a life without her.

For an instant, her blue eyes softened, as if reading the words stuck in his chest. Then the sentiment vanished and only the Moscow-trained operative remained. Darien almost pitied the pair of men walking toward them. They probably thought they had Darien at a disadvantage.

For their sake, Darien hoped they didn't give Katerina a reason to demonstrate otherwise.

"As-salamu alaikum," Darien said, greeting the two men.

"Wa alaikum assalaam," the nearer man replied, his response sounding somewhat

grudging to Darien's ears.

Then again, neither man looked like the epitome of joy.

Unlike most of the inhabitants of this part of the world, the men weren't dressed in the faux-Western style of city occupants. Instead of jeans, shirts, and tennis shoes, the men wore clothes from another era: brown *aba* robes complemented by white turbans. The AK-47s slung across their chests were the pair's only concession to modernity, a suspicion reinforced by the way they both studiously ignored Katerina.

The men had the bearded, weather-beaten faces of those who lived exposed to harsh desert conditions. Their frames were identically slender, as if any excess fat had long ago been scoured away by the unrelenting sun and wind.

The man closer to Darien had facial hair that seemed to begin at the base of his throat and extend all the way up to the single eyebrow that bridged the gap between two distrustful eyes. In contrast, his partner had more peach fuzz than whiskers, and the feeble facial hair did little to soften his pinched features. Taken together, the two resembled a bear standing next to a weasel.

Their countenance was just as friendly.

Then again, Darien supposed that a sunny

personality wasn't a prerequisite for membership in an apocalyptic cult.

"Who is the woman?" the Bear said.

"My whore," Darien said. "Forgive her dress. She's Russian and doesn't speak Arabic."

As one, the men turned their backs on Katerina, who mumbled something in Russian before shuffling to a point behind the men. It took everything within Darien not to smile. That easily, the former SVR operative negated their numerical advantage while giving herself a clear view of the shooter on top of the hill.

Good didn't even begin to describe his partner.

"You were supposed to come alone," Bear said.

Darien shrugged. "I don't often do what I'm told. Take what I've brought or don't. I don't care. I'm sure your imam will be very understanding if you return without it."

Bear glanced at Weasel, who gave a short nod.

"Fine," Bear said. "But you can explain her presence yourself."

"What?" Darien said.

"You're supposed to deliver the cargo," Bear said.

"That was not the arrangement," Darien said.

He delivered his line with a bored tone, but his heart rattled against his ribs like a snare drum. If a double cross was to occur, it would happen now. Katerina took a half-step to her right as she gave another delightful stretch.

"It is now," Bear said. "Your boss, the general, told the imam that you would deliver the cargo in person. The general said to tell you *saa'at.* But feel free to call and ask for clarification. I'm sure he will be very understanding."

Saa'at, or "clock," was the recognition code word for this operation. The only way these two goons would know it was if Ahmadi really had given Darien new orders. He paused, considering his options while keeping his face expressionless. He'd intended to simply vanish with Katerina after providing Ryan to the cultists. But if he balked now, the two men would be on the phone with Ahmadi the moment Darien climbed back into the car.

Knowing the crafty old fox, Ahmadi had probably arranged some sort of check-in with the men. Meaning that even if Darien killed them, the general would still know something was amiss, and he wasn't ready for the Quds Force operative to know that he'd been betrayed.

Not just yet.

Which meant that his only choice was to keep up this façade for a little longer.

"Fine," Darien said. "Let's go."

50

Jack awoke with the kind of hangover that
made him want to swear off alcohol even
before he'd forced his crusty eyelids open.
Though he'd thrown back a couple from
time to time, he'd never let things get this
far out of control. Hell, he couldn't even
remember what he'd been celebrating, let
alone where he was now.

Not to mention that his pounding head
was only part of the problem. His inner ear
was convinced that the world was bucking
and sliding, and he had yet to open his eyes.
This was going to be one of those times
when it was fortunate to have a doctor in
the family, even if she was an ophthalmolo-
gist.

A particularly vicious jolt sent Jack smashing against a decidedly unforgiving section
of steel. He instinctively tried to shield his
face, but couldn't.

His arms were handcuffed behind him.

Banging his head against something hard wasn't the preferred method to clear away the grogginess, but it seemed to work. The nauseating smell of gasoline, ever-present darkness, and tight confines suggested that Jack was stuffed in the trunk of a car. As his foggy brain came back online, stimuli crashed over him. The noxious odor of car exhaust competed with damp, mildewing carpet. A bundle of rags by his head smelled of motor oil, while the sour scent of body odor and fear permeated everything.

Definitely a trunk.

Stretching as far as he could, Jack tried to flex in order to get his blood circulating. He was partially successful. His legs and back announced their displeasure with a series of muscle cramps, while his arms were still masses of unresponsive jelly. Turning his hips, Jack shifted from his back to his side, gritting his teeth against the pins-and-needles sensation.

Whatever the waitress had injected him with had been a doozy.

Thousands of invisible wasps venting their frustration on his arms and hands helped drive away the remaining mental fogginess. But much like the returning blood flow to his contorted limbs was a mixed bag, full mental functionality came with a price.

Though the semidarkness prevented Jack from getting an accurate depiction of his surroundings, he could sense the trunk's metal confines enclosing him like a coffin. A debilitating claustrophobia struck without warning, forcing Jack to take shuddering breaths through his mouth to confront the phobia. Closing his eyes, he concentrated on his other senses, fighting against the feeling that the metal walls were pressing in around him. His heart rate and respiration were both accelerating.

In an effort to combat the panic, Jack focused on his breathing, sucking fetid air in through his mouth, holding it for a two-count, and then exhaling it out through his nose in a long, steady breath.

While the breathing exercises helped control his physical stress, they were less effective against his mental foes. The sudden feelings of isolation and helplessness were almost overpowering. He'd been snatched in a city infamous for devouring the unwary and unlucky. The Campus's required reading list featured *Beirut Rules,* cowritten by former DSS Agent Fred Burton. The work of nonfiction was a primer on Middle East terrorism, and it covered the kidnapping, torture, and the eventual murder of the Beirut CIA station chief, William Buckley, in excruciating detail.

Unlike many victims whose kidnapping represented their first encounter with violence, Bill Buckley was a former Green Beret who'd served in Vietnam. He'd understood the primeval nature of combat, but even he hadn't stood a chance against his Hezbollah captors. After being traded from one jihadi group to another, Bill's discarded body was finally discovered more than a year after his initial capture.

While Jack knew it was dangerous to draw conclusions based on events separated by thirty-five years, he also knew that the recovery rate for kidnapping victims in this part of the world was minuscule. Now was the time to be bold. To take life-or-death chances even if the odds of success seemed remote, because this was when the kidnappers were also most vulnerable. Once his captors reached wherever they were taking him, the odds would be stacked in their favor.

But now both parties were in a kind of no-man's-land. Jack was cut off from his allies, as were his kidnappers. This might be his only chance to escape, and Jack intended to take it.

As if the car's occupants could read his mind, Jack heard the engine's constant thrum lose its roar as the vehicle began to slow. This was not ideal. Jack had hoped for some time before confronting his captors. Time to plan, or, at the very least, discover what he might put to use in the cramped compartment.

One of Ding's famous adages came to mind: The enemy always has a vote.

Fumbling with his still-smarting fingers, Jack felt along the damp carpet, searching for something, anything that might aid him. He wanted a lug wrench or at least a stray screwdriver, but his fingers touched only rags and threadbare fabric.

While his situation was far from ideal, Jack still possessed one very potent weapon — hope. Jack had access to something that Bill Buckley had not. Just before his capture, he'd activated Gavin's Eye of Sauron. As he understood it, the app turned his cell phone into an electronic black hole. A clandestine collection device that vacuumed up and logged all the surrounding digital traffic across the width and breadth of the electronic spectrum before forwarding the take to Gavin.

If the Eye worked as planned, the hacker would be able to sic The Campus's machine-learning algorithms on the data, sorting IPs, MAC addresses, and globally unique identifiers. Once its targets were acquired, the Eye launched cyberattacks designed to penetrate and compromise each device's operating system.

If a bad guy had a phone in the Eye's vicinity, Jack would own it.

While Jack had been separated from his phone soon after he'd been captured, he was hopeful that the hacker's electronic soldiers had cataloged the bad guy's devices and compromised them. Best-case scenario, his captors' cells were now live mics.

Worst case, Gavin was now tracking their location in real time.

At least Jack hoped that was the worst-case scenario. But worst-case or not, Jack was operating on the assumption that his comrades-in-arms knew he was in trouble and were even now bringing The Campus's considerable resources to bear on rescuing him. But technological wizardry aside, his fellow operatives weren't miracle workers. They'd need time to execute a rescue, and Jack intended to give it to them.

At least that was the plan, anyway.

The vehicle stopped and the slamming of car doors echoed through the trunk. Jack flexed his fingers and wiggled his toes, trying to bring his deadened extremities to life, but searing pins and needles were his only reward. This was unfortunate, but not the end of the world. Once he got vertical, gravity would help to restore his circulation.

Until then, he needed to keep his wits about him and watch for a chance to act.

The trunk popped open and rough hands dragged him from the darkness.

Blinding sunlight played havoc with Jack's already throbbing head, stabbing through his eyeballs with an icepick's compassion. Somehow, the outside air smelled worse than the trunk. A stench Jack associated with day-old roadkill clogged his nose, and his stomach threatened to empty. Struggling not to gag, Jack blinked past the tears streaming down his face, desperate for a look at his new surroundings. For a long moment, the blurry world refused to resolve into something recognizable.

Then it did.

At first Jack saw what he expected — the waitress and her VC boyfriend. The woman smiled at him in a way that made his heart rate accelerate. Then Jack saw a trio of men standing next to the operatives and felt his stomach drop. He was not in Kansas anymore.

Or even Beirut.

Dressed in the *thobe* robes and *sirwal* trousers of desert Bedouins and armed with

AK-47s, the men introduced themselves via a series of blows to Jack's unprotected head and torso. One guard held Jack upright while the other two went to work on him with their fists and their rifles' wooden stocks. When it ended, Jack found himself supported by two of the men, his ability to stand on his own beaten out of him.

Determined fingers grabbed his hair and wrenched his lolling head upward.

"That was for the men that you killed at the apartment," the waitress said, her face inches from his. "My men. Good-bye, Jack Ryan."

She released his hair, and Jack fought to keep his head upright, watching as the waitress and her master-spy boyfriend walked off in the company of two more of the robed jihadis. For the first time since he'd been dragged from the car, Jack took in his surroundings. To his left was some sort of compound resembling a medieval fortress, complete with fifteen-foot earthen berms. But it was what was in front of him that Jack found most troubling.

Death.

Stephen King–style death. Rows upon rows of leafless trees stretched out before him. But they weren't trees. They were crosses. Crosses adorned with the decomposing remains of countless corpses.

The searing image and horrific smell of rotting, bloated meat overpowered Jack. Ducking his head, he spewed a burning stream of bile onto the parched earth. This earned him a strike to the back of his head that turned his legs to rubber. But his inability to walk didn't stop the guards from dragging him toward the killing field.

As they drew closer, Jack was forced to change his earlier assessment. Most of the crosses were occupied. But not all. A length of freshly cut wood lay on the ground next to a tripod-mounted camera.

And Jack was headed straight for it.

51

"Reaper Seven, this is Reaper Fourteen, over."

"Go for Seven," Cary said, not so much whispering his reply as sending it telepathically.

Originally, Cary had thought Jad's concern about their hide site's proximity to the compound was unfounded. The plateau on which the men were located was only three hundred meters from the structure's imposing walls, but it offered an excellent view of the compound's dormitory and newly constructed truck park.

Tarps still stretched overhead, obscuring the MLRS from drones or satellites, but Cary had a perfect vantage point. In fact, he'd already tried out the ground laser target designator, or GLTD, and was satisfied with the return signal. The hide site was much closer to the fortress's walls than Cary would prefer, but the location was, in a word, perfect.

Unfortunately, the dozen or so cult members who'd decided to use the plateau for a pickup game of soccer seemed to be of the same opinion. So far, the soccer players had been too engrossed in the game to notice two Green Berets squatting in a hastily dug chest-deep hole covered with camouflage netting less than fifty meters away, but Cary didn't know how much longer his good fortune would last.

Though neither Cary nor Jad had so much as batted an eyelash in the last thirty minutes, their hide site was situated just beyond the nearest goal. As luck would have it, the keeper on their side of the field wasn't very good. Sooner or later, the ball was going to roll just a little too far.

When it did, hell would roll with it.

"Reaper Seven, Reaper Fourteen, a vehicle just rolled up to Pet Cemetery. They popped the trunk and unloaded a new customer. He's in pretty bad shape. They're dragging him toward an empty cross now."

"Fourteen, Seven, roger all. The F-15s will be on station in one-five mikes. Until then, we can't afford to be compromised, over."

"Roger that, Seven. Understood. It's just

that this guy isn't one of the usual suspects. He looks . . . American, over."

Cary felt his blood pressure spike. Like most of his teammates, he'd been drawn to Special Operations to satisfy a very primal need. He wanted to take the fight directly to the bad guys in a way that conventional forces could not. *De oppresso liber,* the motto of Army Special Forces, means "to free the oppressed," and Cary had fulfilled this creed in a variety of different ways since donning the green beret years ago.

Even so, there was one mission that was considered sacrosanct — hostage rescue. Specifically, the rescue of American hostages kidnapped by terrorists or their ilk. This mission set was one of the reasons Delta Force was formed. Nearly every special operator longed for the day when he might be the one kicking in a door and saving an American hostage.

Even so, the mission brief for Triple Nickel's current operation had been pretty unambiguous. Get into position, clear the cruise missiles of collateral damage, and guide in the F-15's small-diameter bombs. If the payloads on the Iranian missiles really did carry chemical or biological agents, tens of thousands of lives were at stake.

And yet . . .

"Fourteen, Seven, did you get a shot of the victim's face?"

"Seven, affirmative."

"Roger that, Fourteen," Cary said. "Break, break. Reaper Six, this is Seven."

"Go for Reaper Six," Alex said.

"Roger Six, we've got eyes on a potential American hostage, and from the looks of things, our boys are about to nail him to a cross. Reaper Fourteen's got imagery. Can you pass it up the chain of command? He could be a kidnapping victim, and we've still got time to intervene."

"Reaper Six copies all. Send the pic, and I'll see what I can do. But unless we hear otherwise, our mission priorities do not change for the next fifteen mikes, over."

"Reaper Seven acknowledges. Continuing mission."

Cary was frustrated, but he knew his team leader was right. He imagined that Alex didn't like giving the order to stand down any more than Cary liked hearing it. But they were both soldiers, and soldiers followed orders.

A vibration at his chest announced an incoming data file from Reaper Fourteen.

Cary unfolded an Android device about the size of a cell phone from its holder on his plate carrier. Mounted in the center of his chest and wired into his radios, the device provided Cary with both situational awareness in the form of a moving map display and real-time access to the suite of sensors his team employed.

Cary swore as he looked at the picture. American or not, the man was on his last legs. Cary couldn't help but think that this simple observation mission was about to become much more complex. No Green Beret was naïve enough to think that an operation would go exactly as briefed. Change was the one constant, but in this case, Cary welcomed the chance to deviate from the operations order.

He just hoped that the change of mission came down before the poor bastard got himself nailed to a cross.

52

Jack had heard people talk about the moment your life flashed before your eyes, but he'd never experienced it. Perhaps because when his life was truly in danger, he'd been too busy trying to stay alive to contemplate his existence. Or maybe it was because he'd never been in a situation he hadn't thought he'd somehow survive.

Until now.

As the three men hustled Jack toward the waiting cross, he knew that this time there was no escape. He had no weapons and no hope of the cavalry riding to the rescue. He was completely and utterly alone.

With the exception of his captors.

The men dragging him across the densely packed soil weren't much on casual conversation, but the jostling was beginning to force blood into Jack's extremities. The pins-and-needles sensations had largely subsided, and feeling had returned to his

404

hands and feet. He could probably walk if need be, but he didn't try.

Better that his executioners thought he was still incapacitated.

Unfortunately, they weren't taking any chances. The burly one to his left fired a punch into Jack's ribs that sent him to his knees. Then the base of his skull exploded. The rabbit punch had been expertly delivered and didn't so much knock the fight out of Jack as destroy his ability to think about anything but the blinding pain.

By the time his thoughts cleared, Jack was on his back against a coarse length of wood. One man was pinning his wrist to the crossbeam, while the other was straddling his hips. Jack tried to buck free and received two punches in the jaw for his trouble.

And then a third man stepped into view. He'd been fiddling with the camera while his friends were working Jack over, but now seemed ready to join the party. Jack squinted, trying to make out what the man was holding in his hand.

A hammer.

A motherfucking hammer.

The man with the hammer squatted next to Jack's left arm, and then Jack felt a cold pinprick of steel against his biceps.

The nail.

405

53

"Reaper Seven, this is Reaper Six."

Cary jerked as if he'd been slapped. Alex was calling on the command frequency, which meant that only he and Cary were privy to what was being said. Things were about to get interesting.

"Go for Seven," Cary said.

"Roger Seven," Alex said, "I've got some hinky shit here. That picture is definitely of an American. In fact, he's an agency case officer who was kidnapped in Beirut."

"No shit?" Cary said, his surprise causing him to break radio protocol.

"I shit you not, Reaper Seven. We are cleared hot to rescue him . . . as long as we also complete our assigned mission, over."

"Whiskey Tango Foxtrot," Cary said, feeling his neck beginning to flush. "What are we supposed to do with that?"

"I know," Alex said. "It's bullshit. Higher headquarters is trying to cover their ass and leaving us hanging out to dry in the process."

"What do we do?"

"Negative, Reaper Seven. It's what I'm going to do. As the on-scene commander, I'm going to exercise a bit of tactical discretion. You're the man on the ground and I trust your judgment. If you think we can save him, do it. If not, guide those bombs in, and we'll do what we can for the American after those launchers are smoking holes. No matter what happens, I'll take the heat."

In that moment, Cary would have walked through fire for Captain Alex Brown. The ODA team leader was behaving exactly as an officer was supposed to — giving his men the latitude to do what they did best while running interference. While Cary loved his captain, he still wasn't all that crazy about the hand that he'd just been dealt.

Five hundred meters to his right, a trio of cultists had the American on his back. Three hundred meters inside the compound, a black tarp snapped and popped in the desert wind, showing glimpses of the heavy-duty trucks with the boxy MLRS in their cargo beds. Less than fifty meters away, the soccer game continued unabated, the players drifting ever closer to his hide site. Oh, and he couldn't forget the sortie of F-15s streaking toward him as they prepared to loose their cargo of small-diameter bombs in just under ten minutes.

Cary closed his eyes, thinking through the various scenarios, trying to find a way to thread the needle. But he already knew that there was no magic solution. He either let the American die or didn't.

The choice was binary.

Snapping open his eyes, Cary keyed the radio transmit button and began to speak.

"All Reaper elements, this is Reaper Seven. Stand by for change of mission."

54

Clearing his throat, Jack spat at the hammer man's looming face. His aim couldn't have been better. A glob of blood-encrusted saliva blossomed on the man's cheek. The hammer that had been hanging in the air retreated as the man wiped the spit from his face with his shoulder.

Success.

Or at least success in the only way that Jack could currently measure it. Every second he wasn't nailed to a length of lumber was an additional second for someone or something to change the balance of the equation. In the grand scheme of rescues, the tiny ember of hope wasn't much, but Jack would take what he could get.

But his victory didn't last.

The hammer man cuffed Jack in the face with his closed left fist.

The fist with the nail.

Jack's teeth snapped together as blood

filled his mouth. Fire burned the length of his cheek where the nail had furrowed his skin. But his cheek was the least of Jack's concerns. The hammer man had shifted, now kneeling on Jack's forearm. The hammer blurred upward, and Jack knew there was no distracting his would-be executioner from his task.

So he didn't try.

Instead, Jack timed the hammer's swing and bridged, pushing off the wood while throwing his hips to the left in the moment before impact.

Then metal tore through flesh.

55

Cary paused mid-transmission as the event he'd been dreading finally happened. The opposing team's scrappy forward gave the dusty ball a full-legged boot that went sailing past the subpar keeper. The black-and-white ball kicked up a dust tail as it blazed an unwavering path toward the commando's hide site like it was a guided missile.

"Whatever you're going to do, do it fast," Jad whispered, his cheek welded to his rifle's stock.

The ball skipped along, the keeper pumping his legs in pursuit.

Five hundred meters and a world away, one of the thugs pinning the American to a wooden cross raised his hammer for a second swing while the CAS mission clock on Cary's Android read nine minutes and thirty-seven seconds.

Sunlight glittered across the hammer as it began its downward swing.

The ball bounced into the mesh camouflage netting concealing Cary's hide site and rebounded.

The pursuing cultist skidded to a halt.

"Boss?" Jad said, moving his rifle's safety selector switch to *fire*.

A black tarp flapped in the breeze, sheltering a forest of launchers.

Who lives?

Who dies?

"Cary!"

"Take the shot," Cary said.

56

The pain was exquisite. The tempered steel slid into his arm, parting skin and muscle like a knife sliding through butter. Jack screamed as the rational portion of his mind registered a deep *thunk* followed by the hammer man's grunt of surprise. It was only as the man toppled forward that Jack noticed he was missing the back of his head.

The hammer clattered to the ground next to Jack's arm. The arm that was nailed to a wooden cross.

Fuck.

Time stood still as the remaining executioners looked from their fallen comrade to Jack, as if he were somehow responsible. Then a second *thunk* and the man straddling Jack's hips tumbled to one side, blood spurting from his shoulder.

The man pinning Jack's arm crouched, lowering his silhouette.

Jack finally recognized the significance of

the *thunk*s. Someone with a suppressed high-powered rifle was trying to even the odds. Jack was still half nailed to a cross with a madman pinning his arm and a wounded fighter thrashing in the dirt beside him.

But his feet were free.

Groaning against the pain, Jack crossed his legs over the remaining fighter's neck, cinching them tight. The man grunted, threading an arm between Jack's legs in an attempt to steady himself. Jack struck like a mongoose, seizing the arm one-handed and yanking it toward his chest, pulling the fighter into a modified triangle choke. The man's eyes bulged as Jack tightened his legs, applying more pressure to the blood choke.

For a moment, Jack had him.

Then the man rocked to his left, dragging Jack's torso with him as he pitted their combined weight against the nail pinning Jack's flesh to the wood.

The pain was electric. An all-consuming agony he could taste. Jack screamed as he fought to hold the choke, bearing down with his thighs and hamstrings, desperately trying to ease the strain on his arm by engaging his core.

The man's eyes glassed over. He slumped farther to his left, dragging Jack with him.

The nail's head tore into flesh.

It was too much.

Caught between the nail and the man's dead weight, Jack loosened the choke in an attempt to ease the strain on his arm. The pain radiating down his shoulder subsided, but the man's eyes fluttered as blood rushed back to his oxygen-starved brain.

Then the look of animal fear on the fighter's face was replaced by something else.

Cunning.

With a snarl, the man gathered his legs and pushed off the ground, rocking from side to side. Each oscillation jarred Jack's arm against the nail, the agony stealing the air from his lungs. Jack tried to breathe through the pain, tried not to focus on the feel of his flesh ripping or the torrent of blood soaking his shirt.

But he couldn't.

The larger man had leverage and momentum on his side. He was growing stronger by the second, while Jack was getting weaker.

It was time for the unthinkable.

Gathering his courage, Jack coiled his legs to his chest, dragging the fighter closer. The man responded by exploding upward and to Jack's right, attempting to escape the

415

choke once and for all. But rather than constrain the man's motion, Jack amplified it. He kicked both legs straight up in a modified kip, using the man's momentum to wrench himself upward.

Flesh pulled away from metal with a hideous ripping sound and Jack nearly fainted. He'd intentionally shifted his body just before the nail had gone in to take the wound on the fleshy part of his arm near his triceps instead of through the bone.

He'd succeeded.

Sort of.

The arm ripped free in a gush of blood.

The sudden lack of resistance sent the fighter stumbling to his knees, Jack's legs still draped around his neck like a feather boa. A jiujitsu purist would have cinched down the triangle again, but Jack wasn't a martial artist.

He was a brawler.

So while his attacker wasted precious seconds clearing Jack's legs from his neck, Jack dedicated the time to a more pressing matter.

Finding the hammer.

Grabbing the mallet with his right hand, Jack swung the tool in a tight arc, catching the fighter in the knee. Bone crunched against metal, and the man screamed,

416

forgetting about Jack's legs as he pitched to the ground. Jack rode the fighter into the dirt, raining down blows as he worked his way from knee to thigh to arm and then, finally, to the ultimate prize.

The head.

Two strikes and it was done.

Jack clambered unsteadily to his feet, blood snaking down his arm in fat, wavering drops. For the moment, equal parts adrenaline and shock were shielding him from the worst of the pain. But those fickle allies would change allegiances soon enough.

He needed to stanch the blood flow.

Now.

Jack followed the crimson tracks up his arm and swallowed. His shirt was matted with blood, partially obscuring the wound, but Jack could still see the jagged tear running the length of his triceps. Gritting his teeth, Jack turned what was left of his shirt into a makeshift pressure bandage, looping the fabric around his wounded arm before tying off the knot one-handed.

As he put the finishing touches on the ad hoc compress, Jack had the disconcerting feeling that he was forgetting something. Like a buzzing static, his survival instincts were screaming at him, but Jack couldn't understand why. The light-headedness made it hard to concentrate, and he turned in a wobbly circle.

Then he understood.

The third attacker.

Jack had forgotten the unseen sniper's second victim. The fighter who'd been wounded in the shoulder. Now the forgotten man was on his feet, facing Jack. One arm dangled uselessly at his side, but the other held an AK-47 by its pistol grip.

The gunman was about ten feet away. Much too far for Jack to close the distance with a rush, even if he had the energy. More than close enough for the man to fire the rifle one-handed. The muzzle bobbled as the fighter struggled against shock and blood loss, but at this distance, he could fire blindfolded and still put a round through Jack's breastbone.

Jack roared, hurling the hammer while waiting for the inevitable punch in his chest. It never came. Instead, the man's head disintegrated in an explosion of brain matter and gore as Jack's hammer flew harmlessly by.

Jack stared dumbfounded as the fighter crumpled. A moment later, his overloaded brain registered the dull *thunk* that had accompanied the destruction along with the

418

more distinct *crack* of a rifle bullet breaking the sound barrier.

Turning in the direction of the sound, Jack raised a hand in thanks.

Then he grabbed the dead man's AK-47 and faced the compound's looming walls. He was alive, but this was far from over. One way or another, he was going to find Becka and Tommy. He didn't know where they'd been taken, but he knew someone who did.

And those people were inside the compound.

Wedging the AK-47 between his knees, Jack charged the bolt to the rear one-handed, ensuring a round was chambered, and then he put the weapon on safe.

As plans went, this wasn't his finest. But like his SEAL friends said, the only easy day was yesterday. Except yesterday hadn't been much of a cakewalk, either. Maybe he'd have better luck tomorrow.

If he lived that long.

57

"You got our precious cargo?" Cary said, fitting his rifle to his shoulder.

"Affirmative," Jad said. "He's a scrapper. I nailed two of the bad guys and he finished off the third with a hammer. Oh, shit. What is that crazy fucker doing?"

Cary panned his optic across Pet Cemetery just in time to see the man getting unsteadily to his feet.

"Turn around," Cary said, attempting to will the American back toward the desert and safety in the form of the remaining members of the A-team. "Turn around and get the hell out of there."

But the American did not get the hell out of there. Instead, he shook his head twice like a dog shedding water from his coat. Then he squared his shoulders and charged into the compound, one arm dangling limply at the shoulder.

Without waiting for his spotter-turned-

420

shooter to respond, Cary ignored the bare-chested man just ten meters away, who was still staring at the hide site in disbelief in favor of the men seventy-five meters distant. Men running toward the pile of neatly stacked AK-47s they'd abandoned next to their shirts.

Jad's rifle had been suppressed, but it was not silent and at least one of the soccer players recognized the sound for what it was. Cary took a breath, centered the red dot hovering in the center of his holographic sight on the man nearest the rifles, and squeezed the trigger.

The rifle kicked.

The man fell to the ground.

And all hell broke loose.

58

"Sit down, please," the greasy-haired man said, indicating a pair of camp chairs resting against the wall. "The imam will be with you shortly."

Darien shot a glance at Katerina and then settled into the closest seat as she took one on the far side of the room.

For a fortress so meticulously constructed, the furnishings were rather threadbare. The revetments fortifying the compound consisted of reinforced concrete fronted by tons of bulldozed rocks and soil. The access points were manned by competent-looking shooters and crew-served weapons while pricey surveillance cameras were strategically positioned to observe high-speed avenues of approach.

Just inside the compound, a motor pool showcased a fleet of well-maintained vehicles, many of them outfitted with heavy machine guns, recoilless rifles, or grenade launchers. Darien had even noticed a collection of American Humvees. When it came to weapons and equipment, the cult had spared no expense.

The same couldn't be said for sittable chairs and couches.

Darien shifted his weight, trying to get comfortable. Katerina also squirmed, but Darien imagined this had more to do with positioning her hidden pistol for a quick draw than easing the burden on her posterior.

Not that he blamed her.

While Darien knew that the madmen living in the compound played an outsized role in the general's equally mad plan to forever alter the balance of power in the Middle East, he'd never imagined meeting Ahmadi's pawns face-to-face. Though he'd grown up in Iran under a Shia-inspired theocracy, Darien, like many Iranians his age, wasn't particularly religious. What he'd done as an intelligence operative had been for the betterment of his country, not the power-mad men who ruled her.

But this compound seemed like a distillation of what the Ayatollah and his ilk wanted for Iran if left to their own devices. A select few who heard directly from Allah giving instructions to the masses, who had no choice but to do their bidding. From Darien's perspective, these fools would certainly accomplish at least one of their goals. This would be the site of a grand battle, of that Darien was certain.

He was just as certain that he had no intention of being here when it happened.

"Ah, Darien, thank you for joining us. I hope your journey was pleasant."

The magnetism radiating from the man who strode into the room was palpable. Though he went to great pains to wear the traditional robes and black turban in order to appear like the reincarnated imam he was pretending to be, there was nothing poor or downtrodden in the quality of his wardrobe. Clearly the money saved by skimping on simple furnishings had been reinvested in Mahdi Husseini's person.

Then again, Darien supposed that an imam reborn after a twelve-hundred-year absence needed to look the part.

As had been the case with the other male cultists he'd encountered thus far, Husseini swept by Katerina without acknowledging her presence in the slightest. Within the fortress's four walls, women didn't even warrant inclusion into the category of seen but not heard. That distinction was reserved for children. Here, outside of domestic duties and procreation, women were nonentities.

Katerina wasn't acknowledged, because to these Neanderthals, she didn't exist.

"Pleasant enough," Darien said as he stood and extended his hand. "But still unexpected."

"Oh," Husseini said. "How so?"

"I was originally supposed to deliver the American to your men," Darien said. "Not bring him here myself. I'm curious why the plan changed."

Darien was not just curious — he was desperate to understand what the cult leader was thinking. Or, perhaps more important, what new machinations the cult leader's puppet master, General Ahmadi, was scheming. If his goal was just Darien's death, the Quds Force commander could have ordered Husseini's minions to take care of business in the middle of the desert, far from prying eyes.

No, something else was at play here. Something much more insidious.

At Darien's request, Katerina had put the Beirut safe house where the American scientist and her child were being held under surveillance, but she hadn't yet sent her mercenaries to recover them. Putting himself in the old fox's place, Darien had to

425

believe that Ahmadi had some sort of check-in procedure in place with his Quds Force henchmen.

The Iranian vessel wasn't due to dock for several more hours, which meant that Darien had to play this game very, very shrewdly. Act too soon, and Ahmadi would know that he'd been betrayed. Knowing the Iranian, he would probably exact his vengeance on the most valuable commodity Darien had to offer his new employer — the American scientist. But if he waited too long, Darien risked forfeiting something even more consequential.

His life.

"That plan hasn't so much changed," Husseini said, scratching the luxurious black beard that covered his chin, "as become better."

"How so?" Darien said.

From her forgotten corner on the other side of the room, Katerina uncrossed her legs, placing both feet flat on the floor. For a moment, her pale blue eyes found Darien's. Then she stared off into space as if she hadn't a clue what was transpiring.

Darien kept his expression suitably nonchalant as his heart rate accelerated. Katerina didn't get jumpy. If she, too, felt the tension-saturated air, something wasn't right.

"Are you a believer?" Husseini said, his brown eyes peering into Darien's as if trying to discern his thoughts.

"You'll have to be more specific," Darien said. "I believe in a great many things."

Darien kept his tone light, judging distances. The distance from his hand to the pistol secreted in his belt. The distance from the two goons flanking Husseini and the door behind him.

And, most important, the distance to the car.

On the whole, the distances did not favor him.

That needed to change.

"In me," Husseini said. "Do you believe that I am one of the Twelve Imams reborn?"

The cult leader asked the question with the kind of offhand manner one might use to inquire about the weather. Darien wasn't fooled. This was exactly the type of nonsense that had made him caution his MOIS superiors about getting involved with Ahmadi's mad plot to begin with. Unfortunately, here again the general had prevailed. With a little encouragement, Ahmadi believed that he could persuade the cult to become a thorn in the Americans' side. A powder keg of fanatics just waiting for a match.

Then the Quds Force commander had envisioned a way to further up the stakes while remaking the entire Middle East in the process. After all, if the cultists were dead set on triggering Armageddon, why not help them achieve their goal? As Ahmadi had patiently explained to the supreme leader of Iran, even if they failed, the cultists' actions would force the American President's hand. He would have to either make the unpopular decision to increase his military's Syrian footprint or, more likely, abandon the region altogether.

Either outcome was a win, but to Ahmadi's way of thinking, an American occupation of Syria was the ultimate prize. In addition to miring the United States in yet another unwinnable war, this scenario would allow Ahmadi to build on what he'd perfected in Iraq — the wholesale slaughter of American servicemembers.

But if Husseini and his band of idiots actually succeeded, Syria would become the flashpoint for a firestorm that would engulf the entire Middle East, with Iran's greatest enemy as ground zero. Apparently, even this audacious plan hadn't been enough for Ahmadi. Rather than simply light the powder keg's fuse and hope for the best, the general wanted to guarantee a U.S. response.

In this regard, Ryan, the U.S. intelligence officer, had been an answer to prayer. By handing him over to the cultists to be tortured and executed, Ahmadi was ensuring that, whatever happened next, Husseini would have an American target on his back.

And now Darien was standing squarely within the bull's-eye.

"What I believe," Darien said, "is that I brought the American to you. Now, I believe I'll be leaving."

"Of course, of course," Husseini said, grinning. His white teeth were a startling contrast to the charcoal-black of his beard. "But I'd like you to witness something first."

Darien thought of the American and the crucifixion field. Of course. Ahmadi would want to teach Darien a final lesson in the power the general could wield over those who displeased him. A way of ensuring Darien's further compliance. It wasn't enough for Husseini's cultists to video the American's brutal death. Darien's Quds Force commander nemesis would want him to watch in person.

"What do you want to show me?" Darien said, thinking he already knew the answer.

He thought wrong.

59

Cary's **FN SCAR** heavy rifle also sported an interceptor suppressor, but the 7.62-millimeter round still gave a telltale *crack* as it broke the sound barrier. Even so, it was still a hell of a lot quieter than the sound of a fully automatic AK-47.

Like the one rocking and rolling less than seventy-five meters away.

Cary was an exceptional shot, and he dropped the first three soccer players before they reached the stack of AK-47s. But he was still human. The fourth man zigged when Cary thought he was going to zag, and the round meant for the cultist's heart struck his shoulder instead.

The man fell to the ground, bowling over the stacked rifles. Cary put two more into his prone form, but not before the fighter grabbed an AK and squeezed the trigger. The rifle spat half a magazine harmlessly over Cary's head, but the damage was done.

Every swinging Richard in the compound now knew something was amiss.

Men poured from the gated entrance like fire ants defending their mound.

Cary selected his targets with analytical precision, panning his red dot from man to man, making each round count. But he might as well have been pissing into the wind. There were simply too many.

This wasn't working.

And then Jad gave a wet-sounding gurgle. Cary looked over to see his spotter and best friend slouch over the lip of the hide site, a rapidly expanding bull's-eye of red staining his shirt. Cary let his sling catch his rifle. He grabbed Jad and pulled the limp Green Beret into the relative safety offered by the hide site's dirt walls.

Then he keyed the radio.

"All Reaper elements," Cary said, as he frantically ripped a pressure bandage from Jad's trauma kit, "this is Seven. Avalanche, Avalanche, Avalanche."

The radio came alive with excited voices, but Cary didn't reply.

He was too busy trying to save his friend's life.

Sergeant First Class Brian Martin didn't bother confirming his team sergeant's

Avalanche call. The background noise of AK-47s firing seemed confirmation enough. Instead, he stabbed a gloved finger on the Reaper 7 icon displayed on the LCD screen in front of him. Beneath his feet, the gun's hydraulic-enabled servos rotated the 120-millimeter cannon to the required heading.

Originally developed in response to the tragedy that occurred at Combat Outpost Keating, the EMTAS, or enhanced mortar target system, was a GPS-aligned, 120-millimeter mortar system controlled by a tactical computer. The gun was capable of servicing multiple targets in a 360-degree-range fan in less than ten seconds. In this incarnation of the formidable weapon, the gun's frame was mounted to a JLTV, or joint light tactical vehicle, flatbed truck. Though the configuration looked more Mad Max than high-tech, Brian didn't care. For the first time in his Special Forces career, he had a mobile, dedicated fire support asset allocated solely to his team.

And he intended to put it to use in spectacular fashion.

"Avalanche," Brian said. "Fire mission. HE quick fuse. Five rounds fire for effect. Charge two."

To either side, Brian's fellow gun crew members, Staff Sergeants Greg Glass and

Jeff Mishler, were already moving. Grabbing a thirty-five-pound mortar from the stack next to the gun, Greg hoisted the munition onto his shoulder, verifying the fuse, charge, and round type. Jeff stood next to him, the second shell in his hands.

Waiting.

Brian confirmed the gun tube's azimuth with his own compass, double-checked the target's grid coordinates, and validated that the cannon's target line was clear of obstructions.

All three actions took just seconds.

"Gun up," Brian said. "Hang it."

"HE," Greg said, "charge two, quick fuse."

Brian verified a final time that the round, fusing, and charge combination that Greg had selected mirrored what he'd requested. Then the Green Beret gave the command they'd all been waiting for.

"Fire."

Greg released the round into the gun's gaping maw, tracing his now-empty fingers along the tube as he ducked into a crouch. Brian followed suit, hunching beneath the meager cover offered by the tactical computer as he keyed the transmit button on the radio and said, "Shot over."

A moment later, the gun belched, and the mortar shell rocketed skyward. The recoil was enough to rock the five-thousand-pound truck against its suspension, but the three men didn't notice.

They were too busy feeding rounds into the cannon's hungry mouth.

60

"I want to show you the apocalypse," Husseini said.

"Thank you for the offer," Darien said, "but I'm going to have to decline all the same."

"Oh, but I insist," Husseini said. "Or, more specifically, your General Ahmadi insists."

As the cult leader spoke, his two bodyguards fingered the rifles strapped to their chests. The gesture's meaning wasn't difficult to discern. Darien kept his eyes on Husseini, but the whole of his attention was focused on the bodyguards. His lips formed a germane response, but his mind was calculating angles and times. Notably, the time it would take to interdict the bodyguards and the angle of the shot required to render them a nonentity.

His calculations weren't reassuring.

Both men wore perfectly adjusted three-point tactical slings. Either guard would easily have time to pivot his rifle to a firing position long before Darien cleared his concealed pistol. If the odds were one against one, Darien might have chanced it. But with two guards, the math didn't add up. Any way he figured it, one of the guards would get off a shot.

Perhaps both.

At this range, that was two shots too many.

From behind the men, Katerina gave a bored yawn.

To the untrained eye, she was the epitome of ease — a cat lazing in a puddle of sunlight. But to Darien, the Russian's lithe body vibrated tension. Katerina altered the equation, but not enough. The margins were still too slim. Darien had two choices: One, pull up a chair and watch as madmen brought about the end of the world. Or two, do something to shift the balance of power.

He chose two.

"I'd be delighted to be your guest," Darien said, taking a step toward the cult leader while loosening the carbon-fiber blade strapped to his forearm.

"Excellent," Husseini said. His surprised expression suggested that he'd expected Darien to choose differently. "Launch your little birds."

The cult leader directed his command to a wiry man hovering near the room's single doorway. Darien had originally dismissed him as a chief of staff or something of the like. The man had a hummingbird's mannerisms, and his slender fingers were constantly in motion.

At the sound of Husseini's voice, the man's face brightened. Unclipping the handheld radio at his belt, the man mashed the transmit button and issued a series of instructions. Darien couldn't follow exactly what the man said, but he knew where this was heading. He flicked his gaze toward Katerina.

Then he moved toward Husseini.

"Imam, I —" Darien said, drawing the room's eyes to him.

Except for the pale blue pair attached to the forgotten woman lounging in the corner.

The bodyguard closest to Husseini smoothly slid between Darien and the cult leader. A sound decision if this were a crowded Baghdad street and Darien a raucous protester. But this was not that. By blocking Darien's access to Husseini, the bodyguard had inadvertently stepped into his fellow protector's gunline. Much like the Israeli police officers Darien had encountered earlier, the bodyguard had completely misjudged Darien's intentions.

Extending his right hand to draw the man's eye, Darien gave his left wrist a quick twist.

The blade strapped against his arm slipped into his fingers.

"Stop," the bodyguard said, further closing the distance between them.

Plastering a confused look on his face, Darien did as ordered. Inwardly, he smiled as the bodyguard moved to within knife range, placing his outstretched hand against Darien's chest.

Everything was going exactly as planned.

Right up until the moment the world exploded.

61

At the "shot over" call, Cary stretched his body across Jad, sheltering the wounded man as best as he could. Cary had just enough time to wish that he'd shoveled the hole a bit deeper when thunder fell from the sky.

"Should have dug the hole deeper," Jad said, echoing Cary's thoughts. His normally brown face was an appalling shade of white from blood loss, but he still managed a smile.

"Always the Monday-morning quarterback," Cary said, cinching down the pressure bandage on Jad's shoulder. Another round detonated, showering both men with sand and grit. The bullet wound looked like a through-and-through, but Cary wasn't about to start counting his blessings just yet.

"Reaper Seven, Reaper Twelve, rounds complete."

"Reaper Seven, roger," Cary said, acknowledging Brian's transmission. Leading with his SCAR's muzzle, Cary popped his head above the earthen berm.

Hellfire and brimstone waited.

Each fin-stabilized 120-millimeter round was packed with high explosives contained in a shearable metal casing. When the shell detonated, superheated gases expanded outward at several times the speed of sound, turning the metal casing into shrapnel with a lethality radius of greater than seventy feet.

The first five rounds had more than done their job.

Where before the soccer field had been swarming with fighters, now only unrecognizable bits of flesh remained. The compound's main gate drunkenly hung on battered hinges two hundred meters distant. The ground oozed tendrils of gray smoke, and the accompanying stench and gore was something straight out of Dante's *Inferno*. The hide site was no longer in danger of being overrun.

That was the good news.

The not-so-good news was that cultists were racing along the compound's walls to man crew-served weapons as the rumble of engines filled the air. Cary had been hoping that the pure unadulterated violence visited by the fire-for-effect mission would have had a pacifying effect on the cultists.

Instead, the compound looked like a hornet's nest that had just been poked with a stick.

"How's it look?" Jad whispered.

Cary started to reply when the radio interrupted him.

"Reaper Seven, this is Reaper Thirteen. I've got activity in sector seven. I say again, activity in sector seven."

Sector seven. The launch pads.

Not good.

"Thirteen, this is Seven," Cary said. "Can you be more specific?"

"Roger that, Seven. Teams of men are running to the trucks and tearing down the tarps. I think they're going to launch, over."

"Seven copies all," Cary said. "Reaper Twelve, immediate suppression. Target reference point Bravo Nine."

"Reaper Twelve acknowledges immediate suppression Bravo Nine."

Cary could picture Brian selecting the TRP and the gun rotating on its hydraulic struts in response. Rumor had it that the automated system driving the EMTAS could lay the gun even faster than the world's premier mortar men from the Ranger Regiment. For the first time in his

441

life, Cary found himself rooting for a machine in the perennial man/machine contest. By now Greg should be hanging the first round.

It was going to be close.

"Seven, Twelve, shot, over."

"Shot out," Cary replied automatically, his eyes glued to the target area.

In the truck park, the cylindrical containers housing the missiles were elevating from the backs of the semis. The deadly cargo pivoted skyward as swarming groups of men ripped covers from launch tubes and cleared the remaining tarps from the missiles' flight path.

"Splash, over."

"Splash, out," Cary said.

The target area erupted in flashes of orange and yellow as the rounds fell from heaven like God's hammer. Secondary explosions tore through the staging area, sending crew-served weapons and bodies cartwheeling through the air. Thick, greasy smoke billowed into bright blue sky like India ink spilled across a canvas of cobalt.

"Seven, Twelve, rounds complete, over."

Once again, Brian and his mortar men were precisely on target.

But they were also a second too late.

Four telephone pole–sized missiles clawed

their way skyward, leaving sheets of rolling flame in their wake.

62

It took Darien a moment to process the significance of the earsplitting thunderclaps. Then the sound of automatic-weapons fire clarified things. Someone was attacking the compound. Someone with the wherewithal to coordinate an assault employing both direct and indirect fire.

Americans.

It had to be.

The unexpected noise caused everyone to look toward the source of the explosions. Well, almost everyone. With a snarl, Darien plunged his knife into the side of the lead bodyguard's neck, twisting the blade and opening a horrific wound channel. Blood fountained from the man's neck, but Darien ignored him.

The bodyguard was already dead on his feet.

Instead, Darien slid past the gasping man to his startled principal. For the first time since he'd made the cleric's acquaintance, Husseini seemed less than sure of himself. The confidence that normally blazed from his eyes was gone, replaced by a look utterly foreign to his charismatic face.

Fear.

"Wait," Husseini said, his hand fluttering toward his pocket like a startled bird. "I —"

Whatever the cult leader was going to say next was lost to all eternity.

Or perhaps not.

If he really was an imam reborn, he'd certainly find his way back in another millennium or two. Even so, Husseini's eloquent speech became much harder to decipher after Darien opened several holes in his throat.

Then there were two men in the throes of death at Darien's feet.

Turning from the cleric, Darien saw that Katerina no longer lounged in the chair. Instead, the former Russian SVR officer was throttling the life out of the scrawny man with the radio. She'd used the cover of the exploding artillery rounds to fire both barrels of her Derringer-style pistol, reducing the second bodyguard to a slab of meat.

Unfortunately, that left no rounds for the cleric's personal assistant. But a lack of ammunition hadn't deterred the Russian.

Instead, she'd tackled the fleeing man and now had him in a rear naked chokehold. Already his struggles had grown more feeble. Within minutes, the hummingbird of a man would join the cleric in the afterlife.

But those were minutes Darien didn't have.

"Let him go," Darien said, tapping Katerina on the shoulder.

For a moment she just stared at him, her face quizzical. Then she released her hold and rolled clear.

The man's eyes, which had been in the midst of closing, fluttered open. His terrified look turned to gratitude. He opened his mouth but found himself unable to speak for much the same reasons as his dead master.

Darien wiped the blade on the dying man's shirt and slid it back up his sleeve.

Then he pulled his lover to her feet.

"What now?" Katerina said, her accent sending shivers down his spine.

"Freedom."

63

Israeli Restricted Operating Zone Alpha
Mediterranean Sea

"All elements, this is flight lead, knock it off. I say again, knock it off."

"Daisy copies, knock it off."

Natalie "Daisy" Smith unhooked the oxygen mask from her flight helmet and smiled. To judge from his voice, flight lead was pissed. He should be. She'd just handed him his ass twice in a row.

The first time, Natalie had held back out of respect for her Israeli counterparts, allowing the furball to go several minutes longer than necessary. But the cocky Israeli pilot had lasted all of ninety seconds in the second go-round.

Natalie was on a roll.

Truthfully, she could have bagged her counterpart within the first thirty seconds after the break, but hadn't. She was a liaison pilot, and her job was to improve coopera-

447

tion between the U.S. and Israeli Air Force. You didn't do that by downing their best pilot straight out of the gate.

The second time was on him. The two fighters had begun the engagement with a head-to-head pass, and the Israeli pilot had hesitated a moment too long before commencing his turn after the break. It was a stupid mistake, and Natalie made sure he knew it. International cooperation was all fine and good, but at the end of the day, the men and women piloting the F-35 Lightning II were fighter pilots, not kindergarten teachers. In the words of her favorite instructor at weapons school, if you couldn't stand the heat, fly tankers.

"Daisy and Gnat, climb to Angels 30 on a heading of 270 to rejoin the flight. In the meantime, Slammer, please tell me how Daisy smoked you before I even turned inbound."

"Angels 30 for Daisy," Natalie said with another smile as she advanced the throttle while pulling her side-mounted stick rearward. "And don't be so hard on Slammer. I'm sure he was just taking it easy on me."

A series of chuckles echoed across the airwaves as the other two Israelis, both men, hazed poor Slammer.

To be fair, Slammer probably had been

taking it easy on her. Standing barely five feet, two inches tall with Daisy as a call sign meant that Natalie was perpetually under-estimated. But contrary to the public's im-age of tall, strapping fighter jocks, Natalie's slight frame was built for the crushing g-forces that were part of her job.

Unlike men, women carried the majority of their weight and muscle in their hips and legs. This was of particular importance to a fighter pilot, since combating g-forces required a strong lower body capable of forcing blood back into the head and heart. A typical male's heavy chest and shoulders looked great at the beach but were worth jack shit in a dogfight.

Natalie had made a career out of being underestimated. Graduating in the top ten percent of her flight school class, she'd had her choice of aircraft. She'd started with F-16s, but had made the transition to F-35s as soon as the fifth-generation fighters were fielded.

Ten years later, she was coming off a rota-tion as an F-35 demonstration pilot looking for a change. Maybe a permanent one. She'd already put in her discharge paper-work with the intention of marrying her fiancé and starting a family. But when her assignments officer had come to her with one last deployment, to Israel as an exchange pilot, no less, she'd agreed.

After all, it wasn't every day you got to make some of the finest pilots in the world eat crow.

Natalie edged the throttle forward another detent even though her closing speed on the two-ship formation five thousand feet above and four miles distant was more than fast enough. Though she'd been flying the F-35 for more than a decade, she still loved to hear the single Pratt & Whitney F135's afterburner roar.

Producing just over forty thousand pounds of thrust made the turbofan growling between her legs the most powerful jet engine in the world. With a flick of her wrist, Natalie could send her fighter screaming to one-point-six times the speed of sound. Not setting the beast loose at least once a flight was the equivalent of puttering around at forty miles per hour in a Formula 1.

Over the course of her career, Natalie had piloted half a dozen jets, but none of them compared to the combination of raw power and matchless grace offered by the F-35. Her father had once asked her what the jet was like and Natalie had answered that the plane was part ballerina, part racehorse, and all killer. With the cloud-free skies above her, a blue Mediterranean Sea below her, and a snarling engine reverberating in her chest, there was literally nowhere on earth Natalie would rather be.

"Viper flight, this is Weasel Main, come to Angels 40, heading 330, immediately, over."

The unusual call from the Israeli ground control radar tracking the flight came across the net just as Natalie and her wingman, Gnat, slid in behind Slammer and flight lead Rhino in a fluid-four formation. Rhino acknowledged the call and the four ships collectively turned to the new heading.

Once again, Natalie was reminded of how small Israel really was. At two hundred ninety miles wide by eighty-five miles long, the country was barely the size of New Jersey. This meant that remaining in Israeli airspace while flying a fighter required near-constant turns. As such, the flight of four Lightning IIs were currently over the Mediterranean Sea. Conducting air-to-air training in Israeli airspace would have been impossible, and though relations were improving with the Jewish state's neighbors, an overflight by four fifth-generation stealth fighters would not have been welcomed.

"Weasel Main, this is Viper flight," Rhino said. "Please state the nature of our deviation."

451

Up until now, the communications had been conducted entirely in English. This was both for Natalie's benefit and because the international language of aviation was still English. But flight following's response was in Hebrew, and while Natalie didn't speak the language, the tenseness of the transmission wasn't lost on her.

After waiting for flight following to finish, Natalie keyed the radio from her throttle, transmitting on the flight's internal air-to-air frequency.

"Rhino, this is Daisy. Everything okay?"

"Negative," Rhino said. "Early-warning radar is picking up some kind of bogeys with inbound trajectories tracking toward Tel Aviv from heading 315. We need to clear the airspace so the Iron Dome can go to work."

Natalie clicked the transmit button twice in response, but her fighter-pilot mind was already picturing trajectories. Bogeys coming in from the northwest made zero sense. Nothing but ocean stretched to the northwest of Tel Aviv. Touching a button on her multipurpose display, Natalie slaved her sensor suite down the heading flight following had dictated.

The F-35 deservedly received a lot of attention for its stealth capabilities, but that wasn't the reason why the aircraft was such a game changer. In fact, its elder brother, the F-22 Raptor, was both stealthier and a better all-around air-dominance aircraft. No, the real secret to the Lightning II's sauce lay with its sensor packages.

In a first for a weapons platform anywhere, the F-35's mission computer correlated data from its distributed aperture system radar, electro-optical targeting system, and active electronically scanned array radar into one coherent picture that was projected onto the pilot's visor. Rather than dividing her time between a threat warning system, an infrared targeting pod, and a radar display, Natalie was presented with just one image that was a culmination of everything her aircraft's sensor package could "see."

But that was just the tip of the iceberg.

In addition to information gathered by its onboard suite of sensors, each F-35 was data-linked to its wingman's sensor feeds as well. When Natalie followed the cueing dots in her helmet-mounted display system, she "saw" a compilation of the best sensor picture from each aircraft in her flight.

What greeted her wasn't good.

Four bogeys were on the deck hurtling across the ocean at wavetop level.

And they were headed straight for Tel Aviv.

64

"Rhino, this is Daisy," Natalie said, still watching the four airborne entities tracking across her field of view. "What are we looking at?"

The flight of four F-35s was currently flying the reciprocal course of the inbound bogeys, away from Tel Aviv on a northwesterly heading, while the unidentified objects were generally tracking to the southeast. Though forty thousand feet of altitude and fifty miles of lateral separation segregated Natalie from the bogeys, her F-35 was undeterred.

The data fusion engine that drove the sensor integration in Natalie's aircraft had already tagged each object, providing a direction of travel and airspeed beneath the icons. This had Natalie a bit confused. The four objects were traveling at about four hundred knots on a straight and level flight path. Much too slow, with too flat of a ballistic trajectory, to be rockets or guided missiles.

Then the bogey flight rose as one, ascending from just above the water to a height of about one thousand feet off the water.

"Don't know, Daisy," Rhino said. "But the Iron Dome has them. Get ready to see Israeli technology at work."

"Roger that," Natalie said. She was more than familiar with the Iron Dome's awesome capabilities. The antimissile system really was a technological marvel — capable of downing the cheap Katyusha rockets the Palestinian terrorists lobbed into Israel at a fraction of the cost of the much larger Patriot systems. Truth be told, she was actually looking forward to watching the fireworks. After all, it wasn't every day you got a bird's-eye view of one of the most formidable antiaircraft systems ever developed in action.

But what happened next wasn't the stuff of marketing commercials.

After verifying once more that the sortie of four F-35s was clear of the danger zone, Weasel Main told Rhino to stand by. He had no sooner acknowledged than five fingers of flame vaulted skyward from the Israeli coast. The Lightning's onboard computer instantly marked each Iron Dome interceptor missile, showing direction, speed, and cueing data.

But rather than intercept the four missiles, the streaks of fire flew right on by.

"What the hell?" Natalie said, as six more streaks of flame clawed their way skyward. But like their predecessors, these interceptors also buzzed straight past their intended targets, drawing gray smoke trails across the azure sky.

Natalie was about to key her transmit button, but Weasel Main beat her to the punch. A burst of Hebrew jammed the airwaves and Rhino responded in kind. But that was fine. It didn't take a genius to understand the ground controller's intent. A moment later, Rhino transmitted on the air-to-air frequency, confirming her suspicions.

"Viper flight, this is Rhino, flight following is asking us to take a closer look. Stay on me. We're going to see what's what."

"Daisy copies all," Natalie said, cranking her Lightning over in a tight turn to the right as she stayed on flight lead's wing. Her carefree training mission had just morphed into something decidedly more serious.

65

Jack leaned against a slab of dirt-encrusted concrete to stay upright. The ground bucked beneath him and artillery rained down across the compound. The same compound he'd willingly run back into instead of escaping.

Mr. C. was going to have a field day with this mission debrief.

Sheltering beneath the roof's thin metal overhang, Jack set the AK on the ground and tightened the strips of cloth winding around his injured arm. As wounds went, this one wasn't his most serious, but it was probably the ghastliest. The arm throbbed with an unholy agony. Every jostle or bump only further enraged his already angry nerve endings, and Jack had neither the materials nor the time to fashion a sling.

Until he found Becka and Tommy, his

457

only choice was to suck it up and keep moving.

Even so, he couldn't help but think that he was due for some good luck. Moving through a compound full of armed men with a hole in one arm was challenging enough. It'd be great not to have to dodge artillery at the same time.

Retying the bandage gave both his body and mind a chance to regroup. For the first time, Jack tried to piece together what exactly had happened out in the killing field. Someone had saved his life, and that someone had been attached to a precision long gun. Probably a suppressed one since rifle reports hadn't accompanied the first two shots. A skillfully employed suppressed rifle suggested an American Special Operations unit. This in turn probably meant that the indirect fire barrages pummeling the compound also originated from a friendly unit.

But even the most skillfully directed artillery was still an area weapon. Unlike a sniper who killed with a surgeon's precision, unguided shells had no way of distinguishing friend from foe. Jack's rescuers had probably expected him to escape, not run back into a potential kill zone. But they'd still fired the barrage, which suggested operational priorities that outranked Jack's survival.

Like maybe their own.

To avoid becoming an accidental casualty, Jack needed to coordinate with whoever was on the other side of the American firepower. Unfortunately, that was easier said than done. The phone Gavin had outfitted with the Eye of Sauron was long gone, and he hadn't had the time to search his executioners. Reacting had kept Jack from getting the rest of his limbs permanently attached to a cross, but perhaps now he needed to exercise a bit of tactical patience.

He already had one new hole.

He wasn't in a hurry to add more.

Maybe it was time to give the new, less impulsive Jack a try.

But the AK-47-carrying fighter rounding the corner had other plans.

The man skidded to a halt and screamed out a question in Arabic. Jack shrugged. The man stepped closer and repeated himself. His gaze shifted from Jack's face to his bandaged arm, eyes widening at the blood-soaked fabric.

Then he went for his gun.

66

The fighter had been running with his rifle, holding it with the barrel pointed toward his left foot. This meant he first had to swing the AK up and to the right to bring the muzzle onto target, buying Jack precious seconds.

Jack rushed him, choosing to close the distance with his attacker instead of reaching for his own rifle. He might not be a master tactician capable of moving men and machines across the battlefield, but his aptitude for brawling would never be in dispute. Jack was down an arm, but he still had two hundred twenty pounds of rage.

Jack slammed into the fighter like a locomotive demolishing a car on a railroad crossing. As their bodies collided, Jack resisted the urge to punch his elbow through the man's solar plexus. Instead, he pinned the man's rifle against his midsection while driving with his legs.

The pair crashed into the building's concrete wall, and Jack ignored the searing jolt from his wrist. The fighter's head rebounded with a wet-sounding *thunk.* His eyes fluttered and his grip on the rifle loosened, but he wasn't done yet. Shifting his one-handed grip from the rifle to the nape of the man's neck, Jack jerked the fighter downward while rocketing his knee upward into the man's jaw.

Bone shattered and blood flowed.

Releasing the fighter, Jack grabbed his own AK-47. He considered firing a burst into the man's chest, but didn't. Though sporadic automatic-weapons fire still echoed beyond the walls, the inside of the compound was strangely quiet in the aftermath of the second artillery barrage.

The last thing Jack wanted to do was draw attention to himself.

Instead, he reversed the rifle and drove the wooden shoulder rest into the fighter's shattered face. After the second blow, the man quit moving, but Jack gave him two more just to be sure.

Hand-to-hand combat wasn't for the faint of heart.

Then again, neither was crucifixion.

Setting the rifle aside, Jack frisked the fighter, moving from pocket to pocket until his searching fingers found what they sought — a phone. Jack used the fighter's finger to unlock the device, and then dialed. Three rings later, a familiar voice answered.

"Hello?"

"Hey, Gavin," Jack said, wedging the phone between his shoulder and ear as he picked up his rifle. "Got a minute?"

67

"Jack? Oh my god — is it really you?"

"It's me, buddy," Jack said, the portly keyboard warrior provoking a smile. "I need your help. I —"

"Hang on a second, Jack. Mr. Clark is here. He said that if you called again and I didn't let him know, he'd reach down my throat and tear out my tonsils. I think he means it, Jack."

"Nah, Clark's just a big teddy bear," Jack said.

"The hell you say?"

"Oh, hey, Mr. C.," Jack said. "I didn't realize you were on the line."

"Goddamn, Junior, but it's good to hear your voice. The Baghdad chief of station had a walk-in who dumped some pretty nasty pictures of you on his desk. I don't have to tell you that folks here have been a bit worried."

In spite of everything, Jack smiled. The

infamous Mr. John Terrence Clark was worried about him. The man who'd cut his teeth stalking NVA in the jungles of Vietnam was capable of human emotion. Who knew?

But just as quickly, Jack's mirth faded. When Mr. C. showed concern, the average person was already shaking in terror. If Clark was worried, Jack was probably in more trouble than he knew.

And that was saying something.

"I had a rough go of it, Mr. C.," Jack said. "And I'm not out of the woods yet. I don't even know where I'm at —"

"Syria. You're in Syria, son. We've already got your phone locked down, but we were guessing you were there even before you called. Or at least we were hoping you were — Jesus, but you gave us a scare. Anyway, Gavin compromised several phones in the vicinity of your kidnapping. We tracked two groups of folks leaving Beirut. One got on a plane to Iran, but the other headed for Syria. We can do story time later. Right now I need you to unass that compound. You've got friendlies on two sides. Head south, and I'll coordinate a linkup."

"Sorry, sir," Jack said, "no can do. There are two innocents still at risk — a mother and child. The man who knows where they're being held is inside this compound. I'm not leaving without him."

"Junior, listen to me. Things are at play here I can't go into. You need to trust me, son. Get the hell out of that compound."

"Can't do it, Mr. C."

"Goddamn it, Jack. You're putting your father in a no-win situation. Your father. Do you understand what I'm saying?"

Jack looked up into the cloudless sky, searching for the UAV he was certain was orbiting somewhere overhead. He saw nothing but blue, but that wasn't surprising. Jack knew that many drones had declassified loitering altitudes of greater than fifty thousand feet. That put the bird at more than ten miles away. No way he'd see it with his naked eye.

Even so, knowing his old man was probably watching brought Jack a strange sense of comfort. One of the many reasons Jack Patrick Ryan, Sr., was such a great man was that he was exactly the same person in public and in private. But growing up as the son of a great man was not an easy yoke to bear.

Jack loved his father, but he was also terrified of him. No, that wasn't right. Jack would never fear his father, but he was terrified of not living up to his father's reputa-

465

tion. This was the burden borne by the sons of all great men, and while Senior had done everything in his power to lighten that burden, its crushing weight was never far from Jack's mind.

But in this moment, Jack felt an unaccustomed lightness. His father was watching.

Good.

Let him see.

"I read you loud and clear, Mr. C., but you always said that a great commander knows when to trust the guy on the ground. I'm the guy on the ground, sir. I need you to trust me."

The ensuing silence was short, but significant. Then John Terrence Clark spoke.

"Okay, Jack. I trust you, son. Do what you need to do."

"Thank you, Mr. C. And please give Dad a message for me. Tell him that sometimes a good man has to be willing to pay a price for doing what's right. He'll understand. Now I've gotta get to work, and I could use Gavin's help. Please ask him to get his *Lord of the Rings* groove on. It would be great if I could talk to those friendlies you keep mentioning. I'll leave the line open. Jack out."

Jack dropped the phone into his shirt

466

pocket. He knew there'd be some explaining to do at the inevitable post-mission debriefing, but that assumed he somehow managed to escape the compound alive.

At this point, that wasn't a foregone conclusion.

68

Israeli Restricted Operating Zone Alpha
Mediterranean Sea

Fighter pilots at their core were visual
animals. Like a falcon soaring over a rabbit,
they have an innate desire to see their
quarry with their own two eyes, regardless
of what the world's most advanced mission
computer coupled with a next-generation
sensor suite had to say about things.

This explained why Rhino insisted on doing a flyby of the four bogeys even though
the Lightning's computer had long since
rendered its verdict. The unidentified inbound aerial contacts were cruise missiles,
probably of Iranian design.

To be fair, Natalie couldn't fault Rhino's
logic, not that it mattered. She might be a
hotshot American pilot, but she was in an
Israeli formation flying in an Israeli aircraft.
She was not in charge of anything.

"Flight, this is lead," Rhino said. "Bogeys

at our three o'clock, low. We'll conduct an overflight and then turn hard right to circle in behind them."

Natalie did the math in her head and figured they'd intercept in less than a minute. She almost clicked the transmit mike to recommend that the flight decrease airspeed, but didn't. At almost five hundred knots, the four F-35s would blow right by their targets. Not to mention that, according to her flight computer, the cruise missiles were slowing, their airspeed decreasing to below three hundred knots. But once again, she reminded herself that she was just a spectator.

"Tally bogeys," Slammer said.

As the starboard-most fighter in the four-ship flight, it made sense that he was the one who saw the targets first. Natalie craned her neck to the right, following the cueing dots provided by her fighter's data fusion engine, with no luck.

Sometimes being five-foot-two really was a limitation.

Giving up on identifying the targets visually, Natalie slaved the infrared video from the aircraft's distributed aperture system to one of the multipurpose displays that formed her digital cockpit. Natalie might not be able to get her eyeball on target, but that didn't mean she couldn't see what they were chasing.

The black-and-white picture resolved into a familiar silhouette as the six infrared cameras mounted across the F-35's fuselage formed a single high-definition composite image. The target's narrow fuselage was capped with an aerodynamic nose cone, but rather than fins, a pair of stubby wings jutted from its body just aft of the halfway point. Tracking along the missile's body, Natalie registered that some sort of turbofan or turbojet engine hung below the missile's centerline, providing propulsion.

As the four-ship formation of F-35s thundered over the formation of bogeys and began a descending turn to the right, Rhino launched another barrage of Hebrew at Weasel Main. Natalie didn't mind being excluded because she was too busy examining the missile's fuselage. Something about its distinctive shape gave her pause.

Sliding in behind and ten thousand feet above the bogey flight, she enlarged the picture. Something still wasn't right. Touching another button, she zoomed in on the front quarter of the missile and sucked in her breath. Now she understood why the enemy flight had abandoned the cover offered by the ocean's waves in favor of a higher altitude and slower speed.

"Break, break," Natalie said, transmitting on the air-to-air frequency. "Rhino, this is Daisy, we've got a problem, over."

"Daisy, Rhino, stand by."

Daisy could hear Rhino's exasperation at being interrupted, but she didn't care.

"Rhino, Daisy, negative. Look at the underside of the aircraft. I say again, look at the belly of the missiles. Do you see the nozzles?"

Once Natalie understood what she was seeing, the series of fire hydrant–shaped nozzles lining the missile's belly like tits on a sow jumped off the screen. But either Rhino was having trouble switching from Hebrew to English mid-thought or he hadn't yet made the connection.

"Nozzles?" Rhino said. "Say again, Daisy?"

Daisy keyed the transmit button to try to explain, but the missiles took care of any misunderstandings for her. As one, the four telephone pole–shaped munitions slid out of their staggered formation and came abreast.

Then the nozzles began to spray.

69

The liquid misting from beneath the missiles billowed outward in a gray-tinged cloud. Set against the blue sky and cerulean waters of the Mediterranean, the vapor looked pastoral. Like the four weapons of war were putting on an airshow for the citizens of Tel Aviv. But Natalie knew that the innocuous-seeming cloud had to be death in one form or another.

So did Rhino.

A burst of Hebrew filled the airwaves as flight lead issued instructions. He didn't bother to translate, but Natalie understood what he was saying all the same. The missiles would make landfall in just under a minute and the Iron Dome had failed to intercept them. The on-call fighters at Nevatim Air Force Base were probably already scrambling, but even at full afterburner, they wouldn't arrive on station until much too late.

Only four aircraft stood between the city of Tel Aviv and the noxious clouds of death.

And as per protocol when conducting air-to-air exercises, those four aircraft were completely unarmed. Conventional wisdom said that this precaution would help ensure that a pilot never accidentally activated a live missile in the heat of a mock dogfight, unintentionally sending a comrade to his or her death.

A prudent gesture that would now result in the deaths of at least four people. If Natalie and her fellow aviators didn't have the stomach for what came next, the body count could surge into the hundreds of thousands or millions, depending on the cloud's lethality.

Natalie thought of the two American Air Force pilots who'd taken off on September 11, 2001, on a suicide mission to bring down the hijacked airliner presumed to be heading for the White House. In the end, the passengers of Flight 93 had done the necessary work instead. In a single bright spot during an otherwise horrific day, Lieutenant Heather Penney and Lieutenant Colonel Marc Sasseville hadn't had to ram their F-16s into a plane full of innocent people.

Today, Natalie was faced with the exact

same choice.

"Rhino, this is Daisy. Which one is mine?"

The airwaves were silent for a long moment and then Rhino's voice flooded her headset. "Daisy, Rhino, this is an Israeli problem. We'll take care of it."

"Sorry, boss," Natalie said, "but that isn't going to work. There's four of them and three of you. One of you might be able to take out two with one pass, but I'm not going to bet the lives of four hundred thousand people on it. Tell me which one's mine, or I'll pick a target myself."

Once again, silence was her answer. Then Rhino spoke. "The one all the way to the left. I wanted to try and knock them out but there's no time. We'll do our run together. God be with us."

Natalie thumbed the transmit button twice in response.

Braveheart speeches were for ground-pounders.

Natalie was an aviator, and she had a job to do.

70

Lining up her F-35's nose on the rear aspect of the leftmost missile, Natalie visualized how this would go, resting her hand on the throttle as she waited for Rhino's call. A jet fighter, while an extremely durable machine, was not meant to survive collisions at four hundred knots. Both aircraft would disintegrate on impact.

As her body prepared to do what was necessary, Natalie's mind was free to roam. She thought about her fiancé, about her post–Air Force plans. She thought about her mom and dad and the sunsets she would never see. But mostly she thought about duty and honor. Unbidden, the words that had been drilled into her during her four years at the Air Force Academy sprang to mind.

Integrity first, service before self, excellence in all we do.

Much like the Royal Air Force during the

475

Battle of Britain, Natalie was about to make the ultimate sacrifice for countless people she would never meet. Winston Churchill's famous ode to the British pilots who'd saved the United Kingdom from Nazi Germany had never seemed more poignant.

Never in the field of human conflict was so much owed by so many to so few.

"Viper flight, this is Rhino, execute, execute, execute."

Natalie nosed her fighter over and fire-walled the throttle, diving toward the cruise missile like a cheetah running down a gazelle. The great Pratt & Whitney surged to life, a fire-breathing dragon whose roar rattled the very marrow in her bones. The skinny missile she'd chosen expanded in her windshield as she aimed for the unmistakable shape of the twin triangle-shaped wings.

Glancing away from her target for a split second, Natalie drank in the sight of Tel Aviv. Four hundred plus thousand people blissfully unaware that their fate was about to be decided by four nameless faces.

Just like in the Battle of Britain.

Natalie frowned, trying to understand why her subconscious had dragged up a reference to the World War II air campaign for the second time.

Then she knew.

"All Viper flight elements, this is Daisy, abort. I say again, abort."

Like every other aviator, Natalie prided herself on the ability to keep her radio voice calm, no matter what was transpiring. In this case she might have shouted. She jerked her stick into a hard left turn, narrowly avoiding a collision with the still-vapor-belching missile, hoping her wingmen had followed suit. After a perilous moment spent regaining control of her fighter, Natalie was able to check on her flight.

Four F-35s still registered on her radar.

"Daisy, this is Rhino, what the fuck?"

In spite of the sweat pouring down her forehead, Natalie smiled. She wasn't the only one who'd lost a bit of radio decorum.

"Rhino, Daisy, stand by. I've got an idea."

71

Within moments of exiting Husseini's quarters, Darien realized he'd been a bit optimistic with the whole *freedom* thing. While he and Katerina were beyond Ahmadi's reach, they weren't exactly home free. Darien had escaped the cult leader, but the apocalypse was still in full swing.

A series of eardrum-rupturing explosions thundered to his right.

Darien pushed Katerina against a nearby structure, shielding her body with his own.

In a testament to the ferociousness of the detonations, the Russian spy didn't object to his efforts to protect her. In fact, Darien actually felt her tremble as secondary explosions provided an encore to the initial bone-jarring thunderclaps.

Darien waited until he no longer heard the telltale shriek of incoming shells before pushing himself up and helping Katerina to her feet.

"Were those the weapons detonating?" Katerina said, her normally sanguine voice still a bit shaky.

"Yes," Darien said, "but they had help. From the sounds of it, the compound is being shelled."

"By who?" Katerina said, her eyes widening.

Darien shrugged. "My guess is the Americans."

"How do you know?"

"It stands to reason. Husseini crucified a CIA operative because he wanted the Americans' attention. I'd say he got it."

"Then they probably have the compound surrounded," Katerina said. "How do we get away?"

How, indeed.

Darien's thoughts instinctively ran to the vehicle they'd used to enter the compound. Then he thought of something else.

"Come with me," Darien said, grabbing Katerina by the hand.

72

Natalie spun her F-35 into a tightening corkscrew as she began the hook maneuver, tensing the muscles in the lower half of her body to keep her blood from pooling and thereby depriving her brain of vital oxygen. Perhaps she had been showing off earlier when she'd pulled eight g's while turning inside Rhino.

But this time the maneuver was for survival.

Her aborted run had brought her well past her target, and the clock was ticking. For her idea to have any chance of working, she needed to start the engagement slightly behind but on the same flight level as her target.

Though she wasn't a history major, there was something else about that Battle of Britain that had always transfixed Natalie's imagination. In addition to the scores of German aircraft that plied English skies at night, the people of London had two other terrors to contend with. Terrors that couldn't be driven off by the courage shining from the hearts of the Spitfire and Hurricane pilots who flew out, usually outnumbered, to confront the rampaging He 111 bombers and their Me 109 fighter escorts.

This wasn't because of their enemy's own courageous conviction. In fact, it was the opposite.

The winged nemeses didn't have hearts.

German scientists had been in a mad rush to find the perfect weapon as the tides of the war turned against them. Something that could rain death and destruction upon their adversaries without endangering a single life loyal to the Reich. Almost a hundred years before the advent of a spindly, Hellfire missile–equipped drone known as the Predator, the Germans had invented their own remote weapon of terror.

The *Vergeltungswaffen,* or Vengeance Weapons.

The first, known as the V-1, was a pilotless drone powered by a pulsejet. The engine made the drone sound like an oversized bee, hence its unofficial name: Buzz Bomb. Buzz Bombs traveled at four hun-

481

dred miles per hour, and the British pilots had a devil of a time determining what to do with them.

That is until one daredevil pilot came up with the idea of all ideas. Sidling up next to a Buzz Bomb in flight, he'd slipped his wing beneath the unmanned aircraft and banked abruptly. The unexpected attitude change was more than the munition's gyro had been programmed to handle. In one fell swoop, the Vengeance Weapon inverted and dove into the sea, where its almost two-thousand-pound warhead harmlessly detonated.

Just like that, a weapon responsible for nearly twenty-three thousand deaths was rendered harmless.

It was this story that was pinging in Natalie's subconscious. Maybe it was time to try her hand at a little drone-tipping. Except that unlike her World War II contemporaries, there wasn't just a fifty-or-so-knot delta between her target and her fighter's cruising speed. No, that difference was about two hundred knots as the missiles' velocity continued to decrease, presumably to employ the toxin cloud they were releasing to greater effect.

Natalie's plane needed to get a whole lot slower.

"Daisy, this is Rhino. State your intentions, over."

"Rhino, Daisy, stand by."

But with the Tel Aviv beach now clearly visible, Natalie knew that Rhino wasn't going to be standing by much longer. Which was fine, because if this didn't work, Natalie planned to shove her throttle to afterburner and plow through as many missiles as possible before her aircraft came apart around her.

Old Rhino and the boys could fight over whatever was left.

But she didn't say that, either, mainly because she was too busy putting every last trick she'd learned on the F-35 demonstration team to use. Cranking her aircraft's nose skyward, she increased the fighter's angle of attack while pulling the throttle back to almost idle.

The jet shuddered and stall warnings blared, but she still wasn't slow enough.

Not quite yet.

Thumbing down the flaps and the speed brake, she dirtied up the plane, making it as aerodynamically unstable as possible, all in an attempt to bleed off the maximum amount of speed.

She flicked a glance at her airspeed indicator and winced.

Still too fast.

Keying a final switch, she dropped the landing gear.

The jet shuddered as the three wheels charged with handling its thirty-five-thousand-pound frame slammed into the slip-stream.

The stall warnings turned into full-on klaxons as the F-35's flight computer attempted to override Natalie's precarious attitude in order to keep the hundred-million-dollar aircraft from becoming a lawn dart. Natalie responded by shaking the stick twice in order to confirm that she had control of her bird while advancing the throttle.

The engine rumbled in response, and her jet remained aloft.

Barely.

The world's most advanced fighter really was a marvel of technology, but it was not meant for the maneuver Natalie was attempting. With her aircraft's nose pointed almost vertical, she was maintaining her position almost exclusively via throttle control. It felt like pulling a wheelie while riding a motorcycle down a train track's single rail. Natalie had put her Lightning through some impressive aerial choreography during her three years as head of the flight demonstration team, but this craziness was in a league of its own.

Ignoring the sweat pouring from her forehead, Natalie jock-eyed with the rudder pedals to keep the nose straight. Then she looked to her right, scanning for her target. She tried not to think about how all of this would be for naught if she'd somehow managed to overshoot the missile.

Tried.

But what she saw caused her stomach to clench as the first curse word of the entire engagement slipped from her lips.

"*Scheisse,*" Natalie said, settling on the word she'd perfected during her deployment to Germany.

Her specially designed canopy boasted the most visibility ever granted a fighter pilot, but Natalie saw nothing but wispy cirrus clouds and blue sky.

The flight of missiles had vanished.

"Daisy, Rhino, your target is beneath you."

Cursing herself as a fool, Natalie cued the infrared picture, using the fused data to actually look *through* the floor of her jet. Sure as shit, the distinctive dual wings loomed just below her belly. Her stomach clenched again, this time for a different reason. Another ten feet and those wings would have punched into her jet's fuselage, rendering all the hotshot piloting she'd just

485

attempted moot.

"Daisy, roger," Natalie said, the calmness in her voice surprising even her. "I'm about to give this guy a nudge. If it works, we should be short one missile. If it doesn't, I'll take him down with me. Good luck with the other three."

This time it was Rhino who replied with two clicks of the radio, undoubtedly to keep his voice from distracting Natalie. It was a nice thought, but totally unnecessary. Natalie had been a good pilot before taking command of the demonstration team.

Three years later, she was great.

But not just because of her ability to wiggle the stick.

Flying acrobatic maneuvers in close confines with other aircraft took a kind of iron concentration of the sort an Olympic gymnast employs just before sending her body hurtling across the floor in a symphony of backflips and heart-stopping twists. Natalie was in the zone, and nothing short of a Russian Vympel missile detonating in her engine's intake would shake her concentration. Which was good, because Natalie had a feeling that getting blown out of the sky would have been infinitely less taxing on her mind and body than what she was about to attempt.

For starters, her positioning was off. When she'd come up with this cockamamie plan, Natalie had envisioned sliding beneath the missile's left wing, and then rocketing up while banking to the left. In theory, this would cause the Iranian weapon to turn to the right, away from Natalie's aircraft. But since she was above the missile, that was no longer an option.

For a moment, Natalie considered just dropping down on top of the missile's right wing while hoping for the best. But that was just foolish. No, if she were going to endanger her plane on the first pass, she might as well make the reward worth the risk. Dipping her right wing slightly, Natalie slid to the right, passing over the missile, even as she jockeyed with the throttle to maintain her precarious position.

The sweat trickling down the back of her neck along her braid had turned into a torrent. That was okay. She'd actually pulled off the maneuver and now was above and to the right of the missile and to the left of the second Iranian weapon.

Still not exactly how she'd planned it, but the time for second-guessing was over.

Gritting her teeth, Natalie idled the throttle while rolling her aircraft to the left. Steel contacted steel with a shriek that sounded like nails on a chalkboard, and then Natalie was looking at the missile through the top of her bubble canopy.

A missile that was tumbling to the right.

For a split second, the Iranian weapon was completely out of control. Then its internal gyro righted the missile, bringing its right wing squarely into the spinning maw of its wingman's turbojet engine.

This time when steel slammed into steel, a fireball resulted.

With a postcard-worthy end, two bringers of death disintegrated into orange flame and clouds of dense, black smoke.

Two down, two to go.

Exhaling the breath she hadn't realized she'd been holding, Natalie flexed her fingers and then gripped the side-mounted stick, preparing to repeat the maneuver for the next missile.

And that's when she realized she had trouble.

Apparently, thirty-five-thousand-pound fighters were not meant to play bumper cars with one-thousand-pound missiles. The vibrations through both her stick and pedals were unmistakable.

The collision had not left her Lightning unscathed.

Natalie's bird had sustained structural

damage. Serious structural damage. The F-35's flight computers were attempting to compensate for the aircraft's sudden aerodynamic changes, but Natalie knew this was a losing battle. The stress on the damaged airframe was simply too great. At some point, the computers would reach the limit of their authority and the flight surfaces would no longer be able to cancel out the unwanted drag.

When that happened, the result would be binary — like switching off a light. One moment her aircraft would be flying. The next it would be tumbling through the sky with the airworthiness of a rock. Assuming, of course, the fatigued metal didn't just give way first.

She had to eject.

Now.

Thumbing the transmit button, Natalie made the call she'd been dreading. Except the words she'd planned weren't the ones that came out.

"Rhino, Daisy, moving to the next target."

Again her acknowledgment came in the form of two clicks of the transmit button. But Natalie was no longer paying attention. If she played it safe and ejected, she would live.

Then again, if Natalie had wanted a life of

safety, she'd have never climbed into a Lightning's cockpit in the first place.

73

Al Tanf Outpost
Syria

Taking a deep breath, Jack edged around the side of the building, peering into the compound's interior. The fighter he'd tangled with lay motionless at his feet, either dead or severely disabled. The melee could have very easily gone the other way, and Jack knew he couldn't afford to be taken by surprise again. If his life as a paramilitary operative had taught him anything, it was that those who relied on luck didn't live long.

Ordinarily, Jack would have led with his rifle, but that wasn't an option. One-handed shooting a rifle was good for making noise, but little else. If push came to shove, he could probably hit a man a few feet away, but any farther and he'd be just wasting ammunition. Jack would have traded the AK for a pistol in a heartbeat, but the compound's occupants didn't seem to be big on secondary weapons.

It was the rifle or nothing.

But that didn't mean that his search hadn't yielded anything of value. In addition to the cell phone, Jack had relieved the man of his turban and outer tunic. While neither item was going to camouflage Jack's blue eyes or fair Irish skin, the hat covered his unruly shock of hair and the shirt hid his blood-soaked arm. His new wardrobe wouldn't fool a close inspection, but it might let him go unnoticed in the confusion gripping the compound.

Jack ducked as another burst of automatic fire echoed across the compound. Most of the shooting seemed to be happening outside the fifteen-foot berms ringing the structure, but sooner or later that would change. Even now fighters were racing along the tops of the walls, pulling tarps off previously hidden crew-served weapons. Whether they saw targets or not, Jack counted at least three heavy machine guns firing long bursts.

The American Special Operations team would take incoming fire for only so long before they responded by suppressing the machine-gun nests, probably with more artillery. When that happened, Jack knew that the compound's high walls would

492

become a death trap.

It was time to move.

But where?

The compound was laid out in a large square built around a mosque. To the left of the mosque, sheets of fire and thick billowing smoke marked what Jack was guessing had once been an ammo or fuel depot. A motor pool sat to the right, and the variety and quantity of vehicles was unusual. In addition to the standard fare of sedans and Hilux trucks, Jack found a number of surprises, including three Russian BRDM four-wheeled armored personnel carriers parked next to a fleet of up-armored Humvees.

The presence of the Russian vehicles, while unexpected, could be explained. Saddam's army had employed many of the scout vehicles, but the Humvees gave Jack pause. If the American Special Operations team had penetrated the compound, his odds of finding the fake VC manager and the Russian waitress would increase exponentially.

Not to mention his likelihood of survival.

But that was a big *if.*

Still, attempting to link up with an American team sounded a whole lot better than crouching against the side of the building and hoping that the next fighter didn't shoot first and ask questions later. From that perspective, he wasn't facing much of a choice at all. Gathering his courage as well as his remaining sanity, Jack sprinted for the motor pool. As Patton liked to say, When in doubt, attack.

Then again, Patton had never been nailed to a cross.

74

Israeli Restricted Operating Zone Alpha
Mediterranean Sea

As Natalie coaxed her fighter beneath the next missile, it was far from the nimble dancer she normally flew. Sports car fanatics made Natalie laugh with their talk of cornering their German-made motorized toys like they were on rails. Her toy, while ten times as large, had the ability to corner faster than the human body could endure. If she truly pushed the fighter to its structural limits, she stood a good chance of bursting her blood vessels just before she lost consciousness.

Except that the aircraft she was flying now was about as far from its normal spry self as a Porsche 911 was from a Pinto. The jostling in her stick and rudder pedals had grown even more pronounced — bad enough that the flight control computers were having difficulties canceling out the airframe's gyra-

495

tions. She'd probably cracked an aileron or two at the very least. In all likelihood, the wing itself was fractured, meaning it was only a matter of time before the prematurely fatigued metal catastrophically failed.

When that happened, the wing would go spinning off in one direction and Natalie, with the rest of the plane, in another. The good news was that the violent roll would probably knock her unconscious. The bad was that she would end her life as a permanent part of her aircraft.

Not much of a consolation.

The stick shook again, this time more violently, prompting a slew of caution lights and several audible warnings. Natalie ignored them, pretending instead that the instability she felt in her controls was nothing so sinister as traveling through the wake of invisible vortices generated by the missile as it plowed through the moist sea air.

Which gave her an idea.

As much as she didn't want to admit it, Natalie knew that the dexterity required to tip the remaining missile into its neighbor was beyond her ability. Like a duck hit with a hunter's shotgun blast, her fighter's fluttering control surfaces were no longer responsive enough to ensure straight and level flight, let alone the precise formation maneuvers she'd earlier employed. Her jet's days of delicate dancing were over, but her Lightning still had one thing in spades.

Thrust.

Raw, unadulterated thrust from the most powerful fighter engine ever made.

Moving the throttle to idle, Natalie let her jet slide below the missiles tail-first as she toggled the transmit button.

"Rhino, Daisy, I'm losing control of my bird. I'm gonna try something. If it doesn't work, the missiles are yours. Daisy out."

Rhino's voice crackled across the airwaves, but Natalie wasn't listening. Her jet's thrust-to-weight ratio was just over one, meaning that it had more power than weight. If need be, she could stand her bird on its tail and transform it from airplane to rocket.

And a rocket was exactly what she needed.

Watching the pair of missiles edge ahead of her, Natalie estimated a firing solution like she was hip-shooting a rifle. Then, when the angle looked right, she firewalled the engine, turning her jet into the rifle bullet. A rifle bullet that weighed over seventeen tons and churned the surrounding air into hurricane-strength vortices. As expected, Natalie lost attitude control within moments as the dynamic stress snapped off her wing.

But with the powerhouse of an engine streaking a pillar of blue flame behind her, Natalie no longer needed wings to fly.

The jet went into a vicious roll, but she was ready. The former demonstration pilot stomped on the pedals to maintain her heading. The wicked centrifugal motion slammed her against the side of her seat as the g-forces increased exponentially.

Natalie's world narrowed as her tiny frame attempted to endure a beating the universe's creator had never intended.

It was a losing battle.

But that was okay. This was a war of attrition, not of dominance. Natalie didn't have to win the fight against the crushing forces attempting to drive the blood from her brain. She just had to delay them for a few precious seconds.

Gritting her teeth, Natalie watched as the world spun and her fighter tore through the air in front of the two remaining missiles, passing from beneath to above while generating invisible shock waves. The swirling vortices spilled over the remaining cruise missiles, hammers of air smashing them together like a tsunami crashing against a rocky pile. Where before misting death had fallen from the sky, now aluminum pieces rained down instead, splashing into the shallows just short of Tel Aviv beach.

A moment later, the ocean erupted in a spray of white as a single F-35 cartwheeled into the sea.

75

Al Tanf Outpost
Syria

The closer he got to the motor pool, the more Jack thought the three Hummers weren't from an American Special Operations team. For one thing, operators hailing from the SOCOM community had long since abandoned mundane Humvees in favor of the sexier, and presumably better-performing, MRZR and GMV tactical vehicles.

Then there was the physical condition of the trio of Hummers. While American vehicles accumulated plenty of dirt and grime, American units were overseen by American non-commissioned officers, or NCOs. No platoon sergeant, first sergeant, or sergeant major would have permitted the vehicles under their care to degenerate to such a sorry state.

The headlight on one of the trucks was

nothing more than shattered glass, while the second vehicle's radiator was held together with equal parts duct tape and chicken wire. The third Hummer fared better than the previous two, but the bits of rust creeping in among the wheel wells paired with the chipped and flaking paint made the vehicle look like the victim of a particularly bad sunburn.

American soldiers would never ride into battle on such a poorly maintained rig.

Which meant that the vehicles didn't belong to Americans.

Unfortunately, Jack didn't reach this conclusion until he was halfway to the motor pool. While the hat and shirt he'd stolen from the disabled fighter made him a bit less obvious, he was hardly a chameleon. The less he did to draw attention to himself, the better. So rather than stop and reverse direction, Jack kept charging ahead.

Besides, the motor pool was as good a destination as any.

Dodging several groups of fighters running in different directions, Jack threaded his way through the outer layer of vehicles, making for the dirty brown Hummers. Like the rest of the compound, the motor pool was laid out in an organized grid. A series of low-slung buildings bordered the far end of the enormous lot, with vehicles parked in neat rows expanding outward.

The vehicles closest to the trio of buildings were in the greatest state of disrepair. The cars ran the gamut from Kias to Hyundais, but all were makes and models commonly seen on the streets of Iraq or Syria. By Jack's quick assessment, none of them were currently road-ready. Several had hoods propped open and most were missing some portion of their frame. The way that the vehicles' vacant panels revealed their underlying skeleton struck Jack as strangely sinister, though he couldn't articulate why.

Even so, he didn't have time to ponder the matter in great detail. Spurts of automatic-weapons fire still ripped through the air, seasoned by intermittent explosions. Everyone seemed to be in a hurry to be somewhere else, and the scurrying groups of people reminded Jack of sailors reacting to a klaxon sounding general quarters.

In that moment, he realized what he was seeing. The compound's defenders expected to be attacked and had rehearsed for this eventuality. Now they were reacting accordingly. To them, Jack was just another obstacle to circumvent as they raced to take up assigned defensive positions. For all intents and purposes, Jack was invisible.

For now.

As Jack drew closer, he saw a congregation of men lining up alongside the hodge-podge of civilian vehicles at the far end of the motor pool. Something about the gathering was out of place. While every other military-aged male was hurrying about with a weapon in his hands, the group of a dozen men was strangely still.

Jack deviated from his path, angling toward the nearest Humvee to avoid getting caught up in the steadily growing stream of men standing at the far side of the motor pool. Then a man wearing a long white *thobe* and a matching white head cover exited the building and, like a blurry picture sliding into focus, the group rearranged itself into neat rows. The man began to speak, and though Jack was too far away to hear the words, the accompanying gestures his audience made were easy enough to recognize.

They were praying.

With artillery shells dropping and automatic-weapons fire echoing across the compound, twelve men were praying.

Why?

Then Jack looked from the group of twelve to a series of neatly platooned cars arranged to the right of the building. Unlike the rest of the motor pool, this section was segregated with cyclone fence and a controlled access point. As Jack watched, the men finished their prayers and walked en masse toward the cyclone fence.

Leading the way, the prayer leader unlocked the gate with a key he wore around his neck, and then patted each man on the shoulder or back as they walked past him to enter. Jack looked from the cars, to the men, to the *thobe*-wearing man, trying to understand what he was seeing.

Then he had it.

Unlike the rest of the compound's inhabitants, these men were clean-shaven. Twelve beardless men had just prayed in the middle of a firefight and were now getting into a segregated fleet of vehicles.

Vehicles that rode low on their tires.

Son of a bitch.

Jack was staring at twelve suicide bombers preparing to embark on their final mission. Just once he wanted the luxury of worrying about a single bad guy. Instead, he always seemed to be outmanned and undergunned as bad morphed into worse. In other words, just another day in paradise.

The thought almost made Jack smile.

But it was hard to smile with a pistol pressing into your back.

76

In a strange way, the round length of metal jabbing him in the spine felt comforting. Unlike being confronted by a knife, where safety lay in distance, the odds of surviving an encounter with a gunman rose exponentially the closer they stood to their intended victim.

This was not because a bullet was any less devastating at close range.

A 115-grain projectile traveling at 1,180 feet per second shredded internal organs with ease, whether the gunman was six inches or six feet from his intended target. No, the advantage offered by proximity was that the closer a gunman stood, the greater chance the intended victim stood of disarming him.

Jack's combatives instructors had taught him an easy way to judge distance even under stress. If you were close enough to touch the gunman's elbow, you were close enough to take away his pistol. As Jack had learned through practice, a gunman standing near enough to shove a pistol into your back didn't stand a chance.

Assuming, of course, you had two working arms.

Once again, Jack was less than impressed with the cards he'd been dealt, but long odds were better than no odds. If the unseen gunman wanted Jack dead, the man would have already shot him. This meant he would soon tell Jack to drop his rifle. Jack intended to comply, and then use the distraction of the AK falling to the ground to attempt the disarming maneuver he'd done countless times before.

Except with just one hand.

It wasn't ideal.

Neither was dying.

Jack readied himself, picturing how he would compensate for his damaged arm while trying to relax the tense muscles bulging across his back and shoulders. Here speed mattered more than power, and it was hard to move fast with clenched muscles. But the command he was anticipating didn't come. At least, not that way he'd expected it. After a final poke to make sure he was paying attention, the pressure in his back vanished in conjunction with the sound of feet crunching on gravel as the gunman moved backward.

Apparently, Jack wasn't the only one who'd had a combatives class or two.

"Put the rifle on the ground. Slowly."

Jack ground his teeth. An American accent. Which meant that he probably looked like a farm boy from Iowa. The fake VC manager. So his Russian girlfriend had to be —

"Very slowly, or the hole I put in you this time will be much larger."

The second, distinctly feminine voice came from behind Jack and to his right. He couldn't see the waitress, but he was willing to bet she was standing well outside elbow-touching distance. And even if she wasn't, unless you were Steven Seagal, disarming two people was notoriously tricky.

Trying it with just one hand might even give Steven pause.

Jack slowly squatted to place the rifle on the ground as his mind raced. The good news was that he'd found the two people he'd been seeking.

The bad news was that they'd found him first.

77

"Reaper Seven, Reaper Six, sitrep, over."

Alex's call again came over the command frequency, and Cary was grateful for the privacy.

"Reaper Six, this is Reaper Seven," Cary said. "At least four of the missiles launched, and I'm still under direct fire from the compound."

As if to punctuate Cary's last statement, a DShK machine gun chattered to life from one of the hardpoints on the compound's walls. Cary ducked as the vehicle-killing bullets tore divots of soil from either side of the hide site, showering him with grit.

"Roger, Reaper Six copies all. What about the American?"

"He ran back into the compound," Cary said, as he rechecked Jad's bandage. The wound had stopped seeping blood, but Jad had drifted into unconsciousness. *Not good.* "I don't know what the American's doing, and I don't have time to care."

"Roger that, Reaper Seven. Some hinky shit on my end, too. Someone pushed into our net, asking us to assist the American if possible. Apparently, he's trying to locate additional hostages inside the compound, over."

"Roger all," Cary said, "but he's on his own. I am pinned down and combat ineffective with one WIA classification urgent. Reaper Seven is requesting the QRF, over."

"Thought you'd never ask, Reaper Seven," Alex said. "Sit tight, my friend. The cavalry is coming."

A moment later Alex's voice echoed over the team's internal frequency.

"All Reaper elements, this is Reaper Six. I have the fight. QRF is launching time now, and we will be moving up MSR Whiskey to relieve Reaper Seven in place. Continue to place accurate fire on enemy positions, but avoid sector five if possible. When I call Release Point Tango, suppress all target reference points with continuous fire until I've recovered Reaper Seven. Acknowledge, over."

Cary listened as each Reaper call sign acknowledged Alex's instructions. Damn, but his team leader was on it. That boy would have made a good NCO.

"Reaper Seven, this is Skillful Two Three. We are a flight of four at Release Point Sierra Two inbound, over."

The decidedly feminine voice instantly cut through Cary's testosterone-fogged mind. After twenty years of continuous combat, women were more fully integrated into all facets of the armed forces than ever before. Even so, the Special Operations community was still overwhelmingly male. As such, pilots supporting operators on the ground had long ago learned the value of passing communication duties to their female counterparts during tense engagements.

Nothing gets the attention of a distracted male brain quite like a female voice.

Speaking of distracted brains, in the excitement of fighting for his life and tending to Jad, Cary realized that he'd completely forgotten about the F-15s and their bellies full of small-diameter bombs. Keying the radio, Cary was preparing to transmit the wave-off brevity code when he had a wild thought. Maybe there was something he could do for the crazy American after all.

"Skillful Two Three, this is Reaper Seven," Cary said. "Change of mission. I say again, change of mission. Stand by for new instructions, over."

"This is Skillful, send it over."

Gathering his thoughts, Cary pressed the transmit button and began to speak.

78

Jack was surprised by how helpless he felt as the rifle slipped from his fingers. He didn't normally measure his well-being by the weapon he carried, but there was something to be said for the security offered by the AK's worn wooden stock. Especially in comparison to what his fingers felt now.

Nothing.

"Turn around. Just as slowly."

For the first time since he'd been jabbed in the thigh with a syringe full of ketamine, Jack felt a bit of satisfaction when he saw his tormentors face-to-face. The normally cool and collected VC manager looked decidedly less so. Dark splotches coated his sleeves, and his hands were covered with partially congealed blood. While he hadn't been nearly crucified, the man's wild eyes and unkempt hair seemed to suggest that he wasn't having such a great day, either.

The waitress-turned-executioner didn't

look any the worse for wear, but she no longer oozed sex appeal. Her cheeks were flushed, and her eyes shone with what looked like a barely contained mania. Unlike her partner, the Russian wasn't covered in dried blood, but her blouse had a spattering of incriminatingly rust-colored flecks.

"I'm glad you found me," Jack said, projecting his voice for the phone in his shirt.

"Why," the Russian said.

"Because it saved me the trouble of searching this compound inch by inch to find the two of you. Tell me the location of the scientist and her son, and I'll let you walk away."

"You'll let us?" the Russian said with a laugh. "You're alone with no weapon and one arm. I'm not too worried."

"Then you're a fool," Jack said. "Trust me when I say that you don't want me as an enemy. Tell me where they are. Last chance."

The waitress snarled, and Jack turned to face her. Which is why he was completely unprepared for what happened next. With the speed of a striking viper, her boyfriend lunged, smacking Jack across the skull with his pistol. The weapon's front sight post furrowed the side of Jack's head, tearing open the flesh from his ear almost to his temple.

Jack growled, squaring off with the man, but he'd already moved beyond Jack's reach.

"Enough," the man said. "We're leaving and you're driving. Your American friends will be much less trigger-happy with you at the wheel. Get in the Humvee and start the engine. Now."

"No," Jack said, pressing his good hand against his aching skull. Head wounds were notorious bleeders, and he could already feel a wet stream snaking down his cheek.

"Kill him," the waitress said. "I'll drive."

And then the sky split in two.

79

The sky didn't actually split in two, but it felt that way to Jack's aching head. One moment he was facing down two gunmen. The next, he was lying flat on his back, contemplating the flawlessly blue sky.

But that wasn't quite true.

Four objects marred the otherwise perfect view. Swept-wing aircraft with twin columns of fire lancing from their engines. Jack had never been on the receiving end of a sonic boom before, and his tired body thought that stretching out on the hard soil for a spell was a fine idea.

But there was no rest for the wicked.

Rolling away from the prone forms of the Iranian and the Russian, Jack grabbed for his rifle. His fingers had just touched the scarred wood when bullets snapped into the ground, raising dirt plumes inches from his face. Abandoning the AK, Jack continued to roll, sliding beneath a Humvee as rounds

516

sparked off its metal frame. Scrambling to his hands and knees, Jack put as much of the armored three-ton vehicle between himself and his attackers as possible.

While he hadn't anticipated a flight of F-15s buzzing past at supersonic speeds, Jack had been hoping for a distraction of some sort. He'd left the line to Mr. C. open for a reason, and it appeared that Gavin and the intrepid John Clark had come through yet again. When Jack made it home to Virginia, he might just take the cyberninja up on his long-standing invitation to play a round of Call of Duty.

At the very least, he'd buy the hacker a case of Mountain Dew and a carton of Twinkies.

With a sortie of F-15s overhead, a Special Operations team outside the compound, and two angry operatives trying to kill him, Jack decided it was past time to establish communications with the outside world. Duck-walking away from the Hummers, he scurried toward the looming Russian scout car.

The BRDM was about double the size of a Humvee and much more heavily armored. It would make a great place to hide while he picked up where he'd left off with Mr. C. But when he reached for his phone, Jack's fingers patted empty fabric. It must have fallen out of his pocket.

Still, things weren't all bad. As per the bloodstains on their clothing, the Iranian and Russian must not have been on great terms with the compound's occupants, either. With Americans outside and angry Syrians inside, Jack's tormentors were trapped between a rock and a hard place. If Jack could find his phone, he'd have the kidnappers exactly where he wanted them.

But the sound of a Humvee roaring to life suggested otherwise.

80

The throaty diesel rumble changed to a full-fledged growl as the hummer lumbered away from the motor pool. His friends were leaving the party, which meant that his only link to Becka and Tommy was disappearing in a cloud of fumes. Jack was about to retrace his steps in favor of stealing a Humvee of his own when a series of engines cranked over behind him.

Turning, he swore.

The platoon of suicide bombers was now in their respective vehicles. Apparently, the low-flying fighters had galvanized more than just Jack to action. The prayer leader was standing at the front of the gate, waving the first car forward.

Jack had seen the aftermath of VBIED explosions and knew that the victims were just as likely to be women and children as soldiers. Letting those twelve vehicles escape would be the equivalent of emptying a bucketful of rattlesnakes into a kindergarten classroom. If there was any way he could prevent the human cruise missiles from wreaking the death and destruction they intended, Jack knew he had to try.

Turning back to the BRDM, Jack scaled its metal frame as he formulated a plan. As plans went, it wasn't great.

But it would have to do.

81

Unlike the original design put into service by the Soviet Union, this version of the venerable four-wheeled BRDM-2 armored personnel carrier had been modified extensively. In keeping with the same entrepreneurial spirit that had first prompted jihadis to mount machine guns or recoilless rifles to Hilux pickup trucks, the BRDM's standard turret had been completely removed.

In its place sat a formidable weapon.

Jack didn't know the nomenclature for the quad-barreled anti-aircraft gun, and he didn't care. What he did know was that the contraption used old-school traversing and elevation mechanisms powered by hand cranks instead of vehicle hydraulics. Even better, the ammunition cans were already mounted next to the guns.

While the antiaircraft system wasn't anything Jack had ever encountered, the weapon at its heart was a variant of the

Soviet-era KPV heavy machine gun, which had seen widespread use in one configuration or another since World War II. Once you understood the basics of how they operated, machine-gun variants weren't all that terribly different from one another.

After examining the weapon, Jack quickly found and actioned the charging mechanism. Then it was simply a matter of cranking the easy-to-spin traversing and elevation wheels to bring the weapon's sight onto target.

Or at least it would have been easy to spin them with two hands. With just one, Jack was forced to crank the elevation mechanism first and then reach across his body to spin the traversing wheel. His jerky adjustments didn't make for a smooth walk of the iron sights onto target, but since he was shooting at a convoy of stationary cars instead of fast-moving airplanes or helicopters, his method of aiming should work.

Should being the operative word.

After switching between the wheels twice, he'd finally centered the crude iron sights onto the first vehicle queuing to leave the motor pool. Then Jack stepped on the fire-control pedal with his left foot.

The guns didn't so much shoot as erupt. Between the gouts of flame and jackhammer-like pounding, Jack thought one of the vintage weapons might have exploded. Releasing the pedal, Jack peered over the front of the machine guns' conical flash suppressors to survey his work.

Destruction awaited.

But not the destruction he'd been trying to achieve. The quads had fired low, and while several vehicles were now on fire, they'd been parked between him and his targets. The gaggle of VBIEDs were untouched. Grabbing the elevation wheel, Jack cranked just as the first VBIED, a Kia, rolled free of the enclosure and made a run for it.

Jack centered his sight picture on the car's hood and hammered the firing pedal.

This time he was prepared for the muzzle flash and was able to look above the fireballs produced by the quads as four streams of emerald tracers converged on the unlucky vehicle. Golf ball–sized projectiles pounded the car, tossing chunks of metal into the air as the armor-piercing bullets shredded the vehicle's thin skin.

A moment later, the car dissolved into a teeth-rattling explosion as one of the incendiary rounds found the car's sinister payload. Ducking as falling metal pinged against the BRDM's armored hull, Jack stomped the firing pedal again as he spun the elevation and traversing wheels, walking the stream of bullets across the line of waiting cars. The ensuing explosions tossed him against the gun's unforgiving metal as shock waves buffeted the BRDM.

The enclosure once housing the suicide vehicles now resembled the gates of hell. Flames billowed from behind the chain-link fence, boiling across the ground in hazy waves. The heat hit Jack like a blast furnace as thick, choking smoke poured skyward carrying the acrid smells of burning rubber and gasoline.

The sprinkling of debris falling from the sky turned into a full-fledged downpour.

A section of metal as long as his forearm clanged against the quad, just inches from Jack's fingers, and he decided this was his exit cue. The roiling black smoke from the VBIED inferno was curling over the BRDM, and Jack now had the entire compound's attention. Random pieces of the car were no longer the only metallic objects pinging off the BRDM's armor plating.

A ricochet bounced off the ammo box to Jack's left, denting the metal before whining past his head. Cursing, Jack looked into the inviting crew compartment beneath his feet but resisted the urge to hunker down. The armored crew space was more than capable of fending off small-caliber rounds; it wasn't connected to the driver's station. Taking a breath, Jack leapt from where he was crouching behind the quad guns and half rolled, half slid over the flat ledge separating the turret from the sloped edge leading to the driver's hatch.

On his first attempt, Jack slid too far and found himself spread-eagle across the thick glass that served as the driver's viewport. Rolling to his side, Jack scrambled back up the ledge just as a bullet smacked into the section of glass on which he'd been lying. Pushed off the hull, he slithered into the driver's compartment headfirst, nearly braining himself on a toolbox. After pulling his feet in behind him, Jack pushed the toolbox out of the way and folded his six-foot-plus frame into the dusty canvas seat.

Then he surveyed the instrument console.

As he should have expected, the gauges and buttons were all labeled in Cyrillic. But this wasn't a showstopper. The BRDM was an armored car with a standard gasoline engine, not a next-generation stealth fighter. Like most military vehicles, there was no ignition key. Instead, he just needed to turn on the battery power and find the ignition.

Simple.

Outside, the steady *ping ping ping* of

small-arms rounds slamming against the BRDM's armor plating sounded like the ticking of a doomsday clock. Scanning the console for a battery switch, Jack noticed something unexpected. A length of chain was looped around the steering wheel and padlocked to the vehicle's metal frame, preventing the steering wheel from turning. So much for simple.

82

Ignoring the chain for the moment, Jack concentrated on something he could control — the battery switch. Even though the BRDM had first entered service long before Jack was born, the dashboard was still a bit intimidating. Gauges covered with Cyrillic letters sat side by side with darkened lights and buttons of indeterminable purposes. The gearshift, gas and brake pedals, and steering wheel were easily identifiable, but the rest was a mystery.

Peering across the sea of dials and switches, Jack found a push button that reminded him of the ignition on his father's old lawn tractor. Jack thumbed the rubber housing, but nothing happened.

Power first, then ignition.

He flipped several switches at random as the metal hailstorm grew louder. A second examination of the instrument cluster yielded similar results. Lots of interesting switches and dials, but nothing that brought power to the lifeless needles and lights. For a heart-stopping moment Jack considered whether the battery was even connected. Just as quickly, he pushed the idea away. If the battery was gone, he was dead in the water. Instead of dwelling on what-ifs, Jack tried to put himself into the minds of the vehicle's designers.

Russian weapons weren't known for user comfort. A Western driver expected to find everything needed to operate the machine at his fingertips. Not so with Russians. Jack needed to think like a Russian.

Twisting, Jack looked above and behind the driver's seat. More levers, knobs, and dials, but nothing that supplied power. In an act of desperation, Jack turned completely around.

Then he saw it.

A solitary switch. With a whispered prayer, Jack grabbed the metal nub between his fingers and pushed it upward. An audible *click* echoed through the driver's station followed by a familiar *buzz*.

Electricity.

Turning back to the dashboard, Jack saw a Christmas tree of lights and flickering needles. Leaning forward, Jack reached for the starter button.

And that was when the RPG detonated.

the same barrel.

And that was when the K-9 detonated.

83

To be fair, it took Jack a moment to diagnose the source of the earsplitting explosion that tossed him like a rag doll across the driver's station. His first thought was that applying battery power had somehow sparked an explosion, but the blast's magnitude put that notion to rest. An electrical short in a vehicle this old wasn't out of the question, but it would have caused a fire first, then an explosion.

The more likely explanation was that his attackers had just upped the ante.

Crawling back to the driver's seat, Jack stabbed the ignition button. The engine turned over, but it didn't catch. Running through a litany of curses that would have impressed his father and horrified his mother, Jack pumped the gas, trying to ignore the choking smoke drifting into the cabin.

On the fifth pump, Jack again jabbed the

ignition button.

This time, the engine caught with a thunderous roar. Slamming the transmission into drive, Jack floored the gas. The BRDM shuddered, lurching forward like a drunken elephant. In a bit of good news, the air flowing in through the open hatches helped keep the smoke at bay.

On the not-so-positive side, the metal behind Jack's seat was getting warmer.

And the steering wheel was still chained to the vehicle's frame.

A snatch of a country song came to mind — *if you're goin' through hell, keep on goin'*. Jack agreed wholeheartedly with the sentiment, but felt like the singer had left out some salient points.

Like what to do when hell was following right behind you.

84

Coughing against the thickening smoke, Jack eased the steering wheel to the right, straining it against the limit imposed by the chain and padlock. Setting aside the question of why a compound surrounded by fifteen-foot walls also needed vehicle locks, Jack concentrated on a more immediate problem.

Steering.

In this department, he was actually doing better than he'd hoped. While the length of chain prevented any drastic manipulations of the steering wheel, whoever had last secured the links hadn't pulled them taut before engaging the padlock. As such, Jack had a bit of give before hitting the limits imposed by the length of steel.

But not much.

Gripping the steering wheel, Jack pulled to the left, straining against the chain while bracing himself for impact. A second later his right front bumper smashed against a sand-filled Hesco barrier. The impact almost threw Jack from his seat, pin-balling his left shoulder against the unforgiving metal frame. Even so, he considered the agony radiating from his damaged arm a fair price to pay once he'd resettled himself behind the driver's viewport.

Like a game of high-stakes bumper cars, Jack had discovered a way to capitalize on the vehicle's mass and speed by using the multiple obstacles in his path to provide gross adjustments to his steerage. It wasn't an exact science, but Jack was able to keep the armored car roughly on course despite the steering wheel's limited play.

Roughly.

The compound's exit loomed in front of Jack like the mouth of some prehistoric shark. Antivehicle barriers deployed waist-high from the concrete resembled jagged teeth, while strands of concertina wire dangled across the entry like bits of seaweed. Gunning the gas, Jack took the BRDM to ramming speed as he bore down on the entrance.

The men guarding the gate decided that living to fight another day beat martyrdom. While both guards sprayed the BRDM with automatic rifle fire, they also retreated to

533

sandbag-reinforced bunkers on either side of the entrance. Jack's escape route was clear, with the exception of the fire hydrant–like antivehicle barriers that had just deployed from the ground.

With the accelerator pressed all the way to the floor and the BRDM's engine redlining, Jack figured he had a fifty-fifty chance of plowing his way through the intimidating structures. Presumably, the devices had been installed to keep the riffraff *out* rather than the compound's occupants *in.* With this in mind, it stood to reason that if the barriers were reinforced, they were structurally strongest when repelling attacks from outside the compound.

In theory.

But theory tended to become a bit abstract when the rubber met the road and bullets were flying.

As if to punctuate Jack's thought, a large-caliber round thudded into the driver's viewport, spiderwebbing the already cracked surface. The armored glass held, but Jack reflexively jerked the wheel to the right. The chain kept his overreaction from completely taking the vehicle off course, but the damage was done. Instead of the single barrier he'd been hoping to power through, the BRDM's grille was now centered between two of the stubby contraptions.

Fantastic.

With less than fifty feet remaining, Jack could try to adjust course and sacrifice speed or just hang on and hope for the best. Neither option was great, so Jack split the difference. Keeping the gas pedal flush against the floor, Jack nudged the steering wheel a fraction of an inch to the left.

And prayed.

Then steel met steel at sixty kilometers per hour.

85

This time the collision didn't jar Jack so much as attempt to dislodge his teeth from his gums. Even though he'd braced himself against the steering wheel with his one good arm and the vehicle's floor with his left leg, he still headbutted the metal frame with admirable vigor.

Unsurprisingly, the frame won.

Jack's vision blurred as a supernova of pain exploded across his skull. Shaking his aching head to clear the fuzziness, Jack sent a splattering of blood across the dusty dashboard. But his new head wound was the least of his worries. He was more concerned with the high-pitched shriek of metal grating against metal.

That and the sudden lack of forward motion.

A quick glance through the viewport told Jack everything. While he'd managed to dodge the rightmost vehicle barrier, the one to the left was wedged under the BRDM's hull. At some point during the crash sequence, the horrific impact had knocked Jack's foot clear of the accelerator. Pulling himself back into the driver's seat one-handed, Jack stomped on the pedal.

The engine raged, and the vehicle rocked forward, but the barrier held.

He wasn't going anywhere.

Releasing the gas, Jack let the BRDM settle and then jammed the accelerator to the floor, rocking the vehicle back and forth. With each oscillation, the banshee wailing of bending metal grew more pronounced, but the stubborn barrier refused to give.

The slew of curses Jack let fly this time would have given even his Marine father pause. He'd been crucified, drugged, shot with an RPG, and left for dead twice. His vehicle was on fire and a hornet's nest of pissed-off jihadis were hosing down the BRDM with crew-served weapons. Undoubtedly some of the bravest of the bunch were chucking grenades at the vehicle's open hatches.

All this and it was a vehicle barrier that was going to stop him?

Not today.

The vehicle shuddered and Jack slipped sideways. Reaching for a handhold to steady himself, he mistakenly yanked a stray lever. In response, hydraulics groaned and part of the vehicle's forward hull shifted downward. Standing in the cramped cockpit, Jack ignored the bullets flattening themselves against the crumbling glass as he peered over the front of the BRDM, trying to understand what had just happened. The armored vehicle's profile had changed. For some reason, the hull was now canted downward.

Then he understood.

"Well, son of a bitch," Jack said.

The BRDM was actually amphibious. Accordingly, the vehicle's leading edge was hydraulically actuated like a bulldozer's blade so that the driver could adjust the BRDM's hydrodynamic profile in order to give the lumbering beast greater stability in rough waters. Grabbing the same lever, Jack wrenched it from the midway position all the way down and gassed the engine.

For a terrifying moment, the BRDM tilted skyward as the vehicle barrier bore the hydraulic force exerted by the lower splashguard with the same stoicism it had handled the rocking vehicle. Then the shriek of steel climaxed into a *crunch* that rocked the armored car from stem to stern. A heartbeat later, the waist-high tires caught pavement, and the BRDM rocketed from the compound's entrance like a cannonball.

He was free.

But the world outside the compound wasn't exactly all peace and serenity. Tracer fire arced from the compound's walls in sinuous, emerald tentacles as impacting artillery rounds raised clouds of dust and destruction. To his left, a pair of muzzle flashes were winking from what appeared to be a compromised hide site while two GMV Special Operations vehicles in overwatch positions poured supporting fire from crew-served weapons. But fireworks aside, it was the familiar object to his front that held Jack's attention.

The Humvee.

The boxy vehicle had run off the gravel path leading from the compound and down an embankment. Now it was fishtailing its way back up, spewing a rooster tail of gravel and dirt. Surprisingly, the Hummer didn't seem to be drawing fire.

Or maybe not so surprisingly.

The American attackers were probably loath to fire on one of their own vehicles, while the compound's defenders likewise considered the Hummer a friendly. Even so, the Humvee didn't seem to have made it through the battle scot-free. The right rear tire was shedding tread in great flapping chunks. The rubber at the tire's core seemed to be intact, but the loss of traction was affecting the vehicle's stability. The Humvee summited the embankment, but swerved from one side of the road to the other as the driver fought to keep the vehicle from pitching back down the levee.

Jack had no such worries. He poured on the gas, bearing down on the struggling vehicle like a charging rhinoceros while ignoring the thickening smoke and heat radiating from the compartment behind him. The RPG-ignited fire wasn't going to just go away. In fact, it was probably even money whether the hungry flames reached the vehicle's fuel cell before he caught up with the Humvee. But Jack put the pedal to the metal all the same, careening toward the oscillating vehicle.

Like a cougar preparing to pounce, Jack felt the BRDM gather itself before surging toward the crippled Hummer. As the distance between the two vehicles shrank, Jack had a single, disconcerting thought.

He was going to miss.

86

Jack was steering the cumbersome armored car with a deftness that bordered on the supernatural, considering the circumstances. But the closer he grew to the Hummer, the more accurately he needed to steer.

The chain had other ideas.

Every time he attempted to make a larger steering correction, the chain snapped tight, thwarting his efforts. Try as he might, Jack couldn't match his target's unpredictable gyrations. The best he could do was aim straight down the center of the road in an effort to thread the needle between the Hummer's side-to-side oscillations.

While this was a great plan to close distance, it didn't offer the precision needed to ram the Humvee. One sharp turn, and Jack would drive right by. Straight lines he could manage, but the dexterity required to hit a moving target was beyond his ability. The Hummer grew steadily closer as something about the notion of straight lines bounced around Jack's brain, refusing to be ignored.

Straight lines.

Straight lines.

Then he had it.

Keeping the accelerator mashed to the floor, Jack released the wheel, allowing the chain to provide the tension required to keep the wheel straight. Then he reached across the cabin for the toolbox he'd shoved out of the way what seemed like an eternity ago.

At first, he tried to stretch from a seated position so that he could keep his eyes on the road. But after twice brushing the pitted metal with his fingertips without securing a handhold, Jack gave up. If what he was planning had a prayer of succeeding, he'd have to quit watching the road at some point.

Might as well be now.

Abandoning the viewport, Jack turned parallel to the floor, stretching for everything he was worth. His probing fingers touched the toolbox's handle and then slipped away when the BRDM hit a pothole. Cursing, Jack tried again, for the first time releasing pressure on the gas pedal in order to increase his reach.

The BRDM decelerated, but this time Jack touched metal.

Dragging the dense container to his seat set Jack's core on fire, but he ignored the pain. After a second of grunting, and even more cursing, he had the box where he wanted it. Now came the moment of truth. Reaching down, Jack grabbed the handle and attempted to one-arm-curl the unwieldy box onto his lap.

He failed.

Miserably.

The box slid to the floor, spilling tools across the compartment.

Jack looked at the debris and then decided that, since he couldn't get the box up to his lap one-handed, maybe the lighter load was a blessing in disguise. Hoisting the box onto his legs, Jack got his first look back out the viewport. The Humvee was less than twenty feet away. It was now or never. With another grunt, Jack slid the toolbox from his lap to his right knee. Then he bent forward and lowered the container onto the gas pedal.

It worked.

Sort of.

The toolbox kept the accelerator depressed, but not flat against the floor. Without Jack's foot keeping the accelerator floored, the armored car was slowing down.

No matter.

So was Jack.

With a final adjustment to the steering wheel, Jack stood on the driver's seat and boosted himself onto the BRDM's roof. What he saw when his head cleared the armor plating brought new meaning to *out of the frying pan and into the fire.*

87

"All Reaper elements, Reaper Six is RP Tango. I say again, Reaper Six is RP Tango, over."

With a final check on Jad, Cary grabbed his rifle and popped his head out of his hole, feeling very much like a prairie dog exposing himself with a hawk circling overhead. Fortunately, the rest of Triple Nickel was doing the same, as every weapons system the ODA team possessed began to continuously pump steel onto target.

Cary could hear the deep *thump, thump, thump* of MK-19 grenade launchers joined by the throaty hammering of .50-caliber machine guns. Shells whistled overhead as Brian's 120-millimeter mortars made their presence known while the unmistakable chattering of SAWs and M4s going cyclic filled the air.

The effects were awe-inspiring. The weapons fire from the compound slackened to a trickle as munitions impacted the length and width of the fortress's walls, sending eruptions of dirt and stone skyward. But this awesome display of precious firepower wasn't what garnered Cary's attention. Instead, he was focused on the two vehicles careening his way. One was a Humvee sliding from one side of the road to the other.

The second was even more interesting.

A BRDM.

A BRDM in flames with a man standing on the roof.

"Reaper Six, this is Reaper Seven," Cary said. "We've got a problem."

88

The rear of the BRDM was on fire. Not the kind of *on fire* that meant a curtain of smoke punctuated by flames poking up here and there. No, this was the kind of *on fire* Baptist preachers thundered about on Sunday mornings. Sheets of flame billowed from the crew compartment framed by columns of choking black smoke thick enough to taste.

If not for the feeble headwind provided by the vehicle's forward motion, Jack thought he would have succumbed then and there. But he did not asphyxiate on the roof of the BRDM, which meant he had to deal with phase two of his plan — the Humvee swerving back and forth just feet away.

The Humvee edged out of the rolling smoke enclosing the BRDM like a phantasm materializing in the early morning fog. One moment there had been nothing but the gravel road passing by at a ridiculous pace.

547

The next, the Hummer's pitted desert-colored frame loomed to his left, almost close enough to touch. But before Jack could react, the Humvee vanished, swallowed again by the churning smoke.

Cursing, Jack edged as far forward on the roof as he dared. His eyes watered from the acrid fumes and his skin reddened from the heat, but he saw the Humvee's frame just ahead. The Hummer was one of the turtleback variants, meaning that rather than rear windows, the back half of the vehicle was a single piece of angled metal. The structure sloped from the turret opening on the roof down to the rear bumper, resembling a ramp of sorts.

Before he could think through the insanity of what he intended, Jack shuffled backward until the heat became unbearable, and then sprinted the length of the BRDM's roof. When he got to the edge, Jack leapt into space, his legs bicycling, his good arm windmilling. For what seemed like an eternity, he sailed through emptiness, wind whistling past his face and nothing but air beneath his feet.

Then the Humvee appeared like a rust-spattered steel wall.

Jack sucked in a breath before smashing into the angled armor plating, instinctively reaching out with his left hand to cushion the impact. Mistake. Pain radiated the length of his arm, and Jack gave voice to the agony in a lung-bursting scream. He reached for a handhold on the Humvee's canted back as he slid down the sloped metal toward the treacherously churning rear tires.

Grasping for support, Jack's fingers closed around a length of flexible steel. He gripped the metal rod like a pit bull. Looking up, Jack realized that he'd snared the vehicle's whip antenna, the top of which was tied off to the Humvee's bumper.

Or at least it had been tied off.

Apparently, radio aerials weren't designed to hold two-hundred-twenty-pound men.

The antenna bowed dangerously downward, resembling the fishing pole of a weekend angler who'd hooked a great white rather than a perch. Jack slid slowly lower in response, edging ever closer to road. He tried to use his left hand, but the damaged arm gave way under the strain.

He couldn't pull himself up and he couldn't stay where he was.

He was screwed.

Turning, Jack saw a steel mesh storage platform about even with his waist. The small enclosure appeared to have been spot-welded to the Hummer's frame, probably to provide space for an extra can of diesel or perhaps additional ammo cans. Regardless of what the designers had intended, Jack thought the steel lattice looked like heaven.

Wrenching downward on the antenna, Jack tried to swing his left leg onto the platform.

Another mistake.

The antenna bowed under the strain, dropping Jack so that his right foot brushed the ground. He screamed as the speeding gravel tried to wrench him from the vehicle and curled both knees to his chest. Something popped in his shoulder. His right hand had slid the length of the antenna as he'd fallen, and now his fingers found the aerial's wider base. Grasping the broader attachment, Jack wrenched himself toward the Hummer with a burst of adrenaline-fueled strength as he again swung his left foot toward the metal grating.

This time his boot wedged inside the compartment.

With a move that would have done a contortionist proud, Jack rotated his body toward the Humvee, locking his left leg out while struggling to find purchase on the slanted surface with his right. For a heartbeat Jack's right leg banged impotently against the Hummer as his strength ebbed. Then, in a moment of desperation, Jack pushed off with his left leg, lunging upward and grabbing the antenna by its treacherous middle.

Again the metal bowed, but this time Jack was ready. The moment his upper body was vertical, he hooked his right leg onto the platform next to his left. Shuddering with the effort, Jack pressed himself upright.

With both legs settled beneath him, Jack had a modicum of stability, but suddenly the fickle whip antenna flexed *outward,* away from the Humvee. In the blink of an eye, Jack was rotating backward with nothing to arrest his motion but his throbbing shoulder and overworked stomach muscles. He was tipping over like a fool trying to balance a chair on one leg. He made a grab for the antenna's base.

It wasn't enough.

He was falling.

Until the BRDM exploded.

The fireball pummeled Jack, singeing his clothes and blistering his skin. But the accompanying blast wave made the pain worthwhile. One moment he was wavering against the back of the Humvee. The next, he was plastered against the sloping metal frame like a bug on a windshield.

Ignoring his screaming body and smoking clothes, Jack reached up, grabbing for the Hummer's gun turret. He snagged a metal handhold and pulled his body flush against the Humvee's canted side while bracing his feet in the wire mesh. For a long moment, he just held himself in place, taking breath after shuddering breath. Then he widened his stance, wedging his feet into the corners of the platform. As he stood on the back of a Humvee hurtling across the desert, Jack had just one thought.

It was time to end this.

89

The Humvee's occupants were both armed and, as far as Jack knew, still had the full use of both hands. But that was fine. Jack lacked finesse, wasn't much of a tactician, and acted impetuously. All of that was true. What was also true was that Jack possessed something harder to quantify.

Something visceral.

Jack was a hammer, and the Hummer had two nails that needed pounding.

After visualizing what he was going to do, Jack swung inside the Hummer through the turret's circular opening and went to war. Leading with his right foot, Jack connected with the waitress's head just as his leg reached full extension. The sickening sound of his boot crunching against her skull was second only to the thud of her face rebounding off the bulletproof glass.

Based on the way she limply slid to the floor, she was out of the fight.

Her boyfriend, not so much.

Whether the man had seen Jack in time to react or had been in the process of correcting for the Humvee's unsteady handling when Jack attacked, the result was the same. He'd jerked the wheel to the left just as Jack swung into the cabin, and the inertia sent Jack tumbling into the rear seats.

No matter.

Jack spun toward the driver, torquing his hips as he swung his massive right hand. This wasn't anything as civilized as a boxing match or even a sparring session on the jiujitsu mats. This was the proverbial fight in the elevator, and nobody did cornered junkyard dog better than Jack.

Well, almost nobody.

Jack's hammer fist was millimeters from the driver's inviting right ear when he slammed on the brakes. Jack crashed into the sturdy seatbacks, bashing his still bleeding forehead against another uncushioned section of metal sheeting before tumbling to the floor.

In keeping with his fantastic luck, Jack landed on his left arm and the flesh ripped open even farther. The electric jolt filled his eyes with tears. Pushing himself up from the metal floorboards with his good hand, Jack found himself face-to-face with the business end of a pistol. Knowing that the gun was too far away for him to grab, Jack did the next best thing.

He channeled his inner hammer.

With a grunt, Jack delivered the mother of all elbow strikes to the back of the driver's seat. He pictured the point of his bone spearing through the canvas seat and cleaving the driver's spinal cord in half. While he didn't achieve all that, Jack did manage to make the man miss when he fired his pistol.

Mostly.

The ricocheting round slammed into Jack's left shoulder with the force of a baseball bat. Ignoring the numbness spreading down his arm, Jack grabbed the man's gun wrist with his good hand and wrenched downward, using the seatback as a fulcrum. The pistol clattered to the floor. The man leaned over the seat, firing a jab at Jack's head. Jack met the punch with his forehead and heard the delightful sound of knuckles breaking.

Now they each had just one hand.

But Jack was meaner.

Releasing the driver's wrist, Jack grabbed a handful of his shirt and jerked him forward while administering a second headbutt. Jack had been aiming for the man's nose, but hit his mouth instead. No matter. The effect was the same.

Blood flowed and bones broke.

Apparently deciding that he'd had enough, the driver opened the Hummer's door and bailed. Jack grabbed the fallen pistol and then shouldered open the rear door. He half fell, half crawled out of the vehicle, landing flat on his back.

Through the smoky haze, he saw a convoy of trucks racing toward him, led by an MRZR sporting a machine gun. The gunner situated in the all-terrain vehicle's passenger seat unleashed a torrent of fire over Jack's head at the compound behind him. A moment later, the fighters manning the crew-served weapons in the GMVs trailing the MRZR joined in the fray, pummeling the compound's fighting positions with ordnance.

The cavalry had arrived.

Which meant that Jack needed to wrap things up.

Turning onto his side, he centered the pistol's sights on the fleeing Iranian and fired twice. The second round blew out the Iranian's knee in a mass of blood and bone splinters, and the spy tumbled to the ground.

Ignoring the approaching convoy, Jack limped over to the driver and stuck his pistol in the man's face.

"Tell me where the scientist is," Jack said. "Now."

"No," the man answered. "You can't —"

Jack drove the muzzle into the driver's shoulder and pulled the trigger.

The spy screamed as flecks of spittle coated his lips.

"Tell me," Jack said.

"You're an American," he said. "You won't —"

This time, it was the ruined knee.

The driver fainted. Jack backhanded him across the face.

On the second slap, the man's eyes opened.

"I have ten more rounds," Jack said, "and I swear to God I'll blow off your pecker next. Where is she?"

The driver moaned, but he told Jack what he knew.

They always did.

EPILOGUE

The helicopters came in hot, flaring mere feet above the tarmac. The downdraft sand-blasted Jack with grit and dirt, but he didn't mind. Choppers that came in fast equated to happy pilots. Happy pilots meant a successful mission.

At least that's what he was hoping.

The Israeli defense minister had offered to let Jack watch the action in real time from a seat next to her in the high-tech command post, but he'd declined. He couldn't stomach the thought of sitting impotently by as strangers attempted to rescue people he cared about. Besides, Jack had more than just Becka and Tommy on his mind. One of the Green Berets who'd helped to rescue him was about to undergo a second round of surgery. If there was a better place to pray for divine intervention than an Israeli flight line while watching a crescent moon rise over the ocean, Jack couldn't think of one.

"Pilots only fly crazy after a successful mission," Dudu said, echoing Jack's thoughts.

"We'll see," Jack said.

Though if anyone had a chance of bringing Becka and Tommy back alive, it would be the two helicopters full of rough men who'd departed hours earlier. In a show of solidarity, the assault force had numbered twenty-two shooters. Eleven from Sayeret Matkal and eleven from SEAL Team 6, the quick reactionary force dispatched from the States the previous day.

From Jack's vantage point during the pre-mission briefing, neither unit seemed terribly happy to be working with the other. But at the end of the day, the military does what politicians say, and both Jack's father and the Israeli prime minister wanted to send a message to the people who'd kidnapped Becka and Tommy. The President of the United States wanted the organization to know that the act of kidnapping Americans carried with it lethal consequences. The government of Israel wanted the Wagner mercenaries to understand that operating on Israeli soil was not conducive to a long life and happiness.

Jack was hoping that both messages had been received loud and clear.

The Black Hawks taxied up to the edge of the tarmac, their landing lights lancing through the darkness.

"Come on," Dudu said.

Jack hesitated for a moment, remembering the explicit instructions he'd received about the harm that would befall his person if he stepped over the double red line denoting the boundary between the tarmac and the flight line proper.

Then he ignored them.

While the gunshot wound he'd sustained during the aborted insertion necessitated a sling, Dudu still radiated an aura of barely controlled menace. Air Force security personnel were notorious for enforcing flight line protocol, but Jack had his money on the Shin Bet officer.

Following in the stout man's wake, Jack made his way to the helicopters as their blades spun down. Jack was now sporting his own sling, and he had to wonder what the disembarking passengers thought of the two observers waiting in the darkness.

A wail cut through the night air. Jack looked over his shoulder and swore as he saw flashing red and orange lights.

"Ambulance," Dudu said, tracking the vehicle's progress. "Not good."

The ambulance screeched to a halt just

outside the lead helicopter's rotor disk, and a pair of paramedics exploded out the rear doors, pushing a gurney between them. Apparently, there were other reasons helicopters came in hot.

Two men exited the Black Hawk, supporting a third between them. The paramedics rushed to meet the gaggle, lifting the wounded operator onto the gurney before the scrum of five headed for the waiting ambulance at a run. Jack intended to hang back in case there were additional injured shooters, but Dudu was having none of it. Squaring his shoulders, the Shin Bet officer headed for the closest helicopter, barking questions in Hebrew at anyone who would listen.

Jack started to follow and then stopped, directing his attention to the second bird, which was also disembarking passengers.

Though it had been billed as a joint operation, the assault team had flown in helicopters segregated by nationality. This was probably due mostly to operational considerations, but it was also symbolic of the state of the two nations' relationship. Israel was still deeply angry that the United States had run an unsanctioned operation on its soil, while the Americans were singularly unimpressed with Israel's operational security, particularly the Shin Bet.

While the initial debriefings with the Iranian spy were far from conclusive, the consensus now seemed to be that there was no mole. Instead, the Shin Bet's hardened computer network had been penetrated in much the same manner as the Iron Dome's air-gapped systems. Apparently, Israel wasn't the only nation capable of pulling off daring intelligence operations. In any case, while the joint rescue operation was a good start, there was still much work to be done.

That said, Jack had a feeling that fences were already being mended. Apparently, an American F-35 pilot had sacrificed her life saving Tel Aviv from the Iranian cruise missiles. The account of her heroic actions was playing endlessly on both Israeli and American television. Accordingly, social media was ablaze with heartfelt messages exchanged between ordinary American and Israeli citizens. It didn't take a diplomat to understand that when the people of two nations thought highly of each other, their politicians would fall in line.

But the international issues at play were way above Jack's pay grade. Instead, he was singularly focused on the figures exiting the Black Hawk.

The first two were kitted-up operators

with the prerequisite broad shoulders, long hair, and furry beards that marked them either as Vikings or as members of the venerable SEAL Team 6. But after three more of their kind hopped onto the tarmac, two seemingly out-of-place silhouettes followed.

Abandoning all decorum, Jack sprinted for the helicopter just as the pair walked into the pool of light cast by the Black Hawk's landing light.

"Becka," Jack said. "Tommy."

Becka turned toward the sound of her name. Seeing Jack, she pulled him into a hug.

"You didn't forget us," Becka said, releasing her embrace. "I knew you'd come."

"Not me," Jack said with a laugh as he held up his sling. "But some friends of mine were able to lend a hand. You okay?"

Becka gave a slow nod. "They didn't hurt us, but it was awful, Jack. Awful. When the rescue happened, I wanted the men who took us to die. I wanted it with all of my heart. But it was still awful."

"I know," Jack said. "Believe me, I know. But in time, the memories will fade."

Disentangling himself from Becka, Jack squatted in front of Tommy.

"How you doing, buddy?" Jack said.

As usual, Tommy's gaze was focused on the ground. But at the sound of Jack's voice, the little boy took a step closer.

"Hey," Jack said, "I've got something for you."

Reaching into his pocket, Jack withdrew a new Captain America figure and placed it into Tommy's hand. Again, the child was silent, but his fingers wrapped around the figure with an intensity that turned his knuckles white.

"Dr. Schweigart, if you'll come with me, please."

Becka looked from the SEAL who'd materialized out of the night to Jack, a questioning expression on her face.

"It's okay," Jack said. "They've got some things they need to ask you."

"I'm sure they do," Becka said. "Thank you. For everything."

The unassuming scientist with the knowledge to potentially upset the world's balance of power gave Jack another violent hug. Then she was walking away, her son in tow.

Jack watched the little family until they vanished into the night. Then he took his new phone from his pocket and made a call.

"Lisanne? Hi — it's Jack."

ABOUT THE AUTHORS

Tom Clancy was the #1 *New York Times* bestselling author of more than eighteen books. He died in October 2013.

Don Bentley spent a decade as an Army Apache helicopter pilot, and while deployed in Afghanistan was awarded the Bronze Star and the Air Medal with "V" device for valor. Following his time in the military, Bentley worked as an FBI special agent focusing on foreign intelligence and counterintelligence and was a Special Weapons and Tactics (SWAT) team member.